PROTECTED IN DARKNESS

by Nicole Edwards

AUSTIN ARROWS

Rush

Kaufman

BRANTLEY WALKER: OFF THE BOOKS

All In

Without A Trace

Hide & Seek

Deadly Coincidence

Alibi

Secrets

Confessions

Bounty

Off Course

Chain Reaction

To Have and To Hold

Missing Pieces

Smoke and Mirrors

CLUB DESTINY

Conviction

Temptation

Addicted

Seduction

Infatuation

Captivated

Devotion

Perception

Entrusted

Adored

Distraction

Forevermore

DEAD HEAT RANCH

Boots Optional

Betting on Grace

Overnight Love

Jared (a crossover novel)

DEVIL'S BEND

Chasing Dreams

Vanishing Dreams

HEROES & HAVOC

Wait for Morning

Beautifully Brutal

Without Regret

Never Say Never

Beautifully Loyal

Without Restraint

Tomorrow's Too Late

MISPLACED HALOS

Protected in Darkness

Salvation in Darkness

Bound in Darkness

OFFICE INTRIGUE

Office Intrigue

Intrigued Out of The Office

Their Rebellious Submissive

Their Famous Dominant

Their Ruthless Sadist

Their Naughty Student

Their Fairy Princess

Owned

PIER 70

Reckless

Fearless

Speechless

Harmless

Clueless

PRIMAL INSTINCTS

Chase (Volume 1-3)

Capture (Volume 4-6)

Claim (Volume 7-9)

THE JAMESONS OF COYOTE RIDGE

Hot Chocolate Wishes

Rough & Dirty

THE WALKERS OF COYOTE RIDGE

Kaleb

Zane

Travis

Holidays with The Walker Brothers

Ethan

Braydon

Sawyer

Brendon

Curtis

Jared

Hard to Hold

Hard to Handle

Beau

Rex

A Coyote Ridge Christmas

Mack

Kaden & Keegan

Trey

Rafe

Violet

STANDALONE NOVELS

Unhinged Trilogy

A Million Tiny Pieces

Inked on Paper

Bad Reputation

Bad Business

Filthy Hot Billionaire

RULE

NAUGHTY HOLIDAY EDITIONS

2015

2016

2021

PROTECTED IN DARKNESS

MISPLACED HALOS

BOOK ONE

NICOLE EDWARDS

Nicole Edwards Limited, a dba of SL Independent Publishing, LLC

This is a self-published title.

Originally published in 3rd person POV - previous print ISBN 9·7·8·1·6·4·4·1·8·0·0·8·2

ISBN: 9781644181225

COVER DETAILS:
Image: © sashkab; © winwinartlab | 123RF.com | *Design:* © Nicole Edwards Limited
INTERIOR DETAILS:
Image: © winwinartlab / *123RF.com*
Formatting: Nicole Edwards Limited

For Zeus.

I know you're still here with me.

PROLOGUE

OBSIDIAN

Some believe angels only exist in heaven.

Some claim to have met one.

Others think they're nothing more than fictional fodder meant to give humans hope.

Being of the celestial, winged variety myself, I can attest to the fact that we do exist. Granted, we're not all floating on clouds, listening to the soft strum of a harp while waiting to greet the next to pass on to their life ever after.

Nope. Then again, neither are those who protect the gates of Heaven but leave it to humans to come up with whatever ridiculous faith-filled illusions they need to feel content about what they hope is their final destination.

As for the eternal resting place ... well, it's much like it is here on Earth. Chock-full of well-meaning folk attempting to maintain order with their policies and procedures. Yes, those are the angels you're familiar with—robes, halos, wings—keeping a watchful eye over your loved ones who've moved on to claim their just reward.

For the record, my brothers and I aren't those types of angels, nor have we set foot in Heaven for some fifteen hundred years or so. Since I spent my first five hundred years there, I learned a thing or two. A few things even that I wasn't meant to learn, but hey, with that many years under my belt, I got bored and curious. Sue me.

I know what you're thinking. *Oh, pity, he's a fallen angel.*

In a sense, I guess you could describe me that way, but try less fall and more push.

See, we're part of what Heaven refers to as misplaced halos, a faction of celestial warriors sent here to walk amongst the humans under the cover of darkness following the orders of our leader: the archangel Michael. You might know him as the protector of humanity, the patron saint of warriors, or even the one who sent the big bad to his rightful destination.

Most of the time, he's a giant pain in my—

I digress.

Yes, Michael is our boss, and he sent us here to watch over you. He refers to us as the Angels of Darkness, his greatest creation. And since we originated from his will, we're far from perfect. Perhaps we were your next-door neighbors at one time or another. If so, you probably remember us. We were the ones with the fast cars and loud music. Not your typical divine beings, no, but we get the job done.

Never fear; we aren't in one place for long. We're drifters, never quite settling in because we're needed everywhere. Small towns, big cities, bayous, mountains, deserts, we've experienced it all. But most importantly, if we stopped in and later disappeared, it was deemed safe for you to keep calm and carry on with your routine nine-to-five, maintaining your cute little house, raising your two-point-five kids, and throwing sticks for Fido.

That's what we were sent here to do. Protect you.

From what, you ask?

Well, demons, of course. Those who escape Hell, working for Lucifer, carrying out his evil deeds in an effort to prove their worth. Stealing souls, wreaking havoc, and trashing lives with absolutely no remorse. I hate to break it to you, but a few probably settled into your quaint little cookie-cutter neighborhood when you weren't looking. And no, Shawn, the drunk guy two doors down, is not a demon. He's just a jackass.

Like I said, that's why we're here. Seeking out the evil and sending them back where they belong.

Why do we do it? It's simple. That's what we were created for. We gain satisfaction by fulfilling our duties, protecting those who need it.

Oh, and because we were promised one thing: a love that knows no bounds. What we refer to as an *amsouelot.* A single soul destined for each of us, the two halves forming the whole, completing one another.

Of course, this carefully guarded secret got out eons ago. Humans use the term *soul mate,* though often the connection for them is little more than hope for everlasting love. In an attempt to force the union, human beliefs are frequently steeped in exploited traditions and trivial efforts. In reality, unless the Fates destined the two souls, those ventures are merely a desperate need to curate a love with little chance of survival. That's not to say your relationship is doomed to fail. Perhaps you're one of the lucky ones who's found your destined love, sealed by the Fates. It does happen.

However, for angels, it's a bit more complicated. For us, it isn't a matter of wining, dining, and roses. We can't use Tinder or eHarmony to track down our one true love. There is no such thing as a chance meeting. And once we come face-to-face with the one destined for us, the interaction's far more intense, a phenomenon that engulfs bodies and souls, entwining them, making it impossible to keep any sort of distance, physically and emotionally. When we mate, we do so for eternity.

Most importantly, without our *amsouelot,* we would have no reason to live. In essence, we would be nothing.

Which brings me to the beginning of this story...

Sunday, June 30, 2019

OBSIDIAN

"Now *that* was a lucky shot," Eclipse shouted, chugging back his beer, then following with a satisfied *ahhh.* "I'll drop a Benji if you can do that again."

"You're on, brother," Aphotic countered, snatching up his glass and tossing back the last of his favored Fireball.

Relaxing in my chair, a chilled bottle of Corona in my hand, I watched my brothers as they poked at each other in their attempt to enjoy one of our few nights off as of late.

While X Ambassadors crooned about the devil you know, Aphotic repositioned the cue ball and pointed his stick at Eclipse, a shit-eating grin pulling at the corners of his mouth. "Watch and learn, son."

It was good to be home, even if it was only a temporary hiatus. Discretely nestled in Darkness, Colorado, this was the one place we could relax and chill, where my brothers could act like idiots, as they were prone to do.

"They just don't quit," Stygian rumbled, casually stroking the top of Zeus's furry black head.

The dog had been glued to Stygian's side since we returned early that morning, minutes before sunrise. As for Aphrodite ... Zeus's much younger playmate was sprawled out beneath the pool table, sleeping soundly despite the ruckus.

"Eclipse is out what? A grand at this point?" Piceous rumbled, his tone relaxed, hooded eyes following the action. "He does know he's being hustled, right?"

Oh, he knew. And if I had to guess, Eclipse had a plan to hustle the hustler.

"Can't blame 'em for wanting to blow off some steam," Shadow drawled, sipping from his third glass of Glenlivet.

"You're right about that." I took a deep breath and watched the males strut and grunt.

It had taken four months, but we'd finally cleared out the demon nest that had taken up residence in New York City. Not an easy feat, mind you. Working under the cover of darkness in the city that never slept required strategy to eradicate more than three hundred demons, but we'd pulled it off, ridding the metropolis of the evil that lurked in the shadows.

To be clear, our responsibility is to the *actual* demons. As for the malevolent humans that resided there ... the human race was in charge of cleaning up that mess, thank God. I was equipped to deal with a wealth of shit, but the humans' behavioral problems were their own. We had our hands full. As it was, it would only be a matter of time before more demons would return, a new group sauntering in and attempting to take over.

The demons did their thing, which allowed us to do ours.

"So where're we headed next?" Cimmerian flopped down

on the black leather recliner, long legs dangling over the side. He tipped his head back, regarded me. "Tucson? Dallas? Maybe we could head down to Miami. It's been a while since we've had any Cuban action."

Before I could respond, the lights flickered, dimmed, the surge of energy flowing through the electrical circuits throughout.

In the true manner of warriors, the seven of us were on our feet, armed and ready to take on the threat. Big or small, didn't matter. We were always ready.

Of course, Zeus and Aphrodite weren't going to be left out. The German shepherds were positioned within the group, snarling softly as they anticipated the threat to their home.

"Relax, warriors," the disembodied voice echoed through the mansion.

"Well, fuck me running," Eclipse muttered, relaxing his stance with a heavy sigh and tucking his deadly half-moon blades away.

"Sounds like a challenge," Michael said, taking form in the center of the room, the feathers of his wings rustling as they settled at his back. "One for another day, perhaps."

Still locked in a fighting stance, I kept my eyes on the archangel gracing us with his presence. It was rare for the male to make an appearance, and when he did, it was never good.

In true Michael fashion, he didn't get right down to business. Instead, he ambled around the space, picking up the eight ball from the table, studying it momentarily. He set it back down, moved on. His steady gaze scanned the entire space, taking it in before returning to us.

"To what do we owe the honor?" Shadow queried, more than a hint of disdain dripping from his words.

"Want to commend us on a job well done?" Cimmerian

taunted. “Not necessary. We patted ourselves on the back already.”

Michael picked up Aphotic’s glass of cinnamon whiskey, sniffed, grimaced, clearly ignoring our rumblings.

“I come with a message,” he finally said, setting the glass down before turning his attention to us. “Sit.”

“Would it hurt you to say please?” Aphotic muttered under his breath.

“We’ll stand,” I told him.

“Don’t say I didn’t warn you.” Michael squatted down on his haunches, motioned the dogs to him.

Zeus and Aphrodite went happily, tails wagging as they cuddled up to the archangel.

“At least someone’s happy to see me.” Michael grinned, giving them each a generous rub before standing tall. His smile fell away instantly as he crossed his beefy arms over his armor-clad chest.

Mirroring his position, I honed my patience. The male wasn’t the sort to jump to the point when he could drag shit out.

“I heard about the stint in New York.” Michael’s dark eyebrows rose. “Impressive. Though not exactly timely.”

We’d long ago stopped waiting for Michael to bestow any sort of praise, so the seven of us remained silent, staring intently at our visitor. Though armed to the teeth, we’d all tucked our weapons away, out of sight but never out of reach.

Michael sighed heavily, smirked. “You boys should relax more. The sticks up your asses aren’t becoming.”

Since the archangel didn’t take well to commands, I kept my lips shut, though I was quickly growing tired of the male’s presence.

“And here I thought I’d injected a sense of humor when

creating you. My bad." Michael dropped his arms to his sides, paced in front of the billiard table.

"Just get to the point," Shadow rumbled, his shoulders squared, eyes narrowed. Clearly, the two were still on the outs.

"Fine. We've recently uncovered a leak." Michael's eyes briefly shot skyward. "Upstairs." He leveled his stare on us once again. "I'd go so far as to say there's a traitor in our midst. Though for the life of me, I can't figure out who it is."

Didn't surprise me. There were tight reins up there, but despite what the gospel wanted everyone to believe, not even Heaven was perfect. It was inevitable that someone would eventually fall through the cracks.

A scroll appeared in Michael's hand before he motioned me toward him, holding it out.

Stepping forward, I took the papyrus, broke the solid gold seal, unrolled it, and scanned the archaic writing. "It's a list of names," I told the others before meeting Michael's unamused stare. "What is this?"

"It's a list of *amsouelots*," the archangel clarified.

I frowned. "How did you get this?"

Only the Fates—Adorah, Nevaeh, and Karma—knew the alignment of souls. The sisters were the gatekeepers of humans' destiny, and they took their roles seriously. They kept detailed lists under lock and key somewhere beyond the pearly gates. Not even the highest order of angels had access to them, not even God Himself.

Or so I'd been told.

"Look at it again, warrior," Michael commanded.

I peered down at the paper once more. It was then that additional names appeared beside those already scrawled.

My eyes narrowed menacingly, shot back to Michael. "What the fuck?"

Stygian stepped forward, glanced down at the page,

inhaled sharply. I passed it over so my brothers could see for themselves.

"Who are they?" Aphotic asked.

"Those, warriors, are the names of your *amsouelots*. The seven humans whose souls are destined for yours."

"Six females, one male," Piceous noted.

"That is correct."

As the implications settled in, so did the silence.

Cimmerian frowned. "These names were leaked?"

"They were," Michael confirmed. "Yes."

"To whom?" I inquired, though I seriously doubted I would like the answer.

"Lucifer." Michael paced away. "And before you ask, yes, it was the only list that made it into my brother's hands, though we're still not sure who shared the information. When we find him, the traitor will be persecuted."

"Damn right he will," Shadow growled.

Michael sighed, then relaxed, his wings fluttering when he turned back toward us. "I don't need to tell you those females are in danger. Lucifer's already sent his demons topside, and they're searching. I've done my best to keep them shielded, albeit temporarily, but you know my father. He gets all up in arms when we attempt to interfere."

"How long have you known about this?" I snarled, not at all pleased with the situation.

Perhaps for the first time in my two thousand years of existence, Michael appeared almost remorseful when he said, "Too long."

"Where are they?" Stygian demanded.

"Unfortunately, warrior, that's not for me to reveal."

"Bullshit," Shadow hissed, stepping forward.

I held out my arm in a gesture for the male to settle. Inciting Michael wouldn't get us what we needed.

"It took some groveling," Michael explained, his eyes narrowing on Shadow, "which you all know I'm not fond of, but I managed to buy you some time."

Knowing I wasn't going to like the answer, I asked anyway. "How long?"

"Unfortunately, I don't have an exact timeline. Let's just say the situation's being monitored closely." He paced across the room, exhaled heavily, then turned to face us once more. "The sooner you find your *amsouelots* and complete the *linta-mair*, the better."

The archangel made it sound so simple. Like making the acquaintance of a human would result in an instant love that could be punctuated by an archaic mating ritual. We all knew humans were a bit more complex than that. Even if the warriors did have the Fates on our side, it would require finesse. Tack on the fact we had to *find* them first...

Michael studied us as though he expected us to spring into action. "You're up against both the clock and your enemy, so I suggest you get to work."

"And if the situation escalates before we locate them?" Cimmerian asked, the dark rumble of his words reflecting his doubt.

"My father has ordered their deaths."

A round of growls sounded.

Michael held up a hand. "Not my call, warriors. My father has deemed their deaths imperative should you not fulfill your duties."

"Meaning mate them," Stygian stated.

"Correct. Should Lucifer take possession of their souls before you're mated ... well, you know what'll happen."

"We'll be up shit creek without a paddle," Aphotic stated.

Michael frowned. "Is that really a thing? Flowing shit? Sounds disgusting."

It was often difficult to remember that Michael wasn't up to speed on human idioms.

Regardless, it was an apt description because an *amsouelot's* soul was tied to that of its mate. In our case, should Lucifer get his hands on an *amsouelot* before mating, he would take possession of both souls, meaning he would own an all-powerful, immortal warrior with capabilities that extended beyond those of an archangel. At least here on Earth. Not to mention, with the soul of the *amsouelot,* he would be able to persuade the warrior to do whatever he wanted.

The only way to prevent that was to bind the souls for eternity, placing them into the hands of Heaven's guardians. So, not only did we have to *find* our *amsouelots,* we each had to get her (or *him,* in Cimmerian's case) to fall in love with us and—yes, as though that wasn't difficult enough—*and* perform the *lintamair,* the official mating ceremony.

"I'd like to put in a formal request for backup," I told the archangel.

Michael shook his head. "As outlined, you may not seek assistance from the humans, and I cannot grant you reinforcements from Heaven."

"So we're on our own?" Stygian groaned.

"Last I checked, you have forty or so angels at your disposal. Plus, the seven of you." Michael cocked one dark brow. "Seems more than fair to me."

"We've also got the Fae," I reminded Michael.

He exhaled heavily. "You know how I feel about that."

I did, but I didn't give a shit. The Fae were meant to be a food source for us, not partners in this war against evil. However, Michael was the only one who saw them as such.

"Fan-fucking-tastic," Eclipse quipped. "Seventy or so heads to weed through seven-point-seven billion."

"A bit overdramatic, warrior," Michael replied. "It's safe to say you can narrow your search to North America."

"Well, in that case..." Eclipse rolled his eyes.

I fought the urge to do the same because Eclipse was right. It was a near-impossible task, and we didn't have nearly enough manpower to tackle it.

"Awesome," Aphotic snapped. "Only five hundred seventy-nine million."

"I didn't say it would be easy," Michael noted, then canted his head. "Might I suggest you utilize other factions of misplaced halos? Perhaps they'll offer you assistance."

"Vampires and witches?" Piceous asked.

Michael nodded as he paced away once more. "But fair warning. Lucifer's proving to be a formidable enemy. Not only to me but to humans and vampires alike. It's come to my attention that the *mesonneir* have made it topside. And I'm hearing rumors the *trielair* won't be far behind."

The *mesonneir* were the lieutenants in Lucifer's demon armies, capable of severe devastation. On the other hand, the *trielair* were a beast all their own. They hadn't come up from the bowels of hell for some six hundred years. It was then that they had laid waste to much of Europe and Asia, rolling out the Black Death, which resulted in the demise of roughly fifty million humans.

"Rumors are spreading that he's looking to acquire your souls in an effort to strengthen that brigade," Michael continued. "Without you defending them, the humans will be wiped out. So, I suggest you waste no time."

"Why not eliminate us now?" Piceous prompted. "Without us, there's no risk."

Michael smirked. "Don't think I haven't considered it. However, the Fates have informed me your souls have already been aligned with your *amsouelots*. The direct link is made.

Should your *amsouelots* die, your souls would still reside with whoever owns their soul."

Which explained why God would eliminate them, ensuring He possessed both souls, regardless.

Michael's eyes slid over each one of us. "Because you've proven yourselves worthy, I requested you be given the opportunity to claim your *amsouelots.* My father's aware that your existence will prove futile should He eliminate them, but He's prepared for that outcome. Don't let me down."

"You know, this could be made simple if you'd just tell us where they are," Eclipse grumbled.

"If it were up to me, warrior, I would," Michael stated, his words ringing with sincerity.

With that, the archangel vanished, the flutter of wings the only sound in his wake.

"Son of a bitch!" Aphotic shouted, grabbing a pool stick and snapping it in two.

Zeus barked once in warning. The canine was not fond of aggressive actions.

However, I understood the male's frustration. We'd been up against incredible odds before, but nothing of this magnitude.

"So much for a vacation," Stygian said.

"Needless to say, our priorities have shifted," I informed my brothers. "We'll divide and conquer."

Stygian nodded, taking the scroll when I offered it. "Good news is, none of their names are Mary Smith."

True. But with a little more than half the population of North America being female ... we had our work cut out for us.

"Bring in the *lieterras,*" I instructed, my mind whirling with things that needed to happen to get our mission underway. "They can start searching."

"I'm on it," Eclipse said before disappearing.

"We need to meet with the *fiestreigh*," I told Cimmerian. "Let them know we're refocusing our efforts."

"Will do," the male agreed, then vanished.

"And someone have Søren bring back up the Misplaced Halos website. We're gonna need all the help we can get."

Six females and one male to locate and an undetermined timeline.

Sounded simple, right?

Too bad nothing ever was.

I

PENELOPE CALAZANS

"Shit." I tossed the bookmark to hold my place and closed the book, dropping it onto the coffee table. "Shit, shit, shit."

I was late. Or I would be if I didn't get moving but I was pretty sure that was the story of my life.

I knew better than to read before work. It never ended well. I always found myself caught up in the fictional world, shoving aside the real world for as long as possible. Why wouldn't I? Fiction was far more fascinating than my mediocre existence.

Luckily, I was ready, so the only thing that stood between me and my shift at the casino was the commute. Being that I worked on the Las Vegas Strip, the amount of time it would take to get there was always a gamble. It depended on the time of year, the time of day, the various special events taking place, and the sheer number of tourists who descended on Sin City.

On top of that, I had to contend with the heat. July in Las Vegas was the equivalent of vacationing on the surface of the sun, yet for some reason, everyone in the known universe seemed to enjoy visiting when the desert was practically on fire. Since I'd grown up in California, my first summer here had hit me hard, but I was adjusting. Slowly.

As I was pulling out of my apartment complex, my cell phone rang. I glanced at the screen.

"Crap."

I debated whether to answer or let my dad go to voicemail. I tried to remember how many times I'd sent his recent calls that direction. Too many, I was sure. Could he deal with one more? Or would that send him over the edge?

Fearing the latter, I decided I would have to suck it up this time. With a huff, I hit the button to take the call, putting it on speaker.

"Hey, Dad," I greeted, focusing on the road.

"Penelope."

Yeah, that right there was the reason I usually let his calls ring through. Despite the fact he called me, I could hear the expectation in his voice. I was hard-pressed to remember a single time in my life when my father was happy to talk to me. To say we had a strained relationship was an understatement.

"What's going on?" I asked, trying to sound casual.

"Work, as usual."

And *as usual*, my father didn't elaborate. That was one of his infuriating qualities. I had little knowledge about what Michael Calazans actually did, aside from owning one of the largest tech companies in the US. He didn't share the ins and outs of his day-to-day, merely ensured we knew that his work was far more important than anything else.

"What a coincidence," I said, forcing a laugh. "That's where I'm headed right now. To work."

"You haven't found a day job yet?"

I chewed on my bottom lip, opting to go with the lie I'd been telling him for the past few months. "Still looking."

Truth was, I was quite content working at Caesar's Palace Casino. Waitressing wasn't nearly as bad as I thought it would be. Working nights was a plus since the tips were usually better.

"You should reach out to Oliver," my father suggested. "I'm sure he can find you something."

Yeah, no. The last person I wanted to talk to about employment opportunities was my twin brother. Oliver and I had a tenuous relationship. As in, he didn't like me, and for whatever reason, I wasn't okay with that. Mostly. I didn't push him too much because it was definitely easier to keep my distance. But he was still my brother. Aside from sharing a womb, we had absolutely nothing in common. I mean, nothing. It was difficult enough to have a conversation with him, much less trying to find common ground.

"I'm sure he could," I agreed, because placating my father was the only real option. "What's up with you, Dad?"

"I was actually looking for Oliver," he stated.

And there went the bubble of hope that always formed when he called. He had an uncanny ability to pop it with a few simple words. The fact that he called me to find Oliver was a testament to how little the man listened to anything I had to say. I'd told him numerous times that Oliver and I were practically estranged. If we talked once every three months, it was only because I annoyed him until he answered.

Kind of like my father did to me.

Not that I expected dear old dad to worry about me. His curiosity sometimes came across that way, but that was because he was trying to disguise his disappointment. Although I'd never asked my father for anything, he still acted as though I was living on his dime. I wasn't exactly proud of the fact I'd lived at home until I was twenty-five or that I moved in with my best friend for a couple of years after that, but I was on the right track now.

"I haven't heard from him," I informed my father as I pulled to a stop at a red light. "But I'll let him know you're looking for him if I do."

We both knew I wouldn't hear from Oliver. I never did.

"Dad?" I said when he didn't respond.

I heard murmurs on the other end of the line and realized he was talking to someone else. Not surprising.

"Okay, then," I said, raising my voice, hoping to get his attention. "I'm almost to work. I'll talk to you later."

"Sorry, Pen. I've got to take care of something. I'll call you later."

The call ended and I was left shaking my head, wondering why I even bothered to answer in the first place.

OBSIDIAN

"You realize what this means?"

Glaring at the male keeping pace with me, I fought

the urge to roll my eyes. “I suppose this is the point where you enlighten me.”

Taayin smirked. “It’s what you pay me for.”

I tucked my hands in my pockets as we approached the casino entrance. “I don’t *pay* you.”

“We should chat about that. What *is* the going rate for the smart, handsome, right-hand of a celestial being, anyway?”

“At your current pace?” I cut a quick look at the *lieterra*. “I think you should be paying me.”

“You want to trade places for a minute?” Taayin taunted. “I’d like to see you transcribe *one* message from Tenebrous. Just one.” The male sighed. “It’s a wonder I can get a single thing done with his constant chatter. On and on and on. You know what I mean?”

“Better than you think.”

“Shall we?” Taayin asked, holding the door open, his keen gaze scanning our surroundings.

With my senses flaring out, I stepped inside the elaborate resort hotel.

“As for that salary...” Taayin continued, strolling alongside me.

“I let you live.” I headed toward the casino floor. “Seems rather generous to me.”

“Yeah, maybe.” Taayin smirked, an amused gleam in his vivid blue eyes.

I was tempted to thump the annoying angel back to the house—just one flick of my finger and ... poof.

Instead, I sighed. “I think I can handle this outing on my own tonight, Taayin.”

“Yeah. *No.*” The male stopped. “I know you’re a big boy and all, but no way am I letting you run amok. Remember what happened last time?”

The memory brought a smile to my face.

Taayin's displeasure was reflected by the crease on his forehead. "Stop that. Michael will have my head if you wreak havoc in here. Do you even *know* how many views those YouTube videos got?"

"I really don't care."

"The most was six million," he huffed. "Damn thing went viral. And that was Biloxi. Ever consider the hell that'll rain down on this city when the demons catch wind that you're *here*?" Taayin chuckled. "Get it? Hell? Rain down..." Another laugh.

At least someone found him amusing.

"If I promise not to obliterate the masses, will you take your ass home?"

"Promises are like assholes. Everyone's got one." Taayin squinted, frowned. "No, wait. I think that's opinions. Opinions are like—"

"I get it," I snarled.

"Okay, fine. Whatever." Taayin dramatically motioned for me to precede him. "Your Majesty..."

I growled low in my throat, a sound that drew the attention of tourists tossing money on tables like it was in endless supply.

Eyes widened, even a few gasps as I continued on. Not unexpected. My size alone tended to intimidate mere mortals, never mind the fact that I was dressed head to toe in black and looked as though I would rip a throat out with the slightest provocation. Lucky for them, they couldn't see behind the Oakley Radar Ev Paths I sported. The dark sunglasses weren't a means of amping up the coolness factor. They were a necessity. They both protected my eyes from the bright lights and concealed the iridescent silver glow from the humans.

As for Taayin ... well, the angel had a long way to go before *cool* would be a term used to describe him. Truth was, he was a pussycat who had a penchant for classical music, enjoyed tiramisu more than could be normal, and had his Armani suits tailored to fit his six-foot-two-inch frame.

Taayin flashed white teeth. "Don't mind him," he told the humans peering our way. "He can be a bit capricious. Being an angel and all."

"Fuck off." Forcing my shoulders to relax, I strolled deeper into the casino. "If you're not careful, you'll be looking for a new job."

And we both knew the only *other* job for his kind was a number clerk in Heaven. As it was, I didn't need his help. Being that I was a warrior angel cast down by an archangel, Taayin's job as *lieterra*—translation: assistant—was more irritating than necessary.

Try telling him that, though. He was nothing if not a persistent pain in my ass.

The fact of the matter was I could hold my own with the humans. The wide berth I garnered was proof.

Because I was forced to live amongst them, I did not appear to be a threat to the humans who caught glimpses of me. Despite the fact I'd surpassed the two millennia mark, the outward facade reflected a strong, healthy male in his late twenties/early thirties, attractive to all genders, though slightly hardened by time. My hairstyle hadn't changed much over the centuries, though in recent decades, I'd nixed my favored mohawk and simply brushed the thick jet-black strands back on the crown of my head, keeping the sides and back shorn tight to my scalp. Facial hair wasn't a factor because, aside from the hair on my head, I was smooth as a baby's ass, no need to shave whatsoever.

At six foot ten inches, two hundred eighty pounds, I towered over most males. Though I wouldn't be caught dead in one of those ridiculous suits, I garnered the respect my demeanor commanded. Provided the human wasn't intimidated by size, I wouldn't foster fear unless pushed. At which point, I didn't mind rousing their antipathy in an effort to send them running. And while they could even interact if they were brazen enough, they would keep their distance. Which was exactly how I liked it.

Throwing out a mental command for the humans to avoid looking at me, I evanesced my physical form, drifted through time and space to the balcony overlooking the casino floor, and materialized. Taayin appeared beside me, hands cocked on his hips as he scanned the floor below.

Standing at the faux-stone railing, I leaned down, bracing myself on my forearms as I exhaled heavily, praying like hell the tip we'd received would pan out. Unlike the last two dozen that had trickled in through the Misplaced Halos website. I mean, seriously. Penelope Calazans was not a common name. How could so many people mistake it for Callie Peterson?

"Do you really think she's here?" Taayin asked.

"No reason to doubt the validity of the lead." Not until we'd checked it out, anyway.

For the past three centuries, vampires have been our eyes and ears on the streets, passing along intel in return for backup when needed. From my vantage point, this has been beneficial to both species. While the vampires have the numbers, the angels have the powers, and the combination of the two was necessary to keep humans safe.

While the angel grumbled beside me, I scanned the floor below, watching the interactions and keeping my eye out for the female I'd spent the past three weeks searching for.

I turned my attention to the crowd, scanning the one hundred twenty-five thousand square feet of money-sucking games and those who succumbed to their vices. Some were angling to beat the house, hoping against hope they'd hit that multimillion-dollar jackpot, while a couple of wannabe card sharks tried their not-so-skilled hand at the tables.

Then, of course, there were the working girls strutting through the space, looking for their next buck, attempting to dodge the millions of eyes in the sky.

All blending naturally, as though they belonged.

I figured, technically, they did. After all, Las Vegas was a playground for all sinners and saints, was it not?

However, I wasn't here for them.

I was in search of...

A soft growl rumbled in my chest as I stood tall, my eyes seeking the source of the connection I could feel deep in my soul.

"Obsidian?"

"I feel her," I rasped, a desperate need to lay eyes on my *amsouelot* coiling my insides into knots.

This was what I'd been waiting for since we set out on this search-and-rescue mission. To think she could possibly be within reach put a promising twist on what I'd started thinking was a pipe dream.

Taayin pulled out his phone, glanced at it.

"Uh ... Obsidian..." His hand rose, finger pointing.

I followed the direction and exhaled slowly, taking in the most beautiful sight I'd ever seen: Penelope Calazans in all her human glory.

The female was radiant, even wearing the casino's designated uniform for their cocktail waitresses: a silky white minidress that showed off an ample amount of smooth ivory flesh. Unlike the majority of cocktail waitresses who donned comfortable yet ugly footwear, her small feet were tucked into high heels that accentuated her lovely legs.

No more than five-four, she was a tiny little thing. No bigger than a minute. But she carried herself like a goddess who towered over many. Long, shiny hair the color of caramel was curled into silky waves, flowing down her back, the tips brushing her phenomenal ass with every sway of her hips. Wide eyes, delicate cheekbones, and a lush mouth tied her beguiling face together perfectly.

And this particular female, in all her natural beauty, was mine. My *amsouelot.*

"She's a bit smaller than I expected," Taayin muttered beside me.

I could feel the male's questioning gaze as he glanced at me, then her, then back to me again.

Taayin's voice was low when he said, "I think you can hold her in the palm of your hand."

I growled softly, a warning for the male to shut the fuck up.

On the other hand, I understood Taayin's concern because there was a drastic physical difference between me and my soul's beloved. My formidable size and strength dwarfed the fragile human female.

Keeping my attention on the female strolling across the casino floor, I gripped the balustrade and allowed my senses to flare out once more, taking in every detail. Blocking out the irritating music piped in through the speakers, the absurd noise emitted from the slot machines, and the acrid scents arising from the buffet and various cafes, I focused only on her. The soft rasp of her breaths, the steady thrum of her heartbeat, the sweet, powdery scent that beckoned me.

The conversation taking place around her was set to a dull roar, but I shut it out, centering on the golden-haired female taking drink orders from three high rollers at a blackjack table. She smiled sweetly, passed over a diluted Jack and Coke. I gave the receiver a mental push, and he paused, pulling out his wallet before passing over a tip. Her eyes widened, as did her smile when she accepted the one-hundred-dollar bill.

It was the least I could do.

"Well, what are you waiting for?" Taayin mumbled. "Introduce yourself."

It was the only thing I'd wanted since I found out about the list that had been leaked. Like me, my brothers were scattered across the continent, following up on leads on their own *amsouelots*, hoping to make contact and provide protection from the demons set out to acquire their souls.

As I stood there, debating my next move, the female stopped in her tracks, her gaze scanning her surroundings as though looking for someone or something. Liquid gold eyes lifted, stopping on my perch high above her. She remained there for a moment, though she couldn't see me. I had ensured that much.

"Maybe a drink then?" Taayin offered. "Something to help you work up the nerve."

I turned toward the male, smirked.

Before I could poof my ass elsewhere, my phone buzzed in my pocket.

"Yeah?" I greeted Reidar, the *ladeare* in charge of directing the *fiestreigh* under my command.

"We've got eyes on Perfidious."

Son of a bitch. Although Michael had warned us that the *mesonneir* were walking amongst the humans, we'd yet to encounter one.

"Where?"

"Heading toward New York, New York."

I growled. "Keep him at that end of the strip."

"You found her, didn't you?"

"I did."

"Should I take him out?"

I considered it for a moment. In a perfect world, we would eliminate Perfidious, which would keep my *amsouelot* in the clear. Unfortunately, this wasn't a perfect world, and to take down a demon the likes of Perfidious would require more power than Reidar possessed on his own.

"Just keep him in your sights," I told him.

"Fuck. All right, but he's got a handful of *impietans* surrounding him. I've got Gryffyth with me, so we'll do our best to distract them."

Due to the concern in Reidar's voice, I dematerialized, taking form in a darkened hallway to shield myself from the humans. A second later, Taayin appeared beside me. With the phone still to my ear, I strolled out, senses already reaching out to ensure no demons were lurking nearby.

"Whatever it takes," I ordered Reidar before disconnecting and tucking my phone in my pocket.

"I'll go help Reidar," Taayin offered. "You make like glue and stick close to her."

I nodded.

No sooner had Taayin strolled off than I turned around...

And came face-to-face with my destiny.

Well, maybe face-to-face was a bit of an overstatement.

2

PENELOPE

Moving through my section, I offered drinks to the few customers who'd been lingering for a while.

As it was Monday night during the height of the summer season, we were surprisingly slow, not a lot of people lurking about. Then again, the partiers were back in their hotel rooms, sleeping off the hard-core weekend, while the locals kept on with their day jobs. Or night, as was my case since I'd been lucky enough to get the overnight shift.

"Penelope," someone called in a singsong voice.

Turning slowly, I scanned the people milling about, smiling when I saw Chelsea moving toward me. I prepared myself to be slammed with my co-worker's emotions. Wouldn't matter if Chelsea was happy, sad, or sexually frustrated, my senses were so heightened I would feel them with the force of a tsunami.

Thanks to whatever weird curse I'd been born with, my emotional well-being was tied to others, something that had taken me years to come to terms with. Since I was a kid, I'd been able to feel the moods and intentions of those around me, their emotions seemingly becoming my own. It was an affliction I'd grown up with and, over time, had learned not so much to master but to endure.

"Hey, Chels."

The younger woman grinned widely as she held up the tattered paperback I'd loaned her last week. "You were right. It was amazing."

Chelsea's energy was calm with a hint of excitement—nothing I couldn't handle.

"Glad you liked it."

"I'll put it in your locker if that's cool."

"Yep. Oh, and I've got the next book if you want it. I can bring it on Wednesday."

"That would be awesome!"

As soon as Chelsea walked away, I retrieved another empty glass from a slot machine, set it on my tray, and headed back in the opposite direction.

I came up short, nearly plowing into a man.

Righting the tipping glass on my tray, I chuckled to hide my surprise. "I'm sorry. I wasn't watching..."

My words died in my throat as I peered up at him. *Way* up. At close to seven feet tall, he wasn't so much a man as he was a mountain. A sinfully attractive, rock-solid, muscled mountain.

Wow.

As usual, I waited for the assault of emotions, the baggage that came with every person I encountered. After a few seconds, I realized there was absolutely nothing coming from him—zip, zero, zilch. Either he was merely a husk, or his emotions were blocked from me.

Though his intimidating appearance should've had me backing away, I found my feet rooted in place as I studied his striking features. The jet-black hair, the strong, lean line of his jaw, and what had to be the most elegant mouth I'd ever seen on a man. He was, quite simply, scrumptious.

Unfortunately, I couldn't see his eyes because they were hidden behind a pair of sunglasses that should've made him look like a douche since it was night but instead made him look like a badass. My imagination ran wild, picturing the eyes behind the lenses as a dreamy blue or even a jeweled green.

Realizing I looked like an idiot, I tried to move around him, but his massive body, rocking jeans and a T-shirt in a way that should've been illegal, was blocking my path.

"Can I get you something to drink?" I offered, unsure if he intended to say something or merely wait for me to get out of his way.

"No." His voice was rich and dark, the single word dancing over my skin.

"Okay, then. If you change your mind, just let me know."

When I tried to move around him this time, he stepped out of the way, but not before my arm brushed his. The sensation that rocked my entire being drew me up short and had me turning to look up at him once more.

Even though his eyes were covered, I could feel the intensity of his stare. It washed over me, sending a shiver of awareness through all my senses. I didn't recognize him, but I got the feeling I knew him somehow.

Or perhaps it was merely my libido on the fritz. There was no denying the guy hit all the right buttons.

But it wasn't only his striking features that had my senses

on red alert. All of those did come together to form a rather yummy package, but they were more the decoration, what fanned the flames. The real attraction I felt was for the power I sensed in him, the restraint. It shrouded him like an aura, enticing me to interact.

"Do I know you?" I whispered.

He didn't smile, didn't respond, merely assessed, waiting for me to make a move.

Feeling awkward, I offered another smile, and just when I was about to turn away, his hand lifted, rising toward my face. I stood there, breath lodged in my chest as he brushed his knuckles lightly over my cheek.

The first thing I noticed was how enormous his hand was compared to my head. When I said he was giant, I wasn't exaggerating. Even in my four-inch heels, I was only about eye-level with his chest. The second thing I noticed was a shocking wave of desire that warmed me from the inside out, sparked by that simple touch.

Before I realized what I was doing, I covered his hand with mine, leaning into it lightly. His touch was by far the most soothing thing I'd ever felt. Along with the warmth of his skin, there was a deep sense of peace. It was almost shocking in its intensity, making it difficult for me to break the strange but undeniable connection.

"Hey, waitress! Could I get a drink over here?"

A-a-and *there* was the emotion I'd been trying to avoid.

While sadness was difficult to deal with and happiness sometimes caught me off guard, irritation was the worst. It made my skin prickle painfully, and this guy's frustration was buried deep in his bone marrow.

My mystery man's head swiveled, his attention going to the rude guy I'd been catering to most of the night. Knowing I had to take care of him, I dropped my hand and stepped back from the stranger.

"Excuse me. Duty calls."

The sexy guy turned his attention back to me, nodded.

I spun around and sauntered over to Mr. Slot Machine.

"It's about time," he huffed, not bothering to look up from his task. "You'd think I could get some decent service. I've been here all night."

My skin felt like ants were doing the Macarena, and I had to fight to keep from dragging my nails over my arms.

"What can I get you?" I asked, maintaining the polite tone required of me.

"Another vodka and cranberry." He cast a pithy look my way. "Make that two. Since you're taking your sweet time tonight."

Figuring it wouldn't benefit me to get lost in my section before getting his drinks, I headed right for the server station, relayed the order.

"Hey, Pen. How's it going?" Tim, one of the bartenders on duty, asked.

I offered a one-shoulder shrug. "Not too bad." I nodded toward the fresh glass he held in his hand. "This guy's a bit antsy."

Tim smiled. "He said diluted vodka, right?"

When I returned to the floor a few minutes later, the man was still sitting at his slot machine, continuously hitting the button to spin the reels, hoping for the triple sevens that would signal a big payday.

"Vodka and cranberry." I set the two glasses on the shelf near his knees, then turned away.

"Oh, wait, miss," he said politely.

Turning back, I frowned.

He offered a beaming smile. "Thank you."

Confused that maybe I'd delivered the drinks to the wrong person, I studied his face because either he was Mr. Slot Machine's nice twin or he'd received a personality overhaul in the few minutes since I'd walked away. Gone was his frustration; in its place, a sense of remorse, as though he regretted how he'd treated me earlier.

"Here you are." He held out two twenty-dollar bills.

Hesitantly, I took them from his hand, offered a smile of my own, feeling only a tad guilty about the extra water.

After placing the bills beneath the glass on my tray, I peered around, noticed my mystery man was nowhere in sight.

Too bad. He'd been the highlight of my night.

OBSIDIAN

No sooner had Penelope returned to her section than my neck began to itch, a sure sign that things were about to get ugly up in this bitch.

I scanned the interior with all my senses, seeking the anomaly as I moved along the wall, keeping to the periphery of the humans.

It wasn't like I could keep a low profile. By design, I stood out, but I wasn't concerned. The hundreds of cameras throughout weren't capable of catching my image. In fact, I was only seen by the human eye because I chose to let them see me.

With the itch turning into a raging case of eczema, I called out to my *ladeare* telepathically. When it took more than a few seconds for Reidar to answer, I shot out another.

A little busy here, was Reidar's clipped reply.

My gaze swept across the space, bouncing from one face to another as I strolled between machines. I came to a halt when I saw three large males circling the tables, clearly on a mission. To the humans, they looked like ordinary, everyday people. And while *impietans* didn't have demonic faces visible to angels as a true demon did, they lacked a heat signature because they were ultimately dead.

I've got a bead on some impietans. *Here in the casino.*

Yeah? A soft chuckle sounded in my head. *You and me both.*

Son of a bitch.

Taayin?

Of course he was offline, damn it.

Marching toward the threesome scanning the casino floor, I shot a mental command to the humans to keep their eyes averted. How long it would hold was beyond me, considering my focus was for shit. Shielding the humans and keeping them unaware of the demons was usually my top priority. Right now, my only goal was to get these bastards out the door before they located their target. No doubt in my mind they were seeking Penelope.

With a shrill whistle beyond the capabilities of human hearing, I caught the demons' attention, their beady eyes swinging around to locate the source.

Canting my head to the side, I smirked.

The one in the lead snarled as it began its march in my direction.

Never one to run from a fight, I took a leisurely stroll

toward the doors leading out into the night, the things following at a fast clip.

Once outside, I glanced left, right. Content the humans weren't looking my way, I led the band of merry assholes down the walkway in front of the casino. Rounding a corner, I started down a darkened drive separating one casino from the next.

"Come on, you jackasses," I muttered, praying I'd keep their attention long enough to get them out of sight of the humans.

With *impietans*, it was hit or miss. The imbeciles weren't capable of logical thought, so it was an effort just to maintain their focus for longer than a minute. These things were the most vicious of demons if for no other reason than they were idiots. Humans who were turned by a demon morphed into a mindless, soulless monster that couldn't think for itself, unable to speak. It was used for one purpose: to perform a single task. Sometimes as labor for whatever the demons were working on, but usually instructed to kill. And it always left a path of destruction in its wake. We had taken care of our fair share over the centuries.

On the flip side, *impietans* were easy to eliminate because, again, they were idiots. It was the mess left behind that caused the biggest problem. Once stabbed, they dissolved into a thick black sludge that tainted everything.

I felt Taayin's presence before I saw the male stepping out of the shadows.

"Sorry, boss man, got hung up with another one," my *lieterra* explained, moving around so the *impietans* were between us. "These bastards are everywhere tonight."

Which meant Perfidious was busy building an army. It didn't surprise me. I'd go so far as to say the demon was behind schedule.

"I knew I smelled 'em," Reidar grumbled, appearing at my side.

Yes, the *impietans* had a unique odor. A stench so powerful it seeped through your nostrils and coated your tongue. One that was closely related to the sulfur family, only more poignant.

"Where's Perfidious?" I asked Reidar.

A few quick steps and the *impietans* were at the center of our oddly formed circle.

"Gryffyth's keeping an eye on him. He's getting his drink on right now. If I didn't know better, I'd say he was in Vegas to check out the sights."

Or so he wanted us to believe. Perfidious always had a plan, even if it was to appear as though he didn't.

"Would it be too much to ask to find a formidable foe tonight?" Reidar shrugged his shoulders, bouncing on the balls of his feet. "Last ones all but impaled themselves on the blade."

As though they heard him, three more appeared, heading toward us at a jog.

Great. "That better?"

"I could take all six with my hands tied behind my back and my eyes closed," Reidar challenged, a glint in his eye.

"I could always time you," Taayin told him. "Just to make it more interesting."

"If it wasn't closing in on Miller time, I might take you up on that."

"We gonna dance?" I prompted the demon closest to me.

Its dead black eyes narrowed, confusion marring its forehead. Even if it could speak, the thing had no idea how to answer the question.

"Fists or blades?" Reidar asked.

"Fists'll be more entertaining," Taayin mused. "Blades'll get us home faster."

As though bored, Reidar planted his feet wide, tossing one of his custom-made, four-and-a-half-inch push daggers into the air and catching it over and over, the light from the Strip bouncing off the silver blade. The good news was, he hadn't started juggling them.

I kept my eyes on the *impietans* as they began the shifty dance, twisting around, assessing. They glanced between themselves, probably trying to determine who would die first. Then again, I wasn't sure they were capable of determining even that much.

"Hey, T," Reidar called out conversationally. "Remember that redhead from the bar the other night?"

"By bar, you mean strip club?" I asked.

"*Ta-may-toe, ta-mah-toe.*"

Taayin smirked. "Which one?"

Since the Angels of Darkness were forbidden to have interactions with humans, I had to assume this redheaded stripper was either a vampire or a fairy, the only other species willing to tangle with an angel. I figured vampire, knowing Reidar's taste in females.

"The tall one. Big green eyes, even bigger..." Reidar crudely cupped his imaginary breasts.

"Oh, I remember."

One of the *impietans* paused, looked over its shoulder, then stood there as though it had no idea what it'd been about to do. They took *dumbass* to an entirely different level. Sometimes I wondered why the fuck the *mesonneir* even bothered turning them.

"She's been blowing up my phone," Reidar continued as though we were out for a leisurely stroll. "Said you told her I had a surprise for her."

Taayin chuckled. "Did she?"

Reidar stood tall, squaring off with one of the idiots closest to him. "You care to enlighten me on what you told her?"

The *impietan* in front of me glanced down at the eight-inch black steel tactical dagger in my hand before lifting its eyes to my face.

"I might've told her your dick's made of plaster," Taayin replied.

Reidar roared in laughter. "You didn't."

The *impietans* all turned as one, focused on Reidar.

"Yeah." Taayin grinned over at him. "I kinda did."

"Perhaps I'll have to give her a spin on it, show her how wrong you are."

"Well, as soon as we get these jackasses into the light, I'll race you back there. You get to her first, you can plead your case."

Reidar nodded. "Deal."

Ready to get the show on the road, I peered at Reidar, then Taayin. "You two want to quit dicking around and get to work?"

As though choreographed, the three of us stepped forward, closing in on the *impietans*.

"What's up, big boy?" Reidar taunted the blond idiot who'd stopped to stare at him. "Don't tell me they're not even gonna try."

The disappointment in the male's tone made me laugh.

Evidently, that was the trigger because the one nearest me squealed, that high-pitched, obnoxious sound that only came from a demon. The thing lunged, impaling itself on the black blade I wielded, its human form igniting in a flash of blue light, leaving a sludgy mess in its wake.

Too easy.

"You'd think Perfidious would make these things smarter," Taayin called out, another blue light flashing.

You'd think.

Then again, it wasn't necessary because these things were meant purely to destroy. Having no decision-making abilities, they were programmed not to defend but to attack in whatever vicious, vile way they could. Every now and then, we'd encounter one who'd been a thug in its previous life, one familiar with guns. Those were the best because Perfidious failed to inform them that bullets couldn't kill angels.

Another blue light flashed. It was enough of a distraction to have two of the others peering away. Reidar aimed for one; I took out the other. That left one more, and it seemed to be more entertained by the flashing lights than anything else.

I stopped moving, coming to stand beside Taayin.

"Sometimes I feel sorry for these guys," I told the male before impaling the asshole with my blade.

Taayin offered a pitiful wave as the thing dissolved.

I didn't bother sticking around, sheathing my dagger and temporarily erasing my physical existence, resuming my form inside the casino. Now that I'd touched Penelope, I had a direct line on her, so I stuck to the shadows, moving around the space with my eyes on her. I sensed no other demons, but I damn sure wasn't about to leave her. The presence of the *impietans* wasn't a coincidence.

Demons, with the exception of *impietans*, weren't exactly idiots. Sure, one would occasionally go off the rails, but for the most part, they tended to keep a low profile in the communities they occupied, awaiting their orders. Some even managed to live among humans for decades before anyone suspected their ill intentions.

However, when they were on a mission, all bets were off. And since the orders to eliminate the *amsouelots* had come from the king of Hell himself, they were a driving force these days. Ever since Michael had informed us of the leak in Heaven, we'd seen their numbers increasing. Usually wouldn't be a problem, except for the fact we'd had to make some changes. Rather than an army of roughly fifty, including the Fae, we'd split into seven groups. Divide and conquer being the only option to get to the *amsouelots* before the demons could.

Even then, it was iffy as to whether we'd succeed.

However, for the sake of human existence, it was best we did. A male without his mate was about as destructive as a tornado. About as contained as one, too.

Imagine what one would do with an eternal existence before him and no chance of happiness.

3

PENELOPE

By the time my shift was over at four in the morning, I was dead on my feet and grateful to have peeled my toe-killers off. I was almost positive the four-inch heels were designed by the devil himself. And while they weren't a requirement in my job as a casino floor cocktail waitress, they did have magical powers.

Not real ones, of course. Those were simply suggestions by Marvel and DC to give us all hope.

However, the heels had pretty much the same effect as, say, a siren would on the opposite sex. Minus the luring them to their death part. Plenty of men appreciated a nicely dressed woman, and when they were in Vegas, their wallets tended to open wider whenever their eyes did. Therefore, I worked diligently to get the best tips possible.

Tonight, it had been a success.

Grabbing the jeans and T-shirt I'd worn to work last night from my locker, I went to the restroom, locked myself in a stall for privacy, and hurried to change. Once finished, I went to the sink, washed my hands, and pulled my hair up in a ponytail to get it out of my way. When I returned, several people were lingering in the break room. A couple downing sandwiches at the table, one reading a book, another doing a quick round of calisthenics. Their emotional energy pinged me from all directions, but luckily, no one seemed overly maudlin.

"How'd you do tonight, Pen?"

I smiled at Jenny, one of the new girls working near my section. "Not too bad for a Monday."

Taking a seat in a nearby chair, I pulled on my Converse, tied them.

"Hey! Did y'all hear what happened to Jessica Brighton?"

Looking up, I watched as Melissa Miller rushed over, all long legs and bouncing boobs. Her eyes were wild, mouth hanging open, thin brown hair dangling lifelessly around her face.

"Who's Jessica Brighton?" Jenny asked, her curiosity rolling over me like a tidal wave.

"Waitress at OMNIA. Stick-thin blonde? She always wore bright red lipstick?"

That described nearly half the waitresses on the Strip.

Jenny shook her head, clearly not knowing who Melissa was talking about. I was in the same boat she was.

"They said she had a heart attack," Melissa announced in a conspiratorial whisper. "Cleaning crew found her under one of the tables in the club Sunday morning. They think she might've sat down to take a breather. Keeled right over."

"Heart attack?" Jenny's hand went to her chest, rubbing absently. "Oh, my God, that's terrible."

While she appeared at a loss, I didn't feel actual pain coming from her—more keen interest than despair.

"It's horrible," Melissa continued. "She was only twenty-nine. Her boyfriend just moved here last month. They were buying a house." Melissa's voice lowered. "They don't want us talking about it. Said it wouldn't be good for the guests to overhear. Anyway. It's horrible." She forced a smile. "I'll see y'all tonight."

And there you go. Drop the big death bomb and head off to do your thing. Bad news drive-bys were a trend around here.

"See you tomorrow night, Jenny," I offered with a quick wave, eager to get out of there.

Jenny's gaze trailed after Melissa, still stunned by the delivery of bad news. "Yeah, you, too."

I didn't stick around, grateful I hadn't been overwhelmed by the emotional turmoil. I got enough of that on the floor each night. Gambling, or rather the act of winning or losing hard-earned money, was a roller coaster of emotions for most people. Which was why I tended to high-tail it as soon as I could.

With my purse draped over my shoulder, I strolled toward the parking garage, trying not to think about that poor waitress or the fact she would never buy that house with her boyfriend.

The sound of muffled voices had me looking up, noticing the sexy mountain of a man I'd encountered earlier. He was standing near the exit doors, conversing with another man. This one not quite as intimidating with his perfect hair and fancy suit. Unlike the mountain, who reminded me of a warrior, this one looked more like a lawyer. I studied them both for a second, curious.

Evidently, my staring triggered his internal radar because

my mystery man's head turned in my direction. He then nodded to his friend. The second man shot a quick smile before strolling out into the night.

Alone, the big guy's full attention shifted to me. Not sure what I was going to say to him, I considered running in the opposite direction but managed to hold my ground, continuing on my path to the exit.

"Heading out?" he prompted when I approached.

It was one thing to admire the man from the safety and security of the casino floor. Something else entirely to find myself in a dark corner with him. I debated for a moment as to whether this was a smart move. Likely not, I decided, but for some reason, I was compelled to respond.

"I am, actually." I glanced past him toward the door. "Heading home."

"How about breakfast?"

His offer caught me completely off guard. Earlier, he hadn't said more than one word to me. Now he was asking me out on a date?

"I ... uh ... I don't date customers."

The smirk that formed on his sinful mouth had a tingle of awareness spinning and swirling down my spine.

"Good thing I'm not a customer."

Okay, fine. He had me on a technicality. Since I hadn't brought him a drink, he wasn't *my* customer.

But still.

He continued to watch me, evidently waiting for my response.

Not for the first time, I found myself in a dilemma. I'd been in Vegas for nearly two years and had yet to go on a single date. In fact, I'd yet to make any real friends besides my casual acquaintances with my co-workers or my brief encounters with my neighbors. And because I didn't interact socially, I spent most of my time locked up tight in my apartment. Alone.

I glanced toward the door, thought about the empty apartment I would be going back to, the Lucky Charms awaiting me in my pantry, and considered my options.

"Only breakfast?" I asked, and as soon as the words were out, I realized how stupid they were. If this guy were a serial killer, I doubted he was going to outline his nefarious plan in detail simply because I asked.

That ridiculously sinful smirk returned. "Anything else is entirely up to you."

As long as there's no hacking of body parts, I might be persuaded.

Feeling the blush warming my cheeks, I stared up at him. I didn't sense anything malicious, nor had I felt any negative energy when we'd touched earlier.

"Well, I only share meals with men whose names I know."

That sexy smirk returned to his mouth. "Obsidian."

"As in volcanic glass?"

"That's one definition for it, sure," he said, the deep rumble of his voice making my insides quiver.

It was an interesting name, and oddly, it suited him. Sexy, mysterious, and definitely unique.

With a smile, I offered mine in return. "Penelope Calazans."

"I know."

Frowning, I tried to remember when I would've possibly mentioned my name.

He nodded toward my chest. "You had a tag on your dress."

Ah. Right. Name tag. The devilish invention that made those who preferred to remain anonymous *not*.

Obsidian held out his hand, drawing my attention to it. It wasn't offered in greeting, more like... Oh, okay. Yes. I was a little slow on the uptake because it took a second to realize he wanted me to hold it.

"Just breakfast," I clarified, wanting him to know I wasn't about to do anything more.

I only hoped my body remembered that before the morning was over.

Though hesitation coiled in my belly, I slid my palm against his. I inhaled sharply when he linked our fingers, mine fitting perfectly within his gigantic hand. There was no disturbing electric shock, nothing to make me recoil, so I breathed a little easier. I honestly couldn't remember the last time I'd held anyone's hand. It felt surprisingly intimate.

Rather than go toward the exit doors, Obsidian reversed, heading back into the casino.

"I actually can't hang out here," I informed him, inhaling his rich, musky scent. "Since I work here, it's a conflict of interest."

"We're not staying down here."

"Then where are we going?"

"I've got a room."

I pulled up short, stared up into his face. "You realize I'm a waitress, not a..." *Hooker.* I shook my head. "I'm not going to your room with you."

I wasn't one of those chicks in the horror flicks who forged headlong into the woodshed with the dangling hooks and razor-sharp hacking tools. In fact, I prided myself on being responsible, making sound, logical decisions.

"You're safe with me, Penelope." His tone was thick with reassurance.

"So you say."

He seemed surprised, as though he wasn't used to being rebuked by a woman.

"It's a rooftop villa," he explained, regarding me closely from behind those dark lenses. "Complete with patio and butler. If it makes you feel better, I'll invite him to join us."

I actually laughed at the notion. "Rooftop villa, huh?"

He nodded.

The villas—those with their own exterior patios—had a price tag in the tens of thousands per night. I had a strange desire to check it out for myself, if for no other reason than to say I had.

Or that was the excuse I was going with because I did not want to admit I was the chick in the horror flick.

Hmm.

"Okay, but I get to grill the butler."

He grinned, his warm hand giving mine a light, reassuring squeeze. "How long have you been in Vegas?"

"Almost two years," I admitted as we walked. "Traded angels for sin in an attempt to chase down my brother."

He peered down at me. "Angels?"

"Los Angeles? City of angels." I grinned.

He chuckled softly, a sound that made my entire body quiver.

We made it to the private elevator, where Obsidian didn't need to produce identification. Evidently, he'd already made quite the impression on the hotel staff because they knew him by name. It made me feel a little better about my spur-of-the-moment decision to go with him.

Obsidian nodded toward the man guarding the elevator, then motioned for me to step inside before him.

As the doors closed, sealing us inside, I pulled out my cell phone and shot a quick text to Winnie, my best friend back in LA, letting her know where I was and who I was with. Should something ominous happen, at least Winnie would know where to find my body.

After tucking my phone back in my purse, I watched Obsidian's reflection in the mirrored doors. His energy hadn't changed at all. Of course, I was making that up since I still couldn't detect his emotions. But for my sanity, I had to believe there was no deceit, no disdain.

Not the norm for Sin City. Not that I'd seen, anyway. In the time I'd been in this city, I'd learned most people had an agenda —especially those who were visiting. Whether to sow their wild oats or attempt to get something for nothing, it was all a game.

"What brings you to Las Vegas?" I asked as the elevator continued its rapid ascent.

"Business."

I turned to face him, let my gaze rake over him from head to toe. "What sort of business?"

"I'm looking for someone."

"Ah. So you're what? A bounty hunter?" I'd meant it as a joke, but the instant the words were out, I had to wonder.

"No."

I glanced at the mirrored doors as the elevator began to slow, suddenly curious as to how many chicks he'd taken to his hotel room before.

"I assure you, I've never taken a *chick* to a hotel room."

"Never?"

What was he? A choirboy?

Wait.

My eyes widened as I peered over at him. I hadn't voiced the question aloud. So how had he answered it?

Obsidian supplied a seductive smile, took my hand once more, then led me out of the elevator, down the carpeted hall toward the plush accommodations offered to those with tremendous wealth.

I half expected to wake up to find I'd fallen asleep reading. I was a paranormal romance junkie, and this felt surprisingly like many of the plots I'd read.

He opened the door to the villa, allowed me to precede him. I stopped just inside the opulent space. While I knew this hotel catered to the rich and famous, I'd never seen anything quite like it before.

"Wow. It's ... big."

Another smirk was all Obsidian offered as he let the door shut behind him.

He didn't appear at all fazed by the luxurious surroundings, as though they were inconsequential. On some level, I understood. After all, I'd grown up with an affluent family. My mother was a lawyer—or had been before she ran off with a man-child—and my father had built his own tech company from the ground up. My brother and I were not strangers to wealth and privilege, having gone to the best schools money could buy from grade school through college.

"Wine?" Obsidian offered.

"Sure."

As though summoned, a man appeared. Blond hair, aqua-blue eyes, a smooth, chiseled jaw. He was tall, just over six feet, I would guess, but seemed small compared to Obsidian. His black suit was a bit overpriced for a uniform, but maybe that was a requirement when dealing with the upper class.

"Now's your chance," Obsidian stated, nodding toward the man.

Confused, I stared up at him.

"To grill the butler."

Oh, right.

My face heated from embarrassment, but not one to back down from a challenge, I turned my attention to the butler, holding out my hand.

The man's gaze snapped to Obsidian's as though seeking permission before he shook my proffered hand.

"Penelope Calazans," I said. "I work downstairs. Waitress."

The butler smiled. "Alden. It's a pleasure to meet you."

"How long have you been in Vegas, Alden?" I asked when he released my hand.

"He travels with me," Obsidian explained.

Ah. Well, that made sense. Kind of.

"Anything else you'd like to know?" Obsidian prompted.

"I'll hold off for now. Maybe later."

He smiled, clearly amused.

I watched as the man poured two glasses of wine, passing them over in a manner that said he had vast experience with waiting on people. Like Obsidian, I couldn't detect his emotions, and I wondered whether that was something they mastered because of their clientele. Being unobtrusive to the guests was likely a positive.

Once again holding my hand, Obsidian led me out onto the patio.

I instantly knew what all the fuss was about. If I had buckets of cash lying around, I would certainly give them up for a night or two of this. The interior, while spectacular, didn't hold a candle to the outdoor living space. The enormous area was softly lit by the lights in the whirlpool and the gas fire pit, but it was the Vegas Strip that drew the eye.

"It's beautiful. Especially at night," I mused, stepping up to the railing beside the handsome man.

"I'd have to agree," he said softly, his gaze focused entirely on me.

I felt the blush warm my cheeks, so I kept my attention on the lights.

The sound of dishes had me turning. The butler was

placing two covered plates on the table, along with a variety of accoutrements.

I smiled up at Obsidian. “You were serious about breakfast.”

He grinned. “Hungry?”

“Starving.”

Though I wasn’t sure it was for food.

4

OBSIDIAN

Though my intentions were pure when I made the offer of breakfast, now that I had Penelope alone, it took everything in me to remember she had no clue who I was or that the Fates had destined us to be together.

I also had to remind myself that humans prefer to be courted rather than claimed. Penelope was oblivious to the fact that I'd instigated this intersection of our lives. From her perspective, this was a chance encounter—perhaps a happy accident.

When it came to claiming my *amsouelot*, I had little patience. I was ready to move on with the rest of my life with her at my side. However, since human traditions dictated that I wine and dine her and get to know her on a deeper level, I figured that was the least I could do, even if it was trivial, considering we would be together for eternity.

Pulling out a chair, I waited for Penelope to take a seat before moving to my own. Selecting the one to her left, I was able to keep the balcony wall behind me and maintain a full view of the hotel room. One might say I was a paranoid angel. Then again, if the humans were aware of the evil that lurked, they would probably do the same.

Alden, the angel posing as the butler, came over, removed the silver lids from the plates. "Is there anything else I may get you?"

Penelope's reaction to the male was a quick smile, her eyes dropping to her plate.

"We're good for now," I told him, followed by a telepathic order: *Follow up with Reidar. Get a status.*

Alden bowed, then exited quickly.

"All right, Obsidian, tell me something about yourself," Penelope prompted when we were alone.

Since she didn't realize how loaded that request was, I deflected. "What would you like to know?"

"Everything." Her smile was radiant. "But we can start slow. If you're not a bounty hunter, what exactly do you do? For a living?"

"Protection," I said easily, having given the response a million times before.

"Like a bodyguard?"

"In a sense, sure." I picked up my fork, took a few bites, urging her to eat because I could tell she was hungry.

Penelope followed my lead, cutting her omelet into smaller pieces before taking a bite. I was strangely drawn to the way her lips caressed her fork, mesmerized by her soft murmurs of approval.

Her eyebrows lifted. "And how exactly does a bodyguard afford a hotel room on the top floor?"

"I've got connections." That was the truth.

Then again, every answer I gave her would be the truth.

Because Penelope was my *amsouelot*, the Fates were at play here. Though this appeared as a normal date, it was actually the beginning of a cataclysmic union of souls. As we got to know one another, only truth would be spoken between us. Unlike human souls paired together, those linked with an immortal were held to a higher standard. We were incapable of lying to one another. For her, I doubted that was a problem. For me, it wasn't quite so easy. It was imperative to deflect because I had to tread carefully about the details I revealed—such as the fact that I was an angel.

Not that I couldn't tell her. I'd received the go-ahead from Michael to be as candid as was necessary with the humans slated as our other half. However, humans were groomed to classify what they didn't understand, the things they couldn't control, as fiction. Seeing was believing, but when it came to defying the logical aspect of their beliefs, it was imperative that I take things slow.

But that wasn't the only obstacle we had to overcome. That was minor compared to the chemical reaction we would have to one another as soon as Penelope opened up to the idea of loving me. That was all it would take.

On the physical front, her body would lust for mine in a way she wouldn't be familiar with, growing stronger every second she was with me. No other male could instill such a deep-seated hunger within her, and it wouldn't be long before my female would need me on an intensely intimate level. In fact, it had escalated tenfold the moment I'd felt her soft skin, smelled her powdery scent for the first time.

Preferring to keep the topic on her, I nodded toward her leather handbag. "What are you reading?"

Penelope reached for the paperback sticking out of her bag. She set it on the table. "I loaned it to a friend. It's one of my all-time favorites."

"What's it about?"

"Fallen angels. It's a paranormal romance." She blushed beautifully. "Don't make fun of me."

"I wouldn't dare."

The female ate with such grace, her hand movements minimal, chewing slowly, sipping from her glass. I could hardly focus on my food long enough to remember the social niceties of sharing a meal.

"I've had this fascination with the paranormal since I was a teenager," she explained. "I'm not sure what spurred it, but I devour everything I can get my hands on. I even majored in mythology and folklore in college."

"In the realm of vampires and werewolves? Or more so Greek gods?"

She smiled. "All of the above. Among other things. And no, I don't believe they exist—at least not vampires and werewolves, but I enjoy the escape from reality."

Probably not the time to tell her my closest friend was a vampire then.

"And your interest in angels?" I nodded toward the book. "Are you active in the church?"

Penelope shook her head. "No. I ... uh ... I just enjoy the romanticized versions of angels in fiction."

"Fascinated by angels and vampires." For some reason, that pleased me.

"Don't tell me you're not."

Fascinated wouldn't quite be the term I would use, but I smiled anyway. "Do you believe in God?"

She nodded. "I do, yes."

Her conviction surprised me.

"But I've never been to church."

"Never?"

Penelope lowered her eyes as though embarrassed. "My father doesn't believe in God. Says if He did exist, my mother wouldn't have left him."

Ah. A common misconception among humans. They believed God had a hand in everything they did, and when it didn't turn out as they hoped, some turned against Him.

While I could've gone down that path, I tended to avoid religion and politics if possible.

Shifting to a safer topic, I motioned toward the building. "What prompted you to work here?"

"It was convenient, and they were hiring. I also thought it would be temporary until I could get on my feet." Her smile disappeared, her gaze dropping to her plate. "I tried to tell myself I moved to Vegas to be closer to my brother, but it was more so because I needed a change of scenery. When I got here, I needed a job. This was the first offer I received. It pays better than I expected, and until I figure out what I want to do with the rest of my life, I'm enjoying it."

"And your brother? He's here in Vegas?"

"Yep. Living the high life. Met a woman about a month ago, claims he's in love."

"But you don't believe it?"

Penelope shook her head, finished chewing. "First of all, Oliver falls in love two or three times a month." She laughed. "Which isn't usually a problem, but something about this one puts me off."

"Seems fitting for a sibling to think that."

Penelope's gaze locked on my face as she set her fork down. "I'm not judgmental. Or I try not to be. I mean, I love my brother, but he's his own person. He can do what he wants. And he does. Secretly, I think he hates me."

I wanted to ask why she thought so, but she continued.

"It's not that. Truly. We've never been close. I've never judged him for the women he's dated. And he's entertained some real losers. But this one..." She shook her head. "I don't know what it is about her, but she's not right. Maybe it's her name. Seraphina. It just reminds me of... Never mind."

I paused, my fork halfway to my mouth. "Have you met her?"

"Only once. A couple of weeks ago. He brought her to the casino. He doesn't talk to me for weeks on end, ignores my texts, but then one day, there he is, eager to show off the woman on his arm." Penelope dabbed her mouth with her napkin. "They've only been together for about a month, but Oliver's already talking about marriage."

"Marriage?"

"I know, right?" Penelope huffed a laugh. "To be honest, she doesn't seem the marrying sort."

Frowning, I waited for her to elaborate. When she didn't, I realized she was hoping for a subject change.

"Well, I'm glad you're here. More so that our paths crossed," I told her.

She smiled sweetly, picking up her fork again. "So am I."

I shot a telepathic command to Alden, requesting him to have Taayin look into Seraphina. If two of the *mesonneir* were here in Vegas, and one was courting Penelope's brother, we had a much bigger problem.

For a few minutes, we ate in silence, the sounds from the Strip drifting up high. While Penelope would hear the horns from the cars, perhaps even the music from a nearby casino, I could decipher the conversations taking place on the street below. It took effort to block it out, but it wasn't too difficult with Penelope close. The only thing I wanted to focus on was her.

"So your job ... do you see it as something you'll do long term?"

"Doubtful." Penelope set her fork down once again. "Interacting with so many people isn't normally my first choice."

"Not fond of people?"

"I like them fine." She picked up her orange juice glass. "It's their emotions that cause me problems."

"How so?"

Another shy smile. "It's not a medical diagnosis or anything, but I've got this heightened sense of emotion."

"Meaning what? You can feel when someone's sad?"

"Actually, yes. That's exactly it. Almost like their emotions are my own. Too many at once can overload my system." She nodded her chin toward the casino below. "Quite a feat when you're dealing with something as emotionally charged as gambling."

Good point. "How do you deal with it?"

"For the most part, I'm used to it. Anger and frustration are difficult because they make my skin crawl. Sadness is... It consumes me. Thankfully, I don't encounter that much from tourists." She took a sip of her juice, set the glass aside. "The worst is when someone has ill intentions. Especially if I touch them. It's like an electrical shock." She gave a soft smile. "Needless to say, I don't touch many people."

The admission pleased me. More so, she'd taken my hand relatively easily when I offered it.

"What emotions do you get from me?"

"I don't."

Canting my head to the side, I considered that. "None at all?"

"It's like you're blocked from me." She laughed, clearly

seeing my concern. "That's not a bad thing. It's quite nice, really. I'm free to feel what I want to feel."

I extended my arm toward her. "And when you touch me?"

Her gaze shifted to my arm as her soft fingers brushed over my skin. Tingles erupted where her fingertips settled, my entire being lighting up.

"A sense of peace," she acknowledged. "I noticed it when you touched my cheek downstairs."

She pulled her hand back, and I instantly missed her touch. I finished my omelet, pushed my plate away, and waited for her to steer the conversation.

"Do you come to Vegas for business often?"

"I do not." I sat back, watched her. "But I do travel a lot."

"You said you were here looking for someone? Did you locate them?"

"Yes."

When she didn't say anything, I slipped into her mind, curious as to where her thoughts had gone. She was reliving the scene down in the casino. When I'd touched her. I hadn't intended to do it, but I couldn't help myself. Even now, it took tremendous restraint not to reach for her.

Her thoughts instantly shifted to me leaving town, never to be heard from again. She thought I had no reason to stick around because I'd found who I was looking for. Of course, she wouldn't know I'd come here to find her.

Before I could come up with a way to broach the subject without letting on that I'd read her mind—a slip I hadn't avoided earlier in the elevator—Penelope shifted her chair back.

She finished her orange juice before tucking her book back in her purse. "I hate to eat and run, but I really should be heading home. I promised my neighbor I'd feed her cat."

Since the sun would be rising shortly, I needed to do the same.

"How about breakfast tomorrow morning?" I offered, pushing to my feet.

"I'm not working tonight. I have Tuesdays off."

"Then the next day."

"Really?"

I took her hand after she put her purse on her arm. "Really."

I loved the way her small hand settled in mine so easily.

"Up here?"

I paused, glanced back at the Strip as we stepped into the hotel room. "It offers a nice view, no? Plus, it's private."

"True."

"So, that's a yes?" I opened the door, escorted her out into the hallway.

"We'll see."

I liked that she was playing hard to get. Not a trait I often found in females I encountered. Then again, Penelope was unlike any female I'd ever met.

"Thank you for breakfast," she said softly, as though not sure what else to say.

"Thank you for joining me," I replied.

When the elevator doors opened, I put my hand up to ensure they didn't close on her. Penelope's head turned my way, her eyes lingering on my mouth when she passed by, as though she was hoping I would kiss her. Once inside, I joined her, a move that took her by surprise.

"You don't have to walk me down."

"But I do." Her safety was paramount, but I also wasn't quite ready to leave her yet.

Another blush colored her cheeks as she ducked her head shyly.

The doors closed with a soft whoosh, and I pushed the button for the casino floor.

After slowing the elevator with my mind, I put my finger under her chin and tilted her head up. "I really hope to see you again."

"Likewise."

As we stood there, I felt that inexplicable pull. I realized I'd leaned down, my hand curled around the side of her neck, thumb gliding along her jaw.

Her eyes glittered. I could sense her intrigue. She was surprised by her reaction to me, but she wasn't disappointed. Knowing that made it easier to do what I wanted to do.

"I'm going to kiss you, Penelope."

Although I didn't phrase it as a request, I wouldn't force her. I lingered, waiting for a response.

She nodded, going up onto her toes, offering me permission. Having waited for this moment for what felt like an eternity, I leaned down and pressed my mouth to hers.

I didn't intend to do more than brush my lips against hers, so when Penelope's hand slid behind my neck, pulling me toward her, I nearly stumbled. And while I could be a gentleman, I wasn't at that moment. My tongue slid past her soft lips, gliding over her teeth, seeking hers. She kissed me back, turning the gentle press of mouths into a full-blown mating.

I was completely in sync with her—every breath, every heartbeat, even the vibration of lust that coursed through her veins. I wanted to feel her beneath me, undulating, writhing, her body melding with mine.

It took tremendous restraint to hold myself back, but I managed.

When I released her mouth, I stood tall, looked into her eyes, memorizing this moment for all eternity, then allowed the elevator to resume its natural pace.

"I'll be here Thursday morning," I told her. "Have breakfast with me again."

This time, my *amsouelot* didn't resist.

She smiled. "I'd like that."

It took roughly ten minutes to make the twenty-mile trek back to the house the *fiestreigh* claimed as our own during our stay here in Vegas. I could've reduced it to a fraction of a moment if I hadn't chosen to drive, but I'd needed that time to process all that had happened in the past few hours.

As I pulled into the small two-car garage and shut off the engine, I instantly missed home. I missed the twelve-bay garage at the mansion, the row of muscle cars and motorcycles my brothers favored, and, more importantly, I missed them. Having spent centuries alongside my brothers, it was taking some time to get used to not having them around.

When I stepped into the house, I was assaulted by the Red Hot Chili Peppers blaring through the sound system wired throughout, which meant Gryffyth was there. I strolled through the wide-open space, heading for the kitchen, peering around to see who'd arrived before me.

"Hey, you're back," Acadia called out, a brilliant smile on the Fae's face. "I heard the good news."

Her eyes scanned the space behind me as though she expected someone else.

"Where is she?"

I opened the refrigerator and pulled out a beer. "At home."

Acadia pouted. "Well, that's no fun. I was hoping to meet her."

Tilting the bottle to my lips, I studied her. Tonight, the fairy was decked out in a silky, pale blue gown that covered her from neck to toe, clinging to every curve, the skirt flaring out around her feet, which no doubt were bare.

"I thought she would return with you."

"Not yet."

"Why not?"

"It doesn't work that way."

"Why not?" she repeated. "You've finally located your *amsouelot,* and what? You just let her go back to her regular life?"

"Not like he can expect her to fall at his feet, Acadia," Gryffyth rumbled as he joined us. "She's a human. She expects things."

Acadia, ever innocent, turned her attention to the male. "Like what?"

"Dinner, dancing. Dating."

Her amethyst eyes darted my way. "But her soul is destined for yours."

"It is, yes," I agreed. "But she's human, Acadia. We have to respect human traditions."

"Dinner, dancing, dating," she said, her gaze dancing between Gryffyth and me.

Gryffyth grinned. "Exactly."

"That makes no sense," she said softly. "I think the *lintamair*'s more than enough to convince her."

The Fae was referring to the mating ceremony to unite a mortal soul with an immortal's, which was both complicated and ... not utterly romantic in every manner.

I sighed, took another pull of my beer. "In time."

She frowned again, spinning around to the stove. The sound of burners being clicked off punctuated her heavy sigh. "I guess there's no need for a feast then."

"Hey," Gryffyth told her. "You want to cook, I'll always eat."

She shook her head. "I'm going to my room." Her eyes lifted to mine. "Unless you need me."

"I do, actually."

Acadia nodded. "I'll meet you in your quarters."

The Fae had been with us since the beginning of our mission fifteen hundred years ago. The command for their presence had come from God, insisting the Fae provide their services to the warriors. Since the Fae had been categorized as misplaced halos somewhere along the way, it was likely the big guy's way of ensuring they didn't veer too far off the path as they'd been known to do.

Though they were good with a blade, the Fae had long since turned in their swords. While the human females were asserting their dominance, the Fae had opted to ease off the front lines, returning to their roots, providing comfort to the angels. While the males in the house often accepted their offers of sex, I had never allowed myself to succumb to their advances. Not those who were part of our mission, anyway.

Not because I was a saint by any means. No, more like I preferred less complicated relations. When it came to sex, I ventured outside to sate my baser urges. Now that I'd made the formal introduction to my *amsouelot*, I wouldn't be able to bear the touch of another female, Fae or otherwise.

However, I did require a Fae for feeding. At least until my *amsouelot* provided her blood as nourishment.

The thought had me remembering Penelope's fascination with vampires. I wondered if she'd be surprised to find out how much the Angels of Darkness had in common with them.

"Where's Taayin?" I asked Gryffyth when Acadia disappeared.

"In the library. Doing research. With Asmia."

I nodded, though I seriously doubted the *lieterra* and the Fae were nose-deep in a book.

“And Reidar?”

“He sent me and Gerran back here. Said he’d be along shortly. He’s making a detour after he chats with Penelope’s guardian.”

Curiosity got the best of me. “Who’s her GA?”

“Stig.”

I didn’t know the angel personally, but I suspected the male was a suitable guardian for my female. I’d yet to meet a guardian angel who had failed at his or her duties to protect the humans they were responsible for. Considering the rules they had to follow when it came to interfering, I doubted it was an easy job.

After finishing my beer, I tossed the bottle in the recycle bin. “Tell Reidar I want a meeting at nightfall.”

“Of course.”

Without further ado, I headed up the stairs to my private quarters, otherwise known as the largest bedroom in the five-bedroom house. It was nothing compared to the Colorado compound, but it worked for our needs.

I sensed the Fae before I stepped inside. Acadia had changed out of her gown into her white robes, which covered her from neck to toe. Her dark hair was secured on top of her head in some sort of intricate knot, fingers clasped tightly as she sat primly on the bed, awaiting my arrival.

Although Acadia didn’t see herself as anything more than a servant, she was one of my oldest and dearest friends. Because of that, I preferred feeding from her. She respected boundaries, and not once had she ever propositioned me. I wasn’t big on conversation, and I had no desire to turn an already intimate act into something more than it needed to be. However, I wasn’t so selfish that I couldn’t provide her with what she needed.

“When’s the last time you fed?” I asked her.

Purple eyes lifted. "Two days, but Alden's offered."

Grateful she wouldn't need to siphon my emotions, I nodded, then sat beside her as she pulled the sleeve back from her wrist and held up her arm.

Because I'd interacted with my *amsouelot*, the touch of another female would cause tremendous pain, so I did my best not to touch Acadia more than necessary. She must've realized because she used her other hand to hold her arm securely. The instant I leaned forward, my fangs elongated, preparing to pierce her vein. A second later, I sank into her flesh, fueling myself on the blood required to maintain my existence.

Fifteen hundred years ago, back when Michael had presented his idea to God, requesting that an army of warriors be sent to Earth to guard humanity against Lucifer's demons, the Father of Creation was against the idea. However, Michael, being the steadfast leader that he was, pushed until God came around to his way of thinking, but not before putting a few rules in place.

After all, someone had to keep us in line, did they not?

First and foremost, we could not make our existence known to humans. To keep our secret, Michael agreed that his warrior faction would only venture out into darkness. To ensure that happened, God made it so that the sun could and would eliminate us should we violate the rule.

Secondly, we had to be monitored at all times to ensure we didn't go rogue and take over God's finest creation. As a means of keeping track of us, He required us to feed on the blood of a Fae. His theory was it would keep us from going rogue if we were tethered to others. Plus, with the Fae's blood flowing in our veins, He would always have a bead on us. The only human blood that could sustain an angel was that of their *amsouelot*.

Considering my vast capabilities as a warrior, I knew the pros far outweighed the cons.

Several minutes passed before I released Acadia's arm. She quickly sealed the wound on her wrist, then nodded before disappearing as she was known to do.

As expected, it only took a few minutes of quiet before my body hardened, the need for release becoming my main focus as thoughts of Penelope invaded. I'd done well to ignore it back at the hotel, though I couldn't deny I'd hoped she would end up in my bed tonight.

I set aflame two candles using my mind, needing a distraction. From my perch on the bed, I stared at the wall, replaying the events of the evening in my mind. I already missed Penelope, but it helped to know I had a direct link to her emotions. She would also have a direct link to mine, should she figure out how to tune in.

My body was assaulted with sensual heat, the need to assuage the desire powerful enough to steal my breath. When clothing became too much to bear, I stripped it off and started to pace. It was the only option for fighting the all-consuming need.

The fact that the heat was hitting me so hard already did not bode well for my future. I'd heard stories about this but only knew a few angels who'd experienced it and were willing to talk about it. I could only hope that Penelope wasn't enduring this yet. At some point, it would be inevitable, but for now, I wanted her desire for me to grow organically.

Walking eventually became too much of a torment for my cock, forcing me to drop to the bed, feet on the floor, flat on my back, staring up at the ceiling as the sensual pain called to me. There was only one way to eliminate it, albeit temporarily. The instant I gripped my cock, I hissed. The damn appendage was so fucking sensitive; the simple stroke had pleasure darting through every limb. It wouldn't take long, but as had been the case in recent weeks, I closed my eyes, envisioned Penelope.

The female I'd already dedicated my life, my love to. One day she would be my *ereswa,* and I would cherish her until the end of time.

I didn't ravish Penelope in my fantasy, knowing that would only make things worse. The more I wanted her, the more intense the need would become, so for now, I was satisfied with picturing her in my mind as I stroked my cock faster, harder. Seconds turned to minutes as I held out, enjoying the pleasure of my own touch, thinking of my *amsouelot*, forcing the erotic fantasies away.

Despite my best efforts, an image slipped into my mind, and my hips jerked upward, driving my cock into my fist. I envisioned Penelope kneeling before me, her sweet lips...

"Fuck!" My teeth clamped together, back bowing as my release tore through me, ripping a howl from my throat.

It took me long minutes to settle, to force myself into the shower. That was all I would allow myself, knowing that once Penelope was with me, I would be relieved for all eternity.

Once clean, I padded to the bed, fell into it. Closing my eyes, I thought of Penelope for as long as possible before succumbing to sleep.

5

PENELOPE

Nine hours later, after an uneventful night at work, I was making my way up the stairs to my apartment, my phone to my ear. Although I pretended I didn't care that my brother ignored me most of the time, it wasn't true. And phone calls from my father only reinforced the fact.

Hence, I was calling Oliver for the second time since I talked to my dad last night.

"Hey, Oliver, it's me," I told the voicemail. "Thought maybe we could grab breakfast. I just got off work, so give me a shout when you get this. I'll be up for a while if, you know, you're checking your messages."

Disconnecting the call, I pushed my key into my door,

disengaged the lock. With a heavy sigh, I stepped into the darkened space, flipped the switch.

The room brightened, as did my mood.

That had been the case for the past year, every time I walked into the apartment I called home. Not that it was anything uber fancy, but it was seven hundred square feet that belonged to me and only me. I could sleep when I wanted, wake when I wanted, eat what I wanted, and there were no hovering roommates looking to pillage my food, borrow my clothes, or steal my perfume.

All mine.

When I first scrounged enough money for a deposit and the first month's rent, I spent a solid month looking at a variety of apartments in and around Las Vegas until I finally settled on two that would work for me. It wasn't until my best friend Winnie came for a visit that I finally decided to make the leap, and with her help, I decided on this one. At her insistence, of course. Winnie had promised we'd throw a huge party, though deep down, she knew I would never allow it. But Winnie was the fun-loving, *shuck-all-responsibility* type that people gravitated toward, while I was the *hide-out-in-my-apartment, speak-only-to-those-I-had-to* sort. Polar opposites.

Even though I hadn't allowed a naked free-for-all to take place, Winnie had taken a week off from work and helped me move in.

Truth was, this was a far cry from where I'd imagined myself being at this point in my life, but hey, that was the way things had played out. On a high note, I did feel as though I was officially adulting, and at twenty-eight, I figured it was better late than never.

In a last-ditch effort to get in touch with my brother, I shot him another text to go with the two I'd sent since last night, before I started my shift at the casino. Praying it wouldn't go unread like the others, I huffed a sigh and deposited my purse on the small table near the door. I tossed my keys beside it, staring at the phone in hopes of seeing those three dots bounce around to show Oliver was messaging me back.

He wasn't. But that wasn't new.

SERAPHINA

"You dumbass," I hissed. "It's not hard. Get in the car and drive. Wait until she's walking out in the open, then run. Her. Over."

Though the empty eyes merely stared back at me, I hoped the *impietan* could process the simple order. It was about as reliable as a rat, but short of handling the task myself, I had no other options. I didn't care who the orders had come from; I was not going to waste my time or energy on that little prissy princess. For one, I couldn't understand what any male worth his salt would see in her. She was *human*.

"Do I make myself clear?" I glared at the thing still staring back at me.

The *impietan* cocked his head to the side as though he couldn't translate the words.

"Fucking idiot," I mumbled.

Since I'd rendered it mute upon turning the pathetic male into a mindless, soulless demon, I'd get nothing in return. I'd found this little bastard in the back alley behind a casino. He'd just relieved another stupid human of her purse and was digging through it to claim his bounty. I had enjoyed raining on his parade.

Though it remained in the human husk, that was about the only trait it shared with them. Inside was a cold, dead mass covered in the skin from its former life. Unlike the demons who emerged from Hell, the *impietans* had no worth other than extreme disruption and violence. As a means of self-preservation, the things expired after three days, their souls banished to Hell for eternity, where Lucifer could do cruel and unthinkable things to them.

"Go! Run her over."

It turned and left.

I grabbed the glass of wine, tapped my fingernails on it as I peered at my reflection in the window. I smiled, admiring my upgraded body. Even a month in, it was holding up well. Thanks to the slutty waitress at the strip club, I was blessed with long black tresses, big tits, a tiny waist, and a rather impressive behind. The first thing I'd done was discard the hideous wine-red lipstick and atrocious fake eyelashes, which had been an immediate improvement.

I licked my glossy, fire-engine-red lips and smiled.

"It's true what they say. The devil *is* in the details."

I remembered how worked up the human male had gotten when he first caught sight of me. Truth be told, Oliver Calazans wasn't as pitiful as I'd thought he would be. Quite the opposite, really. The male had stamina to rival that of any demon I'd encountered, and quite frankly, I happened to enjoy his selfless acts. Especially those that involved that wicked tongue.

It was going to suck when I had to kill him.

I fluffed my hair, seeing the light blue eyes peering back in the glass. "But orders are orders."

Perhaps I could keep his apartment when I was finished with him. Not like he would need the place.

Even thinking about that shithole I'd been shacked up in made me shudder. Back before Oliver had invited me to move in with him. Rather quick, in my opinion, but who was I to deny the male his last wishes? If he wanted me in his bed every night, we could both reap the benefits until his dying breath.

Now it was up to Perfidious. He'd finally arrived, his sole focus on the female we'd been sent to eliminate. One of the many *amsouelots* of those godforsaken warriors, all targets, their demise at the top of Lucifer's agenda.

Honestly, it had been ridiculously easy to find Penelope. Probably had a lot to do with the fact her brother was a sinner of the highest order, even if he was rather good at hiding his many vices, including a sizable debt to some very unsavory people. And once I had homed in on him, finding the bitch had been easy-peasy.

My cell phone rang, drawing my attention from the window.

"Yes, my lord," I greeted Perfidious, using the title he insisted I use.

"Rather cheerful, are you?"

I grinned as I spun around to survey the living room. "If you must know, I'm enjoying my current assignment."

"Good. Because I expect you to hold on to it for a while."

With a controlled breath, I hid my disappointment. "How long's a while?"

"Until I tell you. For now, keep the male busy."

"Oh, that won't be a problem." My eyes shot to the full-length mirror. I eyed the tiny scrap of lace that covered my sex, the demi bra that supported my tits, and the stilettos on my feet. Oliver would be home any minute, and I had a few surprises in store for him.

"I didn't think it would. In the meantime, I'm going to cozy up to the female."

I was tempted to call him out on the bimbo waitress he'd eliminated recently, but figured it was best to hold my tongue. I knew him. He did what he wanted, consequences be damned.

I frowned. "That's not the task. You're supposed to eliminate her."

"All in due time, Seraphina. All in due time. There's no reason I can't enjoy my job, is there?"

I didn't respond, knowing the question was rhetorical. Perfidious didn't need my permission to do anything. Not to mention, I wasn't about to get on his bad side. Though I worked for him, Perfidious gave me plenty of room to roam. Crossing him would likely get me confined to whatever hell-hole he was hiding out in.

"That's what I thought. However, I am going to need something from you."

"Anything, my lord."

"I'm going to require access to your body."

Heat bloomed inside me. "I'm looking forward to it."

"Be careful what you wish for," Perfidious rasped. "I'm feeling a tad *mean* these days."

"Mmm." My scalp tingled with thoughts of Perfidious's hands pulling my hair. Unlike the human, the demon had no problems asserting his dominance over me.

"Are you thinking about me? About all the dirty things I'm going to do to you?" he asked, his voice deeper than before.

"Just let me know when and where, my lord."

"Soon, my pet. Very, very soon."

The last thing I heard before I disconnected the call was a promising growl.

PENELOPE

When it became apparent Oliver wasn't going to respond, I shrugged off my irritation and went next door to Janice's to feed Bill, the fat, fluffy gray cat my neighbor fancied.

"Good news is, your mommy'll be home later today," I said aloud, though I knew Bill wasn't listening.

The feline didn't care much for people, so even when I called out to him, he remained in hiding. I'd learned the first day that it wasn't worth sticking around to see if he'd make an appearance, so I rinsed out his water and food bowls, refilled them before locking up and going back to my apartment.

With energy to burn, I made a quick yet thorough pass through my apartment, cleaning from the baseboards to the ceiling fans and everything in between, finishing up with a pass of the vacuum cleaner. The effort relaxed me, though it did nothing to shut off my brain. More specifically, the delicious thoughts of Obsidian. I could still smell his rich, exotic scent, hear his deep, rumbling voice. For the first time in my life, I was completely enthralled by a man.

Those lingering thoughts were what drove me to make a cup of coffee and settle into the thick, velvet-soft cushions of my sofa. It was my favorite piece of furniture in my apartment.

The deep red with white pipe trimming the cushions made me happy.

I stared around the room, my thoughts drifting back to Obsidian. He'd certainly piqued my interest in the short amount of time I'd spent with him. I hadn't meant to rush out of there so quickly, but I'd had no choice. Not only because I really did have to feed my neighbor's cat, but also because I wasn't sure I trusted myself in his presence.

Never had I met a man I'd considered sleeping with on the first date. Not before Obsidian. Yet the entire time I'd been with him, I'd imagined his hands on my body, the two of us falling into his bed, tangled in a heap as we moved together. Even before he'd kissed me in the elevator, I had wondered what his lips would feel like. Now I could think of little else.

Part of me wished I'd gotten his phone number. I would've loved to hear his voice right then. A giddy feeling trickled through me at the thought of having breakfast with him Thursday morning. Though only two sleeps away, it felt like an eternity from now.

With the urge to tell someone about what had happened, I grabbed my phone and dialed Winnie, the one and only friend I had back in California. She was a bartender, so Winnie's schedule aligned with mine almost perfectly.

"Hey, chickadee," Winnie greeted with a laugh. "I was just about to call you. Make sure you're alive after that cryptic text. I take it this isn't a forced call seeking a ransom?"

Chuckling at my friend's odd sense of humor, I assured her I was safe and sound.

"Always a good thing," Winnie said.

I settled into my sofa, stared at the television. "What are you doing?"

"Watching *Supernatural.* Hold on, let me see which episode this is." There was a brief pause. "Season nine, episode eight."

I grabbed my remote, clicked on the television, and hit the Netflix app, then searched for *Supernatural*. "Is it just starting?"

"Yeppers."

It only took a second to pull up the episode Winnie was referring to and I smiled. "Start it over. We'll watch it together."

"Done."

Back in California, Winnie and I would hang out on the weekends, binge-watching shows like *The Originals* and *Supernatural* as well as others we'd come to know and love over the years. When we weren't watching television, we were devouring paranormal romance like it was going out of style.

For a few minutes, we watched Sam and Dean gearing up to tackle another monster while Winnie went on and on about how hot Sam was. I was more of a Dean fan, personally.

"I think I'm in love," I blurted, a silly giggle following. It was our code for meeting a man who might possibly involve a second date.

"Pause the show!" Winnie squealed.

I hit the pause button. "Why?"

"Because this requires my undivided attention. The guy from tonight? Some rich out-of-towner?"

"Yep. Well, I don't know about his financial status or anything." Nor did I really care.

"Where's he from?"

"He didn't say. But he's staying in this wicked nice hotel room."

"Did he say why he was there?"

"Business."

"Oooh. What's his name?"

"Obsidian."

"Like volcanic glass?"

I snorted. "Exactly what I said."

"Sounds mysterious. What does he look like?"

"Tall, dark, ridiculously handsome." I sighed. "He's so freaking big, Win. Like bodybuilder big. Enormous arms. And holy crap, he's tall."

"How tall?"

"I don't know. I didn't measure him."

"Well, to you, everyone's tall," Winnie teased.

True, but I'd never in my life met a man who towered over me like he did. During that exquisite lip-lock in the elevator, I noticed that he'd had to bend at an awkward angle just to kiss me. And I'd been up on my toes.

"And you met him while you were at work?" Winnie asked. "I think it's fate."

"Fate? I seriously doubt fate had anything to do with this."

"So? What happened? Did you get hot-and-sweaty naked with this guy?"

"Of course not. I just met him." Though the idea of being hot-and-sweaty naked with him was rather appealing. "We did have breakfast, though. On his fancy patio overlooking the Strip."

"Uggh. I'm looking for some dirty details, Pen. I assume those'll be coming in the future?"

I sincerely hoped so. "Maybe."

"And I'll be the first person you call, right?"

"Of course." I took a sip of coffee. "What about you? Any appropriate suitors?"

"Ha!" Winnie snorted. "I wish. I'd be open to *in*appropriate, even. Although there is this one guy..."

"Do tell."

"He started coming in a week ago, I guess. Every night, he takes a seat at the bar. He doesn't talk to anyone but watches everyone," she explained.

"An alcoholic?" I teased.

"Probably. But he's hot. Tall, blond. Nice smile."

"And his name?"

"Sirius."

"Of course I am," I countered.

Winnie laughed. "No, dummy. That's his name. Sirius. Like the radio."

"Oh." Odd name.

"Hey, what are you reading right now?" Always changing the subject, that Winnie.

"*Acheron*," I told her, referring to the *Dark Hunter* series by Sherrilyn Kenyon.

"Swoon. I'm going to have to reread that one next."

"What are *you* reading?" I inquired.

"The Warden herself," Winnie said with a chuckle.

"*Black Dagger Brotherhood* or *Fallen Angels*?"

"BDB. It's delish."

That it was.

"God, it's good to talk to you," I admitted. Though we hadn't spent much time together since I moved to Vegas, Winnie and I had remained friends. Long distance, but we talked on the phone often. Winnie was the only person I could open up to, share my thoughts with. I was hoping to make friends like that here but had yet to have the time.

"Likewise. One of these days I'll have to get out that way. Have you show me the town."

"I will. In a heartbeat."

For the next half hour, we chatted about the show. When it was over, we said our goodbyes, promised to catch up next week.

Once again, I was left sitting alone in my apartment, my thoughts instantly drifting to Obsidian.

As I stared around the quiet space, reliving the kiss we'd shared, I remembered I needed to make a grocery store run. My gaze swung to the window, to the sunlight peering in through the blinds. It was still early, so the best time to avoid most of the shoppers.

With a sigh, I got to my feet.

Time to do that whole adulting thing again.

Half an hour later, I was perusing the grocery store aisle, tossing a few things into the cart. More Lucky Charms, a half-gallon of two-percent, grapes, a Hershey bar. I didn't have a long list because I didn't spend much time at home. Most of my meals were on the go in the form of granola bars or yogurt. They were quick and easy and didn't require dirtying up a bunch of dishes to make a meal for one.

That was one of the downsides of living alone. Probably the *only* downside, though.

Now that I thought about it, I couldn't remember the last time I'd actually cooked.

I made a trek down the freezer aisle, stared through the frosty glass in search of some comfort food.

Lasagna. Yum.

I snagged one of the boxes of frozen goodness and set it in the cart. If anything could comfort, Stouffer's would do the trick.

Plus garlic bread. Homemade.

Well, not completely homemade. I wasn't exactly an over-achiever, and making bread from scratch required a trait I lacked. Fortunately, the bakery would have exactly what I needed.

Feeling eyes on me, I paused near the rack of freshly baked goods, glanced around. There weren't many people there at this time of morning. A little old lady testing the softness of a loaf of bread before delicately setting it in her cart as though it were a newborn baby. A guy behind the bakery counter, pulling what appeared to be donuts out of the oven. I'd passed others in the aisles but only a couple of people, none having exerted any odd energy.

Still, I searched the area, trying to find the source of the weird feeling, but ended up with nothing.

"Get a grip," I mumbled under my breath, dropping some sourdough into my cart and heading toward the front.

Seriously. I was being absurd. Who in their right mind would be watching me? And why?

Shaking off the paranoia, I made my way to the front register, stood patiently while the fuchsia-haired young woman chomping gum rang up my groceries. After swiping my debit card and sliding it back into my wallet, I slipped the two plastic bags over my arm and headed for the doors.

The sun was even higher in the sky, another scorcher of a day well underway.

"Good morning," someone said on their way into the store.

"Morning," I called back, smiling to myself.

It *was* a good morning. A really good morning. I'd had breakfast with a fascinating man, and said man had asked me out again. Maybe I should consider making him a meal. Perhaps tonight. He could come over for dinner. Did Obsidian like lasagna?

Of course, I had to nix the idea because I didn't have his phone number. Shame.

As I stepped off the sidewalk and into the crosswalk, I heard the sound of an engine being gunned. I glanced out at the parking lot, looking for the idiot who was making so much noise, and that was the very reason I didn't notice the vehicle in question was plowing toward me at a high rate of speed.

I looked over just as I expected to feel the impact.

As the air in my lungs slammed to a halt, my feet left the ground. I was launched through the air, but the car wasn't the culprit. Pain didn't erupt from my body. There was no impact with the asphalt. Instead, I was set on my feet a couple of yards away.

I spun around to see who my savior was, but there was no one. The car peeled out of the lot on the other side while I was left standing alone, my groceries dangling from my arm.

What the hell just happened?

6

OBSIDIAN

I woke to the sound of music blasting through the house. The Red Hot Chili Peppers from this morning had been replaced by Kendrick Lamar, who was ordering the bitch to sit down, be humble. Not surprising considering Gryffyth's eclectic taste in tunes.

While the thick drapes were still covering the windows, I knew the sun was finally going down. Since it was the height of summer, the nights were quite a bit shorter than I would've liked, but I'd learned to deal a long time ago.

With a groan, I forced myself out of bed, stretched, then took a moment to let my senses flare out, seeking my *amsouelot*. Penelope was asleep, tucked safely in her bed, deep in a dream. It was tempting to slip into her REM event, interact with her there, but I refrained. While dream walking had its perks, I would rather take the opportunity to interact on a more personal level, when she was aware of me on every level.

After a quick pit stop in the bathroom, I pulled on jeans and a T-shirt, socks, boots, then headed down to the kitchen. Asmia and Acadia were fluttering around, the Fae cooking up a meal for the eight of us. Not quite the same as the meals prepared by the *heurosp* back at our mansion in Darkness, Colorado, but for the time being, it would suffice.

"Where's Reidar?" I asked, hoping someone could give me an answer because I was ready to get the night underway, and an update from the *ladeare* would get the ball rolling.

"He'll be down shortly," Acadia replied, offering a sweet smile.

Alden joined us, a smile on the male's face when he caught sight of Acadia. Being that the Fae had feasted on Alden's emotions last night, he looked downright happy. Then again, I suspected the two of them had done more than provide sustenance.

"Will you be needing me tonight?" the male asked, his question directed at me.

"No. Penelope's not working tonight, so we won't be going to the hotel."

Alden nodded as he opened the refrigerator, retrieved the jug of orange juice.

Before I could say anything more, my cell phone rang. Seeing that it was Stygian, I hit the button to answer, then stepped out on the back patio for some privacy.

"What's up, brother?" I greeted the male, unable to stop the smile on my face.

"I heard the good news. Congratulations," the gruff voice said through the phone.

"Don't go getting ahead of yourself yet. I just met her."

"And? How'd that go?"

"Better than I expected, honestly."

Not one to wax poetic, I didn't go into the details of my interactions with Penelope, though I was already looking forward to the next opportunity. I knew there wasn't a chance I could go a single night without seeing her, so I was already forming my plan to show up at her apartment.

"And you?" I prompted my brother.

"Still no luck," Stygian said with a heavy sigh. "But Aphotic's got the scent of his female. He's heading to Texas as we speak. What's your plan?"

"For now, I don't have one. The second I can get her out of town, I'll head back to Colorado."

"Good. If we're as lucky as you are, we won't be far behind," Stygian stated. "There's safety in numbers, and the *amsouelots* will be better off with all of us protecting them."

I agreed. It was the reason we lived on the thirty-five-acre ranch, situated in an easily defendable area known as Darkness, Colorado, which didn't exist on any map. We'd built the mansion from the ground up, modified it so it was a modern-day fortress.

"We're dealing with Perfidious," I informed Stygian. "And from what I gather, he's working with Seraphina."

"Son of a bitch. They make a move yet?"

"I think he's playing games. Probably thinks he's got the upper hand." Though we'd been making valiant efforts to eliminate the *mesonneir* for centuries, they proved elusive. There was a reason Lucifer had selected them as his lieutenants.

However, Perfidious's one major flaw was his need to drag shit out, to play with his prey. In this case, it would likely work in my favor.

"Let me know if you need backup," Stygian offered. "We can be there in a breath."

"I will." Hopefully it wouldn't come to that. "What about you? How're things going?"

"Slow. Too damn slow. And I think we picked up a tail a few days ago. Mordecai's almost positive he detected Valdis."

"Hopefully you can keep him back." As it was, that particular demon made Perfidious look like a boy scout.

"That's certainly the plan. I'll check back in with you soon."

"Keep in touch," I told my brother.

"You do the same."

The call disconnected and I headed back into the house. I found Reidar sitting at the kitchen island, scarfing down the meal the females had put out.

"Sit. Eat," Acadia ordered, her voice soft and sweet but rife with insistence.

"I'm good for now, but I'll take coffee."

"Coming right up."

"Tell me about Stig," I commanded Reidar when the male pushed his plate away.

Reidar wiped his mouth. "I apprised him of the situation. He said he'd keep his eye on her, but he's inundated with the other forty-nine he's looking after."

"Wow. They're taking on fifty souls now?"

There was no doubt the guardian angels were overloaded. Because of the extensive requirements, they were in short supply. Those who'd been doing it for a while were being overloaded with more assignments. But it paid to have them as backup since they were capable of going out during daylight hours.

While I would've preferred Penelope to be Stig's only human to look after, I knew it wasn't possible.

"And Perfidious?"

Reidar rolled his eyes, exhaled heavily. "Bastard's sneaky. Penelope's definitely his prime target, but I think it's safe to say he's distracted. He's like a kid in an amusement park, not sure which ride to hop on first but wanting to try them all."

"Might keep him looking elsewhere temporarily, but he's not alone." I took a sip of the coffee Acadia handed me. "Penelope informed me her brother's dating a female named Seraphina."

Reidar's blue eyes widened. "No fucking way. You think it's the demon?"

"No doubt. They're getting their claws in her family. Probably intending to use the brother as leverage."

I could practically see the male's brain working. "I'll have Gryffyth keep an eye on him. See if we can figure out what she's up to. And you? I assume you'll be sticking close to the female?"

"As close as she'll allow." I smiled, thinking about Penelope's abrupt departure this morning.

"Stig said she's independent. But she's a homebody. Doesn't get out much, nor does she have much contact with her family. Including her brother. It's only a matter of time before Perfidious gets bored, and we all know what that means."

Yes, I did. And we were all aware of what the demon was capable of.

After everyone was caught up on the situation, I wasn't in the mood to sit around, but I hung back long enough to catch up with my brothers, checking in, getting a sit-rep on their *amsouelots*. They were still searching, following every lead that came in on the females destined as their mates. Though we were only three weeks in, the website was getting numerous hits and leads, mostly from vampires looking to get in our good graces.

Rather than wallow in the disappointment that my brothers had yet to get the satisfaction they sought, I headed out. No surprise I ended up standing in front of Penelope's apartment door, hand raised to knock.

I'd seen her little compact car out front, and I could hear her moving around inside, so I knew she was home. The question was, did knocking on her door make me look like a stalker? Technically, she hadn't given me her address, which put my impromptu arrival in that category.

Never one to second-guess my actions, I rapped my knuckles on the door, then took a step back and waited for her to answer. I listened to her bare feet moving across the laminate flooring, her breaths as she paused and peered through the security hole.

She opened the door, those big, beautiful eyes wide with surprise. "Obsidian. What are you—? How did you know where I live?"

Yep. Stalker.

"I've got connections."

She smiled sweetly. "So you said."

"May I come in?"

Penelope stepped back out of the way. "Of course."

I strolled into the small apartment, taking in the living room and kitchen in a single breath. Though she didn't have much, her personal space was spotless and organized, clearly a place she enjoyed spending her time. I let my senses expand through all seven hundred square feet, listening for noises that might suggest someone else was there.

I was greeted only with silence.

"I'm ... uh ... actually glad you came over," she said after locking the door behind me.

I peered down at her when she moved around in front of me. She was wearing a thin tank top that showcased her smooth shoulders, her toned arms. And those little shorts gave me a great view of her sexy legs. Her little toes were painted a brilliant blue, which made me smile. Whoever bitched about the heat of summer being brutal clearly hadn't caught sight of Penelope in her summer wear.

Her lashes fluttered, her eyes shifting to my neck as though she couldn't look me in the eye. "I was thinking about you."

That single admission had every cell in my body roaring to life.

"I'd considered inviting you for dinner," she added, a slow smile forming as her gaze lifted. "But I didn't have your number." Penelope motioned toward the living room. "Please, come in. Have a seat. Can I get you something to drink? Are you hungry?"

Her nervousness was endearing.

"What did you have in mind?" I asked, clearing the three feet to the living room.

"I bought lasagna. It's frozen, but ... well, it'll take about an hour."

"Lasagna sounds perfect." I would've been open to eating raw meat if that was what she offered me.

While she padded to the other side of the island that separated her kitchen from the living room, I headed for the red sofa, ensuring I had a view of both the windows and the door. As well as Penelope.

"This is a nice place."

Penelope glanced over her shoulder as she punched buttons on the oven, pride making her face glow. "Thanks. It's the first place I've had all to myself. A little small, but I like it."

It suited her. The furniture was minimal, but it matched. The few knick-knacks she had held a gothic flair, catering mostly to angels and fairies. I paused next to a two-foot-tall statue that looked remarkably like Acadia. Right down to the wings that resembled snowflakes.

I picked up a picture frame on the end table, stared at it.

Penelope was standing beside a man, the Las Vegas sign behind them. They were both mugging for the camera. "This your brother?"

"Oliver. Yes. We took that back when I moved here."

Though I knew all the details, I still asked. "Is he older or younger?"

"My twin, technically four minutes younger, though he sometimes thinks he's older."

Aside from their light hair and golden eyes, there weren't many similarities between them. Penelope was a good six inches shorter than Oliver, her features softer, more delicate.

"Do you spend time with him?"

"Not really. We talk on the phone every now and again, text every few days. Even before he started dating Seraphina, we didn't spend a lot of time together. Believe it or not, we're polar opposites." Penelope opened the oven, shoved in a pan, then closed it. "He's the life of the party. I'm more of a homebody."

She joined me in the living room, carrying two glasses of wine. She passed one over, then took a seat on the opposite end of the sofa. She pulled her legs up underneath her as she angled her body toward me.

"Do you work nights?" she asked.

"I do, yes."

"But not tonight?"

"Every now and again, I wrangle some time off." I took a sip of wine, pulled the glass back and looked at it. The fruity taste surprised me.

"Sorry, it's the cheap stuff. Not quite the same caliber as what we had this morning."

I held her gaze. "If you're serving it, it's perfect."

Her cheeks turned a lovely pink.

In an effort not to stare, I peered around. "What do you usually do on your nights off?"

"Mostly chill, watch TV. Read." She nodded toward the end table. "I was reading when you got here."

I picked up the hardback book. "What exactly is a *Dark Hunter*?"

Penelope grinned. "Basically, an immortal who protects humans from Daimons."

"Is that so?"

"Sherrilyn Kenyon's one of my go-to authors. I love that series."

I set the book down.

She shifted, as though nervous. "Do you read?"

"Not as much as I used to," I admitted.

When Penelope lifted her wineglass to her lips, I noticed a scratch on her arm, roughly two inches long and not very deep. Seeing it mar her perfect skin bothered me.

"Something happen?"

She turned her arm over, twisted her wrist around, glanced at the red mark, frowned.

"Huh. I must've gotten that this morning."

"This morning?"

Her eyes returned to my face. "The weirdest thing happened. I went to the grocery store to grab a few things. When I came out, I was nearly run over in the parking lot. I actually thought I was a goner, but ... right before I was certain the car was going to hit me, I was moved out of the way."

Every inch of me tightened with barely restrained fury. I knew there was a target on her back, but thinking that the demons had gotten close to her made me see red. Good thing she couldn't see my eyes. No doubt they were glowing brightly.

"Maybe you got that when you hit the ground?" I said, working to keep the growl out of my voice.

"But I didn't. I didn't fall, didn't stumble. Something *moved* me."

Sitting up straight, I narrowed my eyes, though she couldn't see them behind my sunglasses. "Some*thing*?"

"I know it sounds crazy, but it's true. Something moved me out of the path of that car seconds before I would've been plastered to the pavement."

"What time was this?"

She shrugged. "A little after eight, I guess."

I made a mental note to follow up with the guardian angel. Although Reidar hadn't mentioned the situation, I could only assume Stig had intervened. The male deserved my gratitude, but he also needed to know I expected to be informed of these situations. ASAP.

"I thought I'd imagined it." Penelope turned her arm over again, studied the scratch. "It looks like I'm not crazy after all." She looked back at me, nodded in my direction. "Do you wear those sunglasses all the time?"

"Sensitivity to light."

"Oh." Her gaze darted to the lamp dangling overhead. "Would you like me to turn it off?"

"No. It's fine." Not like I could take them off and reveal that my silver eyes glowed naturally. The lamp merely gave me an excuse because my eyes *were* sensitive to light.

"Well, if you change your mind..."

I wouldn't.

Feeling the need to find a safer subject, I glanced back at the book. "Tell me more about this *Dark Hunter* stuff."

PENELOPE

An hour and a half later, we were sitting at my kitchen island, sharing dinner and trading stories. I'd been enjoying the interaction, the easy conversation.

"It's true." I giggled. "I didn't mean to call him out like that, but I did. I remember the way his eyes blazed with anger. He hadn't been too happy that I'd confronted him in front of the entire class, but I couldn't help it. I mean, what mythology professor can't remember the name of Zeus's father?"

"Cronus," Obsidian said.

I pointed my fork at him, grinned. "Exactly. He said it was a momentary lapse. I call bullshit. Honestly, I think the guy was hitting the bottle before class. So you know about the Greek gods?"

"Not really. But I've got a dog named Zeus. Back when we were picking a name for him, I got an earful about Greek mythology."

"A dog?" The idea warmed me.

"Two, actually. Zeus and Aphrodite. They're at home right now."

Obsidian's smile held me captive, and the warmth in his voice when he spoke of his animals made me smile in return.

"What about you?" I asked. "Do you have any crazy college stories?"

He shook his head. "Didn't go to college."

"It's not for everyone. My brother gave up after two semesters. Ended up here a few days after." I pushed my plate away, wiped my mouth with a napkin. "Would you like some more?"

"I'll get it." Obsidian got to his feet and moved around the island to dish more lasagna on his plate.

For such a large man, he was graceful, as though every move was choreographed.

Before he returned, he walked over to the refrigerator, pulled out the wine. After refilling my glass, he returned the bottle and took his seat on the barstool beside me.

I couldn't resist watching him. There was something innately sexy about him, the way he moved, the way he talked, the sheer size of him. Until Obsidian had shown up, I'd considered my apartment a relatively decent-sized space. With him here, it felt small, cramped. Even the oversized island felt minuscule. He just took up so much real estate.

And boy, could the man eat. He was on his third serving, each one at least twice what I'd scarfed down, and I was stuffed.

"Do you mind me asking where you live?"

Obsidian peered over, held his fork suspended. "I've got a house in Colorado."

A bit vague, but I'd gotten quite a bit of that from him tonight. It was as though he preferred to talk about me. Not that I minded. His curiosity made me feel important, like he cared about me and what I had to say. Granted, that was likely the wine talking. I was on my third glass and feeling no pain.

Once he was finished and pushed his plate away, I got to my feet and grabbed our plates. Walking around to the sink, I flipped on the water, began washing them, sneaking quick glances at him every now and again.

"I would've done that," he said, his attention on me as he lifted his wineglass.

"I don't mind." It gave me something to do with my hands.

For the better part of the evening, I'd been fidgety, nervous. Since I couldn't remember the last time I'd been on a date, it wasn't surprising. Not that I was disappointed by Obsidian's impromptu arrival. It was as though he'd been reading my mind.

My gaze swung to him and I smiled, recalling how he'd responded to my thought about bringing chicks to his hotel room. I'd thought about that endlessly, and I knew I hadn't said the words aloud, yet he'd answered as though I had. What if he could read my mind?

I barely held back the laugh as I shifted my attention to the book on the end table. Clearly, I was confusing fantasy with reality.

Obsidian's phone rang, his head turning toward it. Rather than silence it like he had the other times it had rung, he reached for it.

"Excuse me for a minute."

I nodded, watched him get to his feet and stroll into my bedroom, ducking his head slightly as he moved through the doorway.

The thought of him being in there made my body flush. He was simply seeking privacy, but it seemed intimate. I hadn't had the chance to make my bed since his impromptu arrival. And that was rare for me. The only time I ever skipped the step was on my nights off. In case I opted for a nap.

After hand-washing the few items we'd used, I turned off the water and grabbed the dish towel. I could hear Obsidian talking but couldn't make out the words. The language he spoke ... I didn't recognize it. Then again, I didn't know much about languages. I'd taken French in high school but couldn't speak enough to do anyone any good.

Focusing my efforts on putting away the dishes, I smiled because, for the first time in a really long time, I was happy. Genuinely happy. Tonight had been nice, having dinner with someone, sharing conversation. It was easy with Obsidian.

Sure, I was nervous around him, but it wasn't an uncomfortable feeling. The butterflies in my stomach weren't on a rampage, but they were making themselves known. But most importantly, I wasn't overwhelmed by emotions. Obsidian's were still shielded, and I didn't have to worry about feeling the repercussions of his answers should I ask the wrong question.

"I'm sorry to eat and run," Obsidian said from behind me.

I shrieked, surprised by his return. I hadn't heard him come back into the room.

Turning to look at him, I laughed off the shock. That died in my throat when I realized how close he was. My thoughts instantly reverted to the kiss we'd shared in the elevator. I wanted him to kiss me again.

Obsidian held up his phone. "Duty calls."

"Sure. Yeah." I stared up at him, wishing for the thousandth time that I could see his eyes.

"When's your next night off?" he asked, tucking his phone away.

"Thursday. I'm off Tuesdays and Thursdays."

That sexy smirk had me staring at his mouth.

"And we're still on for breakfast Thursday morning?"

I nodded, swallowed when he took a step closer.

"Thank you for dinner." His words rasped over my skin like a physical touch.

"You're welcome."

I inhaled sharply when his hand lifted, long fingers gliding over my neck as he moved my hair back, his thumb brushing the underside of my jaw. It was such an intimate move, one I could so easily get used to.

"I'm going to kiss you again, Penelope."

Yes, please.

Obsidian leaned down, his warm hand curling around my neck. I could feel him watching me from behind those dark lenses. I shifted up on my toes, trying to meet him halfway. When his lips met mine, all thought fled. I sighed, leaning into him. His other hand moved to my lower back, pulling me closer, holding me there while his tongue dipped into my mouth, sliding against mine. Every nerve ending in my body came to life, dancing a jig, warming me from the inside out.

His lips were soft, his skilled tongue taking control. His dominance was subtle yet unmistakable. The man could kiss, and the sensuality of it made me want more. To feel his hands on my skin, his big body covering mine. Hell, I'd settle for feeling his bare skin against my palms.

Somehow, I managed to rein in my thoughts, to focus on the kiss. The same couldn't be said for my hands. I reached for Obsidian, my fingertips grazing his smooth cheeks, then on to the soft bristle of his hair. My thumbs glided over his ears as I wound my arms around his neck, trying to get closer. It was a wanton move, but in that moment, I didn't have the brain power to be concerned.

The dark rumble in his chest made my sex clench, my thighs squeezing together to stave off the desire.

The next thing I knew, Obsidian lifted me off my feet. My butt met the granite countertop, our lips never separating. The new position brought me closer to his mouth, the position far more comfortable. I moaned softly as his lips caressed mine, his tongue taunting and teasing. I tried to pull him closer, but he was a mountain and I was a breeze. He kept himself in place, not quite giving in to whatever was transpiring between us.

The same could not be said for me. I was falling. Rapidly. Everything about him spoke to me.

When his lips separated from mine, we were both breathing hard. Embarrassment at my behavior chilled me, made me realize how needy I'd been. I barely knew this man, and here I was, practically climbing him in an effort to get more.

"I don't want to leave," Obsidian whispered, his thumb brushing over my cheek.

I tried to look away, to hide my shame, but he kept his hand on my neck, his long fingers keeping me from turning my head.

"You're so sweet," he said softly, pulling me closer as his arms moved around me.

I buried my face in his chest, inhaled his delicious scent. A rich, musky fragrance mixed with what I assumed was fabric softener. The combination made me light-headed. His big arm curled around my neck, his palm cradling my head. It was a move that felt far more intimate than anything I'd experienced before. As though he was keeping me within the protection of his arms. I sighed against him.

Obsidian finally released me and I hopped down from the counter, straightening my T-shirt, messing with my hair, anything to keep from reaching for him again.

"What's your cell phone number?" Obsidian prompted, his phone in his hand.

I rattled it off.

A second later, my phone rang but cut off almost instantly.

"Now you have mine."

I nodded, followed him to the door.

"Good night, Penelope."

"Good night."

The kiss he pressed to my lips was soft, chaste, but it did nothing to diminish the heat flooding my veins.

Obsidian studied my face once more before he opened the door and slipped out. I closed and locked it behind him, then leaned back, my fingers touching my lips.

I could still feel his mouth on mine long after he was gone.

7

OBSIDIAN

I stared at the guardian angel, confused by the conversation we'd just had. "You weren't there? At the grocery store when she was nearly run over?"

"Unfortunately, no."

At least the male had the sense to appear remorseful. Had he been flippant, I couldn't have promised Stig would leave the house in one piece.

"Do you have a backup?"

Stig shook his head. "I wish. We're so overloaded right now it's ridiculous. It's a wonder I haven't lost more than two souls in the past decade. I can tell you, it wasn't from anything I've done. The humans are as good as on their own at the rate we're going."

I paced from one side of the small room I'd commandeered

as my office to the other. "So if you didn't come to her aid, who did?"

"That would be me." The disembodied voice sounded seconds before Michael appeared.

Stig inhaled sharply, and for a second, I thought the angel would drop to his knees before the archangel.

"Leave us," Michael ordered, not giving the guardian angel a second glance.

"Of course, Your Grace." In a flash, Stig was gone.

Though I wasn't fond of Michael's impromptu arrivals, I couldn't find it in me to give him hell for it. In fact, I stood stone-still, hands clasped behind my back as I stared at the male.

"I'm forever in your debt," I told the archangel.

"You're in my debt no matter what." Michael's cheeky response was relayed with a dismissive flutter of his hand. "I will tell you that was a fluke."

Fluke, accident, I didn't care what Michael called it. The male had saved my *amsouelot's* life, and for that, I was forever grateful.

"Do you know who was driving the vehicle?"

"One of those idiot demons."

"*Impietan*?"

"That. Yes. It made it around the block before I ensured it went headlong into a concrete divider." Michael's dark eyes met mine. "I'd say it's in your best interest to get your female to safety. Not that I'm the best to give relationship advice, but she's in grave danger as long as she's out there on her own. That damn GA is useless to her right now."

"Why are you telling me this?" It wasn't like Michael to offer assistance without an argument.

"I happen to like you, Obsidian. You've been a fair and honest leader. I've got a vested interest in your happiness. But like I said, I won't be able to assist in the future. If my father catches wind of this..."

Yeah, I didn't want to know what God would do if he found out Michael was interfering with the humans. It was a point of contention between them. Always had been.

"If you want my advice," Michael continued, "I'd put some extra protection around her. More eyes."

"I'll do that." And I knew exactly who would be perfect in the role.

Michael held my stare for a second before vanishing in a rustle of feathers.

With a sigh, I marched around the desk, brought my laptop to life, and sent a telepathic message to Asmia, requesting her to join me ASAP.

The Fae appeared less than a minute later.

"You asked to see me?"

I peered up from my computer screen, watching as the female moved gracefully into the room, her luminous purple eyes hesitant.

"I did." Motioning toward the seat opposite my desk, I waited for her to sit.

Asmia was one of the youngest Fae to become a member of the *fiestreigh*, and she'd been the last one to join our clandestine team. I couldn't recall her exact age off the top of my head, but she was likely rounding the century mark. Like all Fae, as well as angels, she didn't physically age past twenty-five, so she was as vibrant as she'd ever been with her smooth alabaster skin, the soft lines of her face.

I still remember the day she'd joined us, waltzing right into a team that had been growing for the past fifteen hundred years. Smart, beautiful, and full of light, Asmia had taken us all by storm, endearing herself to everyone. Her ability to befriend even the hardest of warriors was a benefit, and it had come in handy a time or two over the years.

Once she took a seat, I relaxed in my chair, smiled, wanting to put her at ease. "I have an assignment for you."

The female looked as though she'd been called to the principal's office and feared the reprimand for whatever transgression she'd been caught doing. I found it amusing because I'd never been the sort to inspire terror in those who worked for me.

"Asmia?"

"I'm sorry. I'm just a little"—she seemed to shake it off, added a smile that was most definitely forced—"nervous."

Before I could launch into the details of the assignment, Taayin sauntered in, his gaze zeroing in on the female instantly.

"Where's my invitation to the party?" the male quipped, though there was no humor in his tone.

"Can I help you?" I asked, not out of courtesy, more from irritation.

Taayin's gaze remained on Asmia as he leaned on the credenza to my left, crossed his arms over his lean, muscular chest. "What's going on?"

I smirked, turning my chair in Taayin's direction. "Although you believe I should, I'm not required to clue you in to all my decisions."

Irritated blue eyes shot to my face. "In case I need to remind you, I'm your *lieterra*. Therefore, I should be in the know."

Each warrior had a designated *lieterra*, an angel tasked with tracking, doling out responsibilities, and handling other menial tasks they often bitched about. Though they took orders from my brothers and me, they often believed they were due far more than we thought they were. Sure, as a right-hand or assistant, they dealt with a wealth of shit that gratefully I didn't have to be bothered with, but that didn't change the fact that the *lieterra* were inclined to do so by the roles they'd been assigned.

"And might *I* remind *you*," I told Taayin, "Heaven's gates are always open."

The implied threat that I could send him back at any time hung heavily between us.

Taayin huffed. He was fighting the urge to argue. Not surprising considering that was his most prominent trait.

Only because I felt sorry for the poor sap did I halt my efforts to piss Taayin off the way he did me. Instead, I turned my attention back to Asmia, who was still watching me carefully.

"I need an extra set of eyes on Penelope. Mostly when she's at work. I'm assigning you the role of temporary *ritarro* to my *amsouelot.* Effective immediately."

Her eyes widened, mouth falling open.

Taking on a role as a *ritarro*, even temporarily, was one of the highest honors among the Fae. It was the equivalent of a *lieterra,* but on a more personal level.

"It would be my honor," she said softly, bowing her head briefly before meeting my gaze once more. "Please forgive my ignorance, but I'm not sure exactly how I go about such a task since Penelope is not living with us."

"For now," I explained, "I want you to focus on watching over her, keeping me apprised of anything that seems off."

"What about Stig?" Taayin asked.

"He's still her guardian, but he's overloaded. I need someone closer, someone who'll clue me in immediately if there's an issue."

Asmia glanced at Taayin, then back to me. "Did something happen?"

I relayed the information I'd received from Penelope regarding the incident in the parking lot. Both Taayin and Asmia were watching me intently.

"Michael acted on Stig's behalf?" Taayin asked.

"It would seem that way." I looked at Asmia. "I want you to be present while Penelope's at work. Keep an eye on her. And in the event I'm not with her, I want you to follow her home, ensure her safe arrival. I'm not sure what Perfidious is up to, but I'm not willing to risk her life because the demon wants to play games."

"Should I introduce myself to Penelope?" Asmia asked.

"Not at this time, no. There's no need."

"It would be helpful if I had all the information you have on her," Asmia said, squaring her shoulders, as though preparing to take the weight of the world on them.

An iPad appeared on the desk, conjured out of thin air by none other than one irritating *lieterra* who prided himself on always being one step ahead. On the screen, an image of Penelope.

Asmia picked it up, skimmed the details. Her quick perusal would enlighten her to the fact Penelope Jane Calazans was twenty-eight, born to Michael and Marisol Calazans on February 2, 1991. She had one sibling, a twin brother named Oliver. Her educational background was lengthy, but her employment history was relatively short. It reflected a couple of odd jobs prior to her being employed at Caesar's Palace Casino as a cocktail waitress for the past five and a half months, earning a shitty hourly wage, though tips tended to make up some of the difference. Her medical history reflected a clean bill of health. Birth control was the only medication she took routinely, and according to the details, it was due to the irregularity of her menstrual cycle. The last time she'd visited the doctor had been for her yearly physical, and the last illness she'd been treated for was bronchitis, diagnosed eighteen months prior.

"She has a brother," Asmia noted.

"She does," I confirmed. "Though he's not in the picture."

Asmia's eyes widened. "Did he die?"

"Not yet," I muttered, then offered up the details I had on Seraphina.

"Someone needs to protect him," Taayin insisted.

Though I agreed, my one and only priority was Penelope. It wasn't that I didn't care what happened to her brother, but I was programmed to put my *amsouelot* above all others, including myself.

"Reidar has Gryffyth keeping an eye out, but find Oliver's GA," I ordered Taayin. "Check in with him. See if he's got any information."

"It's not Stig?"

Being that they were twins, I understood why Taayin would've assumed as much. "No. Changing of the guard a few years ago."

"What did he do?" Taayin asked, knowing there was only one reason a human's guardian angel would change during their lifetime.

"He's been headed down a dark road. Addiction. Gambling and alcohol."

"Shame."

"Just get what info you can," I told the *lieterra*.

Taayin nodded, clearly understanding my intentions were not to interfere with the male unless Penelope specifically asked me to.

"Does she have any close friends?" Asmia's eyes lifted. "Ones I should be aware of?"

Taayin answered with, "She has a few acquaintances from work whom she spends very little time with. Her closest friend lives in California. A Winifred Drego, a.k.a. Winnie. They speak often but haven't seen one another since she moved here."

"So she's a loner," Asmia surmised.

"Very much so," Taayin stated.

"Like I said, I expect you to look out for her," I explained. "If at any time you feel she's in direct danger, I want to know. Provided all goes well, I'll look to you as her *ritarro* once we're back at the compound. Should you happen to interact with her, she's to be treated with the utmost respect, regarded with the highest authority."

Taayin began his spiel regarding the responsibilities of a *ritarro.* As they conversed about the details, I observed the pair. In recent months, it'd been brought to my attention that they had grown closer, developed a relationship, one might say. While there were no rules restricting them from pursuing one another, they were both cognizant that their souls were not destined to be together. I suspected they wished that weren't the case.

I couldn't deny that their relationship had worked in my favor when it came to selecting Asmia for this assignment. Because she cared for the male, but her loyalty was not tied to Taayin's well-being, I knew I could trust her to keep her focus. And because Asmia was important to Taayin, he would ensure she succeeded, which meant they would work doubly hard to ensure my *amsouelot's* safety.

"I'm honored to've been selected for this role," Asmia said, drawing me from my thoughts.

Leaning back in my chair, I regarded her. "At no point should you take this lightly, Asmia."

Her perfectly plucked brows lowered. "Of course not. I'll dedicate my life to her health and happiness."

I considered her for a moment. It would've been easy to dismiss her, to allow her to walk out, prepare for the role. The female would do the job as she understood it, protecting Penelope as best she could. I trusted her. Otherwise, she would not be sitting there.

However, I felt it necessary to ensure she understood my expectations.

"While Penelope's not aware of her status as my *amsouelot*," I explained, "that doesn't change the fact. She is my utmost priority, above all else. Do you understand what I'm telling you?"

Asmia swallowed hard, nodded.

My voice dropped an octave. "Without her, Asmia, I will cease to have reason to live. And since I'm doomed to exist for eternity, her absence would ultimately endanger every living, breathing species on the face of the planet."

I paused, my eyes glowing brighter as emotion churned within me. The mere thought of something happening to Penelope had rage slicing through my gut.

"Should something happen to her, I will not hesitate to destroy everything in my path as a repercussion of losing my only reason for being. Penelope Calazans is my heart and soul. Without her, we shall all cease to exist. I will make it so."

And that was not me being dramatic. It was simply fact.

ASMIA

"Why did he select me for this?" I asked Taayin once we'd approached the main hall after leaving Obsidian's office.

"Because you're the most qualified."

I choked on a brittle laugh. "Why in Heaven's name would you think that? Everyone here is older than I. Far more versed in the hierarchy."

As with all living beings, especially the Fae, knowledge was acquired with age. And while I was just past the century mark, I was a newborn compared to the others in Obsidian's *fiestreigh*, the group tasked with supporting the warrior angels. All had far more powerful abilities, could ensure Obsidian's *amsouelot's* safety with minimal effort.

Taayin paused, turned to face me. His eyes were warm with affection, and I felt the intensity deep in my soul. This male... I'd come to care for him greatly, which was both a blessing and a curse.

"You have nothing to fear, love," he whispered. "I trust you. As does Obsidian. For now, keeping Penelope safe is the priority. However, befriending her is equally important." He smiled, his blue eyes glittering. "You're most qualified in that department."

He twined a lock of my hair around his finger, tugged me toward him.

I moved without hesitation, leaning in and accepting the warmth of his lips upon my own. As was the case whenever we were near, passion ignited. I still found it difficult to believe he was not my *amsouelot*. I could not imagine wanting someone more than I wanted Taayin.

Granted, I was appreciative in many ways that he was not my soul's other half. Along with the tremendous pleasure enjoyed between two who had been mated by the Fates, an equally devastating pain was associated when they were apart. The only reason Obsidian had not been subjected to this was due to the fact his relationship with Penelope was in its early stages. Once they consummated the relationship and until their *lintamair*, any separation they endured would give the same impression of mourning a part of oneself.

I didn't wish that upon anyone. Least of all Taayin.

"Tonight, I'll take you to the casino, show you around," he said. "I won't be able to stay for long. Now that we've located Penelope, my responsibilities have expanded. With the demons hot on her trail, I have to maintain my focus."

I understood that much. There was no doubt in my mind Obsidian would leave a wide trail of death and destruction in his wake should something happen to his *amsouelot,* and it was our responsibility to support him.

"I will not fail either of them," I assured Taayin. "Although I shall miss you terribly."

His smile was sad. "We've always got the daylight hours."

That we did. But I was hoping we'd be spending those together back in Colorado. Truth was, I missed home, missed Zeus and Aphrodite. And the *heurosp*. Vegas was so different from what I was used to, and I was eager to get back to the mansion.

"Do you think Perfidious will make his move soon?" I asked.

Taayin pulled back, stared into my eyes. "Hard to tell. Perfidious likes to play games. Always has. Since both sides are playing for her soul, it's possible he'll drag it out."

"Or catch us off guard," I acknowledged.

When an angel became ensnared by their *amsouelot,* they lost their overall focus. And without the others around to watch his back, both Obsidian and Penelope were at risk. Not only were they up against Perfidious, who was out to get Penelope, there were other demons who would love to get their slimy paws on Obsidian.

"Fear not, love," Taayin said softly. "Focus on Penelope."

I nodded in agreement, forcing thoughts of world destruction from my mind.

The gleam in Taayin's eyes told me his thoughts had already ventured down a different road entirely. Somewhere with salacious intent.

"You're thinking about taking me right here, aren't you?" I whispered, stepping in closer.

"It had crossed my mind."

"Well..." I didn't bother to look around, not caring who might be lingering. When it came to sex, I wasn't shy. "What are you waiting for?"

TAAYIN

This female taunted me in every way.

Asmia was quite possibly the most stunning fairy to have ever graced Heaven or Earth. Not only physically, though it was near impossible to deny she was otherworldly with her waist-length blond hair, the stunning amethyst eyes notorious to Fae, those cupid's bow lips, and a body to fucking die for.

No doubt about it, Asmia had wrapped me around her little

finger the very day she stepped into my world. The fact that she wasn't shy, spoke her mind freely, and sought the natural pleasures most of us forgot existed was only a bonus.

I found myself wanting her with a desperation that wasn't normal.

Without regard for consequence, I pushed Asmia up against the wall, crushed my lips to hers. Didn't matter that she'd slept in my bed through the day, I still wanted her again. My cock ached with the need to feel her wrapped around me, to be buried to the hilt in her sweet, welcoming heat.

Asmia's soft moans were a direct contradiction to the way her fingers ripped at my clothing. She was as desperate for physical contact as I was, the need overwhelming.

Answering her aggressive movements, I tore at her blouse, her bra, freeing her breasts from the constraints before gripping them firmly, kneading her soft flesh as her tongue mated with mine. In my eight hundred years of existence, I'd never met another female who could inflict such a painful desire within me. Back when things first got physical between us, nearly a year and a half ago, I'd thought she was my *amsouelot*, caught completely off guard by the emotions she churned within.

Unfortunately, I'd learned after our first parting that she wasn't mine to have and hold for all of eternity. However, she was mine for this moment in time, and I chose to be content with that, looked forward to the time I did have with her.

When she freed my cock from my slacks, her hands slowed, wrapping firmly around me, caressing my throbbing shaft.

I released her mouth, my head falling back as undiluted pleasure consumed every cell. Pumping my hips, I drove into her soft hand, sought the release she could so easily draw out of me. When my own pleasure became too much my focus, I stepped back, dislodging my aching erection from her grip.

"Strip," I hissed.

Not wasting a moment, she removed her ruined clothing, tossing it to the floor before leaning back against the wall. My hand curled around my cock in a vicious grip while hers snaked downward, between her thighs, teasing me as she pleasured her slick flesh with her fingers.

I chose to watch her, to admire the long, lean lines of her beautiful body, the way her eyes glittered as ecstasy coursed through her, driven by her own touch and my perusal.

Footsteps sounded beyond where we stood, but I ignored them. Whoever it was could watch for all I cared. My own need to satisfy this female far outweighed the worry someone might indulge in their own voyeuristic fantasy.

I relocated a chair using the powers of my mind, not wanting to look away.

Asmia giggled. "In a hurry?"

"You have no idea." My desire for this female was never curbed, no matter how many times I had her.

I took a seat, turned her away from me, then pulled her down, guiding my throbbing cock between her slick folds, angling for optimal penetration.

"Taayin," she moaned softly, impaling herself on my erection. "Yes."

Focusing on the exquisite torment, I let the euphoric sensations overwhelm me as the tight clasp of her body held me there. The silky glide of her sex over mine caused my hips to involuntarily shift upward, trying to go deeper inside her.

"Take your pleasure," I ordered the female. "Take everything."

Suffering from euphoric bliss so intense it bordered on pain, I focused on the graceful shift of her toned body working down on me, her hands gripping the chair's arms, giving her better leverage. I refrained until I was nothing more than a rubber band stretched to within seconds of snapping.

I could feel her siphoning my emotions, drawing them into her. It was what fueled the Fae, and during times like this, when emotions ran high, Asmia absorbed the excess.

Wrapping my arms around her, I jerked her back against my chest, kneading her firm breasts in my hands, pumping into her from beneath with rough, punishing thrusts of my hips. Slipping one hand downward, I teased her clit with my middle finger while I drove us both to the edge of insanity found only through the joining of our bodies.

"Taayin ... I'm so close. Make me come. Please ... come inside me."

Driving upward, I held her down with my palm on her pelvis, my finger thrumming her clit as I propelled toward release. Mine. Hers.

When I reached the pinnacle, I held myself there, driving into her harder, faster, deeper. The sweet female screamed my name, succumbing to orgasmic ecstasy. Her clit pulsed against my finger while her sex clamped down on me, a velvet vise that ripped my orgasm from me in a rough growl.

Desperation was replaced with satiation. I relished the comfort I felt with her, my arms embracing her as we relaxed, enjoying the moment.

"We should do that more often," Asmia whispered, turning her face toward me.

I pressed my lips to hers, smiled. "I won't argue with you."

However, it would have to wait. For now, we each had our assigned duties, supporting the warriors we'd taken an oath to protect, putting our own needs aside for the greater good.

And despite the inconvenience, it would be worth it in the end.

8

PERFIDIOUS

As I strolled through the casino, observing the tourists, I envied their ignorance, wondering how many would remain in their seats if they were aware a demon was amongst them.

Granted, I wasn't just *any* demon. The direct spawn of the ruler of Hell himself, my rank among the demons was at the very top. Well, maybe not the *very* top, but pretty damn close. Had I actually given a shit about status, perhaps I would've aimed higher, sought the coveted position within the *trielair*.

No, thank you very fucking much. I happened to enjoy my role exactly as it was.

"Drinks?" a female wearing a skimpy white dress and far too much makeup offered as she passed by.

"Jack and Coke," I called out, drawing her attention.

The female nodded and winked, then followed it up with some not-so-subtle eyeballing that reflected her approval.

Not giving her a second thought, I focused my attention on the empty blackjack table.

"Well, you look rather bored." I glanced at the name tag on the older female's shirt. "Beatrice."

The blackjack dealer smiled, though it didn't reach her eyes. There wasn't an ounce of friendly on her aging face, but I didn't mind. I wasn't looking for a friend.

"Perhaps I could keep you company."

She motioned toward the end seat as though I actually needed her permission to sit.

"I'm curious, Beatrice, what do you think?" I asked, tilting my head to each side, urging her to look at me as I eased into the chair.

"About?"

"Well, my face, of course."

"It's ... uh..." She peered over her left shoulder, then her right, as though she hoped someone would come save her from this conversation.

"Go on," I urged. "Tell me what you think."

"It's a ... a very nice face."

I grinned. "It is, right? No hideous demon here, thank you very much."

I was in a good mood; otherwise, I would've given the female a quick glimpse of my demon face, hidden beneath the facade of a human.

Beatrice's dark eyes saucered before dropping to the table. "Care to place your bet?"

I had to give her credit; her voice only wavered slightly. Cool as a cucumber, this one.

"I would, yes."

I pulled out a one-hundred-dollar chip from my pocket. A gift from the male whose body I now sported. After passing it to Beatrice, I waited as she called out to the pit boss to note she was making change. A minute later, she returned smaller chips.

A quick shift, and I'd successfully placed the minimum bet.

While Beatrice did her thing, I clasped my hands and stared at her. "What exactly do you find most fascinating about this face?"

Her forehead wrinkled in confusion.

"Maybe it's the eyes? The nose?" I touched the knobby protrusion. "Perhaps a tad big, but I think it works well."

"It does," she said quickly, eyes never leaving the cards she was dealing.

"Granted, I can't take any credit," I explained. "That goes to the male I misappropriated it from last night. One of the perks of being a demon, you know."

Her eyebrows lifted as though she was not sure what I meant.

"The ability to take on the appearance of any human I've stolen a soul from?"

Beatrice nodded as though she'd expected me to say that.

"Comes in rather handy, really." I scanned the humans nearby. "Around here, there's quite the selection, too."

I motioned for Beatrice to deal me a card.

Chuckling, I smiled up at her. "There for a while, I entertained myself by exchanging bodies like clothing. But admittedly, I have a type, which requires a bit of patience." I exhaled heavily. "It's rare to find a human who realizes the true gift he's been given. That whole *my body is my temple*." I met Beatrice's stare. "Where are *those* guys? I'd be happy to keep them in my closet."

Her eyebrow rose, gaze dropping to my cards. I waved a hand, refusing the offer of another.

"I know, I know," I continued. "A picky demon. Probably don't run across a lot of those, huh?"

Beatrice shook her head, but she'd lost the surprised look in her eyes. Likely saw all sorts here at her table.

"The last body I had ... it ran its course after only a few weeks. Not quite as endowed as expected." I squeezed my cheeks. "But I found this pathetic loser sitting alone in a bar. Had the look I was going for. And quite the heft, if you know what I mean."

Beatrice paid out my winnings for that hand, then pulled all the cards back before dealing more.

"For such a handsome male, he was quite the drain, though. Totally see why his wife left him."

Her eyes widened once more, followed by a smile that said I could've been speaking any number of languages and she wouldn't have cared.

"I'm making much better use of it now. If I'm lucky, I'll get quite a few miles out of it before it's time for a new one."

Beatrice nodded, waiting for me to decide whether I would hit or stand. I waved my hand over the cards. She dealt herself another, then paid me out once more.

A female approached, peering down at the table, clearly considering her options.

"Have a seat," I urged before turning my attention back to Beatrice. "The only reason I've yet to soil it with the flesh of a female is because there's only one I'm really interested in." I waited until Beatrice met my eyes. "Penelope Calazans. You know her?"

Beatrice shook her head while the female who'd started to sit strolled off.

"Pity," I said as I tracked the lithe brunette. "Probably

could've had a bit of fun later." I turned back to Beatrice, tugged on the lapel of my suit. "What about the suit? Like it?"

The dealer nodded.

"Brioni Vanquish II," I told her. "Quite the price tag, but can't beat the feel of it."

While waiting for the waitress to return with my drink, I divided my attention between the cards Beatrice dealt and the waitresses moving about, attempting to sight the female whose mere existence had summoned me to Sin City.

"I don't know Penelope," I admitted to Beatrice, rolling one of the chips through my fingers. "But word around the campfires in Hell is she's met her angel."

Beatrice nodded, though it was clear she couldn't care less what I had to say.

"It's the reason I'm here tonight. To introduce myself. See if Penelope's all she's cracked up to be. After all, why should the angels have all the fun?"

A gentle tap on my shoulder had me peering over, meeting the eager, hungry eyes of the waitress.

"Thank you, beautiful." I took the drink, passed her a five-dollar chip.

As she sauntered off, I returned my attention to Beatrice. There was a temporary lull in the game as an older man took the seat at the end, requested change, then placed his bet.

"If you've met one," I continued, "you know why angels are a crappy choice for a female. Possessive, domineering. Think they're hot shit because they're almighty." I shuddered. "Irritates the hell out of me."

I chugged my drink, motioned for Beatrice to pass me another card.

"I figure for him to devote so much attention, she must be worth checking out. Risky, I know. I mean, he could see me, right?" I grinned, leaning in. "That's the best part. He *can't*."

Beatrice peeked at her cards to ensure she wasn't holding a ten beneath the ace. She pushed them back in place, waited for me to hit or stand one more time.

My waitress passed by again, and I reached out, touched her arm. "Can I get another?"

"Sure." With a smile, she continued on.

I watched the cards as Beatrice dealt them. "I'm sure he's going apeshit, as you humans like to say, because I'm here, but that's what makes it fun. I mean, what's the point in going to work if you don't have fun?"

Both Beatrice and the male weren't paying much attention to me.

No matter.

"It's your turn, buddy." The male nodded toward his cards.

"Hit me, Beatrice."

She smiled, dealt another card, the sum of the four coming to twenty-one.

"How many is that now?" I asked. "Oh, right. All of them."

My gaze was snagged by a caramel-haired beauty as she moved toward me. The small name tag on her dress was what prompted my smile. Then again, her bountiful cleavage deserved some added wattage. She was quite lovely.

"Excuse me," I said, keeping my tone polite as I shifted in my seat to face her.

She paused, her gaze slamming into mine. "I'm sorry. I don't work this section. I can get Vivian for you, though."

"Oh, no need," I told her, visually caressing her face. "She's already getting my drink."

Those honey-gold eyes remained locked on mine.

"I was wondering if I could borrow a lighter," I lied.

She took the one sitting on her tray, passed it over. I used it to light the cigar I magically conjured inside my jacket pocket.

"Are you new here?" I asked in an attempt to make conversation.

"No." Her eyes shifted to Beatrice briefly, then back to me.

"Hmm. A shame I haven't seen you before now."

Her eyes dropped to the lighter, as though that was the only thing she was waiting for. When she held out her palm for it, I ensured my fingers brushed her skin. Those beautiful gold eyes swung back to my face, even as she jerked her hand back.

"I'm sorry. I have to get back to work."

As she walked away, I admired the gentle sway of her hips, the way the tips of her golden hair brushed the luscious upper curve of her ass. I could definitely see what the angels were all up in arms about. However, I was a tad curious how a behemoth like Obsidian had ended up with such a tiny little thing. Seemed to me things could get a bit awkward.

I reclaimed my position at the table, addressed Beatrice. "She's lovely, don't you think? And the sparkle in her eye." I grinned. "Feisty one, I'm sure."

We played several more hands before the thrill faded for me.

"Looks like I'm going to call it a night, Beatrice. Cash me out?"

She took the pile I'd amassed, called out her intention to the pit boss, then traded smaller chips for larger ones before passing them over.

I shifted a one-hundred-dollar chip back in her direction. "Thanks for listening, Beatrice."

Her smile was wide and approving.

With cigar in hand, I got to my feet, glanced around.

"Sir? Your Jack and Coke."

I spun around to see the bottle-blond waitress smiling brightly, lifting a glass from her tray.

Setting the cigar in the ashtray on Beatrice's table, I offered a grin of my own.

Taking the glass, I ensured my fingers brushed hers. Had I wanted, I could've used that brief touch to hold a connection to the human, allowing me to monitor her every move. And while I did that on occasion, it was rare. Most humans bored me, this one included.

What was perhaps the most interesting was when I'd done the same to Penelope ... I'd been unable to make that link. Meaning she'd already been touched by an angel.

Pity.

"Thank you, Vivian," I said, keeping my voice low and seductive. The charm wasn't necessary, but it was fun. "Lovely name to go with such a lovely creature."

"Thank you."

Holding the female's dull blue gaze, I willed her to follow me. No, she wasn't Penelope Calazans but she would do in a pinch.

"Have a good night, Beatrice," I told the dealer, offering her a quick wave.

Once we'd made it closer to the exit, the waitress set her tray down while I downed the watery shit they pretended was free alcohol, then discarded the glass. Once outside, I strolled toward a set of bushes used to decorate the monstrosity they called a hotel. As I studied the rather hideous arrangement of greenery, I came up with the perfect way to spruce them up.

"Come here, beautiful," I whispered, waiting until the loose-legged female approached. "Do you know Penelope Calazans?"

She nodded, her eyes blank.

"Is she a friend of yours?"

"Co-worker."

Not close, then. Too bad. "Vivian, I'd like to send Penelope a message."

"I really don't talk to her much," she said softly.

"No worries. I won't need you to talk to her." I moved closer, ran my finger over her cheek.

Vivian didn't say a word as I leaned in, let my lips brush hers. The female sighed, her eyes glazed from the trance she was in.

Aware we were in direct view of the dozens who meandered in and out of the nearby doors, I backed the female against the wall, crowded her with my much bigger body.

"I would give you an orgasm," I informed her as I peppered kisses on her mouth. "However, I'm not in a giving mood tonight."

So, rather than thrust my fingers between her skinny thighs, I sealed my lips to hers. As my tongue stroked into her mouth, she relaxed in my arms with a contented sigh. Figuring she deserved at least a little tease, I sucked on her tongue, allowing the kiss to warm her, to make her squirm with anticipation.

After all, it was the last thing she would ever feel.

With our tongues dancing, our lips fused, I did what I do best. I inhaled her soul, drawing it right out of her body and into mine. As I felt the life leave her, I pulled back, stared. This was the best part: when their life dissolved into nothingness. The unlucky female wouldn't see Heaven or Hell because I'd consumed her very essence.

"Nothing to write home about," I assured her, tossing the lump of skin and bones into the bushes.

Turning away from the garden's new decoration, I straightened my suit jacket and sauntered out into the night.

Perhaps that would give those warrior assholes some idea that I was here, that I knew where the *amsouelot* was. Admittedly, I enjoyed the games. It made my existence far more interesting.

However, the list was a long one, so I knew I couldn't stick around indefinitely.

Which meant Penelope's time was almost up.

OBSIDIAN

"You know we're not gonna find any action out here," Reidar griped as we strolled down the strip.

I felt the *ladeare's* disappointment.

We passed a group of human males stumbling along, laughing when one all but face-planted on the concrete.

"I didn't realize we were looking for any," I replied, ignoring the human idiots.

"I guess I'm just twitchy," Reidar grumbled.

I could understand what he was getting at. We'd spent so much time looking for Penelope, always moving, chasing one lead after another. Now that we'd found her, it was a matter of going on the defensive. Not something any of us were good at.

"Whoa, dude," a human male crooned, stopping directly in front of me. "How freaking tall are you?"

Rather than answer the intrusive and completely asinine question, I met the male's dark stare, held it. *Apologize for your rudeness, then pretend you don't see me. Oh, and don't ask any more fucking questions for the rest of the night.*

"I apologize for my rudeness," the male said, his gaze darting to the left as he eased around me, going about his business.

"Please tell me you fucked with him," Reidar said with a wide grin.

"Nothing that'll cause him discomfort," I admitted. Of course, the human's friends would probably want to thank me later. The mind control would last for several hours at least.

"That's too bad."

Grinning, I tucked my hands in my jeans pockets and paused as the Bellagio fountains rose high over the water in front of us. "Don't you ever just want a night off?"

The water danced along with the music, the lights offering a show as well. Humans tucked themselves against the concrete railing, trying to get a better look as cell phones captured the scene so they could boast about it on social media.

"You forget who you're talking to," Reidar stated, smiling for the first time since I insisted he accompany me on this patrol. "Admit it," the male continued. "You hate it as much as I do."

"Yeah, I do." There was no denying it. Over the centuries, I'd come to enjoy the hunt. Prowling for the predators who preyed on the innocent was a responsibility none of us took lightly.

Granted, there weren't nearly enough of us. Keeping an eye out for so many humans required an army. We were more of a brigade, made up of a battalion in the double digits, not triple.

Then again, our powers made up for numbers.

As we passed a row of trees shooting up from the concrete, I felt the presence of a demon, my senses flaring out, categorizing all present until I located the young female standing alone in the shadows of a tree.

Reidar sensed her a second later, his hand going for the blade on his belt.

With an arm across the male's chest, I paused him from doing anything rash.

"Possessed or *neilloh*?" Reidar inquired.

"Possessed," I confirmed, referring to the fact the female's body had been taken over by a demon rather than having been sent back from Hell to carry out an order.

With minimal effort, I entered the female's mind, searched for her intentions. She wasn't working under Perfidious's orders, which meant she was on her own, likely attempting to settle into the area. Her outing tonight was about boredom, not instructions.

"Think we can spring a trap? Get her out of the eyes of the humans?" Reidar asked.

"Good plan."

Being that dawn was only a few hours away, the Strip was not as crowded as usual, most of the occupants intoxicated. It only took a minute to locate a human male straggling behind his buddy, who was putting the moves on a frustrated female. The male was sober and bored, a bit irritated after spending the night putting up with his annoying travel companion, who'd imbibed far more than he should have.

The mental push I sent his way had the human glancing over at the female, pausing. Her eyes darted around as though looking for the trap.

Cloaking myself and Reidar, I remained where I was, waited for her to take the bait. As expected, the demon locked onto him, her lip curling as she scented her prey.

I shot a mental command for the male to take a detour. Rather than follow his friend into the casino, he continued past the doors, leading the demon down the sidewalk around the side of the building.

With Reidar at my side, I followed close behind.

Evidently proud she'd trapped her prey, the demon didn't bother looking around, even as I dropped the cloak and approached her from behind.

The human male stopped, stared at the elevator before him, the only way to go unless he turned around.

I've got this one, Reidar informed me.

Keeping the human peering straight ahead, I stepped back as Reidar daggered the demon from behind. A flash of light, followed by sludge the only evidence it had ever existed.

I released the hold I had on the male's mind, sending him back in the direction he'd come. The male turned, gave the sludge a wide berth, then walked between Reidar and me, his eyes glazed, confusion contorting his face.

"Such a waste," Reidar grumbled, his voice low. "That girl was what? Twenty-one? Twenty-two?"

Probably. And Reidar was right, it was a waste. The female had once been human, but she'd hit a crossroads at some point. It was the only way a demon could occupy a vessel. They waited on the fringes, seeking a ride with an occupant worthy of their deception. Once they found one, they bided their time, slipping in only when the human opted for the wrong direction at the crossroads. And while I detested the idea of eliminating a human, the fact that they were doomed for evil eased the guilt somewhat.

I cast a sideways glance at Reidar. "Get anything more on Seraphina?"

The male sighed. "We now know what she looks like. At least until she takes another form."

"As long as she's with the brother, she'll stick to the same one."

"True. And from what I can tell, he's moved her in with him."

"Fucking hell."

"That's what I said. Poor fuck has no idea he's shacking up with a demon. If only he could see her true face." Reidar shivered dramatically as he stopped in front of the fountains. "Word came in a little while ago that a human female was found in the bushes at Caesar's."

I cocked an eyebrow, silently urging him for details.

"Her name was Vivian Matthews. Thirty-two-year-old female." Reidar's gaze slid past me toward the fountains. "Soul drained from her body. Second in a matter of days."

The rough growl escaped before I could tamp it down. "Perfidious?"

"Has to be. I figure he's sending you a message?"

That he knew where Penelope was, yes. Message received. Loud and clear.

"I know it's a delicate situation," Reidar said, "but I think we need to get her out of town. Take her to the mansion."

If I thought it was possible, I would. Except I was not going to make Penelope feel as though she was a prisoner. And if she learned that I had whisked her off for her protection and left her brother behind, I doubted she would ever forgive me. Not how I wanted to build a relationship with the female I intended to spend eternity with.

Turning my attention to Caesar's, I paused. "I'll be with her for a few hours at least. I want you to check on the brother, but make sure Seraphina doesn't catch a whiff of you."

Reidar's grin turned wicked. "She'll never sense me."

"Then I want you to find a way to track Perfidious. We need to know his movements to eliminate him once and for all."

"Will do. See you back at the house?"

I nodded.

The male strolled around the corner, concealed himself before vanishing.

Rather than do the same, I opted to walk to my destination. Penelope would be getting off work in a few minutes, and I had every intention of picking up where we'd left off the other night.

An hour later, I was walking Penelope into the hotel room. She'd been oddly quiet since I encountered her near the elevators, where I'd asked her to meet me.

The moment we stepped into the room, she seemed to relax somewhat.

"Hungry?" I offered.

"Not really. Well, not yet, anyway."

I nodded. I was starved, but it had absolutely nothing to do with food. From the instant I laid eyes on her again, I'd thought of that make-out session we'd had in her apartment. The ache I had for her had renewed, intensifying, and it took tremendous effort to ignore it.

"Why don't we sit outside? Relax for a bit?" I motioned toward the patio doors and allowed her to precede me.

"So, how was your day?" she asked.

"Uneventful." I was hoping that would change in the near future. "And yours? Any irritating customers tonight?"

"Not really, no. But it's only Thursday. Most of those wait for the weekend."

I came to an abrupt stop, surveying the patio at the same time Penelope did. At least two dozen candles flickered around the whirlpool, and steam billowed up from it in the gentle morning breeze.

"Did you do this?" Penelope asked, glancing from the water to me, a rosy tint to her cheeks.

"I wish I could take the credit, but no." If I had to guess, Alden had been attempting to set the mood. "Why? Care to take a dip?"

I'd actually intended to sit out here near the fire pit, enjoy some of the unseasonably cool night with the beautiful female. We had roughly an hour and a half before the sun rose, so I figured it was the safe thing to do. The mere thought of getting into the water with Penelope—

I cut off the mental image the thought invoked.

"I didn't bring a swimsuit," Penelope stated. "Otherwise, I'd be game."

I fumbled for something to say, then mumbled, "Clothing optional."

She huffed a laugh. "I am not getting in naked, Obsidian."

"I will if you will," I teased. Mostly.

"Not naked," she insisted.

Okay, so we were doing this.

Figuring she would follow my lead, I made the first move, tugging my T-shirt off. "Suit yourself."

It was bold, perhaps, but I could think of no better way to spend the morning.

Her golden eyes caressed my chest, and I felt the warmth as though her hands were making the trek. The way she scanned every inch hardened my body instantly.

"Not naked," she repeated.

Oh, I'd heard her the first time, but I offered a nod of agreement as I sat down and removed my boots, my socks. She was still watching me when I stood and unbuttoned my jeans.

"Wait!" She placed her hand over her eyes.

"Not naked," I assured her. *For now.*

She giggled, but it sounded a bit strained.

Offering her a bit of privacy, I took off my jeans, then made my way into the water, my boxer briefs doing little to conceal my erection. Since I couldn't do anything to eliminate it, I did my best to hide it by sinking into the warm water.

"You're still fully dressed," I reminded her.

Penelope lowered her hand, scanned the area. A second later, she had clearly come to a decision.

"Turn around," she insisted.

In an effort to appease her, I did as she asked.

Evidently, she didn't realize I could see her perfectly in the reflection of the glass.

9

PENELOPE

I could not believe I was doing this. Stripping down to my underwear outside, where pretty much anyone could see me…

Yes, I was aware my underwear wasn't much different from a bikini. But still. It felt strangely taboo.

Yet I'd been firmly on board from the instant Obsidian made the suggestion. After all, this was a rare opportunity, right? To overlook the Vegas Strip while submerged in water with a sexy man by my side.

Plus, I was being bold. Taking chances. It was the promise I'd made myself before I left for work last night. I'd done little more than think about Obsidian since we had dinner at my apartment, and I'd been eager to see him again. I'd come to the decision that I wasn't going to shy away from what I wanted. Not ever again.

So, the last thing I intended to do was tuck my tail between my legs and run when I could enjoy a sexy encounter with an equally sexy man.

Then again, it was likely my hormones dictating my actions, making me reckless. From the moment I saw him downstairs, I'd been set on simmer, warming the longer I was in his presence.

Deep breath.

Clad only in my bra and panties—thankfully, it was one of my nicer sets—I stepped down into the warm water, sinking as deep as I could, most of my hair getting drenched in the process. Good thing it was in a ponytail.

The body of water surrounded by two dozen candles wasn't so much a hot tub as it was a small heated pool. A smooth concrete ledge ran the length of the rectangular tub on both sides, providing seating for at least ten. And being that it was in the heart of Vegas, I could only imagine what sort of action this thing had seen.

As I eased onto the ledge across from Obsidian, my gaze caught on the enormous tattoo that covered his back. An absolutely stunning design, expanding across the entire breadth of his shoulders down to his narrow waist. Two feathered wings, one white, one black, looked almost lifelike thanks to the skill of the artist. There was a shield in the center. The words *Angels of Darkness* were inked inside while a ribbon curved beneath it, with his name in big block letters.

Angels of Darkness, huh? A motorcycle club, maybe? Seemed fitting.

"Can I turn around?" Obsidian asked.

"Yes." The breathless quality of my voice surprised me as I jerked my attention away from the tattoo.

It was Obsidian's fault. I'd gotten an eyeful of his ridiculous physique, and my cardiovascular system had taken a hit. Never in my life had I seen a man that well-built. Every inch of him was muscular, from his neck down to his defined calf muscles. But his upper body was what I was caught up in now. Those thick arms looked strong enough to move mountains, his wide shoulders powerful enough to carry the weight of the world, the hard planes and angles of his chest were cut to perfection, and the delicious ridges of his abdomen made my mouth water.

I had an overwhelming urge to use my tongue to outline every single angle of his body. Twice.

The sound of the patio door opening put an end to my ogling, brought me out of that ridiculous fantasy and back on solid ground.

Footsteps echoed on the concrete, drawing my attention to the butler moving toward us. He had one hand tucked neatly behind his back, the other carrying a tray. Without looking at me directly, he set everything down near the edge of the pool. Two champagne flutes, a dish of strawberries, a small bowl of what appeared to be chocolate sauce, all arranged artfully.

Not exactly the breakfast of champions, but I had no complaints. My nerves were rioting, so I doubted I could eat much anyway.

"Is there anything more I can get you right now, sir?"

"That'll be all," Obsidian told him, though his attention never shifted away from me. "Something troubling you?"

I smiled, allowing my arms to float to the top of the water. "You mean besides the fact I'm nearly naked in a pool with a complete stranger?"

Another laugh, so dark, so rich, I suddenly wanted to kiss him again. My thoughts drifted back to that kiss in my apartment, to the way his mouth had covered mine, owning me for several breathless seconds. I'd actually dreamed about it, waking to disappointment because Obsidian hadn't been there to reignite that passion I was craving.

"I wouldn't say I'm a complete stranger."

My eyes inadvertently dropped to his mouth. "No. I guess not."

Obsidian held out his hand. I stared at it briefly, then put mine in his. He pulled me toward him with ease. Not that I resisted. Touching him was about the only thing I cared about right then.

"Turn around."

Swallowing hard, I turned away from him, the Vegas Strip laid out before me. He pulled me backward, settling me on his lap. The second his arm came across my midsection, just below my breasts, a warm tingle skimmed over my flesh. He kept me there, reclining against his muscled torso.

"Relax, Penelope." The dark rumble of his voice had my nerves dancing. Every inch of skin that met his warmed. It felt good to be in his embrace, made me feel safe.

"Believe it or not, this is the first time I've done something like this," I admitted.

"Like what?"

"Being intimate like this. With someone I barely know."

"Really? No wild romps in your younger days?" he questioned, handing me one of the champagne flutes.

"How old do you think I am?" I teased.

"Age is merely a number."

I took a sip, felt the bubbles fizz over my tongue. "True. Even so, there've been no romps for me."

"No?"

"I've dated some, sure, but ... I guess I've never found anyone who tripped me up."

Not the way you do, anyway.

Obsidian chuckled, as though he'd heard my inner thoughts.

"I've always been the good girl," I explained. "Usually spent my time trying to corral my brother, keep him in line."

"He a troublemaker?"

"You could say that."

"You only have the one brother?"

"Yeah. I think two at once was more than my parents bargained for."

"And your parents? Where are they?"

"My mother ran off with a man-child, ditching all of us when I was thirteen. I haven't seen her in years. My father ... he's still in LA. He owns a tech company. Spends the majority of his time in the office."

"Do you keep in touch with him?"

"Not really, no. He calls from time to time. Usually looking for Oliver. His company's more important than his family. Our relationship ... it's a bit strained."

"I'm sorry to hear that."

"It's part of the reason I followed Oliver here. Not because we're close or anything. Guess I figured if I was going to have a relationship with one of them, I had a better chance with my brother."

Not that that had worked out for me or anything.

Obsidian dangled a strawberry in front of me. I started to reach for it, but his lips brushed my ear.

"Let me feed you."

I could hardly breathe for the heat that consumed me. The sensation of his breath caressing my neck had my skin feeling two sizes too small.

Opening my mouth, I waited for him to bring the strawberry closer. He teased my lower lip with chocolate, dragging the berry across it. When he paused, I closed my lips around it, bit down. The tangy flavor was softened by the sweetness of the chocolate.

"Good?"

I nodded. "You said you're here on business? How long will that be?"

"As long as it takes."

"But you said you found who you were looking for."

"I did. I've got a few more things to deal with."

"And when you're not here? Do you spend most of your time in Colorado?"

"It's the first place we've purchased with the intention of sticking around."

"We?"

"Me and my brothers."

"How many do you have?"

"Six."

"Wow. That's a lot of siblings. Are you the oldest?"

"Yes."

Based on my guesstimate, I doubted he was much older than I was. Before I could voice my question regarding his age, he held another strawberry up. I took it easily this time, licking at the chocolate that dripped down my lip.

"And you?" he asked. "Are you planning to stay in Vegas?"

I stared out at the lights of the Strip. "I haven't decided yet."

"Regrets?"

"No, actually. It's been a nice change of pace."

"What do you like best about it?"

"The night. It took some time to get used to, the whole sleeping during the day, but it works for me." I exhaled, relaxing against him. "I came here for a change. Wanted a new start. Some excitement."

"And how's that working for you?"

Tilting my head back so I could peer up at him, I smiled. “Things are looking up.”

He was still wearing those dark glasses, and I wondered how he could even see with them on. Despite the lights from the Strip, the patio was shrouded in darkness, our own private alcove.

I hadn’t realized I was still staring up at him until I felt the champagne glass being removed from my fingers. I heard the light clink of the glass on the patio before Obsidian’s warm hand cupped my cheek, his head lowering.

When his lips brushed my mouth, it sparked every nerve ending in my body.

Reaching back, I ran my fingers over his smooth jaw, urging him closer. Our lips melded together, and I moaned softly, lost to the sensual swipe of his tongue against mine.

Unable to help myself, I turned in his arms, tongues exploring, breaths becoming more labored. Obsidian’s big hands curled over my hips, pulling me closer. I straddled his thighs, our tongues intimately entwined. Desire, unlike anything I’d ever felt, consumed me, dragging me under. I was lost to it as I trailed my fingers over the hard muscles in his shoulders, then brushed against the short hair at the back of his head.

His erection pressed against the juncture of my thighs, and I wantonly shifted closer, wanting the friction of his body to soothe the ache within mine. I moaned, this time encouraging him to touch, to taste, to explore. This desperate hunger was not something I was familiar with, nor did I know what to do about it. My mind warred with my body. This was a man I barely knew, but that didn’t seem to matter. I simply wanted him to assuage this painful need, to sate the intense ache.

It took a moment to register the sound of a phone ringing.

When I did, I pulled back, completely appalled at my behavior.

Jerking out of his arms, I backed away, embarrassed that I'd allowed myself to get so out of control. Again. I wasn't sure I even recognized myself when I was around him.

Obsidian's attention remained on me as he reached for the cell phone behind him.

"Yeah?"

God, what in the hell was I doing here? What made me think this was a good idea? The man ... he was the kind who seduced to get what he wanted. And though I was intrigued by thoughts of what he would feel like covering my body, buried deep inside me, I was not that girl. If I gave in to this now, there was no doubt in my mind Obsidian would be gone by nightfall, never to be heard from again.

With him distracted, I rushed out of the pool, grabbed one of the plush towels sitting on a nearby table. I hurriedly dried myself as best I could. My undergarments were soaked and would no doubt show through my clothes if I attempted to keep them on. I could imagine the looks I would get downstairs if I traipsed out of here like that.

With no other options, I wrapped the towel around myself, then stripped off my panties before pulling my jeans on. It took effort with my skin still damp and my intentions to keep covered, but I managed. I did the same with my bra, discarding it before pulling on my shirt. I wrung out the wet undergarments, tucked them into my purse. My hair was a tangled, wet mess, but there was nothing I could do about it now. As I headed for the room, I squeezed out as much excess water as possible.

I was only a few steps from the door when Obsidian called out to me.

"I have to go."

"Wait, Penelope."

I turned to see him strolling toward me, his thickly muscled body clad only in a pair of black boxer briefs and dripping with water. The man was enormous, and even though I was embarrassed by the way I'd reacted, I couldn't stop myself from ogling him once again. He had a weird hold on me.

"Stay," he whispered softly as he cupped my face with one hand.

"I can't." Didn't mean I didn't want to.

I could tell he was staring at me even though I couldn't see his eyes behind those lenses. Suddenly, it bothered me that I'd been seconds from getting down and dirty with a man whose eye color I didn't even know.

"I've got to go."

"I'll walk you down."

I shook my head. "No. Please. I just..."

It took every bit of strength I had to move away from him, but I did. Fueled by concern that I'd do something I would wake up to regret, I walked away from Obsidian.

And didn't look back.

The good news was my heart was still intact.

The bad news...

I felt an overwhelming sense of loss.

OBSIDIAN

Had it not been for the sheer panic I'd seen on Penelope's face, I would've left well enough alone, gone back to the house before the sun rose, settled in for the day.

Okay, that was a fucking lie. Nothing could've kept me away from her. Not her need to run or this bullshit white-knight thing I was dealing with. And certainly not when she was freaked out.

Because I opted to take the fastest route from point A to point B, I managed to catch up to her as she sped toward the exit leading to the parking garage. For such short legs, my female could huff it. Had I been a couple of seconds earlier, she would've likely seen me materialize in the adjoining hallway.

"Penelope, wait."

She came to an abrupt halt, slowly pivoting to face me, her face pinched with confusion.

That she would give me a chance to talk was a good sign.

Maybe.

Of course, now I could see the question in her eyes. I was fully dressed, yet I'd managed to make it downstairs before she could get out the door.

"Wha— I need to go home."

"Stay with me."

She shook her head. "I can't do this, Obsidian. This..." Her hands moved back and forth to encompass the two of us. "It was a mistake. I shouldn't..."

As I moved closer, she drew inward on herself, her arms wrapping around her middle as though she was afraid of what would happen if she didn't.

"Did I do something?"

She shook her head. "Not you. Me. This... I can't do this."

I couldn't deny I'd anticipated her having an issue dealing with *what* I was, but since I'd yet to reveal any details to her, that wasn't the issue.

"What's wrong?"

"This ... it's moving too fast."

Ah. Speed could be a tricky thing. Then again, I was in no rush, so why should she be?

"We can keep it casual," I told her, willing to do whatever it took to keep her with me, to spend just a few more hours together.

Her cautious gaze lifted to my face. "See, that's the problem, Obsidian."

The frustration in her tone had me stepping back, giving her space.

"I'm not sure I can keep it casual. Whatever's happening here ... I can't ... I can't seem to find the brakes."

Personally, I didn't see a problem with that, but clearly she did. Then again, I was aware of the *amnigh*, the overwhelming desire *amsouelots* felt for one another. It wasn't something that could be ignored, and with time, it would only intensify.

"I'm not into one-night stands, Obsidian."

I smiled. Couldn't help it. "Trust me, that's not what this is."

"No?" She obviously wasn't convinced.

"I want to spend time with you," I admitted.

"For now," she countered. "Once I sleep with you, all bets are off. You'll be out the door before—"

I cut her off, my voice dropping an octave or ten. "Don't assume you know who I am or what I want, Penelope. I assure you, you'll be wrong."

She had no scathing retort, but the insecurity was still glittering in her eyes.

Funny how I had a wealth of powers at my disposal, yet I

couldn't use a single one on this female. Perhaps the more accurate term was *wouldn't,* because, technically, I was capable. I wanted Penelope with a passion that rivaled all, but I wouldn't force this. I wanted to take this at her pace because, in the end, she was all that mattered.

Holding out my hand, I waited.

"You terrify me," she whispered, her eyes pleading as though she needed me to confirm that what was happening here was something to embrace, not run from.

When her hand settled on mine, I felt the tremble in her body. Whether it was fear or cold, I couldn't tell, but I pulled her against me anyway, holding her for a minute. Her hair was dripping down her back, her shirt wet and the air conditioner was going full blast. I was going with cold.

"You have no reason to believe me," I whispered, cupping the back of her head as she pressed her cheek to my chest. "But this isn't temporary. What's happening here..."

I couldn't continue without giving away my deepest secrets, and I knew she was in no place to believe me, much less understand this was only the beginning for us.

"Stay with me today, Penelope. We'll go as fast or as slow as you want. I have no agenda, I promise."

Penelope's head tilted back, her eyes searching my face. "I don't even know what color your eyes are."

Well, hell. "I'll show you, but I need you to come back to the room with me."

Her forehead creased, her confusion evident.

"Trust me, Penelope."

Whether she did or not, at least she nodded.

Getting her back to the hotel room didn't require much effort. She walked with me, her hand in mine, as she clutched her purse to her body.

Before we stepped inside, I willed the curtains closed with

my mind, ensuring there was no light peeking through now that the sun was rising above the mountains.

"Are you hungry?"

Penelope shrugged.

"Why don't you sit down? I'll have room service bring breakfast."

"Eggs and bacon," she said, releasing the grip she had on her purse when I reached to take it from her. "Would you mind if I ... uh ... use your restroom?"

I nodded toward the bedroom, then turned back to the phone, giving her some privacy.

It took a hearty breakfast and a dreadful two hours of some vampire chick flick before she was relaxed completely. And while I hadn't a clue what the fuck that whole glittering bullshit was, I would've endured it a million times over just to spend time with her.

When Penelope yawned, I grinned, pushing to my feet.

"Let's go to bed." I held out my hand.

Penelope's eyes widened, a hint of her panic from earlier replacing the serenity I'd witnessed a moment before.

I held my hands up as a sign of surrender. "I promise, completely innocent."

"I have a few questions first."

I could handle questions.

Maybe.

"Hit me."

"What's your last name?"

"I don't have one."

That didn't seem to be the answer she expected, but it also didn't sway her from asking another. "What are your brothers' names?"

"Stygian, Eclipse, Shadow, Piceous, Aphotic, and Cimmerian. Not in order, and no, they don't have last names, either."

"How tall are you?"

I couldn't help it, I smiled. "Six ten."

"Wow. Okay." Her golden gaze bounced over my face as she stared up at me from her position on the sofa. "What color are your eyes?"

I swallowed hard. "Silver."

That evidently wasn't the answer she was looking for because she continued to stare. When she reached for my hand, tugging me toward her, I sat on the sofa once more. Penelope shifted to her knees, moving closer, while I remained where I was. I didn't move a muscle when she reached for the sunglasses shielding my eyes.

Inhaling deeply, I closed them briefly, realizing for the first time in my life I felt genuine fear. The absolute last thing I wanted was for Penelope to be scared of me.

Penelope's cool hand cupped my cheek. "Please let me see."

After a deep, cleansing breath, I opened my eyes.

"Holy..." Rather than move back, Penelope remained where she was, her gaze bouncing back and forth over my eyes, studying them. "They're ... beautiful."

Realizing I'd been holding my breath, I exhaled slowly. "Intimidating's usually the word humans use."

"Humans?" Her head canted to the side slightly. "You say that as though you're not one."

Since she hadn't asked a question, I didn't answer.

Truth was, I was at a loss, terrified that one wrong move would send her running. While I'd always prided myself on my strength, I couldn't deny there was an underlying insecurity. Especially when it came to her. I'd spent centuries waiting for the female I could love with everything I was. Now that Penelope was within reach, that vulnerability was wreaking havoc. I couldn't chance losing her before I ever had her.

"They're so bright and ... they're swirling. Why?"

"It's a long story. One that can wait until we sleep for a bit."

I was surprised when Penelope nodded, accepting my evasive response. Not willing to chance her changing her mind, I got to my feet, reached for her hand, then helped her up. She continued to stare, making me feel a bit uneasy. Like a specimen that required dissection.

Once in the bedroom, I barely caught myself before I used my mind to turn on the lights.

"Are your eyes really sensitive to light?" she asked as I flipped on the small lamp by the bed. "Or do you wear them to hide the fact they glow?"

"Both. Here." I reached behind my head and tugged my T-shirt off. "You can wear this. It'll be more comfortable because ... yours is still damp."

As she'd done the last time I removed my shirt, Penelope's eyes instantly zoned in. Her obvious approval did something for me in a major way.

"I'll ... I'll just go change in the bathroom."

While she went off to do her thing, I reclined on the bed, keeping my boots on to show her I had nothing planned except for sleep.

Good thing, too, because when Penelope returned, she was once again on edge. Right up until she noticed I was still dressed. She, on the other hand, was clad only in my T-shirt. The black cotton covered her from neck to knee—though it did hang off one shoulder and offered a delicious glimpse of her puckered nipples—but it was the sight of her wearing it that did it for me.

"Come on," I urged, patting the pillow.

Cautiously, she crawled into the bed. Just as she was about to lay her head on the pillow, I reached for her, pulling her against me.

"I promise, I'll keep my hands to myself. I just want you close."

She sighed as she relaxed her head into the crook of my shoulder. Her hand rested on my stomach, making the muscles tense.

"Your feet are hanging off the end of the bed," she said softly.

I smiled, staring up at the ceiling. That was a small price to pay. "Sleep. I'll be right here when you wake up."

I'd expected some sort of argument, but Penelope didn't put up a fight. In fact, her breaths evened out shortly after she snuggled up to me.

With my hand covering hers where it rested on my chest, I allowed myself to drift when Penelope slipped into slumber, but it didn't last long. Probably because I didn't want to miss a minute of being with her. Rather than sleep through it, I remained in the darkened room, content to have her nestled close, to listen to her soft breaths and the steady beat of her heart.

The coldness I'd felt in her absence last night was nonexistent because I was with her. Though she hadn't mentioned it, I had to wonder if she'd felt it, too. It was brought on by distance, and as things progressed, the more time we spent together, the more insistent it would become when we were apart. It was the Fates' way of ensuring two souls destined to be together remained together.

Had it not been for the fact she was hesitant to move forward at my pace, I would've taken her back to the house, gotten her into my bed, and kept her there for days. Only, there was so much more she needed to know before I could do that. Revealing to this female that I was not human was going to require finesse, and right now, I wasn't sure I could muster any up.

I drifted in and out of sleep, rousing only to ensure Penelope was still beside me before nodding off again. The minutes turned into hours as the sun blazed high in the sky. My skin prickled as it always did when the sun sank beyond the horizon, signaling it was safe for me to go outside once again.

Penelope stirred, peering around the darkened room. She yawned, stretched. "How long did I sleep?"

I peered at the clock. "Roughly eight hours."

She snuggled closer. "Good thing I don't have to work tonight. Did you sleep?"

"A little."

"What are you thinking about?" she murmured, shifting against me, her soft hand sliding over my stomach, causing every muscle in my body to harden.

"You."

I could feel her smile against my chest.

"Me? And what thoughts are going through that handsome head of yours?"

"That I like the way I feel when I'm with you."

"I know the feeling. It's... You don't think this is weird?"

I turned my head, tried to look down at her. "What?"

"I mean, we just met."

"You make it sound like that's a problem."

"Isn't it?" Her hand disappeared as she moved her hair out of the way. "For all you know, I could be some harlot seeking a sugar daddy."

"Are you?"

Her hand returned to my stomach, my cock twitching in response.

"No. It's definitely not money I'm after."

"So what *are* you after?"

Penelope laughed. "Honestly, I don't know. It's not that I'm timid or anything. I just... I don't want to move too fast. Ruin what might be a good thing."

"So, I don't have to worry about a jealous ex wanting to challenge me to a duel?"

"Not sure what man would be up for that challenge." She giggled. "And no, I haven't had a boyfriend in... Well, the truth is, I've never had a boyfriend. Not anything that lasted more than a couple of days, anyway. And that was back in high school."

"Why not?" I prompted, curious.

"Good question. I don't know, really. I've tried dating, but it's so tedious. Like I said, it's not easy to be around people for too long. And a guy I'm interested in ... not exactly romantic when I can feel their intentions, know what they're after."

"And me?"

"Maybe that's what's throwing me off. I can't read you. I think it scares me."

"Ever think that maybe we're exactly where we're meant to be?"

Penelope's head rose slightly. "No. I'm not sure I believe in fate or karma or the universe's plan."

"But you have a fascination with the supernatural?"

She chuckled. "Touché."

Her head lifted, and even in the pitch-black room, I could see her clearly. My eyesight allowed me to see better in the dark than in the light, hence I was sensitive to artificial light.

"I should be running for my life," she said softly.

Shifting so that I was facing her more fully, I met her eyes in the darkened room. "Why?"

She stared at me, seemingly entranced by my eyes. "I don't know. It's just ... I've never felt anything like this before."

"Anything like what?"

"This connection, like I've known you my entire life. Or from a past life, maybe." Her hand moved to my cheek. "And then ... I can sense something different about you. Not just your eyes. It feels surreal, Obsidian. Like my mind's playing tricks on me. Like it's not real."

"Trust me, *ayreme*, it's real," I assured her, leaning forward, dropping a soft kiss on her mouth.

My hunger for her was all-consuming, and with every kiss, every touch, I wanted one more, and then another. I couldn't resist her, didn't want to. The way her soft lips moved against mine, those sweet mewls sounding in her throat, they spurred me on, made me want to—

Forcing myself out of my thoughts, I shifted away from her.

"I'm sorry," she whispered.

"For what?"

"For coming on so strong."

I laughed. "I assure you, that's not the problem, Penelope."

"Then what is?"

Turning toward her, I cupped her face in my palm and sealed my mouth to hers. I let her taste my hunger, my need. This female rocked me to my very core, evoking emotions I'd never felt before.

I pulled back, met her eyes. "I want you, Penelope. I can't deny it. I won't."

My hand wandered to her thigh, slowly inching upward, cupping her naked hip as I pulled her close.

"But I'm not pushing for anything. I'm here because I want

to be here. With you. Even if it's only to hold you while you sleep."

"Sleep is the last thing on my mind right now."

Before I could put space between our bodies, she reached for my neck, pulled me back down to her. I shifted closer, one knee settling between her thighs, hands flat on the mattress, braced beside her head.

"I like feeling you against me, Obsidian. Everywhere. It's all I can think about."

The sexy rasp of her voice had my cock harder than steel.

I crushed my mouth to hers, inhaling her soft, sweet moans, loving the way she moved beneath me, as though trying to become one. Her ragged gasps were so loud in my ears, her tongue persistent in response to mine. My cock, hard and throbbing, pressed intimately against my zipper, eager to get closer to her. I wanted nothing more than to strip Penelope right there, to lose myself in her for all of eternity.

Except, I knew the pain of separation would be unbearable once that happened, and until I knew she would be with me, I wasn't willing to do that to her.

This time, when I pulled back, I stared down into her face, brushed her hair back. There was no way to tell her that I already loved her. She wouldn't believe me since our introduction had been only recently, and for some reason, she was stuck on the timing of our intimacy.

Didn't make it any less true.

"How about we make a deal," I offered.

She smiled. "What kind of deal?"

"We don't think too hard on the what or the how and simply see where this goes. At its natural pace."

"Natural pace. I like the sound of that."

"Good." This time, I forced myself to get up, to put a safe

distance between us. "Why don't you do your thing, and I'll order us something for dinner?"

"Would you mind if I shower?"

"Not at all."

Her eyes roamed my face as though she was considering her options. When her gaze locked with mine once more, she nodded.

As for what decision she'd come to, I hoped I would soon find out.

10

PENELOPE

I was being silly.

When Obsidian slipped out of the room, I remained where I was for a minute, staring after him. His scent wafted up from the T-shirt I wore and the pillow he'd slept on, surrounding me, comforting me.

I was acting like a virginal teenager, and honestly, I was far from it. Okay, maybe not *far* from it. No, I hadn't been with a lot of men in my life, but I'd never shied away from sex. The few times I'd been intimate with a man, I'd been in it wholeheartedly. No regrets other than I wish I'd been with someone I was more compatible with.

I'd always prided myself on being an independent woman, one who could make sound, logical decisions, especially when it came to sleeping with someone. Yet when it came to Obsidian, getting down and dirty was the only thing on my mind. When we were together, I felt this overwhelming sensuality that confused me. I believed in love, sure, had a strong desire for the opposite sex. But I'd always expected a meaningful relationship to be a slow build, something that took weeks, maybe months, before the peak was even remotely visible.

Reality had smacked me right in the face.

Or perhaps I simply hadn't met a man who could rock my world the way Obsidian could. Time didn't dictate emotions and certainly not sexual desire. I had that in spades, and now that I was alone with Obsidian, I wanted to explore it.

And yes, I had a million questions. Like how and why his eyes glowed like that. The way the silver shifted and swirled, like mercury being melted, the embers glowing from beneath. It was unnatural, and yet I wasn't scared of it. Merely curious.

Hell, I was more panicked at my physical reaction to Obsidian than I was that he could be something supernatural.

"And Dad said my degree was useless." I snorted as I made my way to the bathroom.

After stripping out of Obsidian's T-shirt, I stood beneath the hot water, running my hands through my hair to wet it.

A sound coming from the other room had me pausing. Was that the door closing? No way was room service that fast.

Which could only mean one thing.

Obsidian had left.

Suddenly, a coldness seeped into my bones, an ache forming in my chest. A terrible sadness overtook me.

Oh, crap. Maybe someone was here. Someone who'd recently experienced a tremendous loss. The maid, maybe? In a matter of seconds, my empathy had shifted to DEFCON 1. If they were hurting, it would make sense that I would, too.

I pressed my fist to my chest, attempting to massage the ache. It didn't help.

It couldn't be my empathic abilities, could it? I'd never experienced it that way. Sure, I'd felt emotions in abundance while in the presence of someone, but I'd never experienced them when I wasn't in the same room. I couldn't imagine a sense of loss this overwhelming would simply linger in the air, hitting me from all angles. Certainly not this extreme.

A sob tore from my throat, the ache building. I felt empty, as though I was missing a part of myself. As though the most important thing in my life had been ripped from my arms, never to return. A tear trickled down my cheek, followed by another, until the dam broke and my breath hitched between sobs.

What the hell was going on?

The bathroom door opened, but I didn't turn, keeping my head beneath the spray.

"There's someone in here," I yelled, fearing the maid hadn't heard the water running.

"It's just me," the deep voice bellowed.

I spun around to see Obsidian standing in the bathroom. Although ridiculously sexy, he looked a little worse for wear. Granted, his eyes told a different story entirely. They glittered with desire and approval as they trailed over me.

Suddenly, every ounce of the loss I'd felt was gone. Vanished in an instant. Completely erased as though it had never been there.

Perhaps insanity was the diagnosis.

"How did—"

Obsidian stood tall, held up his hand, his features relaxing. "Don't ask questions."

"Kinda hard since a second ago I was on the verge of an emotional breakdown, and now I'm—"

"Naked," he said, reminding me of the fact.

"Right." A smile pulled at my mouth as my arm came up to cover my bare breasts. "I'm naked."

He exhaled, then slowly turned around. "Perhaps I'll stay right here while you finish up."

A war ignited within me. Modesty had me wanting to order him to leave, but self-preservation won out, the need to feel the peace his presence brought far more powerful than worrying he'd turn around and see all my naked parts. Again.

Rather than boot him out of the room, I focused on my shower. Shampoo, conditioner, shave, body wash—utilizing all the freebies the hotel provided. All while the sexiest man to ever live stood with his back to me, giving me as much privacy as he could while the two of us were confined to this small space.

Satisfied I'd done my due diligence, I shut off the water, squeezed the excess water from my hair.

I turned to find Obsidian holding out a towel, his back still to me.

Quite the gentleman.

Taking it, I wrapped it around me and stepped out of the shower stall, not caring that I was dripping water all over the floor. "About that whole crying jag you walked in on..." I tapped him on the shoulder. "I'm decent now."

He chuckled, turning as he leaned against the bathroom counter, those thick arms crossing over his chest. "You were rather decent before."

Giving in to his innuendo would've been easy considering how hot the man made me, but there were more pressing things we needed to deal with.

"What happened?" I asked, knowing somehow that he had the answer. "Is someone here?"

"No."

"I thought you left."

"I know."

I frowned. "How'd you know that?"

"I just did." Those silver eyes churned, peering into mine.

"So that whole crying thing ... it was because I thought you abandoned me?" I shook my head because that was ludicrous. "No way. I'm not that type of girl. I don't get all hung up—"

Obsidian placed two fingers over my lips, effectively silencing me.

Frowning, I took a step back. "I felt... Obsidian, when I thought you left, I felt—"

"I know." He cupped my face. "I felt it, too. And I want to give you all the answers, but ... right now ... please don't."

There was a plea in his tone that I couldn't ignore. Almost as if giving me the answers would break him somehow.

And oddly, the discomfort I'd felt seemed minuscule in comparison to how I would feel if I hurt him.

"Okay," I acknowledged. "I won't ask." I held his gaze. "Yet."

His touch slipped away when he strolled across the room, stepped into the enormous closet. He returned a moment later with a fluffy white robe. When he neared, he held it out for me.

"Turn around."

I did, and he helped me into the robe, settling it on my shoulders. The towel fell to the floor as I reached to secure the robe, but I was barely able to cover my naked breasts before Obsidian took over, turning me to face him once more. I stared at his beautiful face as he cinched the belt around my waist, securing it so that I was completely covered.

"Can you at least tell me if I'm right about—"

Obsidian leaned forward, kissed me lightly on the lips. "Hold the questions for a little while longer."

Since it was pointless to argue, I retrieved the towel from

the floor, blotted the moisture from my hair while Obsidian walked out, giving me privacy.

I considered that for a moment. He wasn't right there with me, but the painful loss I'd felt earlier didn't return. So did that mean it had something to do with me being certain he was there?

With a sigh, I shrugged it off. I did not want to think about it because it actually sounded crazy. What could possibly make someone feel that sort of pain when they were apart from someone else? It defied logic. Reason.

I wiped away the steam from the mirror and stared back at my reflection.

Hmm.

I flipped on the faucet, grabbed a toothbrush and toothpaste from the small wooden box sitting on the counter, then hurried to brush my teeth. When I finished, I snagged the hair dryer on the shelf below, plugged it in. Another fifteen minutes passed. By the time I was done, I felt better, though I didn't have any makeup handy.

"This'll have to do," I told my reflection. "He'll either take me or leave me, right?"

My reflection nodded, smiled.

When I stepped out of the bathroom a few minutes later, I got a whiff of food coming from the living room.

"Good evening, Miss Calazans," the butler greeted. "We weren't certain whether you preferred breakfast or dinner for your evening meal, so we prepared a little of both. Steak and eggs. I hope it's to your liking."

"It's perfect." My stomach rumbled as I padded barefoot through the seating area.

The patio doors were opened wide, and I caught a glimpse of Obsidian standing near the wall surrounding the outdoor space, forearms resting on the railing, staring at the city moving below.

I paused to look at him.

The man stole my breath. I was fascinated by every single part of him. His tremendous height, impressive breadth. He was masculinity personified. Everything about him alluded to danger, a man who took no shit from anyone, didn't care what others thought because he was secure in his own skin.

He didn't turn when I joined him, but the butler appeared at my side, passing over a glass of...

"It's orange juice. If you'd prefer, I could add champagne."

"It's fine, thank you."

When he disappeared inside once again, I moved toward Obsidian. "It's not often you get to have dinner overlooking the Strip."

Obsidian nodded, cutting his gaze my way. "That's true."

"Certainly not on a patio as grand as this one." I paused to look out at the lights. "But we seem to be making it a habit."

He stood tall, moved to stand behind me. I leaned back against him when his hands settled on my shoulders. I would've been content to remain just like that for the rest of the night. Just the two of us. Alone.

"Are you hungry?"

As though intending to ensure he knew how much, my stomach rumbled again, louder this time, making me chuckle.

"I'll take that as a yes." Motioning toward the table, Obsidian steered me over.

He pulled out a chair, helped me into it, before taking the one to my left. From his spot, he had a full view of the interior, while I had an unobstructed view of the lights from the Strip.

"Why won't you let me ask questions?" I took a sip of my orange juice.

His swirling silver eyes reflected his amusement. "That sounded like a question to me."

I grinned. "You know what I mean."

"Because I can't lie to you."

The butler appeared with a bowl of fruit—grapes, cantaloupe, honeydew—along with a serving dish holding whipped cream. For whatever reason, the sight of the whipped cream made me blush, as my thoughts drifted to some rather erotic images of what Obsidian might do with it.

Foregoing silverware, I snagged a couple of grapes. "What do you mean you can't lie?"

He took a deep breath, exhaled slowly. "Meaning it's impossible."

"So, what? You're one of those men who can't lie to people? Very noble."

A sexy smirk tilted the corner of his mouth. "Not people. You. And it has nothing to do with nobility."

"Rather cryptic," I muttered, grabbing a piece of honeydew melon before I realized Obsidian wasn't eating. "Something wrong?"

He continued to watch me. "Not at all. I find it rather fascinating to watch you eat."

Because my stomach rumbled a reminder, I continued, pausing only to sip juice.

My head lifted as his comment from a moment ago sank in. "Why do you want to lie to me?"

"I don't. It's the truth I worry might be difficult for you to deal with."

I tossed that around in my head, focusing on the fruit. Glowing eyes, strange emotions, ridiculous chemistry. Perhaps mind-reading. Yeah, I could see where he was coming from because there was definitely something he was hiding.

Once I had finished off most of the grapes and the melon,

the butler cleared away the dishes before bringing more. He took his time setting everything out, situating it perfectly.

"All right." I turned my attention to Obsidian. "Time to address the elephant on the patio."

His level stare remained on me.

"Your accent. It's light, but I can hear it every now and again. Where's it from?"

The relief on his face was tremendous. "I honestly didn't think I had an accent."

Not an answer, but okay.

"Everyone says that, don't they?" I mused. "I guess you can't hear your own as much as you can detect others'. But I heard you on the phone the other night. At my apartment. You were speaking in another language."

The butler placed a scone in front of each of us, along with a cup of coffee.

"It's an ancient dialect," he said softly.

Of course he made no effort to elaborate.

While I hoped he could continue, I doctored my coffee with cream and sugar, then snagged a piece of the scone.

"I'm starting to feel weird," I told Obsidian when he didn't make a move for the food. "Being that I'm the only one eating."

"I much prefer the main course," he said simply, his bright eyes glittering from the lights around us.

"As do I." I pushed the scone away, then sipped my coffee.

Obsidian nodded at the butler. He quickly discarded the dishes before bringing out steak and eggs, situated on the plate with an artful flair, a side of hash browns alongside them.

"Now we're talking," I mumbled, my stomach giving an approving rumble. "This looks divine."

The smirk that pulled at Obsidian's lips was perhaps the most attractive feature of his. It was the wickedness in that look, the promise of making my deepest, darkest desires come to life. My body warmed in his presence, my attraction to him on a constant simmer. It was a different type of hunger that I was growing more aware of by the second.

We ate without speaking, the horns and traffic from the street drifting upward on the breeze. There was a comfortable silence between us, as though we'd been together for ages, not such a short amount of time.

My thoughts drifted back to earlier, to the way that lonely coldness had disappeared the moment I set eyes on Obsidian once again.

"It's because we were apart, isn't it?" I questioned, putting down my fork in favor of my orange juice. "That empty feeling?"

His head slowly lifted. He blinked once, twice, clearly considering his response. "Because you thought I left, yes."

"And the moment I saw you were here, it went away. Just like that."

"Yes."

"You said you felt it too. Did you? That hollow sensation. Like you'd lost a part of yourself forever?"

"I felt your suffering," he said softly. "It's why I came to you, so you'd know I was there."

It took a moment for me to form words. "What? You felt... Why... *How* could you feel mine?"

"That's the way it works."

"*It*? What exactly is *it*?"

Obsidian set his fork down. "It's the Fates' way of ensuring two souls remain together once they've found each other."

The Fates?

Wait. "Souls? As in soul mates?"

He nodded.

"Are you saying I'm your soul mate?" I couldn't help it, I laughed. It sounded ridiculous.

"Yes." There wasn't an ounce of amusement in his tone.

"You're serious." A warmth trickled in my veins, though I wasn't sure why.

"Deadly."

Praying he would continue, I didn't look away, took a long swallow of juice. "And how long does it last? That coldness?"

The silence I got in response was deafening. The man was obviously not eager to reveal this phenomenon.

"Look, Obsidian—"

He leaned forward, his steady gaze settling on my face. "Let's enjoy tonight, Penelope. There's plenty of time for explanations and long, drawn-out stories. Enough to last ten lifetimes. And I'm more than willing to share everything with you, but not tonight."

"I'm sorry. I can't. I question everything. I need to know. It's in my nature to want to know how deep the pool is before I take the plunge."

He swallowed hard.

Just when I thought he was going to reluctantly launch into details, music sounded from the speakers mounted in the overhead cover. A soft, romantic instrumental.

Very convenient.

"Dance with me?" Obsidian pushed to his feet, held out his hand.

Sighing my disappointment at his avoidance of my questions, I stood when he pulled out my chair.

Of course, it passed quickly. The moment he drew me to him, my curiosity faded, my questions disappearing. The way one long, strong arm slid around me, the other bending so I could take his hand as he moved with ease and grace, I was lost to him once again. The music, the lights glittering all around us, that sensual scent that was uniquely Obsidian ... it consumed me, made me feel as though I was in my very own fairy tale.

“You did that, didn’t you? Turned the music on?”

“Yes.”

“With your mind?”

“Yes.”

Startled by his admission, I stared up at him, my breath caught in my throat.

“You don’t have to fear me, Penelope.”

“I don’t. I just... I don’t know who you are,” I whispered. “I don’t know *what* you are.”

The vulnerability in his gaze shocked me.

“It doesn’t matter,” I assured him. “This ... being with you ... it feels perfect, Obsidian.”

And oddly enough, I never wanted it to end.

OBSIDIAN

Penelope was right. This was perfect.

Being with her was both intimate and casual, yet the connection we had to one another was potent.

Of course, her questions were what bothered me most. Not because she asked them. I wanted to answer every single one, to tell my female everything about me. To share the stories of my past, to hear hers. It was what I'd been waiting for all these years.

Yet I wanted to keep some of the mystery. It was in my best interest to draw her closer, to make her fall in love with me the same way I was with her. It would help ease the confusion all my answers would invoke. And there was no doubt in my mind I'd already fallen for her. Didn't matter that I'd spent mere hours in her presence; she was my lifeline, the only one I needed.

We moved on the private patio, our own dance floor, as the soft music played above us. I could hear the conversations taking place far below on the Strip, Alden cleaning up inside, the curtains being pulled shut to ensure our privacy. I even heard someone's deep breathing from the room next door. But I managed to block it all out, focus only on the beautiful female in my arms.

"You said before that perhaps we're where we were meant to be," Penelope said, staring up at me. "Do you believe that's true?"

"I do."

A soft smile formed on her lush mouth. "Me, too."

"Yet you question it."

"It's in my nature. How, when, why something happened. Those are things I want to know, even if the answers won't necessarily make sense to me."

"And you think that's the case here?"

Penelope's hand worked its way up my chest, curling around my neck as I peered down into those honey-gold eyes. My breath locked in my throat as she brushed her thumb along my jaw. She wouldn't realize how much I needed that simple touch. I'd spent years wanting to be this close to the female meant only for me, dreaming about the day it would come to fruition. Now that we were here, together, I couldn't imagine a moment spent without her.

"I do. I won't pretend to understand it, but ... is this normal, Obsidian?"

"What?"

"Whatever this is between us."

I waited her out, somehow knowing she would elaborate.

"When I'm near you, I feel complete," she said softly. "As though I've found my other half. I can't imagine not having this feeling last forever. But is that real? Or a figment of my imagination? The fantasy brought on by fairy tales and such?"

"This isn't a fairy tale, Penelope. It's definitely real."

I could see the desire churning in her eyes. It called out to me, tempted me to take what I'd craved for so fucking long.

"Stop thinking so hard," I whispered, urging her closer.

"I want you, Obsidian. I want to be close to you."

Her cheek rested against me, the top of her head not quite reaching my chest. In that tiny package was everything I'd ever wanted. Her nearness and the soft cadence of her voice soothed me.

"Not just now," she said softly. "Always. That's new for me. I've never felt that way about anyone. And like I said, the timing scares me. It feels like I'm moving too fast."

I tightened my grip on her, keeping her close, our movements limited to swaying.

"I don't want to scare you," she whispered. "I'm probably building this up too fast, but—"

I stopped moving, hooked my finger beneath her chin, forcing her eyes to meet mine as I stepped back and bent closer to her.

"You don't scare me, Penelope. And fast isn't the right word."

"What is?"

"Like you said, perfect," I whispered, leaning down until my lips hovered just over hers.

"Obsidian..."

Letting the music move through us, I shifted with her once more, holding her close. With every whisper of her body against mine, the tension inside me ratcheted up another notch. I wanted to feel her, to be inside her, deep enough she didn't know where she ended and I began. It was all I could think about, even as she was plagued by questions.

With purposeful movements, I worked us toward the section of the patio that was shielded from the rest.

I met her gaze as I slipped into her mind, searching for anything to reflect she wasn't ready for this. I found nothing alarming, only a mirror image of what I was feeling. Desire, lust, contentment. As I'd hoped, she was allowing for the natural progression.

Her breaths rasped, her lips parting as though begging for my kiss.

"Don't move," I instructed when I stopped.

Her hands dropped to her side as I walked around behind her. I moved her hair to one side, then leaned down and brushed my lips against her neck.

"I want to make love to you, Penelope."

She moaned softly as I placed my hands on her shoulders.

"I want to touch you, taste you." I dragged my lips over her smooth, warm skin. "To be inside you."

Penelope swayed in my arms, but I wouldn't let her fall.

"Do you want that? To feel me inside you?"

"Yes. Touch me," she pleaded. "It's all I can think about. Your hands on me. Your mouth."

Using the power of my mind, I lit the candles surrounding the lounge chair tucked into the alcove. Two dozen golden flames came to life, dancing in the soft breeze.

Penelope inhaled sharply.

I pulled her back against me, sliding my hands down her chest, my fingers inching beneath the terrycloth, working the robe open until her breasts were free for my roaming hands. I took my time exploring her glorious curves, sliding over smooth, warm skin. She was as soft as I'd imagined, smelled sweeter than the gardens in Heaven.

When she shifted, releasing the sash on the robe and allowing it to fall open, every part of me hardened.

"Penelope..." It was a warning. Or perhaps a plea. At this point, I didn't know.

"Natural progression, remember?" Her hands settled on mine as I cupped her breasts. "Please don't stop touching me."

"Drop your hands, Penelope."

Her arms lowered as I kneaded the soft flesh, teasing her nipples, plucking them gently. Her breath hitched, her chest rising and falling rapidly. I noticed how erotic it was to watch my hands moving over her so intimately. Never letting my fingers leave her skin, I shifted the robe off her shoulders. It slid to the ground at our feet, ignored.

Taking her hand, I led her to the oversized cushioned lounge chair. It was the perfect spot, big enough for two, strong enough to hold my weight. I paused long enough to ease her down onto it before crawling over her, my lips finally seeking solace against hers.

Penelope whimpered softly, her hands moving to my shoulders, my neck as I explored her mouth with my tongue. I only released her lips so I could trail mine over the delicate skin of her jaw. I allowed myself a second to inhale her sweet scent, to listen to the frantic pulse beating just a few inches from where my lips were.

I trailed light kisses down her throat, her clavicle, lingered for long moments between her breasts.

"Please, Obsidian... Don't stop."

"Never," I whispered against her skin before dragging my tongue over the swell of her breast, pausing to circle her areola, teasing the taut peak.

Penelope sighed, thrusting her chest upward as though in offering. I sucked her nipple between my lips, stroked her with my tongue. I took my time, laving one breast, then the other, teasing my *amsouelot* until she was writhing beneath me, begging for more.

Watching her face, I trailed my tongue down her stomach, pausing to dip into her navel briefly before continuing lower as I repositioned so that my knees were on the hard concrete.

To my surprise, Penelope lifted her head, observing as I shouldered her thighs apart, using my fingers to part her slick flesh. Our eyes met, held as I licked her, my tongue grazing her clit. Her stomach muscles spasmed, and her surprised moan drifted in the air. I did it again, loving the way she watched as I feasted on her. She was the only meal I needed, and I intended to show her just how hungry I was.

Penelope's hips punched upward, her head falling back as she cried out my name. The sensual sound had me driving my tongue inside her, thrusting as deep as I could go, my thumb circling her clit as I pushed her to the precipice, pulling her back just before she reached the pinnacle.

"Obsidian, please..."

"Tell me," I ordered, kissing the inside of her thigh.

"Make me come," she pleaded.

Drawing her clit between my lips, I flicked the bundle of nerves with my tongue, driving her higher and higher, this time not stopping until her body drew up tight and she cried out my name.

Crawling back over her, I smiled as she sucked in air.

"No one's ever… I've never…" When she looked up at me, dazed and sated, her smile warmed every inch of me.

"No one's ever what?" I needed to hear her say it.

"Licked me … intimately. Like that."

That admission provoked my possessive instinct. I wanted to be the first of so many things for her.

While she worked my T-shirt up my torso, I sealed my lips to hers, allowed her to taste herself on my tongue, loving the way she purred, her hands roaming when she revealed skin.

"I want to feel you," she whispered. "All of you. Against all of me."

I pulled back, stared down into those glittering gold eyes.

"I'm yours, Obsidian. All yours."

Pushing up onto my knees, I reached behind my neck, pulled the cotton over my head, and tossed it in the direction of her robe. A minute later, I'd stripped off everything else, once more hovering over her, my larger body covering her smaller one.

"You're so"—her eyes skimmed over my chest—"beautiful."

I wasn't sure that was a word anyone would use to describe me, but the approval I saw in her eyes was all I needed.

The sneaky female slid her hand down, curling her cool fingers around my cock, drawing a hiss out of me. I had to close my eyes, not wanting her to see the powerful glow that ignited from the emotion plowing through me. It took a moment, but I managed to rein myself in enough so that I could open them once more.

"Condom?" she asked, her voice soft, hesitant.

I didn't want any barriers between us, not only because they were futile. I couldn't contract any human diseases, and as an angel, there were none I could pass along to her. And as long as she was human, I was unable to impregnate her.

Not that she knew any of that.

I shook my head. "No barriers. I need to feel you."

She nodded, trusting me though she had no reason to.

When she guided the head of my cock to the slick heat between her thighs, I drew my hips back, held her gaze. The desire to drive deep inside her was overwhelming, held back by sheer will.

"You need to know something first," I ground out. "What you were feeling earlier ... the painful loss..."

Penelope nodded.

"Once we do this ... once I come inside you ... being apart from me will be unbearable, Penelope. You need to know that. You won't be able to function."

Her hand cupped my face. "I don't want to be apart from you."

I inhaled sharply, the admission more than I expected, but I knew she didn't fully understand. It was quite literal. When we were apart, at least until we were fully mated, she would feel the loss with my absence, as would I with hers.

"I want to feel you inside me," she pleaded. "I need you, Obsidian. Please..."

"I'm serious," I warned. "What you felt earlier is only a fraction of what it'll feel like—"

She pressed two fingers to my lips. "I don't care. I want this. You. Not only right now, Obsidian. Please..."

Pushing forward, I breached the opening of her sex, her slick heat enveloping me, her small body stretching to accommodate my size. I didn't look away, even as my body claimed hers in the most intimate of ways. I didn't rush, rolling my hips forward, back, her slickness coating my cock, her body accepting me easily. She was so tight, so hot. Minutes ticked by as she relaxed, taking more of me with every shift of my hips.

And when I was buried to the hilt inside her, I dropped my

head to her neck, breathed her in. Her soft fingers trailed over my back as though she was soothing me, when, in reality, I was hiding the fact that my fangs had elongated, seeking the thrum of her blood beneath her skin. I didn't want to hurt her, didn't want to scare her, but the hunger was too great. What she stirred inside me built to impossible proportions, overwhelming me. Love, lust. For the first time in two thousand years, I could see my future. A happy one with her in it, beside me for eternity.

"Hold on to me," I whispered in her ear, keeping my face buried in her hair. "And don't let go."

Her arms wreathed my neck as I withdrew from her warmth. I slid in again. In, out, my pace increased, her breaths matching mine. I focused on the sensuality of it all. The need to feel her, to hear her cry out my name as I drove us both toward climax. My hips slammed forward, pushing in deep, retreating, driving in again and again. My senses were on full alert, intently focused on her every emotion. I sensed no pain, no fear, only pure, unadulterated passion.

"Obsidian..." Penelope's arms tightened around my neck, her fingernails sensually scraping my scalp, her hips meeting mine thrust for thrust. "Oh, God, yes ... oh, don't stop. Please ... harder."

I growled low in my throat, slid one arm beneath her back as I hammered into her, feeling her body clamping down on my cock, drawing me closer and closer to release.

Her sharp cry pierced the night air, her sex squeezing me as she came. I gave myself over to my own release seconds later, barely managing to swallow the howl that attempted to escape.

II

PENELOPE

I was vaguely aware of Obsidian carrying me into the hotel room, closing the door behind him, placing me on the bed, and crawling in beside me. Grateful he was giving me time to recover, to catch my breath and realign my thoughts, I curled up next to him, drifted in and out of consciousness until finally, I felt as though I'd come back to myself.

Mostly.

My body was sated in a way I'd never experienced before. Mentally, physically. Even emotionally. And at the same time, it hungered for Obsidian, craved more of his touch, his taste, the serenity that came with being in his arms. I could've spent the rest of eternity right there beside him, listening to the steady thump of his heart, the even rasp of his breaths.

According to the clock on the bedside table, I'd been out for two hours, but that didn't surprise me. He'd played my body like a finely tuned violin, until I was little more than sensations. I'd never had an orgasm that consumed every part of me, so I figured I was allowed to take some time to bask in the glory of it.

When I opened my eyes, the glow from the Strip through the windows provided enough light to see Obsidian lying beside me, staring up at the ceiling. Clearly, he was lost in thought, because he didn't budge when I slid my hand over his taut stomach, memorizing the ripples of his abdomen. I'd never seen a male specimen quite as beautiful as him. His body was, for lack of a better word, perfect.

My mind shifted to the moment he'd undressed, revealing every golden-brown ripped inch—and there were certainly a lot of those—including the long, hard, thick length of his erection. I'd honestly been at a loss for words. Never having been one to think a penis was an attractive feature on a man, I couldn't deny Obsidian's was a thing of beauty, perfectly proportioned to his oversized body. And while I'd expected to feel pain from penetration, it had never come, my body adjusting to accommodate him with ease.

"I smell you," Obsidian whispered in the darkened room. "Your arousal."

Embarrassment warmed my face, but I pretended it didn't exist, pressing my lips to his chest. "Well, you do that to me."

He turned his head, dropped a light kiss on my forehead. "I was hoping you'd rest for a while."

"I did." But now I had questions.

He sighed, as though he knew what was coming, and I briefly wondered if perhaps he did. There was still that whole possible mind-reading thing I hadn't asked him about.

His eyes were once again locked on the ceiling when he

said, "Ask me anything, Penelope. Just know you might not like the answer."

Where to start?

"What you said earlier ... about me not being able to function if I was away from you. Is that true?"

"Yes." His pectoral flexed beneath my head.

"That wasn't your way of trying to talk me into your bed?"

He smiled, as I'd hoped he would. "No. I'm hoping you'll be there willingly."

Future tense, I noticed. That was a good thing, right?

Propping my head up on my hand, I stared down at him as I trailed my fingers over his smooth chest. "If I can't be away from you ... well, what exactly *does* that entail?"

Obsidian's silver gaze turned my way. "It means you'll have to stay with me."

"For what? The night? A week? Months?"

"Eternity."

I stared at him, trying to figure out the punch line. "Seriously?"

He didn't speak, simply held my stare.

"I mean, I'm not the type of woman to hop from one man's bed to another, but I consider myself well-versed on the gender. I do have a brother, after all. And in my experience, men aren't generally prone to making lifetime commitments after one night of sex." I grinned. "Sure, it was mind-blowing and all that, but..."

His eyes caressed my face, as though he wanted to say something but couldn't bring himself to do it.

"What aren't you telling me, Obsidian? I'm not an idiot. I know that this ... whatever's going on between us ... something's off here."

"What are you talking about?"

"The instant attraction, the overwhelming need, the desire

to be with you at all times. That's not normal. Certainly not the physical pain of being away from you. But I felt it. That first morning, when I left here, I felt it then. It wasn't comfortable, but it was manageable. Then, after we spent all that time together today and I thought you left ... *that* was overwhelming. And you're telling me it'll get worse?"

"If you're not aware of where I am, yes."

"So, what? I can *never* be away from you? That's not even feasible."

"No, it's not." His gaze shifted to the ceiling.

"So I'm supposed to be glued to your side for eternity?"

"No. It gets easier."

"When?"

"After."

"After what?" I snapped, hating that he wasn't really answering anything.

One second I was propped up, staring at him; the next I was flat on my back, his body covering mine. His erection was hot and heavy against my belly as he held himself over me, staring down into my eyes.

God, he was beautiful. The perfect bone structure of his face, those dark, neatly shaped eyebrows, even his nose was in perfect proportion to his face. Almost as though he'd been created, not the product of two people mating.

"This thing between us..." His eyes narrowed. "It's entirely normal. It's exactly what happens when souls are destined to be together. You've never experienced it before because you've always been meant for me, Penelope."

"Have you experienced it?" I whispered, entranced by the seductive tone of his voice.

"No. Not until you. I get that it's new for you, but it's not for me. I've been waiting for you my entire life."

I reached up, caressed the smooth contour of his jaw,

hearing the underlying words. Though I had a difficult time believing we were destined to be together, something in the way he spoke told me I should believe him. I certainly wanted to.

"Even now, Penelope, I can't imagine my life without you in it. I *need* you. In every way."

My heart did a somersault, emotions I didn't expect coming forward, making it difficult to breathe.

"Touch me," he hissed. "Put your hands on my cock."

Confused as to where this was going but eager to have a rematch of our earlier encounter, I did as he instructed, reaching between our bodies and fisting his erection.

Obsidian hissed, his breath rasping through his teeth.

My fingers didn't touch as I circled the thick length of him, but I gripped him firmly, enjoying the velvet smoothness against my palm.

"Stroke me," he insisted.

I did.

"Keep your eyes on mine," he ordered, his hips pumping as he thrust into my hand. "I want you to see me, Penelope. All of me."

Not sure what he was getting at, I didn't release him, my other hand gliding over the muscles in his arm, feeling them shift and bunch as he rocked his hips forward.

"When I'm with you, Penelope, I feel like I belong somewhere. For the first time in my life."

I knew the feeling.

"I know you suspect it," he whispered. "That I'm something other than human. It's true, although what created you and what created me are the same."

Perhaps I was too curious to be concerned, but I didn't dwell on the former part of the statement. Only the latter. "Who? God?"

Obsidian nodded. "And I know you're meant to be mine because just being in your presence ... you speak to my soul."

My breath locked in my throat when his glowing silver eyes began to brighten, beams of light extending outward. It was hard to decipher at first, but the longer I remained locked in his gaze, the brighter they became until the silver hue consumed the entire room.

Oddly, it didn't scare me. Nothing about him scared me.

"Are you making me feel that way?" I asked. "Controlling my emotions?"

"No."

There was something darkly erotic about him in that moment.

"My emotions do this ... make my eyes glow," he admitted. "*You* do this to me. Not just when you touch me. When you look at me, speak to me."

I glided my hand over his shoulder, feeling the tension. He was holding himself back.

"Put me inside you," he growled as he shifted his hips, allowing me to guide him between my legs.

I expected him to drive into me in one rough thrust, but he didn't. Obsidian gently pushed forward, filling me inch by devastating inch, my body softening, growing slicker with every delicious thrust. The hair on my arms prickled as the glorious sensations consumed every nerve ending. I'd never been one to care much for sex, but I was already addicted to Obsidian, was positive I would never get enough of him.

An eternity wouldn't even be enough.

"Your body needs mine," he said smoothly. "Mine needs yours. But this connection ... it's not purely physical."

It wasn't. I knew that.

Reaching up, I touched his face, sliding my palm against

his smooth cheek. His glowing eyes remained on mine as he moved inside me, long, deep strokes.

Suddenly, his upper lip curled back, my gaze dropping to his teeth. Before my eyes, his canines grew longer.

Fangs.

Obsidian had fangs.

I felt him then, penetrating every part of me. Not only my body but my mind. He'd slipped inside.

"I'm not scared of you," I assured him, somehow knowing he needed to hear that.

Chills coursed through me, as though I was becoming one with him. I needed to be closer. He stared down as though seeking my approval. My knees locked over his hips as I reached for him, wrapping my arms around his neck and pulling him to me, desperate to feel his body covering mine as I gave myself over to him.

"Penelope..." His voice sounded tortured as he buried his face against my neck.

Shifting my head to the side, I offered myself up to him.

"No," he growled softly.

I wasn't sure why he was holding back, but I trusted him. For whatever reason, I knew he wouldn't hurt me, and perhaps that was how I knew I'd fallen in love with him in a matter of days. Not only because of whatever was driving us to be together, either. This was coming from within me, deep inside. Obsidian filled me with warmth and light when I'd spent months—no, make that *years*—walking around with a cold chill in my bones.

"Hold on to me, *ayreme*. Don't ever let me go."

"I'll never let go," I promised.

He became feral then. We both did, succumbing to the overwhelming pleasure as his body covered mine, hammering me with ruthless thrusts as I held on. It was the most exquisite feeling in the world, one I wanted to savor. It didn't matter what he was or even what I was, for that matter. We'd been brought together for a reason. There was always a reason.

"Obsidian ... I'm—" I didn't get the word out, screaming in ecstasy as my orgasm obliterated both my body and mind.

The sound that escaped him was something resembling an animalistic growl, sending me over the edge again, the two of us coming at the same time, united in pleasure.

When Obsidian tried to move off of me, I held on, refusing to let go.

He chuckled, then rolled so that I was draped over him, his warm arms surrounding me.

I fought the urge to tell him I loved him, not wanting to play all my cards too soon. Instead, I settled on top of him and closed my eyes, giving myself over to the exhaustion that dragged me into the deep, dark abyss.

PERFIDIOUS

"Well, aren't you a lovely thing?" I crooned at the brunette female occupying the end chair at the blackjack table.

Though I would've preferred to sit at Beatrice's

table, I wouldn't get lucky tonight because my favorite dealer was enjoying a night off.

"Care to join us?" the brunette offered.

"I think I would." Digging a single chip from my pocket, I set it on the table as I eased onto a chair, waited for the dealer to finish the hand.

"Table's not doing so great," the female said, smiling. "Hopefully you'll change our luck."

Oh, I most certainly would be doing that.

With the ease of one who was comfortable in the process, the dealer swept all the cards away, sliding them into the card shuffler before pinning me with a hard stare.

I pushed the one-hundred-dollar chip out, signaling my desire to play.

"Where're you from?" the brunette asked while the dealer exchanged the larger chip for smaller ones.

"Oh, here and there. Been all over, really."

She smiled, her gaze darting between me and the cards being dealt. "Travel for business?"

"I do. And you?"

"Here for a convention. Starts tomorrow."

When it was my turn, I motioned for the dealer to pass me another card, something to better the two sixes I had.

Another six was laid down, making me smile.

"Oh, yuck. Ugly hand," the brunette said, waving her perfectly manicured fingers over her cards to signal she wanted to stand on twenty.

"Eighteen," I told her. "To the dealer's suspected seventeen. I'd say it's not too shabby."

"But six-six-six. That's the devil's number." She shivered, as though a cold chill raced over her.

I didn't bother to tell her Lucifer had never once staked a claim on any number, much less that one. But whatever.

The dealer revealed the nine he had beneath, then drew another card as was the rule. A king broke him, giving the win to all three of the table's occupants.

"Nice," the brunette said, smiling. She held out her hand. "Elizabeth."

I gripped it firmly, giving it a gentle shake. "Jim."

"Nice to meet you, Jim."

I felt more than saw the female who joined on my other side. Her scent intrigued me, had me turning, coming face-to-face with a beauty that defied all. For a second, I was captivated by her, unable to look away. Long blond hair, vivid amethyst eyes, the face of an angel. Though she wasn't a celestial being, I sensed what she truly was.

Fae.

Her shy smile had me turning toward her.

"I'm Jim and this is Elizabeth. You would be?"

"Asmia." She nodded kindly. "Nice to meet you both."

"Please, join us," Elizabeth urged. "Jim here seems to be shifting our luck."

Asmia glanced over at me, her gaze sweeping my face as though attempting to see through the outer shell to the inside. I felt the mental push, her attempt to get inside my head, then saw the frown of disappointment that tugged that generous mouth downward.

"Drinks?"

My attention was pulled in another direction, this time to the black-haired waitress as she neared, leaning in to take the drink order of the male at the end. I stared as she jotted down Asmia's request for a glass of wine.

When those green eyes met mine, I held them for a moment. "Where's Penelope? Isn't she on the schedule tonight?"

The waitress studied my face. "Not tonight, no. She has Thursdays off."

Ah. Good to know.

While the dealer went through the process of shuffling the cards with the machine, I pulled out my cell phone, shot a text to Seraphina. Something told me tonight would be the perfect time to eliminate the human once and for all. Though I enjoyed the game, I wasn't one to overlook an opportunity when it presented itself, and truth be told, I wasn't all that fond of the desert.

Although Asmia was certainly bringing me around.

"Can I get you something to drink?" the waitress offered, her tone clipped. Evidently, I was holding her up.

"Scotch on the rocks," I said, not caring what she brought.

She offered a fake smile, moved to Elizabeth before gliding over to the next table.

The dealer was waiting for me to place my bet, so I forced my attention back to the table.

"What brings you to Vegas?" I asked Asmia as I situated my chips. "Business or pleasure?"

"Pleasure," she said, the word coming out as a purr. I didn't think it was intentional, but it drew my attention all the same. "And you?"

"Like Elizabeth, I'm here for business."

Asmia's gaze swung over to the brunette, then back to her cards.

This evening was turning out far better than I'd expected. I had only come to gauge the situation, to get another glimpse of Penelope. Instead, I was getting something far better.

"How do you know Penelope?" Asmia asked, her perfect eyebrows lowered.

I studied her momentarily. "She was here last night. I found myself quite taken by her."

Asmia maintained her composure, turned her attention back to the table, but I couldn't decipher what she was thinking.

"Do you know her?"

Asmia nodded, keeping her attention forward. "You could say she's a friend."

Oh, really? Which meant the Fae was implanted in the Angels of Darkness. And if I had to guess, she was here tonight to keep an eye on the human.

My gaze swung to the elevator. Was she somewhere up there now? Hiding out with her angel in one of the rooms? Why else would Asmia be there?

I glanced back at the otherworldly female, smiled.

Looked as though my luck truly was changing.

For the next hour, I plied Asmia and Elizabeth with alcohol and generously tipped the waitress to keep her coming back. While the other chairs maintained a continuous rotation of guests, I managed to keep the females beside me, regaling them with bullshit stories, ones they would expect from a well-to-do businessman who traveled the world.

It wasn't that I cared whether they knew I was a demon, but in an effort not to use mind control so as not to tip off the Fae, I had to resort to charm.

Granted, my efforts hadn't garnered me any points with Asmia. She was keeping a polite distance, even while contributing to the conversation. On the other end of the spectrum, Elizabeth was all but sitting on my lap, batting her eyelashes anytime I spoke.

When it was apparent the human female had had too much to drink, I figured it was the perfect time to make my move. Sure, it was still early, but that left more time for other engagements.

"How about a nightcap?" I offered Elizabeth.

Those dazed brown eyes lifted and locked onto mine. "Perfect idea."

Yes. I knew it was.

I glanced over at Asmia. "Care to join us?"

She frowned beautifully. "Oh, no. You two enjoy yourselves."

I got to my feet, smiled down at Asmia as I held out my hand.

Though her confusion was evident, she offered hers in return.

"It was a pleasure to meet you, Asmia." I took her fingers, brought them to my lips.

"Likewise," she said with a sweet blush.

"Come now, Elizabeth. Let's move this party somewhere more private."

With a single parting glance to the dealer, I took the human female's hand, headed toward the elevators. I could feel Asmia's eyes on me but was unable to detect what she was thinking. Her mind was blocked the same as mine was, not allowing me to peer inside. Such a pity, too. Even now, I was thinking about all the wicked things I wanted to do to that lush body.

"Patience," I mumbled under my breath. "All good things come to those who wait."

"Did you say something?" Elizabeth leaned into me as we waited for the elevator.

I shook my head, forced a smile.

The lift arrived, half a dozen humans stumbling out, laughing, smiling, enjoying themselves.

Exactly what I was about to do.

"God, you smell good," Elizabeth crooned, all but throwing herself at me when we were sealed in the elevator.

Having enjoyed the evening, I was in a giving mood, allowing her to practically climb my body as she fused her lips to mine. She was quite intoxicated and more than a little reckless taking a stranger up to her room, especially in this town, but I did enjoy a female who liked to walk on the wild side.

When the elevator stopped, I peeled her off me. "Show me your room, beautiful."

Fifteen minutes later, Elizabeth was naked beneath me as I drove us both toward climax. In my mind's eye, I saw the alluring Asmia lying there, golden hair spread out on the pillow as I rocked her body with every thrust of my hips.

"Jim! Oh, God! That feels so good."

I could've told her God had nothing to do with it, but I refrained. No sense ruining the mood just yet.

Closing my eyes, I lived out my fantasy, driving Asmia closer to orgasm as her soft hands moved over me.

"Jim ... yes! Make me come!"

The female's voice shattered the fantasy, rage building inside me. Even as I tried once more to pretend, the human's grating voice laid waste to the attempt, pissing me off more.

Ramming into her, I didn't aim for finesse. I was driven by pure frustration and righteous fury, fueled by a desperate need to have the Fae beneath me. I wasn't sure why I was so enamored with her, but for the first time in years, I had a new fixation. Something other than the long list of transgressions I was making right for my father.

"Fuck me, Jim!" Elizabeth squealed. "Harder."

Realizing she'd outlived her usefulness, I gave her what she asked for, slamming into her hard enough to have her muddy brown eyes widening, the pain I saw there ratcheting up my desire. Not at all worried about her pleasure, I took everything

I wanted, thrusting in deep, hard, the human's hisses drawing my release nearer.

Now that was better. If I couldn't have Asmia, I'd settle for a terrified human.

"Jim! That hurts! Ow!" Her hands clutched my shoulders, her attempt to stop my relentless efforts to bring myself to orgasm futile.

I didn't let up even as she thrashed, attempting to shove me off her. The feeble human thought she stood a chance.

"Jim ... please." She cried out in shock, the sound rich with agony.

Only when she started to panic did I lean down, let her see the evil that lurked within me. Seconds later, I erupted deep inside her, coming with a roar that would be heard throughout the entire floor.

The female didn't come, scrambling to get away as I rolled off her.

Dropping one arm over my eyes, I worked to regulate my breathing. "Very nice, Elizabeth. Not the best I've ever had, but worthy."

I heard her desperate sobs, felt the mattress shift, relished the sounds of her trying to escape. Unfortunately for her, the door was locked with the power of my mind, impenetrable by her or anyone else.

"Is that any way to say thank you?" I taunted, getting to my feet.

In an effort to evade me, Elizabeth darted toward the bathroom.

I halted her with my mind.

Tears dripped down her cheeks as she stood frozen in place, naked as the day she was born.

"Much better. Don't worry, beautiful, it'll all be over soon."

The female recoiled as though I'd slapped her, making me laugh.

I grabbed her arm, jerked her back to the bed, positioned her so she was spread out wide, giving the impression she'd endured one hell of a fucking. Terrified brown eyes stared up at me, her mouth open. I leaned in close, covered her mouth with mine, and eased her fear in an instant, sucking her pathetic soul right out of her.

Perhaps it spoke to my depravity, but I did enjoy a terrified soul. There was a sweet taste to it that I found enticing.

Leaving the crudely posed naked heap on the bed, I dressed, ran a hand through my hair to ensure it was in place, before strolling out of the room.

A smile on my lips.

If I were lucky, Asmia would still be downstairs.

12

PENELOPE

After spending the entire night and the following day with Obsidian, it took tremendous effort to remember I had a job, a life, and neither could be ignored, though Obsidian had made quite the argument, especially when he insisted I wouldn't be able to function if I wasn't with him. While I didn't doubt the accuracy of that prediction, I got the feeling he was being a tad dramatic.

As much as I would've preferred to remain holed up in that hotel room, being treated like royalty and driven insane by his exquisite lovemaking, I managed to extract myself from his arms long enough to come home to get ready for work. After all, makeup was a rather important aspect of my nightly costume, and I wasn't about to fresh-face it on the casino floor.

Strolling down the wide corridor to my apartment, I paused when the door diagonal to mine opened.

"Good evening, young lady," the older man greeted, his eyes scanning the hallway.

"Good evening, Mr. Murphy."

His attention turned to me, visually assessing me from head to toe. "Are you working tonight, dear?"

"Yes, Mr. Murphy. I am." I smiled kindly as I relayed the information for the hundredth time since I'd moved into this building all those months ago. "It's Friday, remember?"

"It is, yes." The elderly man flashed teeth a tad too large for his mouth. Whoever he'd gone to for his recent denture upgrade hadn't done him a great service. Unless he'd *asked* for the beaver edition, which I doubted.

"But you've been gone a lot lately. I thought it changed."

A lot in Mr. Murphy's book being the equivalent of two days, mind you.

"It hasn't. I've just been ... staying with a friend," I explained when it was obvious he was waiting for more. "I came back real quick to get ready."

And already, I was missing Obsidian immensely. The coldness had started to make my bones ache from the minute I'd stepped out of the hotel, growing stronger with every mile I put between us. An overwhelming sadness was making my chest tight, but now that I knew what it was, I could force it down. The longer I was away from him, the more I understood his disappointment when I insisted on returning to my apartment. Obsidian had fought tooth and nail, but finally, he'd relented. Clearly not without just cause.

The thought of him aching with longing the way I was didn't sit well.

Honestly, I'd expected him to come with me, but at the last minute, he said he had something he needed to take care of.

"Sorry then." Mr. Murphy's eighty-seven-year-old smoker's lungs took a brief moment to hack before his lips pulled back in another toothy grin.

"Sorry for what?"

"I told your friends you'd be back soon."

I pivoted to face him more fully. "My friends?"

"Three gentlemen." His dark gaze bounced toward my door. "Stopped by a couple of hours ago."

I glanced over my shoulder at my apartment door, a warning tingle dancing along my spine. "Did they happen to mention who they were?"

Mr. Murphy shook his head. "Not too friendly. I asked, but they refused to answer my questions." His bushy brows lowered. "In fact, they didn't utter a word. Rather unpleasant fellows."

Since I didn't have a single friend who had ever come to visit me here—Obsidian being the exception—the entire conversation was moot. "Thanks, Mr. Murphy."

"Anytime, young lady. But you really should tell them to keep the noise to a minimum when they visit."

"Did they go inside?"

My elderly neighbor nodded, his fuzzy gray hair waving. "They did. Stayed for about thirty minutes. Like I said, you should tell them to keep it down."

Concerned as to what was going on, I nodded. "I'll be sure to do that."

His door closed with a gentle click, and I angled my way across the wide hall. Based on the appearance of my door, there was no sign anyone had been there. Or if they had, they hadn't forced their way inside. Good news was, it wasn't damaged.

But it was unlocked.

Maintaining my position outside, I pushed the door open, allowed it to hit the wall with a thud.

That was when the good news ended.

"Son of a bitch," I grumbled, taking in the destruction.

Remembering the outcome of the dumb girl in nearly every horror movie ever made, I paused and listened. Other than the loud hum from the cattywampus refrigerator, there were no sounds coming from inside.

"What the hell?" Glass crunched beneath my feet as I stepped inside.

The devastation was endless. My apartment was in shambles. The red sofa with white piping had been shredded, cushions tossed around, bleeding stuffing all over the floor. The lamp that had once curved over the sofa was lying on its side, the brass shade crushed. My television had joined the lamp, tossed on its face, while the stand that had once been its home was splintered into dozens of pieces.

The two short stools at the center island hadn't fared any better. The contents of my kitchen cabinets were strewn across the counters, and in the sink, pots, pans, and utensils were decorated by the slivers of glass sparkling in the glow of the overhead lights.

When my cell phone rang, my vertical leap would've made an Olympic athlete proud. I snagged my phone from my purse, my hand covering my heart, hoping the damn thing didn't jump clean out of my chest.

"Penelope, what's wrong?" Obsidian's tone was rife with panic.

"Someone..." I scanned the devastation. "Someone broke into my apartment. They... God, Obsidian. They destroyed it."

"Get out of there now," he insisted.

"It's fine. They're gone. My neighbor saw them leave."

"Penelope."

"I'm fine, Obsidian. I just... I need to call the police."

"No. Wait for me to get there."

I wasn't sure what he could possibly do that the police couldn't, but I assured him I would wait, then tucked my phone back in my pocket.

Needing to see the extent of the destruction, I headed for the bedroom, utilizing the fancy maneuvers I'd picked up in those cop shows: keeping close to the wall, peeking around corners. When I deemed it safe, I strolled into my bedroom and inhaled sharply. The damage in there was ten times worse than in the living room. Everything was destroyed. The mattress upended, springs sticking out of the various holes that had been made. The small bedside lamp was shattered, alarm clock gutted, the stand that held them smashed to bits. Even my comforter was ripped down the middle.

Of course, my neighborhood intruders hadn't stopped there. My closet was puking up clothes, all of which now resembled ribbons. Even my shoes were in pieces, heels snapped off, my favored Converse sliced and diced, boots sheared in half.

"Nice. Just what I don't need right now."

I turned toward the bathroom, freezing when my eyes landed on the fractured pieces of the mirror. More accurately, the words written in red lipstick across them: *He will not have you.*

"What the hell does that mean?"

In an effort not to hyperventilate, I focused on the rest of the space. Makeup littered the floor, stomped to smithereens. Shampoo, conditioner, and body wash were bleeding out into the bathtub, coating the shower curtain that lay in a heap. Even my bath bombs were pulverized into dust.

My knees were weak, so I leaned against the doorjamb, my attention shifting back to the mirror. *He will not have you.*

"Who's *he*?"

For the life of me, I couldn't fathom why anyone would be out to ... do *this*. There were no angry boyfriends from my past, no disgruntled prior roommates. I didn't have enemies. Probably had a lot to do with the fact that I didn't have friends. Well, not many, anyway. The only real friend I had lived in LA. The next closest would be the pizza guy, and truth be told, I didn't even know his name. But clearly someone was attempting to send me a message.

Just as the ache in my chest built to astronomical proportions, I stumbled back into the kitchen. Perhaps I should've stayed with Obsidian. It would've kept this ridiculous ache at bay, plus put off seeing ... this.

Surveying the littered space, I felt a slight tremble beneath my skin. An inkling of fear, sure. But there was something else. Anger, frustration. Betrayal.

I screeched like a banshee when Obsidian poofed into existence, right there in my kitchen.

I clutched my hand to my chest, stumbled back, eyes wide as I stared at him. How... Why... *What the fuck?*

As though it was completely normal for him to appear out of thin air, Obsidian scanned the room, his eyes hidden behind his sunglasses. "Did they take anything?"

"I... How'd you do that?" The squeak in my voice wasn't intentional.

His attention shifted to me momentarily, but he didn't answer my question; instead, repeating his own.

I could hardly breathe, shocked to the roots of my hair, confused beyond belief.

"Penelope. Did they take anything?"

Forcing my eyes away from him, I took a deep breath, exhaled slowly. "I'm not sure how I could tell. Everything I own's smashed or slashed."

With Obsidian there, at least that irritating ache had disappeared. And yes, fine, a little of the fear dissipated as well.

I didn't bother following when he made a detour through my bedroom.

With a deep exhale, I kicked a cushion out of my way, then moved to grab my iPad from the couch. The screen was shattered, but it was there. Of course, the hardback copy of *Acheron* had been slaughtered, too.

Obsidian strolled out of my bedroom.

"I don't think they took anything." I glanced around at all the expensive things they'd left in their wake. "Now can I call the police?"

"No. We can't."

I jerked my head toward him. "What do you mean, *can't*? This is my stuff, Obsidian. It needs to be replaced. I'm not even sure renter's insurance'll cover it, but at the least, I need a police report."

A sound outside the window caught my attention. I peered through the broken blinds to see three large men slamming car doors, their eyes fixed on my Honda. Since it was now dark outside, the lights in my apartment beamed out, all but shouting my presence. It wouldn't have been a problem, except the biggest one's eyes lifted, met mine through the window. There was something definitely wrong about him, and not just the eerie malevolence I sensed in him.

When they took off at a jog, I muttered a not-so-delicate *oh, shit.*

Obsidian grabbed me from behind. Plucking me right off my feet like I weighed nothing. Before I could ask him *what the hell*, he was depositing me in my bedroom.

He lifted his sunglasses, met my gaze with narrowed eyes. "Do not move, Penelope. No matter what. Stay here."

I glared at him, but the only response I got was the door shutting in my face.

Lovely.

A few seconds later, I heard the sound of a crash. Like someone had kicked in the front door.

Instinct had me grabbing the closest thing I could find, which happened to be a slender wooden vase. I doubted it would do much damage, but hey, it was something. I flattened my body to the wall behind the door, my goal to be hidden in case someone came in.

My heart was pounding, blood racing in my veins, the roar in my ears reminding me that I was alive and, for the time being, well.

"Don't move," I muttered, mocking Obsidian's stern tone.

To be fair, I considered waltzing right out there like some goddess of the Amazon, taking them on with my fists. If I thought for a second I could mete out my own brand of justice, I would've gone after them.

Sound exploded from the kitchen. More glass shattering, a few grunts as though the exertion was taxing on the body.

Something hit the wall with a heavy thud, followed by a screech that had my eyes widening. More grunts and groans erupted, the distinct sounds of a fight.

Then everything went eerily silent.

Seconds turned to minutes, and I started to panic, worried something had happened to Obsidian.

I reached for the doorknob but came up short when it opened, nearly knocking me on my ass. I stared up into Obsidian's face, relieved that he was in one piece. In fact, he didn't look fazed. Certainly not like he'd just gone hand-to-hand with three guys.

"Where'd they go?"

"They've been dealt with."

Obsidian pulled me against him. I was about as resistant as a leaf in a hurricane and shaking almost as much. With my head on his abdomen—he really was ridiculously tall, wasn't he?—I allowed his strength and warmth to console me.

"Can I call the police now?" I asked when I mustered up the energy to pull back.

"No."

Stepping into the living room, I frowned. "Why not?" I came to an abrupt halt and nearly tipped ass over teakettle. "Ew. Gross. What *is* that?"

There on the floor was... I wasn't even sure what to call it. Thick, black goop—it looked like tar and smelled just as ripe—coated the floor and part of the wall.

"Close your eyes," he insisted.

Odd request at a time like this. "Why?"

"Close them, Penelope."

With a huff, I squeezed them shut. "What are you doing?"

"Taking care of the mess."

Well, in that case...

Even through my closed lids, I could see a brilliant light. There was a warmth that went along with it, but it disappeared as quickly as it had come.

"Okay. You can open them."

When I did, I stumbled back against the wall, scared I'd just fallen down the rabbit hole and into an alternate universe.

My apartment looked exactly as I'd left it before I left for work Wednesday night, nothing out of place. Even the bowl I'd left in the dish drainer was there, the spoon beside it. My iPad was still on the arm of the sofa, no longer shattered, the book in one piece. My television...

"How did you do that?"

"I need to get you somewhere safe," he said, his voice calm and cool.

"Like where? Your hotel?" I shook my head, letting it swivel on my neck like my eyes were tracking a paddleball. "Not happening, Obsidian. I..." Hell, I didn't even know what I wanted to say. I was all mixed up, confused. Between the destruction, Obsidian's inexplicable—not to mention, physically impossible—appearance, the way he'd magically repaired everything...

Slapping my hands on my hips, I pinned him with a stare. "I need you to be straight with me."

"I will. I'll answer all your questions, but not right now. I need to get you away from here."

"Why? Because someone broke in?" I huffed, fought the urge to look at my poor decapitated fairy statue.

Wait.

Nope. No longer decapitated. That was good news, at least.

"I'm sure this is normal," I said, spinning back to face him. "It's not really the best neighborhood. Probably some hoodlums looking to..." I shut down that train of thought before *make off with my electronics* came out because it was evident they hadn't been here to steal my crap.

Hands once again firmly on my hips, I squared my shoulders. "What's going on?"

Obsidian's lips pursed, and I could tell he wasn't eager to fill me in.

"I'm not going anywhere until you tell me."

"Someone's after you, Penelope."

"Who?"

"Not *who*. What."

I frowned, waiting for him to elaborate.

"I need you to trust me," he said softly.

His big hand cupped my face and I could see the plea in his eyes. This man was worried about me.

"I do trust you," I assured him.

"Then pack your stuff. I'll explain everything on the way."

Though I wasn't keen on the idea, I couldn't detect any deceit from Obsidian. And while I couldn't feel his emotions like I did others', there was a connection between us. One that told me I'd be wise to do as he requested, if for no other reason than to save my own life.

"Fine. But you have to promise to answer all my questions. No evading."

"I promise."

Comfortable he would remain true to his word, I hurried to my bedroom, stunned when I opened my closet to see everything exactly as it should be. All my clothes, my shoes ... no damage whatsoever.

"This is crazy," I whispered, snagging my suitcase.

Really, really crazy.

OBSIDIAN

While Penelope packed her things, I stepped out into the hall to call Reidar.

"We're out of here. Tonight," I informed my *ladeare*.

"Wow. That was fast."

A quick rundown of the destruction to Penelope's apartment, as well as my dealings with the *impietans* I'd encountered, was all it took to have Reidar's full attention.

"Shit. All right. I'll have Gryffyth and Alden pack everything up. Gerran and I will be right behind you."

"Send Asmia, Acadia, and Taayin ahead," I instructed. "I want the mansion on lockdown. Have them check and recheck everything. Let the *heurosp* know to prepare it for our arrival."

"Will do."

I paced down the hall, lowered my voice. "One more thing, Reidar. Before you head out, I need you to grab the brother."

"Grab him?" Reidar's tone reflected his amusement.

"I don't care what you have to do. Knock him out if necessary, but bring him to the mansion and make sure Seraphina's not on your ass."

"All right. Mind if I ask why?"

"She's involved for a reason. Either to torture Penelope or use him against her. He's safer with us."

"Understood. Will you make it by sunrise?"

"Night's not long enough." Being a nine-hour drive, we'd already lost too much of the dark. "We'll get as far as we can before the sun comes up. I'll keep you updated."

"We'll stick close," he replied.

After tucking my phone in my pocket, I walked into Penelope's apartment. She was grabbing a handful of books along with her iPad, stuffing them into a duffel bag.

"Ready?"

She glanced around once more, then nodded. "I think so."

"We'll need to take your car back to the hotel."

When she agreed, I retrieved her keys from the hook near the door, then took her suitcase and the duffel bag while she grabbed her purse. A few minutes later, I was crammed behind the wheel of her tiny Honda.

"Okay, time to spill it," Penelope stated, her attention

directly ahead. "I've tossed it around in my head and come up with... I don't even know *what* to think."

I glanced her way briefly, confused as to where she was going with this train of thought.

"The fangs, the glowing eyes, that whole teleporting thing. Then there was the snappy cleanup. My first thought is vampire."

"Not a vampire," I assured her.

"No? But the fangs. Okay, fine. What then?"

Obsidian kept his eyes on the road. "Angel."

Though I expected some sort of disbelieving retort, Penelope made no such sound.

I cut my gaze to her momentarily to see she was staring out the windshield.

"An angel? A *real* angel? From Heaven?"

"Yes."

"Here? On Earth?"

"Yes."

She was silent for a moment. "I thought you were in a motorcycle gang."

The words were spoken so softly, I doubted she intended for me to hear them. But I did and I couldn't help but chuckle.

"Motorcycle gang?"

Her head swung toward me. "The tattoo, glasses. The brooding. Angels of Darkness. Don't tell me I'm the first person to make that assumption."

No, she wasn't.

"Then I thought vampire. Do vampires exist?"

There was a hint of hope in her voice. "Yes."

"Werewolves?"

I nodded.

"Holy crap."

By the time we reached the parking garage at the casino, I

could tell Penelope's brain was working overtime. After helping her into my car, I transferred her stuff to the trunk, then eased in behind the wheel. My fingers gripped the steering wheel lovingly before starting the engine and throwing it into reverse.

A few minutes later, we were heading out of the city.

"Where are we going?"

"Colorado."

Her head snapped over. "Are you serious?"

"I can't lie to you, remember?"

"Right." Her attention focused out the window for a moment before she reached for her purse. "I need to call my brother. Let him—"

I gently took the cell phone from her hand, not wanting to alarm her. "You can't call him."

"What? *Why?*"

I exhaled slowly as I removed the battery from the phone.

"Hey!"

"I can't risk them tracking you. I need to get you to safety first."

"Who...? Or rather, what? You said it wasn't a who. So, *what* do you think's tracking me?"

Glancing over at her, I met her gaze, held it. "Demons."

A rough laugh exploded out of her. "Demons? Are you crazy?"

"I wish I was." I focused on the road laid out before us, put my foot to the floor when there was a break in traffic.

"If what you say is true—"

"It is."

"Okay," she huffed. "If demons *are* after me, then tell me why. What do they want with me?"

Figuring I had to get the information out sooner rather

than later, I leaned back in my seat, relaxed. “Remember how I told you your soul’s destined for mine?”

“Yes.”

“Well, the Fates have a list—”

“Who are the Fates?”

“Adorah, Nevaeh, and Karma. Angels. The Fates. They’re responsible for pairing souls, watching over them.” I peered at her, then back to the road. “Anyway. They keep lists of all souls that’ve been paired. Those lists are carefully guarded. Or they’re supposed to be. The list for the Angels of Darkness ... those of us who’re here on Earth ... somehow it got into Lucifer’s hands.”

“Lucifer? You mean Satan? As in the devil?”

“One and the same, yes. He got his hands on the list, and he’s ordered the execution of the *amsouelots* belonging to my brothers and me.”

“*Amsouelot*? What does that mean?”

“Soul mate.”

She nodded. “Why would he do that?”

I stared at the darkened road. “Payback.”

“For what?”

“A number of things. The fact that we work for Michael, whom he despises. Or because we take out his minions for a living. Who knows. There’s no rationalizing what Lucifer does.”

“You work for Michael? The archangel?”

I nodded.

“I really need to call my brother,” she said after a few minutes of silence.

“He’s being taken care of,” I assured her.

Obviously *that* wasn’t the right thing to say, because Penelope twisted in her seat so fast the move surprised me.

"What do you mean he's being taken care of? Are you going to kill him?"

"What?" I glanced her way, frowned. "No. Of course not."

She relaxed. "Oh. Thank God. What're you doing with him?"

"He's being picked up."

"Why?"

"Well, for starters, the female he's shacking up with ... she's a demon."

"I *knew* there was something off about her."

Her lack of surprise at the revelation made me smile.

"Is that who destroyed my apartment? Demons?"

"Yes. Under the orders of Perfidious."

"Perfidious?" She chuckled. "That sounds terrifying."

"He's not a boy scout."

"So why'd they destroy everything? Why didn't they just kill me?"

"Perfidious likes to play games, but more than likely, they'd intended to. Since you weren't home..."

She gasped. Evidently she hadn't considered that outcome.

"I'm not willing to wait around for him to make his next move," I continued. "Once you're safe, I'll deal with him."

"You said there's a list. How many are on this list?"

"Seven, including you."

"And the others?"

"My brothers are out looking for them. It's the only reason we separated. The sooner we're back together, the better off we'll be."

"And when you're not out looking for your soul mates... When you said you worked in protection, you meant on a grand scale, huh?"

I peered over at her once more. "Yes. I protect humanity from demons."

Penelope sighed. “My dad warned me I’d meet some strange people in Vegas.”

13

REIDAR

Finding the brother didn't take much effort.

Getting him away from the demon was another story altogether.

Luckily I had a few tricks up my sleeve.

After making a call, pretending to be one of his co-workers who needed some information, I managed to lure Oliver Calazans out of his apartment. Of course, I didn't have time to play games, so rather than wait for the human to make the trek across town, I hijacked him in the parking lot of his complex.

Initially, I'd considered taking the friendly route but ended up stuffing Oliver into the backseat of my Camaro, which required more effort than I was willing to admit. The human had a wicked fight-or-flight instinct; I would give him that much. A punch or two might've been thrown. And received.

I wouldn't admit to Obsidian who'd done which, though.

"Who the fuck are you?" Oliver snapped.

"Nice language. Perhaps you could rephrase that. And maybe use your inside voice."

"Fuck you. Who the hell are you?"

Clearly the human wasn't going to respect his elders, but considering the circumstances of our meeting, perhaps I could be lenient on the male.

"Believe it or not, a friend," I muttered under my breath as I eased into the front seat, snatching my phone.

When Oliver thought he'd be funny, shoving the passenger seat forward in an attempt to jump to freedom, I put a big fist into the chair, throwing him back. The power I wielded surprised the human because he flopped back with a grunt.

"What the hell do you want from me?" Oliver groaned.

"Technically, nothing. Now shut up."

"Fuck you."

The human got brave then, his hands coming around my seat and settling on my throat. I chuckled, then snapped my fingers, which resulted in the male being hog-tied on his belly.

"Now just lie there and be a good little boy till I tell you otherwise."

With the miles increasing between me and Obsidian, I knew I couldn't wait around, so I shot a message to Gerran, instructing the angel to meet me. He appeared a few minutes later, a wide grin on his face as he stared at me through the windshield. When he climbed into the passenger seat, his gaze instantly swung to the cargo in the backseat.

"Trussed him up, did you?"

"Figured it was easier than knocking him out. At least until I know what we're up against."

The human mumbled through the tape covering his mouth. With a snap of my fingers, I silenced him.

Gerran barked a laugh, then retrieved his phone when it buzzed in his pocket.

Throwing the car in first, I peeled out of the parking lot. It took some bold moves, but I managed to weave through the traffic, aiming for the highway out of town.

"Taayin says they're settled. The mansion's secure."

"Tell him to send a message to the brothers," I instructed. "Let them know we're relocating."

Gerran's fingers flew over the letters on his screen as he tapped out the text.

Focusing my attention on the traffic, I steered through the streets of Vegas. By the time I hit the highway, I was wound tight as a bow. It took effort to relax, but I finally managed.

"Alden said there's been another death at the casino," Gerran stated. "Police are claiming it's a heart attack. Human female. Died in her hotel room. Think it's a coincidence?"

I didn't believe in coincidence, and knowing Perfidious was on the loose, there was no doubt in my mind that the demon was laying waste to humans simply because he could.

Before I could respond, my cell phone rang. I hit the button to take the call through the Bluetooth speaker.

"It's Asmia," the Fae said when I answered. "I wanted to give you an update. I just heard about the death at the hotel. I actually met that woman tonight."

"At the casino?" I knew she'd been there, anticipating Penelope's arrival before the shit had hit the fan at Penelope's apartment.

"Yes. Played blackjack with her. And a male. He ... uh... I think it was Perfidious."

I glanced over at Gerran briefly.

"He was cloaked, Reidar. I had no idea who he was. But he left with the female. Now she's dead."

Not sure what to do with that information, I thanked Asmia and ended the call.

"So, what's the plan?" Gerran asked as he settled back against the seat. "We gonna drive straight through?"

"Obsidian said he'd shoot us his coordinates. Even pushing it, we'll never hit Darkness before daybreak. Have to hole up somewhere for the day."

Gerran grunted. "Kick my chair one more time, little human, and I'll strap your ass to the roof."

I chuckled. "Maybe we should fill him in on what's going on."

Gerran glanced into the backseat. "Or we could just knock him out."

"Or we could do that," I agreed.

"How much time do you think we have before Seraphina gets suspicious?"

I shrugged. "Between Penelope not showing up for work tonight and the brother missing, I doubt we've got long."

I snapped my fingers, unmuting the human.

"If I take the tape off, you think you can be civil?" I asked, not bothering to look back at Oliver.

A rumble sounded.

I took it as an affirmative, then snapped my fingers to have the tape fall away and the ropes unwinding from Oliver's wrists and ankles.

"Who are you?" he demanded the instant he could speak.

"Angels," I told him simply.

"Are you high?"

I didn't dignify the idiocy with a response.

"Look. My father's got money. If you just let me call him, I'm sure he'll pay whatever ransom you want."

"Believe it or not, we're taking you to your sister," I informed him.

"My sister?" Oliver's voice shifted to a rough growl. "What did you do to her?"

Gerran chuckled. "Humans," he huffed. "Always thinking the worst."

It was true; they were a suspicious lot.

PENELOPE

"Any chance we could stop?" I prompted Obsidian, doing my best not to cross my legs in agony.

I had to pee like a racehorse, but I'd been holding it for the past hour, hoping we'd come to our destination before I had to ask him to make a detour. We'd been on the road for four hours, so I figured I'd held out long enough.

"Of course."

"I really need to stretch my legs. Maybe grab something to eat." Both were true, though my bladder was making the loudest request.

Granted, I hadn't seen any signs of civilization for quite some time, so I wasn't even sure there was a place for us to stop.

As though conjured out of nowhere, a sign for a truck stop appeared, making me breathe easier.

When Obsidian pulled up to the gas pump, I couldn't hold

it any longer. Even as he called my name, I made a beeline for the inside, heading right for the restroom.

A few minutes later, I emerged to find Obsidian leaning against the wall in the hallway, his face intense, eyes shielded behind those dark glasses.

"I'm sorry," I said quickly, feeling my face heat with embarrassment. "I couldn't wait."

A smile formed as realization dawned. "My apologies."

Taking my hand, he led me through the store, snatching up snacks as he went.

"How much longer?" I wondered if we had time to stop for a real meal.

"I wish I could say we'll make it before dawn, but that won't be the case. We'll have to take shelter for the day."

My shoes squeaked on the tile when I pulled him up short. "You can't be out in sunlight?"

His eyes were hidden, but I felt the intensity of his stare. "No. I can't."

Which explained why he hadn't come with me to my apartment. He'd been waiting for the sun to set.

Stepping closer and lowering my voice, I said, "And what exactly makes you *not* a vampire?"

Obsidian leaned down, his mouth close to my ear. "Wings."

Wings.

Great.

Nodding because, you know, what else was I going to do, I settled on a blueberry muffin and a Coke, figuring it would provide sufficient fuel for however long he intended to be on the road.

Once we were in the car, Obsidian wasted no time getting us back on the highway.

I relaxed into the seat, doing my best not to clutch the *oh shit* handle or shriek from the sheer velocity of the car's speed.

It wasn't that I minded the fact he could've been auditioning for Formula One, hitting triple-digit mph, but only because he seemed to know what he was doing.

"Are there any other idiosyncrasies I should know about?" I prompted. "I'm finding it difficult to understand the whole angel thing. Wait." I cut my eyes to him. "Do you drink human blood?"

"No."

"Then why the fangs?"

"Because I do require blood, just not from humans."

"Then from who?"

"Fae."

"Fae?" I frowned, relying on my studies to put my finger on the entity. "Fairies? You drink the blood of fairies?"

"Yes. However, we don't call them fairies. Only Fae. They consider themselves a different category."

"So, are we talking human-sized fairies? Or Tinkerbell?"

He chuckled. "Human size."

Angels getting sustenance from fairies ... er ... Fae. Surely nothing could surprise me now.

"You said you have wings?"

Obsidian nodded.

"Where are they?"

I could see his smile in profile. "Wouldn't be all that easy to blend if I walked around with wings, now would it?" He glanced my way. "I can bring the wings out when I need them."

Oh. Holy moly.

"So why can't you go out in sunlight?"

"When Michael made his proposal to God to send us to Earth, there were a few stipulations. God wanted us to blend, so he made it impossible for us to be out in daylight. And we feed from the Fae so He can keep track of us. With their blood in our veins, it's like a homing beacon. He did the same with vampires when he created the race. However, they're not required to feed from Fae. They prefer their own race, although humans suffice just fine."

"You're telling me God created vampires?"

"Yes."

Wow. That was... *Wow.*

"Do you know any vampires?"

"Quite a few, actually." His eyes slid to mine briefly. "My closest friend is a vampire. His name's Kaj. Good male. You'll like him."

I was sure I would. What human wouldn't want to be friends with a vampire? No risk there, right?

"And these Fae?" I studied my hands for a moment. "Are they female?"

"Male and female."

"Do you feed from the males?"

"I have, sure. Just not recently."

For some reason, that bothered me. I did not like the idea of Obsidian feeding from a woman. Fairy or not. The thought of his mouth on...

I shook off the thought.

"The only human I can feed from is you, Penelope," Obsidian said. "Because you're my *amsouelot*, your blood will sustain me and allow me to be tracked."

It took a moment for my heart to resume its beat. When it did, I glanced over at him. "Will you?" Sure, there was a slight tremble in my voice. Could you blame me?

"Not until you allow me to. And not until it's absolutely necessary."

"What does that mean? Absolutely necessary?"

Obsidian's attention remained on the road, his gaze shifting to the rearview mirror every now and then.

"Once the desire gets to be too much, feeding from you will ease the heat somewhat."

"Heat?"

"What we refer to as *amnigh*. As my *amsouelot*, your body has a natural craving for mine and vice versa. Over time, it'll intensify."

While I wanted to think he was making that up, I couldn't ignore the fact I'd been on a constant simmer since I left his hotel room to go back to my apartment. Even now, my skin tingled, my breasts were sensitive, and there was an insistent throb between my legs.

"How long does that last?"

Obsidian reached for my hand, twined our fingers. "Indefinitely."

Oh, great. He'd turned me into a sex fiend, and there was nothing I could do about it.

Obsidian's phone rang. He answered by hitting a button to allow the Bluetooth to sync.

"Where are you?" he asked without greeting.

"Thanks to your pit stop, only about a half hour behind you. You driving all the way through?"

I watched Obsidian as he spoke.

"As much as I want to, we won't make it. We'll hole up in Flagstaff."

"Perfect. I'll have Gerran grab a couple of rooms. I'll text you the details. Hey, Penelope," the voice on the phone called out. "This is Reidar. I wanted to let you know we've got your brother. He's a bit surly. Thought maybe if he heard your voice, he'd chill."

"Oliver?" I smiled. "Are you okay?"

"I've been better," my brother grumbled. "Mind telling me why you had me kidnapped?"

"She didn't," Obsidian stated. "I did."

"Before you rip him a new one," Reidar said, "be mindful of your manners."

"Fuck you," Oliver hissed.

"Oliver?" I said softly, hoping to rein in my brother a bit. "I promise, I'll explain everything when I see you."

"You're damn right you will," he snarled.

Obsidian growled low in his throat, and I knew there was no doubt everyone heard it.

"Watch yourself, kid," Reidar warned. "He's the most tolerant of them all, but that's not saying much. Hey, Obsidian, we'll drop the info on the hotel. See you in a bit."

"Yep," Obsidian rumbled before disconnecting the call.

"Who's Reidar?" I asked when the radio began to play again.

"He's my *ladeare*. One of the leaders in the *fiestreigh*."

"So there's a hierarchy?"

"You could say that. My brothers and I have a designated assistant, known as a *lieterra*. And when we're fighting, we rely on the *ladeares* and the *lieterras* to coordinate efforts, ensuring we've got appropriate backup."

"Who's your *lieterra*?"

"His name's Taayin. You'll meet him at the mansion."

"And what are *fiestreigh*?"

"Soldiers. Or more importantly, family."

Speaking of family...

I gave Obsidian's hand a squeeze. "I'm sorry for Oliver."

"No need to apologize. I get that he's pissed. I would be, too. Doesn't give him the right to talk to you that way."

Well, Obsidian was going to be in for a treat, because Oliver might've been my twin, but he had very little respect for me. It had always been that way, though I wasn't exactly sure why. I did my best to keep the peace between us, but it never seemed to matter to Oliver.

Staring out the window, I tried to process the information. I wasn't sure I'd ever get used to this, but even now, I was getting more comfortable with Obsidian.

I figured that was a good start.

OBSIDIAN

I had to admit, Penelope was a rather decent travel companion. I thought for sure she'd give me shit about my speed, but if she had a problem with it, she'd held her tongue. However, the *oh shit* handle had undergone some serious grip action for the past three hundred or so miles.

When I pulled the car into the motel parking lot, I thought for a minute Penelope was going to hug the asphalt and send up a silent thank you for getting her there safely. She didn't, but I heard her sigh of relief nonetheless.

"Why don't you go in and grab the keys—ours and Reidar's. I'll shoot him a message to let him know we're here."

Penelope nodded, then sauntered into the small rental office.

While she chatted up the night clerk, I sent Reidar a text, letting him know we had arrived. Though we still had a couple of hours of night left, I wasn't willing to risk the chance of getting pinned down by daylight. Even the thought of leaving Penelope unprotected made my stomach churn.

Penelope returned a few minutes later, holding up two keys, each dangling from a plastic tag. “Bottom floor, the two units at the far end.”

“Perfect.”

I drove through the empty lot, backed into the space directly in front of the last door before climbing out.

“You unlock it, I’ll get the bags.”

“Holy moly,” Penelope called out when she stepped inside. “The seventies called. They want their decor back. This place is... Wow. Just wow.”

I grinned as I followed her through the cracked and peeling doorjamb. I couldn’t deny the decor was atrocious, with the mustard-yellow flowers and paisley print on the walls. The brown carpet had seen better days, and the mirrored closet doors were pretty much useless, but the bed was solid, and there was a bathroom. So long as we had running water, I figured, as far as places to sleep went, it would work.

“The guy said there’s an all-night diner about a mile up. They’ve got sandwiches and stuff.”

I passed Penelope my phone. “Text Reidar what you want. Have him get enough to make it through the day. I won’t be able to leave until close to eight tonight.” Though my statement implied I was the only one who’d be pinned in the room, I had no intention of allowing her to wander the streets without me.

While Penelope typed up the information, transcribing my requests as well, I pulled out the blackout film from my bag. The curtains were thick and would likely do the trick, but I wasn’t about to take any chances. Once that was taken care of, I retrieved the additional locks for the door, which I would add after Reidar delivered the food.

“Do you use that on all windows?”

"Only when we're not at home. The mansion has built-in shutters that close and lock during the day."

Penelope flopped onto the bed, stared at me. "This feels weird."

I went to work putting the film on the window. I'd done it enough, it was second nature at this point.

"What does?"

"All of it. Running for my life, *abandoning* said life."

I hoped that in time, she would want a life with me and the past would be right where it was, behind us.

"Part of me thinks we should've stuck it out," she continued. "Fought these demons. Won't they eventually catch up to us?"

"It's possible." I tucked the remainder of the film in my bag, then sat on the edge of the mattress beside her. "I'm sorry for upending your life, but I have to keep you safe."

Penelope nodded, then reached up and removed the dark shades from my eyes. She set them on the particle-board nightstand before coming to stand in front of me.

I brushed her hair back over her shoulders, cupped her neck in my hands. She was the most beautiful female I'd ever laid eyes on, and by the grace of God, she'd been reserved for me and only me. I figured I owed some time on my knees, thanking the man upstairs for being so kind. Unfortunately, that would have to wait until I got her to safety.

"What's on your mind?" I asked as her gaze skimmed my face.

"I feel safe with you." Her words were a soft rasp.

That was a start, I figured.

"I won't let anything happen to you, Penelope. You're the most important thing in my world."

Pulling her toward me, I melded my lips to hers, then shifted to the side, dragging her down to the mattress. A soft sigh escaped her as her arms slid around my neck. I got lost in her warmth, the sweetness of her kiss. The hunger was a flash fire, igniting in an instant. I was seconds away from ripping her clothes from her body when a knock sounded on the door.

Instinct had me on my feet, gun in hand, aimed at the door. "Who is it?"

"Reidar. I've got food, and I need a key."

I glanced through the security hole in the door before unlocking it and allowing Reidar inside. When I passed over the key, my *ladeare* sauntered back outside, returned a minute later.

"Where's Oliver?" Penelope asked, running her fingers through her hair as she stood beside the bed.

"Gerran's getting him settled in." Reidar turned to face her. "Look, Penelope. I can promise you I won't hurt your brother. He's a major pain in my ass, but I can assure you, I'll get him to the mansion in one piece. Not sure how long he'll survive once we get there. But he's safe in transit."

She laughed softly. "He can be a pain, but he's harmless."

"More so because he's tied up," Reidar informed her. When she frowned, he added, "For his own safety."

I was surprised when Penelope didn't come to her brother's defense. Instead, she smiled, thanked Reidar for the food and drinks, then snatched the ice bucket.

"May I?" she asked, moving toward the door.

The only reason I agreed was because the ice machine was in the alcove between the two rooms. While she headed that way, I stepped out onto the sidewalk and kept an eye on her.

"How long until Seraphina gets suspicious?" I asked Reidar, dividing my attention.

"I shot her a text from Oliver's phone, said he was tied up for a few hours." The male smiled, clearly realizing the double meaning. "I figure she's realizing he's gone right about now.

Which means, if she's planning to follow, we've got a decent head start."

It certainly helped that demons didn't have the ability to teleport, nor could they venture out in the daylight.

"They'll follow," I assured Reidar.

"I figure as much. We'll seal up the room for the day and take shifts sleeping. Not willing to risk the male slipping out on us."

My gaze settled on Penelope as she walked toward the room. "Do whatever it takes. And thanks for the food."

"No problem."

Penelope gave Reidar a sweet smile before she stepped into the room.

"Stay safe," I told him before closing the door, locking it, and working to install the extra safety measures.

"Looks like Reidar's a bit of an overachiever. I'd be surprised if the restaurant has any food left."

"He's proactive," I told her, keeping my attention on the door and the sensors I was positioning.

Once everything was in place, I tucked my tools in my bag, then set it on the floor beside the bed. When I turned to see what Penelope was doing, my breath lodged in my throat.

"Lord have mercy," he whispered.

To my surprise—and delight—my *amsouelot* was standing completely naked at the foot of the bed.

She smiled shyly. "Unless you wanted to eat first."

Within a second, I had her flat on her back, my lips fused to hers.

I wanted to take my time, to graze every delicious inch of her with my lips, but my body ached for hers in a way that shocked me. Based on the way she clawed at my T-shirt, fumbled with the button on my jeans, she felt the same. With surprising dexterity, we managed to strip off my clothes, and finally … *finally*, I was sliding into the warm haven of Penelope's body.

A rough growl erupted from my chest as heat coursed through me. This was the only place I ever needed to be, right here with her, our bodies joined as one. I propped her knee over my forearm and angled my hips, pushing in deep, retreating slowly, our tongues gliding, dancing.

Every muscle trembled as I slowed my pace, wanting to drag Penelope up to the height of exquisite ecstasy before sending her over. When she cupped my face, I pulled back, stared into those beautiful eyes. We were locked together both physically and emotionally, the high unlike anything I'd ever felt before, stealing my breath.

Riding that razor-sharp edge, I thrust into her again and again, slow and deep, as her body clutched mine. The sound of my name on her lips sent me over, following her right into oblivion.

14

PERFIDIOUS

I watched the female stroll across the crowded casino floor, offering drinks to the pathetic humans feeding the slot machines. I turned my attention to the others wearing the same sad outfit, seeking one in particular.

Okay, that was a lie. I didn't give a fuck about Penelope, though she should've been my only concern. Without a doubt, Lucifer would be sending for me if I didn't complete my mission within a reasonable amount of time, and it was obvious our definitions of reasonable were far from aligned. Of course, since Lucifer was the big boss, I couldn't argue that I preferred a more relaxed working environment. The devil didn't much care about my preferences.

Unfortunately for all, I was far too preoccupied to worry about the human right now. Even as I should have been looking for Penelope, my eyes were scanning the area for Asmia, the Fae who'd plagued my mind since our first introduction. Because her presence the other night seemed to line up perfectly with Penelope's shift, I was expecting to find her waiting in the wings, protecting the pitiful *amsouelot*.

"Well, well, well."

Definitely *not* who I was looking for.

The seductive voice came from behind me, causing me to slowly pivot. I caught sight of the statuesque demon strutting my way, damn near every eye in the vicinity locked on her.

Could've been the board-straight black hair that hung to her waist. Or perhaps the voluptuous curves, or the fact that she was six feet tall and wearing a sinful red dress that left absolutely nothing to the imagination. No doubt she'd teased at least a dozen males with her generous helping of tits and ass, which were both spilling out of that tiny piece of fabric.

As she approached, I gave ample attention to the delicious swells of her breasts even as I fantasized about the blonde I craved like a drug.

"I'm glad to see you've shucked the outdated skin," I told her, thinking about the former blond cheerleader Seraphina had been sporting the last time I'd seen her.

Seraphina cupped her breasts. "The human finds it quite impressive. You like?"

"It suits you better."

Her smile was devious. "I found this one downtown at this seedy little place. Much more to my standards."

Seraphina and seedy did seem to go hand in hand.

As we chatted, several men strolled by, their eyes eagerly caressing her as though they stood half a chance.

"Why are you here?" I asked, dragging my gaze away from her to resume my search for Asmia.

"I got tired of waiting for you," Seraphina crooned, stepping into my personal space, her hand sliding around my neck, blood-red nails scraping sensually against my skin.

I probably should've pushed her away, put the demon in her place, but I didn't. There was something about this creature that seduced me, brought me to my knees. And she was right; I had missed her. Despite the fact I'd been in town for a couple of days, I'd yet to make contact with her. I should've known she would seek me out.

Seraphina's hand eased between my legs, cupping me intimately. "I've certainly missed you."

Yes, I knew she had.

But it wasn't her I was thinking about as my cock thickened, the ache reigniting from my previous encounter with Asmia. I would partake of what the demon offered, of course, but in my mind, I was definitely indulging in something I wanted far more.

"Would you like me to take care of this for you?" Her fingers dipped into the waistband of my slacks.

Before she could go to her knees in the hotel lobby, I gripped the demon's wrist and led her toward the casino floor. As usual, Seraphina didn't ask questions. She simply moved, drawing the eye of every human we passed.

I followed the path designed on the gaudy carpet, stopping at a recess in the wall. Had it not been for the fact that Asmia was possibly in the hotel, I wouldn't have given two shits who saw us. However, I figured a bit of discretion wouldn't hurt in this case.

Once partially concealed, I slammed Seraphina against the wall and crushed my mouth to hers. That viper-like tongue thrust into my mouth, but it was the sounds resonating in my head that had my cock rock hard and aching. Asmia's delicious moans, those soft pleas. They were so vivid, if I kept my eyes closed, I could almost see her offering herself up to me, accepting what I so eagerly wanted to give her.

"Why are you here?" I asked Seraphina again, even as I freed my throbbing shaft from my slacks before hiking the demon's leg up over my forearm and guiding myself into the scorching heat of her body.

I grunted as pleasure assaulted me from all angles.

"I figured you'd be here," she rasped. "And I've got some news. But it'll cost you."

Of course it would. The demon preferred the coy seduction. Always had, always would.

"What do you think you deserve?" I taunted.

"One orgasm," she moaned softly. "And you better make it good."

With my hand on her throat, I forced her head back, refusing to look into her eyes. She was merely supplying the vessel to sate my lust. She certainly wasn't the one I was fucking.

Seraphina fought me as she usually did, having a taste for rough, brutal sex, biting my finger as I drove into her roughly.

Though not completely out in the open, we were visible to anyone who took the time to look our way. I wasn't worried about the humans seeing us. Should one be daring enough to interfere, I'd simply absolve them of their soul.

"Harder, Perf," Seraphina hissed. "Fill me up."

Pulling out of her, I spun her around, gripped her hips, and slammed into her from behind. Seraphina adjusted so that she was bent over, that tight red dress hiked up to her waist as I pounded into her. In my mind's eye, I saw Asmia, my hands gripping that luscious ass as I drove us both to an explosive orgasm.

"Fuck yes!" Seraphina shouted, no doubt hoping one of the humans would come looking.

My full attention was on the tight clasp of her sex as I drove as deep as I could. The thought of Asmia's soft body taking every inch of me triggered my release. I came, jerking and pulsing inside the demon, though it was Asmia's body I filled in my fantasy.

When I was momentarily sated, I pulled out, tucked myself away, then headed in search of a drink. The demon followed, righting her clothing, her satisfaction evident in the sexy sway of her hips.

Good thing about Seraphina, I could fuck her all day and all night, and she would never tire. In fact, this particular *neilloh* had been known to take me and Sirius on at the same time and never grow weary. It was about the only thing she was good for. And pretty soon, I wouldn't even need her to indulge some of my darker urges.

An older brunette approached, her smile wide. "Drinks?"

"Why, yes, Judy," I said kindly. "My lovely friend and I would like a Jack and Coke."

"Sure thing."

I glanced over at Seraphina. She was touching up the blood-red lipstick on her lush lips. I couldn't help but envision them wrapped around my cock.

As though reading my mind, her ice-blue gaze swung over to me. "Would you like my lips on you before or after I give you the bad news?"

I frowned. "What are you talking about?"

"You know my lover?"

I narrowed my eyes, ensuring she saw my impatience growing rapidly.

"He texted me a few minutes ago."

I didn't give a shit about the human.

"The angels have him," she hurried to add.

Squaring my shoulders, I stared at the demon, my fury igniting.

"Seems they took a little road trip last night. He's not all that happy about leaving, either."

If they took the brother, I could only assume the entire clan had skipped town. Including Asmia.

"Where are they?"

"He didn't know, but it wasn't hard to locate him." She smiled, white teeth gleaming. "On their way to Darkness, Colorado."

I growled. "Son of a bitch."

"Thought maybe you'd want to get out of town," Seraphina said.

Without waiting for my drink, I headed for the parking garage, the demon right behind me.

PENELOPE

The only thing that was possibly more unbelievable than the fact that Obsidian was an angel was ... well, the mansion he lived in.

After we'd caught some z's during the daylight hours, plus five more hours on the road, our destination turned out to be a massive estate immersed deep within a forest, surrounded by mountains. I had never seen anything like it, which was why I found myself gaping as Obsidian steered the car up the circular drive toward the house.

I wasn't exactly sure what I expected, but it certainly wasn't this.

Closer to the house, the wide circular drive narrowed, the enormous trees giving way to smaller trees and bushes, a few flowers tucked neatly in for color, leading to a covered space, providing the owners with shelter from the elements. Even in the dark of night, the colorful petals and greenery were highlighted by the lights discreetly placed throughout. Ivy snaked up thick pillars, winding overhead in a dense jungle of green, brightly accented by the recessed lights. Three wide steps, bookended by stone borders, led to a set of sturdy, round-top, thick wooden doors. It gave off a very old-world vibe.

When Obsidian opened my door, I stepped out, stretched my aching muscles. The crisp breeze brushed over my skin, chilling me. Considering it was July, I didn't expect such cool temperatures, and it had me wondering if I'd packed sufficiently.

"Where exactly are we?"

"We're only a few miles from Telluride."

Geography had never been my strong suit, so I couldn't picture it on a map.

As we moved toward the porch, the front door opened. A dark-haired man wearing a perfectly pressed black suit stepped out, a smile on his face.

"Welcome back, sire," the man greeted. "Shall I park your car in the garage?"

Obsidian tossed him the keys. "Jeffrey, I'd like you to meet Penelope. Penelope, this is Jeffrey, one of the *heurosp*."

"Very nice to meet you," I greeted and earned an answering, "It's a pleasure to have you here, madam."

Without any additional pleasantries, Jeffrey scurried along, making his way to the car.

"What do you think so far?" Obsidian asked, taking my hand and leading me up to the doors.

"All this is yours?" The sweet scent of jasmine drifted on the breeze.

"It is. Mine and quite a few others, mind you."

"Oh, well, if you have to share it"—I grinned—"then it might as well be a shanty."

Obsidian laughed, and I found that I loved the sound.

"Welcome to our shanty," he said, motioning for me to precede him inside the open door.

I paused in the circular foyer, attempting to take it all in. The Mediterranean theme was carried into the house. Rectangular stones in a variety of gray tones lined the floors and the walls, rising at least four stories to the glass dome overhead. A chandelier the size of a dining room table dangled from up high, an intricate combination of iron and glass to blend with the rest. It was breathtaking, really. Any other time, I would've been in awe of the charm, the design. But right now, I figured a quick peek was far more than my sluggish brain could handle.

"Main stairs to the second floor," Obsidian said, gesturing toward a dramatic curving staircase, its hardwood and wrought iron spindles gleaming.

"What's on that floor?"

"Game room, the *fiestreigh's* private quarters," he said before nodding his chin to the right. "This is one of the libraries."

Sure enough, the walls of books pretty much gave it away.

"You have more than one library?"

"We have a lot of books," he said, the corner of his mouth

tilting upward in a smirk. He gestured toward a wide hallway. "And this leads to the main floor."

"Are these"—I glanced at all the openings leading out of the foyer—"doors?"

"They are," Obsidian confirmed.

It seemed odd in this day and age, considering the whole open-concept theme everyone had taken on.

Then it hit me. "To keep the sun out."

"Yes." Obsidian exhaled slowly. "The doors are an added precaution, kept closed during the day in the event the front doors are to be opened."

"Can the *heurosp* go out during the day?"

"Yes," he answered. "They're human."

Ah. Humans taking care of angels. Not quite what I expected. Then again, nothing was as I'd expected.

I turned to face him. "What happens if you're exposed to sunlight?"

Obsidian removed his sunglasses, his molten silver gaze settling on my face. "We'll burn. And yes, it will kill us."

I studied him for a moment, still unsure how to process all of this information. It was one thing to read about it in fiction. Something totally different to encounter in real life.

Before I could ask another question, Obsidian urged me toward a short staircase that led down to a spacious hallway lined with the same stone pillars I'd seen out front. A beautiful aqua-blue and gold rug ran the entire length, several pieces of furniture sitting atop it, as well as a few doors recessed between the columns on both sides, turning what should've been a hall into another room.

"You mentioned you had dogs," I said casually, wondering if they were inside.

"We do. I'm sure they're around here somewhere."

Obsidian guided me down the hallway with his hand

resting on the small of my back. We emerged through what passed as the mouth of the rest of the house.

The space opened up completely. Probably seventy or eighty feet wide, ceilings at least three stories high, more paved stone walls, rich hardwood floors, decorative beams overhead. The second floor above was ringed with the same wrought iron balusters as the front staircase, the space brightly lit, though there wasn't a single window.

An enormous stone fireplace was the centerpiece of the main floor, rising high above and dividing the large living area and the kitchen on the other side. The furniture in here had a Tuscan vibe. Rich, dark wood chairs with rolled arms and cabriole legs embraced the scrolling acanthus leaf details on the beige cushions. Two matching sofas sat atop a rich blue rug that popped against the light fabric on the furniture. It felt more like a lobby than a living room. The kind where you'd expect to see men wearing suits, smoking cigars, and drinking bourbon.

On the perimeter of the space, more rooms fanned out from the center, all dark.

"I'm assuming Jeffrey's not the only person who works here?" I asked as we continued toward the kitchen.

"No. There're roughly a dozen *heurosp*."

"And the translation?"

"I think the politically correct term is household employees," he said with a chuckle.

I stopped when I'd passed the fireplace, my eyes widening as I took it all in. There was a massive square island—at least eight feet in both directions—that sat with honor in the middle of the space. Barstools lined gray cabinets on two sides, a deep sink the only disruption in the large slab of white granite, with its delicate wisps of gray tying in the colors. On the outer walls, the color scheme was flipped.

White cabinets with gray granite tops formed long rows beneath open shelving and more cabinets. Four ovens, an eight-burner stovetop, and two microwaves were on the left side, and on the right, an industrial-sized refrigerator and freezer.

"That's a ... a lot of appliances."

"It takes a lot to feed the masses," he replied, taking my hand once more.

"How many live here?"

"The mansion was built to house us all. Roughly sixty, including the Fae. Then you add in the *heurosps*."

My attention shot to Obsidian. "Seventy-plus people? Under one roof?"

"I assure you, it's big enough."

Whether by intention or simply chance, the entire house appeared to be vacant. Aside from Jeffrey, I didn't encounter another person during the brief tour. On a positive note, those *heurosps* had earned their paycheck because the countertops were waxed to a shine, the stainless steel gleaming in the decorative pendant lights overhead.

We kept going, passing an enormous dining room off to the right, occupied by a long, wide wooden table to seat two dozen, the stucco walls decorated with dark-trimmed pictures and a couple of sconces that likely dated back to the Middle Ages. The ceiling was lower in there, with three wrought iron chandeliers similar in design to the other light fixtures hanging over the table.

"Do you have meals in there?"

"That's the breakfast nook," Obsidian stated. "The formal dining room holds everyone comfortably."

Breakfast nook. For two dozen.

Wow.

Without elaborating further, Obsidian tugged me toward a

short set of steps leading up into an enormous sunroom that book-ended the main-floor entertainment area.

"We spend a lot of time in here," he informed me, stepping up behind me as I scanned the space.

This room was far more relaxed than the rest I'd seen, even wider than the kitchen space. Though the decor continued with the Mediterranean theme, it felt homier. A nice place to relax and chill. Big enough for several small seating areas, as well as six full-sized sofas, three on each side of the fireplace shaped into U's to allow people to congregate comfortably. Thick rugs sat beneath the furniture, covering the hardwood, while there were televisions mounted on both sides of the fireplace, making two separate areas.

Heavy navy-blue drapes hung from thick iron rods, pulled back to reveal a solid wall of doors that appeared to retract completely, bringing the outside in should Obsidian and his housemates choose. The room overlooked a multilevel pool currently glittering pink and purple.

"Not the colors I'd expect for a manly property," I teased.

"Asmia's the one who plays with the lights. She changes them nightly."

"Asmia? Is she an angel, too?"

"Fae."

I glanced out the doors, seeing the mountains in the distance. "So, you live here, but who owns this place?"

"Technically, it belongs to a company we set up."

Turning to face him, I realized he was a couple of steps lower, our height difference not so dramatic like this. "So *you* own it?"

His gaze shifted away. "I actually don't exist, Penelope. Not in your human world, anyway."

"That makes sense. Probably not easy to categorize angels on birth certificates, huh?"

His attention returned to me, his eyes once more covered by his sunglasses. "I know you have questions, Penelope."

Oh, I definitely did. Far more than I knew what to do with.

Obsidian cupped my face as he leaned toward me, pressed his lips to mine. The kiss went from zero to outer space in a matter of milliseconds. I gripped his biceps, my hunger for him blazing anew. It had been intensifying with every passing second since we'd left the hotel room, but now it was as though someone had hit the switch, turning me into an inferno of need.

Had it not been for someone clearing their throat, perhaps I would've let Obsidian take me right there in the sunroom.

I pulled away from him, then shrieked when my gaze landed on perhaps the most beautiful woman in the known universe, standing just a little too close for comfort. She was so striking she appeared almost imaginary.

"Acadia," Obsidian greeted kindly. "Meet Penelope. Penelope, this is Acadia, one of the Fae."

Acadia curtsied before me, an archaic form of greeting that she made appear as natural as breathing.

"It's a pleasure to meet you, My Queen."

Even her voice was otherworldly.

"The formalities aren't necessary," Obsidian told her. "Where's Zeus and Aphrodite?"

Acadia peered around as though she expected them to be behind her. "No idea. But I can find them for you."

"Please."

Acadia stood tall, her amethyst eyes meeting mine briefly before turning to Obsidian. "May I prepare the feast now?"

Obsidian cleared his throat. "Not yet. Find Asmia and Taayin. Have them meet us in the library in ten minutes. Reidar's not far behind."

"Of course." Acadia looked back at me briefly, then vanished.

I inhaled sharply, taking a step back. "I think warnings should come with that move."

Obsidian laughed. "I'll be sure to let them know."

Hesitantly, I turned my eyes on him. "Is she the Fae you feed from?"

"She is," he admitted, though he seemed to be waiting for my reaction.

It took effort, but I managed to keep my expression passive, even as I acknowledged there was no way I could watch that. That woman, fairy, whatever, made me look like...

"It's not like that, Penelope," Obsidian stated, his voice low, insistent, as though he'd read my mind. Then again, he probably had.

"Yeah, well, try telling that to my insecurity," I muttered, hating that I was jealous, but I pushed it down because it wasn't important. "What else do they do?" I asked, proud my voice remained level. "Cook? Clean?"

"No. That's what the *heurosp* are here for. They manage the house. The Fae are here to serve the *fiestreigh* only."

Oh, God. That didn't sound good. "Serve? That doesn't sound like they're only a blood source."

Obsidian looked away. "It's a give-and-take. They also tend to the *fiestreigh's* sexual needs. The Fae feed on emotions—"

I took a step back from Obsidian. "You have *sex* with them?"

Okay, yeah, it was possible I was going to be sick.

"I do not." He peered down at me, his eyes still concealed. "There's a lot of information about us you've yet to understand. Hopefully, once I've had the opportunity to fill you in, it'll make more sense."

God, I hoped so.

OBSIDIAN

I continued to show Penelope around the first floor. The laundry, the main-floor office, access to two additional staircases as well as exits. After I'd given her a glimpse at the indoor pool, we returned to the kitchen, then onward to the back of the house. I hadn't intended to give her a full tour, but I had sensed she needed a distraction from the information she'd ascertained. For whatever reason, she was not keen on the idea of the Fae being used in a sexual manner.

Then again, humans viewed sex a bit differently than we did.

"Dare I ask where your private quarters are?" Penelope said after I shot a text to Taayin, informing the *lieterra* I needed a bit more time before our meeting.

The male shot a message back, assuring me he would be available whenever we were ready.

"The house was built specifically for our needs," I informed her. "My brothers and I each have our own private quarters on the third floor."

"Three floors?"

"Yes."

Tugging her toward me, I started down the hall that led to the back staircase.

"Where do those go?" Penelope gestured toward the stairs leading down.

"We have an underground facility. Training space, weight room, recreational area."

"But no elevator, huh?" She giggled softly. "Then again, probably not necessary with that whole poofing thing you can do."

The teasing tone had me peering her way, noticing the glint in her beautiful gold eyes. The fact that she was joking lightened my steps. I'd seen the concern, felt it even, for the fact that I fed from Acadia. I'd also seen the way she recoiled at the thought.

Granted, had I been in her shoes, I wasn't sure I would have handled it as gracefully as she had.

"There are two elevators," I informed her.

"Of course there are." She took a deep breath, followed me up the stairs, beyond the second floor, and up to the third.

I motioned to the left. "There's a theater that way, as well as access to the veranda. And over here," I continued, leading her to the wing on the right, "my brothers and I occupy this space. We each have our private quarters, but we have our own separate living room and game room."

I paused, using my palm print to unlock the door.

"Why does it require security?"

"Our *lieterras* have access, but it's mostly for our privacy."

Once we'd made it through the door, it sealed shut behind us, and I texted Taayin to inform him to update the security to include Penelope's prints and iris scan for all secured areas.

I smiled when I heard the familiar sound of Zeus panting excitedly. When we turned the corner into the open living room, I saw both dogs sitting obediently.

"Meet Zeus and Aphrodite," I told Penelope, followed by a command for both to come to me.

Tails wagging excitedly, they trotted over, then sat once again, staring up at Penelope as though she were the only light in their darkest days.

"They're beautiful," Penelope said reverently. "May I pet them?"

"They'll be forever in your debt if you do," I warned with a smile.

When Penelope went to her knees before the dogs, I was overwhelmed by that strange sensation in my chest. I'd come to recognize it as love. Seeing my *amsouelot* petting Zeus and Aphrodite while talking to them made me happy.

"Where do they sleep?" she asked when she got to her feet.

"Wherever they want, basically." I motioned toward two dog beds tucked near the end of the sofa. "You'll find many of those throughout the house."

"They're not locked up here?" she asked.

"No. They have free roam of the house. There are dog doors throughout. They come and go as they please."

Taking Penelope's hand once again, I commanded Zeus and Aphrodite to go downstairs, then led Penelope through the living room toward one of the many hallways that branched off of it. My female was glancing around, her mouth hanging open as she took in the stone and gaslit lamps mounted every few feet down the wide hallway.

"Are those motion-sensored?"

"They are."

"They don't look electric."

"They're not. We use gas in the event the electricity goes out. The motion sensors are just a few modern conveniences we've added."

"Very high-tech," she muttered, stopping when we came to the door to my room.

I opened it with my mind, not thinking anything of it.

Before she walked inside, Penelope peered up at me, shot an amused grin.

"Oh, my God. This is your private quarters?" Her tone was breathless, her mouth agape as she stared at the large space. "It's enormous."

Evidently the *heurosps* had made a few upgrades since my departure. What had once been a comfortable room to sleep in looked more like a romantic honeymoon suite. The king-size bed sported a thick navy-blue comforter that practically sparkled beneath the lights. The nightstands now held lamps, clocks, and reading material for two rather than one. A seating area had been added, perched neatly in front of the doors that led to the terrace, as well as a large dresser with mirror that matched the chest I used.

"If this is where you sleep, I'd love to see the bathroom."

"You can see whatever you want, but first..." Before she could walk away, I gripped Penelope's arm, spun her around, and backed her against the wall, bending down and crushing my mouth to hers. Just as I'd come to expect, she lit up in my arms. I'd recognized the familiar heat downstairs when I'd been seconds from dragging her to the floor and tearing her clothes off with my teeth.

Though we'd indulged in one another numerous times throughout the day in the motel room, it felt as though eons had passed since I'd last had her. The *amnigh* was intensifying, and since I could smell Penelope's arousal, I knew she was feeling it, too.

My *amsouelot's* leg curled around mine as she tried to get closer. I obliged, lifting her with ease. "Legs around me."

Our mouths realigned as I carried her toward the bed, easing her onto the mattress. Taking a moment, I pulled my mouth from hers, admired her as she lay there.

"What?" she asked, turning her head to look around.

"I've been waiting for the day you'd be in my bed."

Her fingers trailed over my cheekbones, my jaw. "You say that as though I'm the only woman you've had here."

Once more, I sensed her insecurity. "You are, *ayreme*. I've never had another female in this bed."

"Never?"

"Never." I placed one knee between her thighs and crawled over her, pressing soft kisses to her jaw, her neck. "You're my *amsouelot*, Penelope. The Fates selected you solely for me. My other half."

Her strangled laugh had me lifting my head.

"I find that hard to believe." Her eyes glittered with vulnerability. "Out of all the women in the entire universe, they picked me?"

Amused, I kissed her lips. "They did. And I've been waiting for you for ... a long time."

"Exactly how old are you?"

I swallowed hard, peering into her eyes as she removed my sunglasses.

"How old?" she repeated.

I fought the urge to slip into her mind to see where she was headed with this.

"You said you couldn't lie to me."

"And I can't."

"Tell me how old you are, Obsidian," she whispered, her eyes imploring.

"I had my two thousandth birthday in June."

Her eyes flared briefly. "Two thousand. Wow. You look *really* good for an antique."

"Does it scare you?"

Penelope shook her head. "Not even a little. I think you're the one who said age is just a number."

She reached for my shirt and I rose, allowing her to tug it off and toss it to the floor.

Before I relieved her of her clothing, I figured I ought to fill her in on a few more details. This time, I rolled so that she was straddling my hips, looking down at me.

"One of the *heurosp* is going to stop by in a minute," I explained. "To see if we need anything."

Penelope reached for the button on my jeans, my breath slamming out of my lungs in a rush. When she continued by lowering the zipper, I fought to fill my lungs again.

"Perhaps you should let them know we're busy," she whispered, dismounting before stripping off her shirt and tossing it aside.

Not intending to miss out, I shoved my jeans down, managed to kick my boots off, then freed myself from the denim before she returned. And when my naked female climbed back on top of me, covering my body with hers and sealing her lips to mine, I knew I was finally right where I belonged.

Hands roamed as tension thickened in the air between us. But that was nothing compared to the elation that consumed me when she sank down on my cock, taking me deep inside her. I hissed, my fangs shooting out of the roof of my mouth as an immeasurable hunger ignited within. She was so fucking hot riding me, it took more willpower than I possessed to remain there, watching her take her pleasure from me, but somehow I managed.

Not for long, though.

My need for her was too great, proven when I reached for her, yanking her down atop me as I gripped her hips, held her in place, and thrust into her from beneath. I loved how she felt laid out over me, surrounding me, all her soft, smooth skin touching me.

"Obsidian!"

When she came suddenly, it stripped me of all control. My hips shot upward as I came in a rush.

"You're breathing hard this time," Penelope whispered, her body relaxed as she remained laid out over me, her soft lips caressing my neck.

"Caught me off guard," I admitted, kissing the top of her head, brushing all that silky hair to one side.

I heard the code being keyed into the panel, knew a *heurosp* was coming to check in, ensure we had what we needed.

"They're here, aren't they?"

"Will be in a second, yes."

She lifted up, smiled. "Mind if I clean up?"

"If you promise to come back naked."

Her eyes narrowed.

"Fine. But I have every intention of keeping you naked for longer next time."

As she strutted toward the bathroom a minute later, I admired her, then dropped my head back to the bed. Already, I was hard and aching for her again. It was intensifying, slowly but surely. Then again, the coming days, weeks, months were going to get brutal for both of us. Pain in the form of intense sexual longing was going to descend until I sank my fangs in her vein, fed from her. Only then would it ease up.

But even that reprieve would be temporary.

Only once the *lintamair*—the formal mating ritual—was completed would we be able to settle, to relax and breathe, spending the rest of eternity together.

I sighed, closed my eyes.

The biggest problem of all...

She had to agree to it first.

15

PENELOPE

After I freshened up and pulled my clothes back on, Obsidian led me down to the second floor via a secret exit. Hidden behind the entertainment center in the living room was an elevator that carried us down one floor, delivering us into what could only be described as a library to rival all. Not that I'd been to many libraries, but if I'd known this was what I was missing out on, I would've made it a weekly trip.

Dark walls lined with books, masculine furnishings, a cozy fireplace ... they fit well within the decor of the house, yet they felt distinctly intimate. A private area to relax and read, should the need arise.

On one wall, floor-to-ceiling windows were opened wide

to allow the night in. With only an hour to go before dawn, I figured they would soon be sealed tight to ensure the safety of everyone within the mansion. Tucked neatly behind the curtains were tracks on either side of the window. Probably the shutters Obsidian had mentioned.

The rest of the walls were lined with shelves and filled with books. A wooden ladder secured to a railing offered access to those on the highest shelves. Most of the books appeared ancient, and I would've bet big money they had come from centuries before.

Obsidian was two thousand years old. I still couldn't believe that. Two millennia. That was a long time. I couldn't help but wonder what he did to pass the time. How much time did he spend here, inside the mansion? For me, cabin fever never seemed to be an issue, and in a place this enormous, I couldn't imagine ever getting bored enough to want to leave. From the outside, it was evident this was more of a palace than a house, so I figured there was significantly more to explore.

"What's on your mind, *ayreme*?" Obsidian asked, his thick arms wrapping tightly around me.

I gripped his forearms, held on. "Just taking it all in. This is a lovely house."

"It does the job."

He sounded so practical, but I knew a lot had gone into building this place. Not only money, but time, effort, and quite a bit of planning. From what I'd seen, it was all electronic. No manual door locks or switch plates on these walls, no sir. When I'd snuck into his bathroom earlier, I'd been in the dark until he informed me I had to request the lights to come on. Verbally.

Like I'd ever get used to that.

Obsidian continued to hug me, and I suspected he was

waiting for my next question. God knew I'd already bombarded him, but I couldn't help it. I was both confused and fascinated with all of it. Like I'd told him at the motel, this entire situation felt strange. More so now that I was here, in this new place. It might've been home to Obsidian, but it felt like a foreign country to me. All new and unexplored.

"I know you're probably growing tired of my questions."

He leaned down, brushed his lips against my cheek. "I'll never tire of them, *ayreme*. Your curiosity intrigues me."

"What does that mean? *Ayreme*?"

His lips grazed me once more. "It's a term of endearment, meaning *my greatest love*."

It was the simple things like that that had my heart filling. Hard to believe I'd only known him a few days, considering how overwhelmed by emotions I was.

I tilted my head back, peered up at him. "Why did you bring me in here?"

"To introduce you to a few people," he said simply as he released me, then took my hand and led me to the sofa.

No sooner had I eased down into the buttery-soft leather than the doors opened.

In walked several men and two women, all eyes locked on me as they stepped around one another until they were fanned out in a semicircle, with me being the item on display.

"Thank you all for coming," Obsidian told them as he placed his arm over my shoulder, pulling me into him. "I figured I'd make the official introductions."

Ah, so an introduction, not a firing squad. Good to know.

"Everyone, this is Penelope Calazans. My *amsouelot*."

For whatever reason, the pride in his voice warmed me.

"You met Acadia," Obsidian said, motioning to the stunning woman I had encountered downstairs.

"Hello again," I said to the Fae, earning a smile in return.

"And this is Asmia, the one who determines the pool colors."

She was as beautiful as Acadia, though they couldn't have been more different. While Acadia was small in stature, Asmia was tall, lithe. Acadia's dark hair was board straight, while Asmia's long blond tresses hung in soft curls down her back, so silky I wasn't sure it was real. The only thing they had in common were their otherworldly eyes. A brilliant shade of purple I'd never seen before.

"It's an honor to meet you," Asmia said softly.

Not sure what to say to that, I offered a smile.

"This is Taayin. He's my *lieterra*," Obsidian explained.

"Right-hand," Taayin explained. "Personal assistant. Not to mention, ass-kicker extraordinaire."

He made me laugh with the last part. "Nice to meet you."

"This is Gryffyth." Obsidian motioned to the enormous man standing off to the side. "He's our resident tech guru. Responsible for most of the equipment in the house."

Blond hair, blue eyes, Gryffyth was what some would call classically handsome. And while he was tall, it was his thick musculature that made him so intimidating, as though he could punch his way through stone with ease.

"And this is Alden."

"The butler," I said, the words coming out more as an accusation.

"Guilty." His blue eyes twinkled with amusement.

"I should've grilled you when I had the chance."

"There's plenty of time for that," he said kindly.

A noise outside the room had all heads turning. A second later, one of the doors swung wide, and in walked the two hulking men who'd accompanied us at the motel. Once inside the room, they stepped aside.

"Oliver!" I shot to my feet and raced to my brother, throwing my arms around him.

Before he could hug me back, I jerked back, hissing as an electrical current hit me from all angles. The equivalent of grabbing a live wire, I imagined. Definitely not a comfortable feeling.

Obsidian's gentle hand came down on my shoulder. "I should've warned you, *ayreme*. The touch of a male will be painful for you."

I turned to face him, frowned. "Why?"

"Because you've mated," Asmia said softly. "It's the same for Obsidian and any female who's not you."

Well, wasn't that convenient? And sneaky.

"Someone care to tell me why I'm here?" Oliver spat, drawing all eyes to him.

"It's for your own safety," Taayin informed him, his voice soft and steady, though his posture had changed to defensive.

"Yeah, well, I think I'll pass," Oliver shot back. "I don't know what the hell's going on, but I've got a life to get back to."

Before Oliver could spin around and march out of the room, Gryffyth blocked his path.

"You might want to rethink that," the big blond man told Oliver. "And maybe ease up on the attitude while you're at it. We're not your enemies."

Oliver's eyes blazed with fury. "No? So, *what*? I should be *grateful* that you crazy fucks kidnapped me?"

Obsidian stepped closer, pulling me into him, my back to his front. His arms came around to cross over my chest in a protective gesture that somehow settled me, though I wasn't intimidated by Oliver or his frustration.

In a strange show of solidarity, the men moved so they

were between me and my brother, the women holding their ground as well.

"I'm only going to say this once," Obsidian began, his voice deep, authoritative. "I understand you're angry, but in this house, you'll show respect to everyone, but most importantly, your sister."

Oliver glared back at him, but thankfully, he kept his mouth shut.

"We'll be more than happy to fill you in as soon as we've all settled in," Obsidian continued. "It's been a rough couple of days, and we all need sleep. I want everyone to meet for dinner at nightfall."

"Then I think I'll retire," Acadia said softly, her gaze pinned on Obsidian. "Unless you need me?"

I felt Obsidian tense behind me, and suddenly, my stomach churned violently. I knew it was the Fae's reference to him feeding, but it felt ridiculously intimate to me.

"I think I'll retire, too," I said quickly, pulling away from Obsidian and heading for the elevator.

"Penelope, wait," Acadia called out.

"You do your thing," I said, my back to the others. "I'll do mine."

Before someone could convince me to stay, I darted for the elevator, keeping my eyes down as the door closed. On the third floor, I stepped out into the living room with its black leather sofas and monstrous television. I hurried down the hall to Obsidian's bedroom, closed myself in, then sauntered into the bathroom.

This was, by far, my favorite room of all I'd seen so far. I'd only spent a few minutes in here, but as far as I was concerned, I could live in this enormous space. From the drop-in tub in the center of the room that looked more like a pool than a bathtub to the spacious shower that stood behind it, the glass tiles on the wall sparkling in the blue lights in the ceiling, it was about as perfect as I could've even imagined it to be. A soothing space meant for luxury and relaxation.

Yet it didn't have any magical powers because the longer I lingered, the more my anxiety grew.

Thinking about Obsidian feeding from the Fae gave me heartburn. Which was odd, considering I knew so little about his kind.

"His kind," I muttered. "An angel. A *warrior* angel, at that."

It made absolutely no sense, and at the same time, it all seemed to fit together.

Though I considered taking a shower, I figured sleep was the best way to deal with the overload of emotions. Not sure where my suitcase was, I ventured into the closet, called out for the lights to come on. They lit up the space, highlighting an entire wall dedicated to Obsidian's clothing, the other side completely empty except for the few items I'd packed. Evidently one of the *heurosp* had unpacked for me.

Figuring it was too cold to wear the tank top and shorts I'd brought to sleep in, I stole one of Obsidian's button-down shirts. It took some doing to get it situated, but I finally managed to get the sleeves rolled up enough so that I could use my hands. When I returned to the bedroom, I came up short. Obsidian stood, hands in his pockets, looking tormented, his sunglasses tossed aside, silver eyes churning.

"We need to talk," he said gruffly.

"After we sleep."

I started for the bed, but he reached for me. "Now, Penelope."

While I was taken aback by his high-handed behavior, I conceded. "Fine."

"In the other room. Neutral ground."

I did not like the sound of that, but I allowed him to lead me out of his room, down the hall, and into the open living room. Flames flickered in the fireplace, warming the space as he directed me to the sofa.

Obsidian took a seat, pulling me down with him so that I was not quite on top of him but close. I leaned into his warmth, held on to his arm when he draped it over my shoulder and across my chest. Despite my anxiety, I still relished the feel of him.

"I know it bothers you that I have to feed from Acadia," he said softly, his torment reflected in the tone.

I stared into the orange flames, fighting the strange twinge in my gut. "Tell me this ... how often do you have to feed?"

"To maintain my strength, daily, but I can wait as long as three days. It's not ideal, but it's sometimes necessary."

"But you can't feed from humans? Or other angels?"

"Angels, no. Humans ... I could, but it's the equivalent of having a bowl of rice when you need protein. We must feed from a Fae or our *amsouelot*."

"Asmia and Acadia?"

"They're the only ones here right now. There are fourteen in total, but we had to split up. Once my brothers are back, the Fae will return as well. There are a couple of males among them, so I could use one of them if necessary."

Oh, great. *That* didn't help.

"Are they all beautiful?"

Obsidian exhaled roughly.

Realizing he wasn't going to answer, I huffed. "Okay, fine. Who do the Fae feed from?"

"Like I said, they feed on emotions."

"So, a psychic vampire?"

"In a sense, perhaps."

"Can they remove the negative emotions?"

"Yes. They have the ability to relieve whatever emotions they want, but that's not their goal. They've learned they can thrive on emotions tied to sexual encounters."

"That's why they're used for sex."

"Not used," Obsidian stated. "It's a mutual agreement. It satisfies both parties."

"No harm, no foul, then," I mused.

"Yes. Or better yet, give-and-take," he noted.

"What about mating? Do they all do it? Like you do?"

"If you're asking whether they have an *amsouelot*, yes, they do."

"So the Fae are here only to act as your blood source and to have sex with you until you mate." Eww. The words left a bitter taste in my mouth.

"We're not allowed to interact with humans, except for our *amsouelots*," he clarified. "Therefore, we develop relationships with other species."

"Fae?"

"Yes. And vampires, fairies. But to answer your question, yes, the Fae are here for a reason. They also have the capabilities to serve on the front lines should we need them. We see them as our partners, not our possessions. We feed because we need to."

Realizing we were approaching a much more important subject, I pulled away and turned to face him, crisscrossing my legs. "So angels can't have relationships with humans?"

He laid his hand on my thigh. "In some instances, yes."

"No, I mean, indefinitely. Since you're two thousand years old, I assume you're immortal. And I'm clearly not. How exactly does that work? I'm not sure how I explain having a young, hot stud on my arm when I'm eighty."

Obsidian looked away, staring at the fireplace. When he looked back, there was a sadness in his eyes.

"You have to turn me, don't you? Like a vampire?"

"Not exactly, but yes. A change is required."

"What do I turn into?"

His eyes lowered. "Exactly as I am."

"An angel?"

"Yes."

"But I thought angels were only in Heaven. Does that mean I have to die?"

His voice was laced with gravel when he spoke. "Yes."

I inhaled sharply, his words sinking in. In order for me to be with Obsidian for eternity, I had to die.

Holy crap. That was ... terrifying. I wasn't ready to die. Not now, maybe not ever.

Obsidian reached for me, his hand cupping my cheek. "I've waited two millennia for you, Penelope, having known since I was old enough to understand that I had an *amsouelot.* There's no rush for more."

"But you've been with other women? Other *humans*?"

I could tell he didn't want to answer that question, but I waited him out.

"Not humans, no. Other females, yes," he said simply. "But there was never a romantic entanglement. Nothing serious, anyway. I'm not a saint, Penelope. But when I learned of your existence, everything changed. I vowed to be the male you deserved. Hence the abstinence."

I had to admit, for him to abstain seemed quite the feat. Especially considering his age and that whole *amnigh* thing.

"How were you created? Do you have parents?"

His eyes shot to mine. "No, I do not. I was the first warrior, brought into existence by Michael."

"And your brothers?"

"God didn't like the fact that I lacked nurturing, so He

insisted Michael do things naturally. My species has what's known as *archsires* and *archdams*. They reside in Heaven. Vitus, the angel of virility, and Asha, the angel of conception, select the strongest offspring in the bloodlines to procreate. The young are raised by the *archsire* and *archdam* who created them, then once they're old enough, they're trained as warriors."

Wow. That sounded so ... clinical. Almost businesslike. A reproduction system for warrior angels. I couldn't imagine.

"When was the last time you fed?" I blurted.

His full attention returned to me. "Yesterday."

"Will you feed from me?"

Obsidian's face twisted, as though he was in pain. "Like I told you, I can. But I won't. Not yet."

I frowned. "Why not? Because it'll hurt me?"

"For *amsouelots*, it's not painful. However, there are other ... complications we must account for."

"What might those be?"

Silence hung between us for the longest time. I was beginning to think Obsidian wouldn't answer my question when he reached for me. With minimal effort, he positioned me over his thighs.

I straddled him, and the instant I did, my desire for him hit me like a Mack truck going full speed down a mountain.

"Because of that," he whispered, his big hands gripping my hips, pulling me toward him until the hard ridge of his erection pressed intimately against me.

My breaths became raspier as my body warmed. "Because you make me hot?"

Obsidian's eyes blazed. "*Amsouelots* have this connection. A need for one another. Most easily identified by their sexual hunger."

"I'm not sure that's restricted only to your kind. We call it lust," I whispered, rolling my hips as the friction between my thighs intensified my desire for him.

"Trust me, this isn't lust. Nothing compares to this. Now that they've found one another, our souls are intent on remaining together. Sex is the most intimate joining. But rather than abate, it only grows stronger. The longer we're together, the more powerful it becomes. It'll cripple us both if we don't satisfy it frequently."

"You make it sound painful."

"It can be. The desire can be so strong it borders on pain."

I was breathing heavily now, a near-desperate ache pulsing between my thighs, but there was nothing painful about it.

Obsidian cupped my face, pulled me toward him. "The only way to satisfy your need is for me to come inside you."

I whimpered, heat blooming throughout me. "What does that have to do with you feeding from me?"

"If I consume your blood, you become a physical part of me." His lips brushed mine. "At that point, when I come inside you, our connection is strengthened. It'll sate you longer, give some reprieve. But only for a bit."

"How long's a bit?"

"A week, a month. Maybe even a few months. It depends on the souls, their needs."

"You're saying we won't want to have sex for a month?"

That sexy smirk appeared. "More like we won't be desperate for it. A couple of times a day should satisfy it."

"Two times a day? Seriously?" I wasn't exactly up to speed on what a healthy sex life entailed, but that seemed like a lot.

Not right now, of course, because I wanted to get my hands on Obsidian as frequently as possible.

"Then it'll return with a vengeance, and we won't be able to quench it, no matter how hard we try. Not until we complete the mating."

"And how do we do that?"

His eyes locked with mine, the silver glow faint at first, then brightening until the entire room was brighter.

"It's a ritual known as *lintamair*. It requires a full moon, a specific setting, some magical stones. We feed from one another while our bodies are joined."

Okay, so I knew I shouldn't find the idea of that erotic, but in that moment, I couldn't help myself. Especially not when his warm hands cupped my hips beneath the shirt I was wearing. The button-down I had on covered me more thoroughly than the dress I wore to work, but I still felt completely naked.

"Obsidian..." I leaned in, kissed him, tried to get closer.

I felt his hands moving between us, but I didn't stop kissing him. Our tongues thrashed as I worked the buttons free on my shirt, wanting to feel his warmth on my skin. His palms squeezed my ass, forcing me to lift up. It was then I realized he had freed his erection from his jeans and he was shoving them down his hips. Finally, the blunt head pressed urgently against my sex, relieving some of the ache within me. I sank down on him, my lips tearing away from his as I threw my head back. He filled me completely, the sensation exquisite, just as it had been every time he penetrated me.

Instead of allowing me to work myself over him, Obsidian rolled us so that I was on my back and he was over me, one knee on the sofa, one foot on the floor, driving deep inside me again and again, his thrusts timed perfectly to deliver mind-numbing pleasure.

When our eyes met, I cupped his face, staring into that intense glow. And when his upper lip pulled back, revealing his fangs, I nearly came. The thought of those sharp teeth at my neck drove me absolutely crazy. It wasn't that I wanted him to bite me, but the thought of it was erotic as hell.

A rough growl sounded in his throat as he drove deeper inside me, making my nerve endings sing.

Feeling bold, I brushed the tip of my thumb over the razor-sharp canine, drawing blood. He growled again, sucking my thumb into his mouth, and I came, my orgasm shattering me.

A second later, he released my thumb, his head falling back as he roared, a sound that made the hairs on my arms stand on end as it rattled the walls with the intensity.

And when he looked down once more, the bright glow was gone, but there was something else in his silver eyes.

Love.

Pure, unfettered love.

I felt it deep in my soul.

ASMIA

I was about to take a shot, to nail the eight ball into the corner pocket, when I heard it.

The feral sound was like a sonic boom through the entire mansion.

"Was that...?" Acadia turned to look over the railing, though I could've told her the sound had come from the floor above us.

"Obsidian," I whispered. "With his female."

Though the sound didn't surprise me in the least, the after-effects that swept through did. A wave of energy passed through the house, stronger than anything I'd ever felt before. Sexual energy.

As soon as it hit me, I felt a tremendous rush. The emotions slammed into me, filling me completely. The equivalent of a human consuming a Thanksgiving feast. Shortly after the high subsided, my womb contracted, my sex clenching fiercely. I gripped the table to keep myself upright even as I noticed Acadia dropping into a chair, a grimace on her beautiful face.

"What *is* that?" Acadia whimpered.

I suspected it was the phenomenon known as *gathenya*, though I'd never witnessed the surge of energy produced by an angel mating before.

Before I could answer, Taayin appeared, materializing before me.

"Do you feel it, too?" he asked.

I nodded, breathing through the overwhelming desire.

"Go away, Acadia," Taayin hissed over his shoulder, even as he moved behind me.

A second later, Reidar appeared. Without a word, he lifted Acadia into his arms, carried her out of the room. A male on a mission, no doubt.

"Taayin..." I sucked in air, but it didn't help. "I need..."

The sound of a zipper being pulled down was overly loud in my ears. Cool air caressed my bare ass when Taayin shoved my skirt up over my hips. The thong I'd been wearing was ripped off, and seconds later, he plunged into me from behind as I was bent over the pool table.

As my mind whirled with lascivious pleasure, I couldn't help but wonder how the others were faring. I'd never felt something so overwhelming before, a vicious need that threatened to unravel the mere structure of my chemical makeup unless it was sated.

"Acadia!" Reidar yelled, his deep voice bouncing off the walls.

Yep, this wasn't good. Whatever had happened with Obsidian had triggered an epidemic.

Taayin's hands curled over my shoulders as he drove into me, deep, hard. The clothing that remained on my body scraped my hypersensitive flesh, irritating it. I willed it gone, freeing myself. The second the cool air caressed my flesh, I came.

Taayin growled roughly and I could feel him throbbing deep inside me.

Crying out as another orgasm bested me, I reached back, gripping Taayin's thigh, urging him not to stop. Two wasn't enough. Hell, I wasn't sure a million would be enough.

"Fuck," he hissed, hammering into me as I came again.

And again.

Lucky for both of us, this male was thorough. He didn't slow his pace, drilling me until we were both weak. Thankfully, the pool table was holding me up; otherwise, I would've been a puddle on the floor, my knees like jelly.

Taayin's hips slammed against me one final time, his cock pulsing inside me as he came. Only then did the painful need subside. I was immensely grateful for the male I'd come to love, knowing he was there for me when I needed him most.

I didn't move, even when Taayin's body covered mine, both of us drained physically. On the flip side, my emotional fuel levels had never been so high before.

"What the hell was that?" he whispered.

"Obsidian." I turned my head, listened for the sounds echoing from below. They had trailed off.

"What about him?" Taayin's weight lifted off me, and I stood tall, grateful some of my energy had come back.

"We heard him upstairs. He roared..." I grinned. "You know,

the sound that escapes after a really good orgasm, but also unlike anything I've ever heard before."

Taayin stared at me.

"It was like the energy was displaced, redirected into the mansion, through all of us." Turning to face him, I rested my naked butt against the pool table. "If I'm right, it's *gathenya*. And I think it's the first of many episodes to come."

"I fucking hope not. I've never felt anything like it."

I wasn't sure anyone had.

16

OBSIDIAN

I'd always thought sleep was overrated.

At least until my body begged for it.

After that last bout of sex, I'd carried Penelope to our bed, placed her beneath the blankets, and crawled in behind her. I'd been too tired to move, grateful to have her in my arms.

That was a little over twelve hours ago. We'd slept through the day, waking twice when our bodies sought pleasure from the other. I'd made love to her both times, keeping her close as I slowly drove us to orgasm before we drifted off again.

Of course, now that my eyes were open, my cock was raging, desperate to feel my female wrapped around me. Since she was still breathing deeply, I fought the urge to wake her, staring up at the darkened ceiling.

Perhaps because I didn't have a blood-born family, I'd

always anticipated the day I would have someone to call my own. Though the *fiestreigh* had become my family over the centuries, I'd never felt complete. Not the way I did now. Not until Penelope.

Before my brothers had come along, Michael had kept me sheltered, with him at all times. Admittedly, the archangel wasn't the fatherly type, nor had he pretended to be. The only thing Michael cared about was proving my worth, ensuring God knew I was everything he had promised I would be. In turn, I had done the same, proving my worth to Michael. I'd never received praise until my first mission with Stygian. My brother had been the one to outwardly express his gratitude for a job well done.

As far as I was concerned, the true praise came from Penelope's love. She hadn't said the words outright, but I could see her emotions in her eyes. Now, as I lay in the dark, it was hard to believe I was home and Penelope was here with me. From the moment I'd learned of her existence, I'd allowed two dozen scenarios to play out in my head. Honestly, I hadn't expected it to turn out quite like this. Certainly not this quickly. Then again, time was relative since I was two thousand years old.

But I couldn't deny it felt as though we belonged there, secure within the walls of the mansion. If all went well, my brothers would arrive soon, safe and sound, their *amsouelots* at their sides.

My cell phone buzzed on the nightstand, and I reached for it, not wanting the noise to wake Penelope.

Taayin: *We need to talk.*

"Mmm, you're awake," Penelope whispered as she moved closer.

I dropped my phone and turned toward her, her curvy little ass spooned against my hips, her head resting beneath my chin.

“Definitely awake.” I leaned forward, kissed her jaw as I rocked my hips, my cock seeking the warm haven between her thighs.

Penelope moaned softly, inching closer, her lips brushing my forearm where it rested beneath her head.

“I need to be inside you,” I whispered against her ear. “To feel you.”

My female angled her hips as she lifted her leg, allowing me to guide my cock into her from behind.

She moaned softly as the slick walls of her sex clutched me, driving the air from my lungs in a rush. Exquisite sensation consumed me. She was wet and hot, her body taking me with ease.

I nuzzled her neck, my lips brushing the soft, warm skin. That sweet, powdery scent was stronger there. I took my time, rocking into her as I hugged her to me, her sweet scent intoxicating me.

“Obsidian ... that feels so good.” She moaned softly. “Just like that.”

Closing my eyes, I allowed the sensations to consume me as I moved inside her. Minutes passed before I shifted my hand between her legs, teasing her clit in an effort to increase her pleasure.

Penelope began rocking against me in earnest, driving her hips back, my cock burrowing deeper.

“Make me come,” she pleaded, her urgency evident.

With my finger on her clit, my cock buried in the tight haven of her body, I drove us both to the edge, then right over the other side.

. . .

In an effort to give Penelope some privacy, I urged her to take her time in the shower while I pulled on my clothes and slipped out of the room. I texted Taayin, told the male to meet me in the main-floor office.

I stopped in the kitchen, accepted a cup of coffee from Phillip, the *heurosp* in charge of the household.

"Good evening, sire," Phillip greeted kindly. "It's an honor to have you home once again."

"It's good to be home." Though I'd only been gone for a few weeks this time, it had felt like an eternity.

"Shall I prepare the evening meal?"

I nodded, took a sip of coffee, then headed toward the office at the back of the house. I'd just stepped inside when I heard footsteps behind me. Taayin walked in, closed the door.

"I expected you to look like you'd been hit by a truck," Taayin joked.

My attention was drawn to the steel shutters that began to open, first those on the interior, then those on the exterior of the windows, the night settling heavily around us.

"What's on your mind?" I asked, not intending to go into the details of my interactions with Penelope.

Taayin took a seat in the chair opposite the desk. "First, I figured we could discuss what happened this morning."

As I eased into his chair, I cocked an eyebrow in inquiry.

"Well, from what I can ascertain," Taayin explained, "something transpired between you and your *amsouelot*."

Another eyebrow arch was all I offered.

Taayin sighed, evidently not impressed with my avoidance tactics and hoping for a response. "A sound reverberated through the entire mansion, followed by an intense wave of sexual energy that consumed every one of us."

I frowned. "What in hell are you talking about?"

"Asmia calls it *gathenya*. I call it brutal." A mischievous grin formed. "The outcome wasn't, but still. An all-out orgy ignited throughout the mansion, everyone scattering, finding the closest available orifice in an effort to assuage the painful hunger."

Relaxing into my chair, I considered what the *lieterra* was saying. "And...?"

"*And*?" Taayin frowned. "What the hell was it? And why did it happen?"

I had no idea, so I offered up nothing.

Taayin's blue eyes remained locked on my face. "It seems the *amnigh's* having quite the effect on ... all of us."

"How's that even possible?"

"You got me. Then again, we've never been in the presence of a warrior who's found his *amsouelot*. I assume that wasn't the first time you got your freak on. Something must've happened to inspire the event."

"What time was it?" I asked.

"Oh, I don't know. This morning. Maybe six thirty. Seven."

About the time I'd been talking to Penelope. My thoughts drifted to that moment when I'd been buried deep inside her, the taste of her blood on my tongue when she'd scored her thumb. Something had definitely transpired between us then.

Not that I intended to explain myself to the male. "I have no idea. You'll have to let me know if it happens again."

"Great." Taayin huffed. "Just what we don't need. Some strange sexual energy plaguing the masses."

"Yeah, well, at least you've got options."

"I'm not sure the *heurosp* are pleased by this phenomenon. It affected them as well." Taayin laughed. "Wonder how the human fared."

Considering Oliver's inappropriate behavior toward his sister, I hoped it was painful.

"What else is going on?" I asked, eager to move on to a more appropriate subject.

"I need to have a few minutes of Penelope's time," he said simply. "For her palm print and iris scan."

"She should be down shortly."

Getting to his feet, Taayin headed for the door, pausing with his hand on the knob. "I know it's not my business, but would it be possible to keep me in the loop once ... once you've determined the timing for the *lintamair*?"

"It'll be a while."

Taayin turned to face me, confusion wrinkling his brow. "A while? But I thought that was the goal. To bring the *amsouelots* here, to undergo the *lintamair*. Ensure their safety. Why—"

Holding up a hand, I cut him off. "She needs time to get accustomed before I look to her to make a decision that will alter the course of her life." And ultimately result in her death.

I could tell Taayin wanted to argue, but for whatever reason, he chose not to.

"Is that all you had for me?" I asked before he could slip out.

"Actually, I wanted to tell you—"

A knock sounded on the door.

Taayin pulled it open and Stygian stuck his head in, a wide grin on his face.

"Well, I'll be damned." I shot to my feet, walked over to the male.

"To tell you Stygian's coming home," Taayin mumbled, evidently late on delivering the news.

An embrace ensued between my brother and me, with some powerful back-slapping tacked on.

"What the hell are you doing here?" I peered around him to see who else had arrived.

"Backup."

"What about your *amsouelot*?"

Stygian shook his head. "No luck. Not yet, anyway. Søren's working day and night."

"And the others?"

"Aphotic's locked in on his." The male smirked. "She's giving him a run for his money."

"Is that so?" Didn't surprise me. Aphotic was the youngest, the party boy, one might say. He had a way with the ladies, so it only made sense that the one he would need most would make him earn it.

"Serves him right," Stygian added. "I talked to Cimmerian a little while ago. He's in California right now, tracking down a lead. Last I heard, Piceous was in New York, but no luck on that front, either. Shadow's in Canada. I think he's closing in."

"And Eclipse?"

A wide grin formed on Stygian's mouth. "Believe it or not, his female's right here."

I frowned. "In Darkness?"

"Telluride. But he's heading home now." Stygian peered around the room. "And Penelope? When do we get to meet her?"

I looked up at the ceiling. "She should be down any minute."

"Phillip said the evening meal's about ready. Perfect timing, huh?"

Yeah. Perfect timing.

"You think maybe you could get a haircut while you're here?" I joked, although Stygian's hair *was* getting long, a few inches past his shoulders.

"I think I'll grow it out."

"Great. You've got long hair, Eclipse has a mohawk, Aphotic's sporting mutton chops. What's next?"

"I'd say you could grow some facial hair," Stygian teased, "but you're the only one of us who can't."

"Yeah, yeah, yeah." I grinned, glad to have my brother home.

A ruckus sounded from the kitchen, drawing Stygian and me out of the office.

"What's going on?" I prompted, scanning the grim faces of all the males standing around.

"We've got a problem," Reidar growled softly, his eyes never leaving Oliver, who was leaning casually against the counter, a glass of juice in his hand, looking like he hadn't a care in the world.

"What?" Oliver asked, grinning. "You're telling me I don't have the right to call my girlfriend? She deserves to know where I'm at. Now she does."

Oh, fuck.

Footsteps sounded from the front of the house, slowing as they neared. All eyes shifted that way, awaiting the new arrival to step into the kitchen.

"I didn't expect a party," Eclipse said, his eyes quickly scanning all the occupants. "Well, fuck me running. What's wrong?"

Reidar relayed the condensed version to Eclipse.

All eyes locked on Oliver again. For a brief moment, I almost felt sorry for the male. He had absolutely no idea the trouble he'd caused.

"How long before she can get here?" Taayin asked, the question aimed at no one in particular.

"Worst case, a few hours," Reidar stated, his gruff tone reflecting the displeasure he found in the fact. "I figure we might as well get prepared."

Which meant only one thing. I peered over at Stygian, then Eclipse.

"Throw it up, boys," Reidar announced.

Nodding at my brothers, I let my senses flare out over the mansion. When I felt my brothers' energies, our efforts combined, effectively throwing up a shield to disguise the mansion from anyone and everyone. Though it was invisible to angels, the *dhira* settled over the property, making it appear as a vast nothingness. The cloak wasn't as powerful as it could've been if all my brothers were there, but it would work for the time being.

"I'm going to get Penelope," I informed Reidar. "You team up with Mordecai and Magnar. Get me a bead on Seraphina."

The male nodded, then everyone dispersed.

PENELOPE

I had just stepped out of Obsidian's bedroom, intending to take the stairs down to the main floor, when he came strolling around the corner, his long legs bringing him down the hall toward me. His brow was furrowed, his mouth a thin line, and I imagined his eyes were glowing behind the dark lenses.

I came to a stop before him, reaching out to touch his chest. His hard body seemed to lean into me. "What's wrong?"

"Nothing yet, but..." He exhaled heavily as he pulled me

into his arms, his lips brushing the top of my head as he bent down. "Your brother called Seraphina. Gave her our location. Or what he *thought* was our location, anyway."

I inhaled sharply, pulled back enough to look into his face. "Why would he do that?"

Obsidian motioned in the direction of the stairs, taking my hand in his. "In his defense, we didn't tell him what's going on. I doubt he meant to cause problems, but..."

Even if it was unintentional, he most definitely did.

"He doesn't realize his girlfriend's a demon, so he called to check in?" I felt weird even saying the words.

"We need to bring him up to speed."

Yeah, unfortunately, we did. I wasn't eager to see Oliver's reaction, but he did deserve the truth. No matter how unrealistic it sounded.

We took the back stairs down to the main floor. As we emerged from the stairway, I could hear the sounds of people working. Footsteps traipsing through, pots being set down, a rush of whispered commands.

When we stepped into the kitchen, the first thing I noticed was the metal shutters at the back of the house had retracted, the lights inside reflecting off the dark glass. The second was that I couldn't see a single thing outside, not even the lights in the swimming pool.

"Why's it so dark?" I moved closer, stepping up into the sunroom.

Obsidian moved behind me, placed his big fingers gently on my temples. Suddenly, I could see clearly out into the night. The pool lights were on, coloring the water a teal blue. The patio lights highlighted the empty furniture. In the distance, a sliver of moon cast the tall trees and mountains surrounding the property in silhouette.

When Obsidian removed his fingers, it went pitch black once more.

"It's an illusion," he explained. "A cloak my brothers and I erected to shield the property. Only angels can see through it."

Well, wasn't that fun?

Obsidian took my hand and led me back down to the kitchen toward a set of pocket doors. He slid them open to reveal what I assumed was the formal dining room. Granted, *cafeteria* was more apt, only far more elegant. Several chandeliers matching the one in the foyer hung from the ceiling, brightening the space. There were several round tables scattered throughout, each large enough to seat probably a dozen people and decked out with white tablecloths and fancy crystal vases in the center. Despite the opulence, everyone was congregating at the long table in the center of the room. The wooden top was covered by plates piled high with food, a few laptops and iPads scattered about.

There were probably three times as many people present as there had been this morning in the library. When Obsidian cleared his throat, the conversation died off, and every pair of eyes seemed to focus on me.

Two men instantly got to their feet, sauntering toward me.

I managed to remain rooted in place, rather than shrink back. Though all the men I'd met were on the larger end of the spectrum, these two were as imposing as Obsidian, just not quite as tall. Both had black hair and dark glasses covering what I assumed were glowing silver irises, though they didn't look much like Obsidian beyond that.

"Penelope, I'd like you to meet Eclipse and Stygian." There was pride in Obsidian's voice. "My brothers."

Eclipse—the one with the mohawk—nodded in greeting. He was dressed head to toe in black, from his heavy combat boots to the leather pants and the black T-shirt that stretched across his enormous upper body. Aside from the intimidating attire, he was jaw-dropping handsome, with his modern goth haircut and the dark stubble covering his chiseled jaw.

Stygian, on the other hand, looked like he'd just stepped out of a board meeting for bikers. He wore black slacks, a crisp white shirt, unbuttoned at the throat, sleeves rolled up to reveal tattoos covering both forearms. His silky onyx hair was parted down the middle and rested on his shoulders, and the sharp angles of his jaw weren't sporting even a hint of a shadow.

Both men smiled in greeting, but neither offered a hand, clearly knowing their touch would cause me pain.

"It's nice to meet you." I tried my best not to stare, but it wasn't easy.

"The pleasure's ours," Stygian said firmly before gesturing toward the table. "Come join us. We didn't mean to start without you, but, well ... growing boys and all."

I smiled up at him. There was a kindness about him that seemed at odds with the hard lines of his face and the intimidating aura.

With Obsidian's hand firmly on my lower back, I moved around to the seat he guided me to, directly across from his brothers. He took the one next to me. As I sat, I briefly glanced over at Oliver, smiled. He didn't return the gesture, instead glaring before dropping his eyes to the table.

"We'll do formal introductions later," Eclipse said, his eyes trailing to the other end of the table. "For now, I'd like an update."

A man wearing a three-piece black suit appeared beside me, setting a plate on the table in front of me. Another did the same for Obsidian.

Pancakes, eggs, and bacon, thank goodness. Needless to say, relief filled me. I wasn't used to eating dinner when I first woke up, though I knew some people preferred it. Then again, it was technically morning for them since they slept during the day—or I assumed they did since they were restricted from going out in the sunlight.

"We'll start with you, Magnar," Eclipse said, even as he began shoveling pancakes into his mouth.

A dark-haired man sitting beside Reidar spoke up. "I've got a lead on Perfidious, Seraphina, and Sirius."

With my fork halfway to my mouth, I peered down the table at the man. "Did you say Sirius?"

"He's a demon—"

Before he could launch into an explanation, I grabbed Obsidian's forearm. "My friend Winnie ... the one in California. She mentioned that name. Said he was visiting her at the bar where she works." I seriously doubted the name was all that common.

Several men began tapping the keyboards of their laptops.

"He's been in Los Angeles for the past couple of months," Reidar stated, meeting my gaze. "Is that where your friend is?"

"Yes."

Obsidian motioned toward Reidar. "Find her ASAP."

He was already pushing away from the table. "And when I do?"

"Keep an eye on her. If push comes to shove, bring her here."

"So, that's a thing with you?" Oliver grumbled. "Just think you can snatch people off the street? You know, they call that kidnapping."

"We call it ensuring you live," Eclipse countered, clearly not amused by Oliver's outburst.

"From where I sit, you're the dangerous ones," Oliver retorted.

"Your girlfriend's a demon," I told my brother.

Oliver glared at her. "Fuck you, Opie. I know you don't like her, but watch yourself."

I cringed when he used the nickname I detested.

Obsidian snarled, silverware dropping to his plate with a clatter. "I suggest you change your tone."

"Or what?"

Obsidian snapped his fingers and suddenly Oliver couldn't open his mouth. His eyes bugged out as he attempted to separate his lips.

"Please don't." I squeezed Obsidian's arm. "He doesn't mean anything by it."

Obsidian peered over at me, eyes blazing with fury. I wasn't sure I'd ever seen him so angry.

"The male lacks respect," the man at the far end said, his blue eyes as hot as Obsidian's. "It was too kind, as far as I'm concerned."

There was a rumble of agreement from the others.

Well, I couldn't very well argue with them. For some reason, Oliver wasn't my biggest fan. And I seriously doubted this debacle was going to change his tune anytime soon.

The man at the end of the table turned his laptop toward Oliver. "This your girlfriend?"

Oliver squinted toward the screen, nodded.

"Did you happen to catch the headline on that article?" The man pointed at the top of the screen, which was still directed at Oliver. "Stripper found dead in bathroom stall at club. Died of natural causes. Five *weeks* ago."

Obsidian snapped his fingers, giving Oliver control of his mouth once more.

"That's not possible," Oliver blurted, his voice pitched higher than before. "She's in my apartment right now."

"No," Stygian said, drawing out the word as though he was talking to a child. "Seraphina consumed the female's soul, took on her appearance. It's one of their tricks. You, my friend, have been getting down and dirty with a demon."

For the first time, Oliver looked surprised, maybe even a little ill.

"And since Lucifer's orders are to kill Penelope so he can acquire her soul *and* Obsidian's," Stygian continued, "we assume Seraphina inserted herself in your life for leverage."

"Lucifer?" Oliver nearly choked. "The devil?"

"Yes," Stygian confirmed, but his attention returned to Obsidian. "I think it's safe to say they'll make their way here."

"At the same time," the man at the other end added, "Lucifer'll likely double his efforts to find the other *amsouelots*."

Obsidian's gaze turned to the man sitting beside Eclipse. "Søren? Any word from Michael?"

The man looked up, pinned Obsidian with a cold blue stare. "He's refused our request."

"Request for what?" I asked, curiosity getting the best of me.

"For reinforcements," Stygian noted with a shrug. "I figured it wouldn't hurt to try again."

Clearly bad news based on their expressions.

"I do have a suggestion," the man at the end said.

"Go ahead, Mordecai," Obsidian urged.

Mordecai took a deep breath, exhaled slowly. "I think it might be beneficial if Obsidian and Penelope hole up here for a little while. We can take Gerran, Gryffyth, and Alden, split them up, help the others locate their *amsouelots*. At the same time, you won't be without backup. With Reidar and Taayin here, you'll have more than enough support."

"I'd like to request I go into the field," Acadia said, speaking for the first time. "Asmia can remain here to serve you."

I noticed the Fae looked everywhere but at me.

"It's not a bad idea," Eclipse said.

"Which part?" Obsidian asked.

"All of it. Since Miklós has tracked my *amsouelot* to Telluride, I'll remain in residence. They can take Stian, Ajax, and Cayden with them. Miklós and Magnar will remain back with me."

Stygian spoke up, his voice lowered as he talked directly to Obsidian. "The sooner we locate them, the better off we'll be."

I couldn't do anything more than stare at the three warriors, waiting for them to come to a decision. It seemed the rest of the occupants of the table were doing the same.

Obsidian finally nodded. "But I want Acadia to remain back. With Ziana. Asmia and Elina can go out in the field."

"May I ask why?" Taayin prompted, speaking up for the first time.

"Asmia's aware of what Perfidious looks like. She can remain in the vicinity."

"Then I'd prefer to go out as well," Taayin said, pushing to his feet.

I could feel the tension ratchet up in the room, though I wasn't sure what prompted it.

"No," Obsidian stated firmly. "You'll remain here."

Based on the look on his face, I expected Taayin to argue, but the man simply took a seat.

"Why don't we reconvene in a few hours?" Eclipse suggested. "I'll call Cimmerian and Shadow, get an update from them."

"I'll call Piceous," Stygian added. "You can call Aphotic. Then we'll chat."

Obsidian nodded.

As everyone else dispersed, I glanced down at my plate. I hadn't eaten a single thing, but then again, neither had Obsidian.

"I'll have something brought to our room," Obsidian said, taking my hand and helping me to my feet.

I felt as though I needed to say something, but I wasn't sure what, so for now, I opted to keep my lips shut.

No sense in making the situation any worse.

17

OBSIDIAN

No one ever mentioned the pain that came with loving someone. For me, the ache came from the fear, the uncertainty of what was around the corner.

In this case, it was the demons out to take Penelope away from me. I had no idea what they were doing, where they were, or when they would strike, and the not knowing was causing this uncomfortable anger to build within me, a rage that wouldn't subside as I tried to come up with a plan to take Perfidious and his minions apart at the seams. Thanks to Oliver's idiotic move, the chances of that happening sooner rather than later had increased tenfold.

After taking my *amsouelot* back to our private quarters, I told Penelope I needed to take care of a few things. She'd seemed somewhat grateful for the reprieve, and I couldn't very well blame her after the disaster that had been disguised as the evening meal. What should've been a getting-to-know-her gathering with my family turned into a bitchfest choreographed by none other than her brother.

And now I needed an outlet for the frustration and anger that were continuing to intensify within me, so I sent a telepathic message to Stygian: *Meet me in the sparring chamber. Ten minutes.*

I think you're reading my mind.

My brother's acceptance eased some of the tension in my shoulders as I took the time to change into athletic shorts, stripping off the rest of my clothes and leaving them in the closet for my return.

Once Jeffrey delivered her meal, I kissed Penelope, then slipped out. I took the stairs down to the second floor, peeked into the library to find Gryffyth, Alden, Mordecai, and Magnar with their heads together, laptops open. That was a good sign, at least, even if Kid Rock was blasting through the speakers hidden in the bookcases.

I heard the sound of pool balls clacking, so I checked to see who it was. When I saw Oliver, I turned and walked away. Speaking to the human right now would not be in the male's best interest.

Another flight of steps down and I encountered Phillip and Jeffrey in the kitchen, going over the planning for the next meal.

All was getting back to normal, but still the restless energy didn't subside, so I navigated down another flight of stairs, deep underground.

Though the house had all the latest technology to protect us from the sun as well as intruders, back when we'd been designing the compound, my brothers and I had opted for a backup plan that included a wealth of rooms underneath the mansion. Everything down there ran on separate water, gas, electrical, and HVAC systems, which were all supplied by a solar backup generator. Should the mansion come under attack, it would require tremendous effort for our enemies to gain access to us, allowing us protection from the deadly rays of the sun and the opportunity to plan our offensive should it be necessary.

Currently, the various rooms were set up as recreation—a full-sized, fully stocked bar complete with half a dozen bar-height four-tops. A Wurlitzer Zodiak 3500 jukebox, circa 1970, fully restored to its original condition and loaded with 45s, maintained by none other than Gryffyth, our resident music guru, sat proudly in the corner. At the back of the room were two grand pianos brought in by Aphotic and Eclipse when they had the idea of a dueling piano bar, along with a plethora of leather seating scattered throughout. Needless to say, this space saw a lot of action when everyone was in residence.

Aside from that, there were a dozen or so rooms used mostly for storage, along with a twenty-by-twenty room utilized as a weapons locker. But my favorite, and one my brothers and I frequented often, was what we referred to as the sparring gym. The nine-hundred-square-foot room was constructed with limestone on all four walls and the floor, lit by four gas torchlights, one on each wall, and sealed by a thick stone door. There was nothing inside, no furniture, no equipment, nothing to distract, which made it perfect for sparring.

Two seconds after I stepped inside the room, Stygian materialized. He'd changed as well, his attire similar to mine: shorts, no shirt, feet bare.

As I moved deeper into the room, I willed the heavy door to close. Once it was in place, I sealed the room with my mind, prohibiting anyone from materializing within. I couldn't risk

Taayin trying to put a stop to what was about to go down. If he knew what was best for him, the male would keep his distance. Especially right now, considering he'd willfully overstepped earlier.

"You sure you're up for this?" Stygian taunted, a grin pulling at his lips. "I assume you're not at full strength with your *amsouelot* keeping you busy."

Stygian was the closest in age to me, though there was nearly a century between us. We'd trained together once Stygian was old enough, learning everything Michael had been willing to bestow on his warriors. And while our brothers were as competent as we were, our younger brothers' training had been left to us.

"I can hold my own," I assured the male.

"So you say." Stygian bared his fangs. "But I accept your challenge."

"Do not hold back," I ordered.

"Of course not, brother."

I squared off with the male, clearing my mind of everything, focusing solely on the rage that was a byproduct of my own fear for my *amsouelot*. Like boxers in a ring, we circled one another, gauging, plotting as we moved closer.

"She's safe here," Stygian said, clearly reading me correctly.

"I know." And I did, but that didn't assuage the concern for her safety.

I let the anger take over, my eyes glowing brighter as emotion built. Here and now, I didn't have to worry that Penelope would pick up on my insecurities or question my abilities. I was free to let it all out.

So I did.

As though invisible tethers were clipped, our bodies collided. Neither held back. Fists flew, knuckles pounded on flesh, knees and elbows cracked against bone. Each landing blows left and right, strategy taking a backseat to the need to punish.

Years of training had honed us both into killing machines designed with one intention. To take out the enemy.

From the moment of my creation, I'd been bred for this. Going toe-to-toe with an opponent, pummeling anything put in my path. Throughout my existence, I'd never backed down, made certain I was the strongest, the fastest, the most cunning. Fists, blades, or bullets, I had mastered them all. Alongside my brothers, we had continued our training over the centuries, never quite content with our abilities despite the fact we were a force to be reckoned with.

I didn't hold back, nor did Stygian. Wounds would heal, for both of us. However, I'd learned there was only one way to rid the body of the rage. Knuckles, elbows, knees. Nothing was off-limits as we fought for dominance.

Stygian stumbled back, then countered with a roundhouse kick, making contact with my chest. I grunted as I regrouped, nailing Stygian with an uppercut to the jaw. My brother's head snapped back, but he didn't fall. Baring his teeth, Stygian charged again.

Minutes ticked by as blood trickled from open wounds, muscles flexed. The only sounds were the reverberation of impact, grunts as pain bloomed from contact, breaths rasping from exertion.

I could feel the push against the magic holding the others at bay. Taayin would no doubt attempt to make entry, but his efforts were no match for mine. The *lieterra* could try for a century and never chip away at the force field I'd put in place. I actually found it amusing that he would try.

Stygian caught me off guard with a series of kicks that sent me stumbling. I slammed into the chipped stone floor before Stygian was over me. I took two blows to the face, managed to dodge the last, then caught Stygian in the chin, sending him flying backward. Our positions reversed as I pummeled him in return, but the male didn't stay down for long.

Grunts and groans ricocheted off concrete as pure will fought against brute strength. Stygian's silver eyes tracked me, assessing, attempting to predict my next move. My fear for my *amsouelot* had a stranglehold and the rage flowed, sending power through my limbs. Unable to hold back, I overpowered the male, driving him into the wall with a violence that rattled the mansion's foundation.

Realizing I was seconds from annihilating him, I dropped to my knees, weak from exertion, then let myself fall to the ground. Stygian stumbled back against the wall, the stone holding him upright.

My breaths soughed through exhausted lungs, my eyes locked on the ceiling above. I felt better. I would for a bit.

Glancing over, I smiled as Stygian slammed his shoulder into the wall, successfully driving it back into its socket.

"Thank you," I told him.

"For what?" Stygian hissed, rolling his shoulder as he bent at the waist. "Kicking your ass?"

I grinned, looked back up at the ceiling. "Yes."

"You're welcome." He chuckled, his gaze sliding to the door. "If you don't let him in, you're going to give the male a heart attack."

With a heavy sigh, I willed the door to release.

As expected, it flew open, Taayin marching in with Miklós and Søren flanking him. The *lieterras* glowered down at us, evidently not impressed.

"We don't need a referee," I informed them, sitting up.

Stygian appeared before me, holding out his hand to help me to my feet. I accepted. Already, the wounds were healing on my body and Stygian's. They would all be gone before we made it to the third floor. One of the benefits of being an all-powerful angel of God. Rapid mending.

Taayin glared at the two of us as though he had any say in what we did or didn't do. The truth was, I held the ultimate power, even above my brothers, though I maintained an even keel between us. I had no need for power or dominance where they were concerned, and they knew it. But every faction had a leader, and somewhere along the way, they'd all looked to me.

"One of these days, you're not going to get back up," Taayin grumbled.

"It would take tremendous effort," I remarked as he started back through the tunnels.

"Maybe. But that doesn't make it smart," Taayin countered.

Evidently, the male had never had to deal with the terror that came along with wanting to protect the one thing that meant more than anything else.

"Obsidian..."

"Let it go, Taayin," I told him.

"We need to talk," the male countered. "About—"

Spinning around, I got up in his face.

Though I had eight inches on him and probably a hundred pounds of solid muscle, Taayin didn't back down.

"I said let it go," I snarled.

Stygian's hand squeezed my arm. "Let's walk, brother."

With a grunt, I backed off, took a deep breath.

"We need to figure out our next steps," Stygian said. "We're all on edge, and rightfully so."

Before I could say anything, I was slammed with a tremendous heat. It moved through me, had me stumbling back against the wall.

"You all right?" Stygian asked, the concern on his face evident.

I shook my head. "Penelope. I have to get to her."

It took two tries before I managed to dematerialize, but I finally did, resuming my physical form on the third floor.

PENELOPE

While Obsidian was off doing his own thing, I was left to explore his private quarters, my thoughts racing a mile a minute after the conversation with the others earlier. It wasn't like I had any idea how to handle a situation of this magnitude. How *did* you deal with demons who were out to kill you?

Hell, a week ago, I'd been oblivious to the fact there *were* demons. Or angels, for that matter.

In fact, a week ago, I'd been living my normal, mundane life, traipsing across the floor of Caesar's offering free drinks and accepting whatever measly tips they were willing to offer.

A week.

Seven days.

Now I didn't even have a job because waitresses were easily replaceable, especially in Vegas. Since I hadn't called in to work, no doubt there was another woman taking my place. I had an apartment, but based on what had happened, I figured it was only a matter of time before a new set of demons paid a visit, destroying it all once again.

I sighed.

And here I was, smack in the middle of Angel Central, trying to wrap my head around it all.

My thoughts drifted to Acadia. More specifically, her abrupt request to go out in the field. From what I'd gathered from Obsidian, the Fae had relinquished their battle garb in favor of manning operations and providing assistance in other ways. So why would Acadia want to go out there? To face the demons head on?

Well, duh. I knew Acadia had made the suggestion for my benefit. More specifically, to put distance between us. There was no denying I had reacted badly this morning. Acadia was simply offering Obsidian what he needed, and I'd become some possessive girlfriend, not wanting the man I loved to feed from anyone else. Certainly not a female. Not wanting—

Before I could finish the thought, desire unlike anything I'd ever known hit me, banishing everything from my mind. It was a sudden jolt that had my muscles tightening. I pressed my knees together as a fierce sexual need exploded in my core, had my sex softening, clenching.

Holy crap. *What the hell?*

I'd gotten somewhat acclimated to how turned on Obsidian made me, how easily I could go from simmer to boil in his arms, but this ... this was not lust. It was powerful, driving the air from my lungs. It was as though my blood was boiling. My skin became ultra-sensitive, the bra I wore damn near painful where it brushed against my tender nipples. Though I was tempted to shove my hand between my legs and quell the urge, I refrained. It wasn't that I was opposed to masturbation, but my body wasn't seeking my own touch. It wanted Obsidian. More so than it ever had before.

"Oh, God," I moaned, my nipples scraping against the lace of my bra as I got to my feet.

In a mad rush, I tore at my T-shirt, needing to get it off. As I tugged it over my head, I stumbled a few steps, fighting to draw air into my lungs. My sex pulsed with an ache that overwhelmed me.

I needed to find Obsidian.

Now.

Before I could get my legs to listen to reason, the door opened, and Obsidian strolled in. Behind him, the door closed, even as he was marching toward me. He was shirtless, his chest glistening with perspiration, and in that moment, I'd never seen a more beautiful specimen.

I stared in awe. All that powerful muscle, the heat in his eyes directed my way.

"I'm not sure what's happening," I told him, the words coming out in a gravelly rasp.

Without a word, he stripped me first, then himself, then dragged me onto the bed with him, his lips a soothing balm to my overheated body.

"I need—" I didn't get the words out before he was pushing into me, filling me so perfectly.

Clutching his shoulders, I stared up into those swirling silver eyes, unable to fight the tears forming. How he knew I needed him, I wasn't sure, but there he was, taking care of me as he had from the moment I'd met him.

"Touch me," I groaned. "Everywhere."

He hugged me to him, the simple feel of his skin soothing mine.

"God, you feel good," I said on a moan as he pushed in deeper.

"Let me love you, *ayreme*," he whispered in that dark, rich baritone.

Oh, God. Those words were a balm to my soul, calming the storm while at the same time igniting my desire for him.

"Love me," I pleaded, burying my face in his neck and inhaling deeply.

He smelled amazing, the scent sending my arousal into hyperspace even as he impaled me, my body rocking with every exquisite thrust of his hips. The pain that had bloomed within me morphed into a delicious pleasure that made me hum. I held on, my arms ringing his neck, his big, hard body covering mine, pressing me deeper into the mattress.

I never wanted it to end. I wanted to stay just like this, wrapped in his arms, filled to overflowing not only physically but emotionally as well.

Obsidian's hand fisted in my hair, tipping my head back. His lips fused to mine as he drove into me, deeper than ever before. I moaned, clearing my mind and allowing my body to take over. That did the trick. With Obsidian moving inside me, the torment was replaced with a beautiful, blinding sense of completion. I was whole when I was with him. Cold replaced by heat, darkness filled with light.

Jerking my mouth from his, I kicked my head back and screamed his name as the orgasm tore through me, leaving me shredded in its wake. Shredded and so completely fulfilled.

Obsidian pushed up onto his arms and I stared at him. The way his thick shoulder muscles flexed and bunched so sinuously, his entire body tense as he pumped his hips, chasing his own release … it had another tremor detonating. That silver glow had become familiar, and I welcomed it, especially when I realized it was a reflection of his emotions. The more powerful they became, the brighter his eyes were.

He was close, I could feel it. I focused on the friction of his body inside mine, and as another tremor began, his thumb brushed over my cheek.

"I love you, *ayreme*," he said gruffly.

My heart somersaulted in my chest, filled to overflowing. "I love you, too," I whispered.

This time, when he came, it was with a devastating growl that was so loud it echoed off the walls. The sound triggered another orgasm, and I cried out, holding him when he fell atop me. His weight was tremendous, but I didn't panic, wanting to feel him over me, if only for a second.

That was all I got before he rolled off, dropping to his back. His lungs worked as hard as mine, panting and seeking the sweet relief of oxygen.

Obsidian chuckled, causing me to glance his way.

"Why are you laughing?"

"Because it happened again."

"What did?"

He peered over, his eyes once again molten silver, a sexy smirk curling his lip.

Then I heard it. Noises coming from somewhere else. Grunts, moans, cries of pleasure. It sounded in my head, not my ears, so I knew Obsidian was projecting it.

"What is that?"

The sound disappeared, effectively cut off from my mind.

"Whatever happens between us ... that powerful emotion... evidently, it's expelled in a wave of sexual energy the entire mansion feels."

Propping up on my elbow, I stared at him, trying to understand what he was saying.

He must've realized my confusion because he continued, "You know that need you felt before I came in?"

"Yes."

"They all feel it."

My eyes widened.

"Somehow, it seems to be directed out of me." His gaze

shot up to the ceiling. "That sound I let you hear, it's what's taking place throughout the mansion."

"Who?"

"All of them."

"Oh, shit." A laugh bubbled up, although I wasn't sure it was funny.

He grinned. "Serves them right." Obsidian's head swiveled my way once more. "Needless to say, we should tread carefully whenever we do that. You never know what we'll see if we venture into the mansion."

"They're doing it in the open?"

Obsidian reached for me. I went willingly, resting my head on his chest while his arm circled my shoulder, his fingers playing in my hair.

"What would you have done if you'd been in the kitchen when that hit? Would you expect me to wait until we were up here?"

I mean, if I were thinking logically, then yes, I would want him to wait. At the same time, I could still feel echoes of the pain that ricocheted through me.

Answering Obsidian, I shook my head. "I couldn't wait."

"Exactly. Add to that the fact that angels have an overdeveloped sex drive."

"By overdeveloped, you mean what? They have sex every day?"

He chuckled, the rough sound echoing in my ear. "Multiple times a day. We need sexual release more than we need blood, in fact. It's the only way to maintain our sanity."

His hand slid down to my hip, fingertips lightly tickling my skin.

"It's not quite as powerful as what we're experiencing now. *Amnigh* is all-consuming, only between *amsouelots*. It affects both males and females who've seen or met their predestined mate."

"Seen? So, what? It intensifies *before* they actually meet?"

He nodded.

I thought back to those first days when I'd been with him. The overwhelming need, the desire. I'd been embarrassed by my actions, but it had been a byproduct of our meeting. Not my fault, after all. Interesting.

Sliding my hand over Obsidian's taut stomach, I pressed my lips to his chest. "How did you know to come up here?"

"I can feel you. Your pain, your need. It's growing stronger."

"Why can't I feel yours?"

"You will. Eventually."

For some reason, that bothered me. It didn't seem fair that he could know when I needed him, but I couldn't return the favor. What if he was in trouble? What if he needed me? How would I know?

"You will," he repeated.

Realizing he'd answered the question I'd only thought, I lifted my head. "You're reading my thoughts?"

"Not intentionally. Usually, I have to mean to do it. With you, it's becoming a constant, something I can't avoid."

"Can you read everyone's thoughts?"

"Yes."

"Can all angels?"

"Warriors, yes. My brothers have the same abilities I do. The others, they have to touch their subject, but then they can."

"Will I be able to? You know, when you turn me?"

Yes, I realized I'd said *when,* not *if*. It was no longer a question in my mind. What I felt for him was so powerful, I couldn't imagine a life without him in it.

“Yes,” he answered. “My powers become yours, making us equals in every way. It allows *amsouelots* to protect one another.”

Obsidian sat up, dropped his feet over the side of the bed, his back to me. Unable to help myself, I reached over, touched his skin, outlined the wings with my fingertips.

“Why is one of the wings black?”

“It identifies me as Michael’s warrior.”

“Does everyone have the tattoo?”

“Technically, it’s not a tattoo. There’s no ink in my skin.”

I grazed the intricate lines, found it fascinating that what looked like ink wasn’t.

“Can I see them?”

Obsidian peered back at her. “See what?”

“Your wings.”

He seemed to consider it for a moment, then got to his feet. I thought he was going to leave, but he merely took a few steps forward. Then, right before my eyes, two enormous wings emerged from his shoulder blades, dissolving the lines on his back. There was a rush of air, a rustle of sound as they spanned open. They arched over his head, extended from one wall to the other, each one likely a good twelve feet from shoulder to tip.

They were absolutely beautiful, one black, one white, the feathers fluttering as he moved.

For possibly the first time since I met him, I was speechless, completely and totally enamored.

18

OBSIDIAN

We managed to pass a few days settling into a routine. When I wasn't spending time with Penelope, getting to know her, exploring the mansion, taking advantage of its numerous amenities, I was working with the *fiestreigh*, trying to locate the remaining *amsouelots*.

Which was where I found myself, making circles around the occupied sofas, glancing at computer screens, and feeling somewhat useless. When it came to technology, I wasn't a beginner, but I wasn't an expert either. I could get by. Mostly.

Suddenly, my phone buzzed in my pocket. A second later, everyone else's were doing the same.

"We've got incoming," Mordecai announced, drawing my attention to his computer screen.

"Who?"

"Well, I ... uh..." Mordecai squinted at the screen in front of him as though he couldn't quite believe what he was seeing. "I'm pretty sure that's Reidar."

Reidar? I wasn't expecting him back yet. The male had informed me he was staying with Penelope's friend to keep an eye on her. Granted, we'd gotten word that Sirius had joined up with Perfidious and Seraphina, but no one had confirmed that as of yet. So why was Reidar back here already?

"He's pulling into the garage now." Mordecai looked up. "And boss, it looks like his charge is riding shotgun."

He brought the human with him?

Son of a bitch.

With half a dozen eyes on me, I snatched my sunglasses off the table, strolled out of the sunroom, and made a beeline for the garage. I made it as far as the main hallway when I heard footsteps coming toward me and the soft cadence of a female voice.

I turned the corner, coming face-to-face with my *ladeare*, who was clearly surprised by the welcoming committee.

"Hey," Reidar said softly, taking an odd position in front of the female, as though protecting her from me. "This is Winnie. Winnie, meet Obsidian."

I peered at the female and offered a nod of acknowledgment.

"Would you excuse us for a moment?" I prompted, then motioned Reidar into the front hall.

"I'll be right back. Don't move," he instructed the female.

The instant we were out of the human's view, I spun around and faced the male.

"What the fuck are you doing?" I ground out, attempting to keep my voice low.

"I know I should've reached out," Reidar said quickly, voice just as low, "but it was a spur-of-the-moment decision."

"To bring a human here. A *human*, Reidar. You understand what the rules are, right? We're not to have contact with them unless absolutely necessary."

Reidar's back straightened, and his blue eyes seemed to shimmer from an unexplained light. Unlike my brothers and me, the *fiestreigh's* eyes didn't glow, although they could when a male was highly emotional.

"And don't tell me you were concerned for her safety," I continued when Reidar didn't speak. "I know Sirius is with Perfidious. The female's no longer in danger."

"You're right." Reidar gave a clipped nod. "However, bringing her here seemed more appropriate."

"As opposed to...?"

"Me leaving the *fiestreigh*."

I stared at the male, attempted to figure out the punch line.

Reidar's voice was barely a whisper when he said, "She's my *amsouelot*, Obsidian."

To use Eclipse's favorite saying ... fuck me running.

"And you know this for a fact?"

"Yeah."

"Son of a bitch." I thrust my hand through my hair, then pivoted and paced away from Reidar. "How much does she know about us?"

"Nothing yet."

Turning to face my *ladeare*, I narrowed my eyes and slipped into the male's mind. I skimmed through Reidar's memories from the past few days, hurrying past a couple of intimate moments he'd shared with the female.

Sure enough, Reidar's *amsouelot* just happened to be Penelope's best friend—what were the odds of that shit?—and was now in the midst of angels, a rule Michael took very seriously.

"The Fates have an interesting sense of humor, huh?" Reidar quipped, his tone lacking the humor he'd evidently been going for.

"You know I have to talk to Michael. Find out how he wants to handle this."

Reidar nodded, eyes lowering. "I understand."

The one and only time a member of the *fiestreigh* had mated with a human, Michael had insisted the male take his leave from the mission. He'd been labeled as *fallen* at that point and relieved of his powers, assuming life as a human.

Of course, that male hadn't been Reidar.

"If it's at all possible, I'd like to make my case to him," Reidar stated. "I believe it's in the *fiestreigh's* best interest if I remain."

I couldn't argue with that. As far as I was concerned, Reidar was pivotal to our success. I trusted him. Perhaps more so than anyone, aside from my brothers.

"You'll have to be ready at a moment's notice," I warned, taking a step closer. "He won't wait around."

"I'll be ready. Just say the word."

I nodded, then couldn't help but smile as I reached out and gripped Reidar's shoulder. "Funny how things work out, huh?"

The somber expression on the male's face said he wasn't sure he was going to like the decision Michael came to.

"We'll figure it out," I told him. "For now, perhaps you could take her upstairs. I'll get Penelope, let her know she's here."

Reidar nodded. "Of course."

Ensuring I was out of the human's field of vision, I dematerialized to the third floor. I found Penelope sitting in the living room, Zeus on one side of her, Aphrodite on the other. She was watching a movie while the dogs snoozed.

She must've heard me because she quickly paused the television and sat up straight.

I removed my sunglasses and rubbed the bridge of my nose, exhaling heavily.

"I'm pretty sure I've figured out how to read your expressions, and this one tells me something's wrong."

"Not wrong," I assured her, meeting her gaze. "Perhaps even good."

I commanded Zeus to vacate his seat before I planted my ass on the sofa beside my *amsouelot*.

Penelope shifted so she was facing me. "You're scaring me, Obsidian."

I took a deep breath, exhaled slowly. "You know how I sent Reidar to find Winnie?"

Penelope's eyes widened and true fear glittered in the golden orbs.

"She's fine," I said quickly, realizing she was expecting the worst. "In fact, she's here."

"She's here!" Penelope shot to her feet.

Before she could step away, I reached for her, grabbing her wrist and dragging her back down.

"I need to see her," she said, attempting to pull away.

"First, we need to discuss a couple of things."

"Like what?"

"Well, for starters, your friend doesn't have any idea who we are. Or *what* we are."

Penelope frowned.

"And until I discuss the situation with Michael, you can't say anything. I've asked Reidar to keep her separated from the others for the time being. You're more than welcome to hang out with her, but under no circumstances can you tell her about us."

"Why not?"

"We took a vow to keep our existence a secret from the humans. And until Michael gives us the go-ahead, we have to protect our identity."

"So why did Reidar bring her here?"

Figuring it wouldn't hurt to tell her, I smiled. "Looks like your best friend is Reidar's *amsouelot*."

A smile slowly formed on her beautiful face, then Penelope laughed. "Seriously?"

"Yes."

"So she's what? Moving in with him?"

I shook my head. "The last member of the *fiestreigh* who found his *amsouelot* was cast out by Michael."

"Cast out?"

"Of Heaven. For the time being, of course. He was allowed to live out the remainder of his days with his beloved here on Earth."

"Where is he now?"

"Who?"

"The one they cast out."

"Oh, they're both in Heaven. This was nearly three hundred years ago." I squeezed her hand. "I have to discuss the situation with Michael. He's the only one who can decide whether Reidar and his *amsouelot* remain with us."

"And if they don't?"

This was the difficult part. "Michael will wipe their memories and implant new ones." I kept my eyes locked with hers. "Winnie won't know you if that happens. It's for your safety, as well as hers."

"Would he do that?"

"He'll do what he feels appropriate to ensure the safety of

the humans we've vowed to protect." Giving her hand another squeeze, I forced a smile. "Why don't you go see her? They're in the game room on the second floor. I've got to meet with Michael before he gets wind of this."

"How come Michael didn't cast you out?" she asked as she got to her feet.

"Because I'm a warrior. My mission must be carried out regardless."

Penelope seemed to study me for a moment before she leaned down and kissed me. "If it'll help, tell Michael I said please."

I laughed. "Go on now. I'll come find you once I'm done."

As soon as the door closed behind her, I sealed off the entire third floor before calling for Michael.

"Well, well, well. Looks like you've found yourself in a bit of a pickle," Michael said when he appeared a minute later. The archangel chuckled. "I always did like that human saying. Though I haven't a clue what it means."

Not sure what to say to that, I remained silent.

"I'm starting to think you're running a daycare for humans. There're what? Three of them in residence?"

I stood tall, facing Michael directly. "You were made aware of two of them."

Michael smiled as he paced across the room, stopped to give the dogs a quick rub. "Warrior, I'm aware of everything that goes on with my soldiers." He turned to face me. "Is that why you summoned me? To discuss this new development?"

"In Reidar's defense, he—"

Michael held up a hand. "I'd prefer to hear it from your *ladeare*."

Without hesitation, I shot a telepathic command to Reidar, then released the seal on the room temporarily so the male could materialize within.

His appearance was instant, as though he'd been waiting for the call. Which he probably had, knowing Reidar.

As they'd been instructed, the *ladeare* bowed respectfully before the archangel, keeping his head down, eyes on the floor.

"Stand, Reidar."

The male stood tall, clasping his hands behind his back, eyes meeting Michael's.

"Care to explain to me why you took it upon yourself to bring a human here? Without discussing this with Obsidian beforehand?"

Reidar's voice was smooth and even when he said, "Because of the situation with the demons, I figured it was in the *fiestreigh's* best interest if I returned. Because Winnie's my *amsouelot*, I wasn't comfortable leaving her behind."

"But you didn't notify him? Is there a problem with your leader that you're not comfortable informing him?"

"No, sire. Not at all. I..." Reidar squared his shoulders again. "Obsidian has enough on his plate at the moment. I didn't want to give him more to worry about."

Michael seemed to process that information, but his expression remained passive. "What are your intentions with the human?"

"I plan to mate her if she'll have me."

I watched the pair.

Michael moved to stand in front of Reidar, his wings flush against his back. "What makes you think your presence is needed here?"

"Because I'm Obsidian's *ladeare*, sire. I serve the warriors and this mission. It's both my honor and my pleasure to remain within the *fiestreigh* for as long as you'll allow me."

Tapping a finger on his chin, Michael seemed to consider the request because it was most definitely a request.

"Do you understand the complications that come with doing your job while being mated?"

"I do, sire."

"And you can vow to put the mission before your *amsouelot*?"

Reidar swallowed, his gaze never wavering from Michael's face. "I vow to give the warriors and the mission my undivided attention, sire. As for my *amsouelot*, she will always be my highest priority."

I felt a sense of pride that the *ladeare* hadn't lied. No male worth his salt would put anyone or anything above his *amsouelot*.

"You've taught him well, warrior." Michael glanced my way briefly before looking at Reidar once more. "You're dismissed."

"Thank you, sire." Reidar shot a quick look at me before disappearing.

"I assume it's your preference to keep the male within the ranks."

I nodded. "Yes."

Once again, Michael paced as though standing still was too difficult for him.

Knowing better than to speak when not spoken to, I waited him out.

"I'll concede your request under one condition."

"Anything."

"You are to undergo the *lintamair* with your female this fortnight."

I knew that fourteen days from now was the next full moon.

"Provided my female's ready," I stated, unable to commit unless Penelope was on board.

Michael's gaze bounced over my face. "Are you telling me

you'll put your *amsouelot's* desires over the livelihood of your soldier?"

I didn't look away. "I'm telling you I'll put my *amsouelot* over anyone and anything."

"And if I command it?"

"I hope it doesn't come to that," I told him. "Because yes, I will put her needs above your command."

For a moment, I expected Michael to strike me down. Instead, the archangel surprised me with a knowing smile.

"She'll be ready, warrior. Of that, I am positive." Michael relaxed somewhat. "I do not envy what you must do, but I know it's what's best for this mission."

I nodded. "And Reidar?"

The archangel sighed. "I'll grant him his request. He may remain within the *fiestreigh* for as long as he proves his worth. I'll look to you to decide otherwise."

"Thank you."

With a quick nod, Michael disappeared.

For several long minutes, I remained where I was, staring at the empty space and wondering what Michael meant when he said Penelope would be ready. I got the distinct feeling the archangel was going to have a hand in how this played out.

PENELOPE

"Oh, my God!" I squealed when I found Winnie sitting in the second-floor game room. "You're really here!"

Winnie shot to her feet and rushed over, embracing me in a welcoming hug. "I'm here! And you're here!"

My friend looked the same as always, although I'd go so far as to say the woman was glowing. Her shoulder-length brown hair was pulled back at the crown of her head, green eyes glittering almost as much as the tiny diamond chips in her ears.

I had to admit, there was a tremendous relief in seeing my friend. Not only because we'd been apart for so long but because I'd been worried about her. Not to mention, I'd been in need of a friend. Someone I could talk to about what was going on with Obsidian. It wasn't that the angels and the Fae weren't welcoming, because they were. But to be fair, I had little in common with them.

"This place is amazing," Winnie said, glancing around when we stepped apart. "And it's massive. I mean..." She motioned toward the high ceilings.

"You haven't seen anything yet." I directed Winnie toward the sofa with a wave of my hand. "Sit. Tell me everything that's happened."

"Well, I met this amazing guy," she said, her face beaming.

"Reidar?"

Winnie nodded. "He's... Oh, God, Penelope. I don't even know how to explain it. I've known him for only a few days and yet..."

I chuckled. "You don't have to explain it. I totally get it."

And I really did.

However, I wasn't sure how to broach the subject because Obsidian had told me I couldn't tell Winnie anything. Granted, I wasn't sure how you casually mentioned that the man you were in love with was an angel, even had the wings to prove it, and that your relationship had somehow been set in motion by the Fates.

Yeah, perhaps I should hold off because it sounded ludicrous, even to me.

"I was surprised when Reidar told me you were here," Winnie said. "I've never known you to be the jump-into-love sort, yet here you are, shacking up with a guy."

Technically, I wasn't shacking up. While we'd talked about plenty, I hadn't had the whole long-term commitment convo with Obsidian. He'd brought me here as a means of protecting me from the demons. Didn't mean I'd been invited to move in.

Not that I could tell Winnie that.

"Where is Reidar, anyway?" I asked, looking around.

"He said he had to talk to someone." Winnie's voice lowered. "I met his boss. Man, he was intimidating."

I smiled. "You met Obsidian?"

Winnie's pale green eyes settled on my face, and a second later, a smile formed. "He's your man, isn't he?"

Unable to deny it, I nodded.

"Holy crap, he's tall." Winnie chuckled. "Probably doesn't help that you're teeny tiny."

"Hey!" I replied in mock irritation. "I'm five-four."

"Five three and a half," Winnie countered. "On a good day."

"Whatever." I laughed, relaxing more. "Do you know if—"

"Excuse me, ladies. Don't mean to interrupt."

I was looking at Winnie as Reidar stepped into the room, which was why I noticed the way my friend's face smoothed out, her eyes twinkling. Yeah, she was a goner.

"Hey." Winnie stood, her grin widening.

Reidar didn't hesitate, stepping up to Winnie and pulling her into his arms. It was a move that surprised me, honestly. While Winnie liked to poke fun at me for not being the type to fall in love quickly, the same could be said about her. However, Winnie had always been the sort to run from relationships, while I simply never found them.

But as long as she was happy, I figured it was none of my business.

The sound of footsteps drew my attention to the hallway. When Obsidian appeared, I scanned his face, attempted to read his expression. He instantly looked at Reidar and gave a barely discernible nod. Had Reidar not exhaled heavily, I wouldn't have known what message Obsidian had been passing on.

"The morning meal's about to be served," Obsidian announced, then held out his hand for me to join him.

Fifteen minutes later, everyone was piling into the dining room.

Reidar took the time to introduce Winnie to everyone who was there while I took my seat beside Obsidian and watched the pair.

"I can assume Michael approved?" I asked, leaning my shoulder against Obsidian's arm.

"For now," he said softly.

"Does that mean we can speak candidly?"

"I'd prefer you not share too much too soon."

"So I guess you shouldn't sprout those wings, huh?" I teased.

He barked a laugh, evidently surprised by my comment. It was then that Obsidian's shoulders seemed to relax.

"Well, if it's any consolation, I'm really glad she's here," I told him. "I've missed her."

"I know you have."

I figured he wasn't simply saying that. If I had to guess, he knew every single thought in my head. Not that I minded. I didn't have anything to hide from him.

The *heurosp* began marching in, some carrying plates, others a variety of drinks. It only took a minute for them to get everyone's food set up before they were slipping out again.

"Reidar?" Obsidian called out, catching the man's attention.

"Yes, I'm sorry." He motioned Winnie to her seat with a smile on his face. "Let's eat."

I didn't have to be told twice. As soon as everyone was seated, I dug in.

As everyone chowed down, conversations picked up. I caught bits and pieces of a few but didn't contribute. It wasn't until I heard a noise in the kitchen that I looked around and noticed Oliver wasn't there. Not unusual because my brother did his best to avoid everyone, especially me. For the past few days, the only time he'd ventured out was when he wanted to bitch and moan, insist that he be let go. More often than not, he ended up storming out and sealing himself off in his room.

All eyes shifted to the doorway when Oliver came stumbling inside, Eclipse directly behind him. "Someone might want to get a leash. Caught this one trying to make a run for it."

Of course he had. That was what? The fourth time? Maybe the fifth.

As though he sensed her, Oliver's eyes shot right to Winnie, then slid to Eclipse. "What? Are you starting a collection? See how many humans you can accumulate?" His eyes darted back to Winnie. "Did you get hog-tied on the way here, too? Or was I the lucky one?"

I glanced at Winnie, noticed my friend's confusion.

Figuring now was not the time to have the whole *angels are real* conversation, I got to my feet and headed toward Oliver. "Can I talk to you for a minute?"

"Oh, look at that. My sister wants to chat. Maybe she can explain why the hell I can't leave."

I motioned him toward the kitchen, careful not to make contact. He was reluctant, but I finally managed to get him out of view of the door. The last thing I wanted was an audience.

"Will you stop it, Oliver?"

"Stop what?" he snapped, stepping toward me. "Stop being pissed off that you kidnapped me? That I'm being held hostage? That my entire life is going to shit because my sister's shacking up with some crazy fuck?"

Feeling my brother's wrath, I took a step back, but Oliver continued to crowd me until I was backed up against the counter, nowhere to go.

"I'm sick of this shit, Opie." He stuck his face right in mine. "I know you don't give a shit about me or my happiness, but the least you could do is stop being a bitch. Tell your boy in there to let me go, and I promise, you'll never have to see me again."

I inhaled sharply. My brother had always been angry, but never had he told me how he really felt about me.

"I'm sorry, Oliver. It really is for your own good."

My brother's hand curled around my arm, and he roughly jerked me toward him. "Sister or not, I'm not going to put up with this shit anymore."

I hissed as pain lanced every nerve ending, his touch as painful as the grip he had on me.

"I'll give you one second to release her," Obsidian growled from behind Oliver.

"Or what?" Oliver spun around, his hand still roughly gripping my arm. "Are you going to beat me to a pulp? Or seal my mouth shut? Huh? You're lucky I don't call the police."

I inhaled sharply, tried to ignore the sharp stabs of pain even as I attempted to pretend I couldn't feel it. No sense inciting Obsidian further.

Obsidian's eyes dropped to where Oliver was holding me. "Off. Now."

Not kindly, Oliver released me before standing tall and facing off with Obsidian.

I rubbed away the ache, regulated my breathing. For a fraction of a second, I considered getting between them, then thought better of it.

Obsidian stepped forward, then leaned down until he was nose to nose with Oliver. "You're lucky I don't send you back to the demon."

Oliver laughed, but I heard the hint of fear. "No, you'd be doing me a favor."

"Is that what you want?" Obsidian stood tall, crossed his arms over his chest. "You want me to send you back?"

I expected Oliver to jump at the opportunity, but my brother didn't say a word. He simply stood there, staring.

"I'll let you think on that for a little while," Obsidian told him, holding out his hand for me to join him. "But I'm only going to say this one more time. You disrespect my *amsouelot* again, your new residence will be the dungeon. Understood?"

I probably should've appreciated Obsidian coming to my rescue, but I felt sorry for my brother. For whatever reason, he'd never liked me, and I honestly had no idea why that was. Whenever I tried to broach the subject, he waved me off and called me crazy. Yet he never denied it.

"Let's eat," Obsidian stated, taking my hand and leading me back into the dining room.

All eyes were averted when I came in, but despite my efforts, I knew they'd all heard what had happened.

And I didn't want to know what they thought of me now.

19

OBSIDIAN

We made it through the weekend without any major incidents, so I considered it a success. While I was still waiting for the demons to make a move, Penelope was proving to be a wonderful distraction. She seemed to have settled in nicely, and I couldn't deny waking up every night to her in my bed was quickly becoming the highlight of my existence.

While I attempted to be of help to my brothers, Penelope spent time with Winnie while Oliver kept his distance. As far as I could tell, the male had gotten the message and he valued his life.

Not that I would kill the human, but I definitely wasn't above locking him in one of the rooms below ground. I couldn't fathom what Penelope could've done to make her brother so angry, so I figured it was no fault of hers. If I was right, the male was fighting his own demons, whatever those may be, and rather than owning up to his mistakes, he preferred to lay blame. Since his sister was the closest to him, she suffered.

One thing I did notice was that Penelope kept her distance. I had to wonder if that was due to the empathy she was plagued with or something else. I didn't even need to be an empath to feel the waves of anger that rolled off the human. For Penelope, putting space between them was likely a coping mechanism.

I headed toward the sunroom at the back of the house. I found Stygian and Eclipse reclined on the sofa, feet up on the coffee table as they stared at the television above them.

"Where is everyone?" I asked my brothers.

"Penelope and Winnie talked them into a movie. They're up in the theater," Stygian said.

"Watching *End Game*," Eclipse added. "I've seen it a dozen times. Opted out this go-round."

I grinned. Aphotic would be proud to know I had mated with a Marvel fan.

I dropped onto the empty sofa. "Any news?"

"On Perfidious?" Stygian's gaze never left the television. "Nope."

Glancing up, I watched the cars speeding along the track. Formula One was Stygian's jam. The male would watch the race live on Sunday and again on Monday in case there was a chance—*there wasn't*—that he missed something.

Eclipse looked over. "However, there was a tip on the message board. It sounds like the vampires are seeing an influx of Shadow Beasts. Word is they took out the Alpha."

I sat up, stared at my brother. "And Kaj?"

"I had Miklós do some digging. He's alive. Sounds like he's reluctant, but he's taking on the role of Alpha."

I breathed a sigh of relief. I hadn't seen Kaj in a couple of years, not since we'd taken the male in when he'd been injured. It pained me to know he'd lost his father, but I was relieved that he was alive.

"Is there anything we can do to help?" I inquired.

"Miklós left a message for him. Told him we're here if he needs us. No response yet."

Good. The vampires had always stepped in when we needed them, and I would do the same. Considering they were the only allies with enough manpower to be of help, I figured the give-and-take was a beneficial arrangement.

Staring at the screen, I tried to relax, but it was futile. I couldn't fight the heat consuming me, though I'd spent the better part of the night attempting to. As it was, Penelope was enduring the *amnigh* relatively well. On a scale of one to ten, I figured we were skating somewhere in the middle at this point, but it was amping up in intensity with every passing day.

A good half hour passed before I could no longer take it anymore.

Completely overwhelmed with the need for my *amsouelot*, I pushed to my feet, strolled out of the room, leaving my brothers to chat.

"Sire, may I get you anything?" Phillip offered when I made my way through the kitchen.

"No," I said, my voice gruff, my need ratcheting up with ridiculous speed.

I took the stairs two at a time, up to the third floor. When I stepped into the darkened theater, I could see the tops of the heads of those planted in the recliners scattered about. All were raptly focused on the screen in front of them.

With only a smidgeon of remorse for ending their movie night early, I stopped the movie with my mind.

"I need my mate," I announced.

The rustle of movement followed as everyone heeded my warning, making their way out without a single argument. Reidar and Winnie were the last two out and they closed the door behind them.

Penelope smiled as I neared.

"I can feel you," she whispered as I lifted her and took the seat she occupied, settling her on my lap.

"You'll feel more of me in the very near future," I promised, claiming her mouth.

My *amsouelot* settled in my arms, her lips grazing mine softly before her tongue joined the mix. I sighed, content for the first time in hours. Her mere presence settled me, renewed the strength that was lost with worry.

As the kiss ignited, Penelope repositioned so that she was straddling my hips in the oversized recliner. My palms itched to touch her smooth, warm skin, so I indulged them, sliding beneath the soft T-shirt she wore. Caressing her back, I pulled her in closer so her breasts were crushed to my chest, her tongue teasing mine.

"I've been thinking about something," she said, sitting up when I tugged the T-shirt over her head.

"What's that?"

She reached behind her, unclasped her bra. My eyes skimmed her perfect breasts as she revealed them slowly. I palmed one, then the other, loving the sweet sighs that escaped her as she pressed into my hands.

"About how I want a future with you."

I held her stare, felt foreign emotions churning with me.

"A family," she whispered, pressing her soft mouth to mine. "But I don't know what you want."

"You've been thinking about this?"

A slow smile formed on her face. "More and more every day."

I was fairly certain my heart tested the strength of my rib cage right then.

"What do you want?" she repeated.

"You," I admitted. "To make you happy."

"What about babies?"

Pausing in my pursuit to seduce her, I studied her face. "There's no rush, *ayreme*. We've got eternity ahead of us, but if you want babies, I'll give you babies."

"But what if it happens now? We're not using any protection."

I grinned, my hands resuming their exploration of her breasts. "I can't get you pregnant yet."

Her eyebrows shot upward. "How do you know?"

"Because you're human."

She nuzzled my neck, her lips grazing the sensitive spot below my ear. "I've been thinking about that, too," she whispered. "About how I want to spend the rest of my life with you. And I want it to be a long one."

I cupped the back of her head, slid my lips over her neck. "You know what that means."

"I do."

She moaned softly, tilting her head to give me better access to her neck. I could hear her pulse as it sped up, her need growing with every passing second.

"I want it, Obsidian. I want to spend eternity with you."

My fangs punched out, the need for her blood becoming impossible to ignore. I teased her, scraping the sharpened points over her neck. I wouldn't bite her. Not yet, but I loved how she gave herself over to me, trusting me completely.

"I need you naked," I said gruffly, barely resisting the urge to sink into her vein.

"What? You can't use magic to strip our clothes off?"

"I could," I admitted. "But I much prefer stripping you myself."

For the next few minutes, I did just that. In a tangle of limbs, I worked her leggings off while she rid me of my shirt. My jeans only made it down to my thighs before she eased down onto me, my cock sliding into the luxurious heat of her body.

"I love you, *ayreme*." I buried my face in her neck, held her against me as we rocked together.

Her fingernails lightly scraped my scalp, sending tingles over my skin.

"Obsidian..." Penelope moaned, pulling back and planting her hands on my knees, her back arching so beautifully.

Gripping her hips firmly, I drove up into her, mesmerized by the bounce of her breasts, the sleek lines of her body as she moved atop me, taking me to the hilt.

"It's not enough," she rasped.

Much to my disappointment, she dislodged me from inside her as she got to her feet. And when she bent over the chair in front of us, her sweet ass teasing me, I forced my weak legs to hold me up. In one quick move, I was ramming deep inside her, holding her hips, angling her for optimum penetration as I fucked her roughly from behind.

"Yes! Obsidian ... more!"

I gave her what she asked for, slamming my hips forward as I jerked her back. In no time at all, I was soaring, my climax just out of reach. I drove into her, surrounded by her sweet cries as she pleaded for more, taking everything I gave her.

And when she came, I plunged forward, draining myself inside her.

Even then, I couldn't seem to stop. Dragging her to the floor, I mounted her from behind, fucking her relentlessly as she begged me to never stop. She overwhelmed me, my love for her strangling me, the fear for her safety blazing in my veins. Her cries of pleasure spurred me on, had my cock throbbing as another climax threatened.

This time when she came, I let it all go, throwing my head back, a thunderous roar escaping as my emotions overwhelmed me once more.

A few miles away in Telluride, Colorado

ECLIPSE

When the others had returned from the theater—evidently exiled by Obsidian—I found myself in need of air. Without telling anyone, I slipped out of the mansion and into the night, dematerializing and taking form a few miles away, figuring some reconnaissance wouldn't be a bad thing.

For nearly an hour now, I'd been wandering Colorado Avenue, not entirely sure what I was hoping to find. I ended up near the Telluride Theatre, where it seemed half the town was. It was an odd outing for a Monday night, but I'd grown accustomed to the frequent gatherings the small town was fond of. On a positive note, it made it easy for me to move around, camouflaged by the humans who were constantly out and about.

As had been the case for the past couple of weeks, my efforts to find my *amsouelot* had been a complete bust, not a single sign of the female I was searching for, though Miklós assured me she was there.

I could admit, when Michael told us we had to locate the *amsouelots*, my first thought was *how hard could it really be?* Sure, I liked to give the archangel shit, so I'd pretended otherwise, but deep down, I figured it would take no time at all. Considering the access we had, it should've been simple.

Not the case.

Searching for a single female was like looking for a specific needle in a stack of identical needles. Even though the names weren't as common as, say, Mary Smith, there were a surprising number of people in North America with the same name. And since we had nothing more than names on a list to go by, it was a tedious process to weed through them all.

Figuring I couldn't put off the inevitable any longer, I was about to dematerialize to the mansion when I caught the scent of a female. I glanced toward one end of the alley, then the other. There was no one there, yet the lavender scent grew stronger.

As I strolled toward Colorado Avenue, I scanned the shadows to no avail. Perhaps I was losing my mind. Maybe knowing Obsidian had found his *amsouelot* was playing tricks on my gray matter. My own desperation to find my female had grown to epic proportions as of late.

I was alerted by a panicked squeak seconds before two humans appeared.

A blond male had his arm around a female as he dragged

her backward in my direction. The streetlight glimmered off dark metal in the male's hand.

A gun. Great.

Good news was, the human male had no idea I was there, even as he jabbed the muzzle into her kidney.

"Don't you dare scream, Amber," he seethed. "I'll shoot you where you stand. Dear old Dad won't be too happy about that, will he?"

The female whimpered, but she didn't scream.

"I figured for sure Daddy would keep a better eye on his little girl, so imagine my surprise when there you were." The male backed her toward the wall, spinning her away from him and pinning her there with his hand around her throat, gun aimed at her chest. His smile was grotesque, as was the scent he put off.

Nothing good was going to come of this.

"Not sure why he never mentioned how pretty you are," the male taunted, his thumb scraping over her chin.

"What do you want?" she asked, eyes wide.

"To warn your father. He owes me quite a bit of money, sweetheart. Makes me angry when he tries to hide from me," he told her, his smile morphing into something vile. "Though a conversation could cover it, I'm thinking something a bit more ... tangible."

"I don't know where he is." Her voice was barely audible, distorted by the hand still around her throat.

"No matter. Once I'm done with you, he'll find me."

The female glared at him, even though her life was at risk, the muzzle of the gun pressing against her chest as the male stepped toward her. His hand shifted from her throat to her jaw, gripping firmly and forcing her head into the brick at her back.

She inhaled sharply, the crack of her head against brick

making me wince.

"Bet you'll be nice and sweet, huh?" he snarled.

"Fuck you," she snapped.

The male cackled. "Got some backbone in there, do you? I look forward to beating it out of you. But first, perhaps we'll have a little fun."

The instant his hand lowered between her legs, I willed him backward with my mind.

The human stumbled a few steps, then spun around, aimed his gun at me. "You better back off, man. I won't hesitate to shoot you in the face."

"Too late. You already hesitated," I snarled.

"Last chance."

Exactly.

Something compelled me to look over at the female. Our eyes met, held, and at that moment, I felt a strange constriction in my chest. I'd never felt anything so potent in my seventeen hundred years, but how could that be? She wasn't the female I was looking for.

Was she?

A gunshot rang out, and it was then that I realized I'd taken a step forward. The bullet slammed into my shoulder. I stumbled back from the force of the round. The bullet wouldn't kill me, but it damn sure had the ability to piss me off.

I glared at the male.

"I warned you. Back off or you'll get another!" The male's voice trembled.

In a move not visible to the human eye, I moved behind him. Without hesitation, I snapped the little fucker's neck, allowed him to fall to the ground.

The female's terrified eyes landed on me, widening in horror. Her chest rose and fell rapidly as she fought for air.

As though pulled by invisible wires, I took a step toward

her. She didn't move, regarding me closely. I wasn't aware of my movements, watching as my hand lifted, brushing over her temple before curling behind her head. Something warm and wet met my touch, and I pulled back, the scent of her blood sending all sorts of red flags.

Had it been any normal night, I would've quickly erased her memory of the event, walked her back to a populated area, and sent her on her way. But there was something in her ocean-blue gaze that held me there, captivated me. Not to mention, the bullet lodged in my shoulder had my vision dimming slightly.

"Are you okay?" she asked, her voice higher than before, her fear and concern evident.

I had to get back to the mansion before I couldn't dematerialize. The pain bloomed hot and bright, my circuits going haywire.

"Go," I snarled at the female. "Run far and fast."

She nodded, even as she took a step to the side. Her gaze dropped to my shoulder once before she glanced down at the dead male on the ground. Her self-preservation finally kicked in as she began shifting away, putting distance between us.

I stared after her, not bothering to stop her retreat, still stunned by this overwhelming need for her. I lifted my fingertips to my lips, tasted her blood on my tongue. A fierce heat bloomed inside me but extinguished a second later, overcome by the pain in my shoulder.

I took a deep breath and set my mind on getting to safety.

PENELOPE

I sat at the kitchen island, sharing the morning meal with Obsidian and Magnar, Eclipse's *ladeare*, the only two who'd stuck around long enough to eat. Everyone else had scattered, likely seeking sleep or some peace and quiet.

"And then," Magnar continued his story, "we were standing there with our..." His gaze shot upward, looking over me. "Whoa, man, you look like death warmed over."

I turned at Magnar's words, surprised when I saw Eclipse stumbling into the room, blood covering his gray T-shirt.

Oh, God. He was injured, and based on his glazed eyes, he was in tremendous pain.

A gasp escaped my throat as I got to my feet, confused as to what to do to help him. A strange sense of urgency overcame me, and I moved toward the injured man. I wasn't a doctor, but surely I could assist somehow.

"Sit down," I urged, nodding toward a barstool.

Magnar retrieved a chair from the breakfast nook, spun it around so Eclipse could drop into it. He didn't.

Figuring he was weak from blood loss, I stepped closer, wanting to offer assistance.

From behind me, Obsidian hissed, "Don't touch him."

I frowned. "He's injured."

"I don't care. You can't... Don't, *ayreme*." Obsidian glared at Magnar. "Where's Stygian?"

"He went out," the *ladeare* told him. "Said he had business to attend to."

"Fuck."

I had no idea why Obsidian needed Stygian. His brother

was injured. Surely he was capable of doing anything Stygian could.

"What happened?" I asked Eclipse, keeping my distance, ignoring my natural instinct to help him.

"Human. Shot me." Eclipse peered down at his shoulder, but he seemed too weak to do anything about it.

"The bullet's still in there?" Obsidian asked.

Eclipse nodded, his expression remorseful, though I had no idea why he'd be sorry. "Tried ... to get it out. Too..."

Weak? Injured? In pain? I wasn't sure what he'd meant to say, but he didn't continue as he finally lowered himself into the chair, hissing.

"Do something," I ordered Obsidian, even though I had no idea what he could do. "He's been shot."

"It'll be fine," Eclipse rumbled. "Bullets won't kill me."

Maybe not, but I figured having one lodged in his shoulder wasn't going to help him, either.

"We need to get the bullet out," Magnar stated firmly, his gaze landing on Obsidian.

A silent communication seemed to play out between them, one I wasn't privy to. Based on Obsidian's expression, it wasn't good.

"Obsidian, you have to help him," I urged, realizing I was quickly moving into panicked territory.

"I can't," Obsidian countered, glaring at the man.

"Because you don't know how?" I prompted.

He stared back at me, silver irises glowing brightly.

"You have to help him," I said, though I didn't think Obsidian meant he physically couldn't do it. Something was going on, something no one was telling me. "You can remove it, can't you?"

"Yes," he said, his eyes narrowing. "I'm capable, but..."

"I tried to get a hold of Stygian," Magnar stated, his voice lowered, his concern evident. "He's not answering his phone. You'll have to do this yourself."

Obsidian shook his head.

"Just do it," I ordered. "Get the bullet out."

Without a word, Obsidian moved toward Eclipse. Although he looked angry, his hand was gentle as it settled on Eclipse's shoulder.

Though I wasn't sure why, I could suddenly feel Eclipse's pain. It was so powerful my knees buckled, dropping me to the floor.

"Stop," Eclipse ordered, teeth gritted in pain.

When Obsidian removed his hand from Eclipse's shoulder, the pain stopped.

Ah, crap. That was why Obsidian said he couldn't do it. The pain Eclipse felt was transferred to Obsidian. In turn, I was feeling it, too. It was something I'd been picking up on over the past couple of days. I was more in tune with Obsidian.

I looked up at the man I loved. "Do it," I insisted. "But be quick about it."

"No," Obsidian refused.

"Will it stop once you've healed him?"

He swallowed, held my gaze. "Yes."

"Then do it. If you don't, I will," I informed him as I got to my feet, though I didn't have the first clue how to remove a bullet. "And we both know what'll happen if I touch him."

No one moved, the only sound was Eclipse's harsh breaths. The man was in pain, and it killed me to see it.

"Do it," I demanded.

Obsidian growled but placed his hand on Eclipse's shoulder once more.

I staggered but remained on my feet, gritting my teeth as my body endured the torment of the bullet Obsidian was willing out of his brother's body.

It only took a minute, but it felt like an eternity.

The sound of metal clanging on the tile signaled it was over, and suddenly the pain disappeared.

"Do that again and I'll kill you," Obsidian growled at Eclipse before lifting me into his arms.

I could see the fury on Obsidian's face. Knew he was pissed at me for insisting he do that.

"I won't apologize," I told him as I rested my head against his shoulder.

His only response was a rough growl as he carried me to the back staircase, up two flights of stairs to the third floor, through the living room, down the hall to his private quarters. The door opened before we got there, then slammed shut behind us with a resounding thud. Obsidian deposited me on the bed, then quickly relieved me of my clothes. His hands roamed over me as though he needed to confirm I wasn't physically injured.

"I'm fine, Obsidian." I cupped his face, forced him to look at me.

His eyes glowed, breaths racing in and out of his lungs.

Not knowing what else to do, I embraced him, bringing his mouth to mine.

His arms banded around me as he eased me down to the mattress.

"Don't do that ever again," he mumbled against my neck.

His torment was so powerful I felt the ache inside me.

"I won't." It was the least I could do.

We remained just like that as we both succumbed to sleep, his arms securely around me.

20

ECLIPSE

I woke to the sound of the shutters rising for the night. I'd spent a restless day in bed, attempting to sleep, though it didn't come easily.

It wasn't my body that plagued my efforts. No, the wound in my shoulder had healed completely, only a couple of hours after Obsidian had retrieved the bullet from my flesh.

As I lay in bed, I stared up at the ceiling, the events of that morning replaying in my head. The humans in the alley, their argument, getting shot, killing the human male. While all of that was fresh in my mind, it was the female I was fixated on. How wide her eyes had been when she stared at the crumpled body of the male whose life I had ended. I figured he'd been found already. Probably by some unsuspecting human who'd stumbled upon it. Leaving it there had been my only option.

Disappearing the body only caused more issues. Missing persons became investigations, the same as murder did.

I could still see the female running out of the alley, glancing back only once before disappearing from view.

Even now, I could smell her, that sweet lavender scent. It overwhelmed my senses, an unfamiliar heat coursing in my veins. I stared at the ceiling, pictured her in my mind, and though I could no longer see her, I could feel her.

Shaking off the weird sensation, I glanced around the room. Everything was as it should be, but it felt different. Like I was somewhere else other than the mansion.

A knock sounded on my bedroom door moments before it opened.

Ziana stepped into the room, a smile on her beautiful face. Dressed in her white robes, the Fae moved toward me, so graceful it was like she was gliding over the floor.

"I heard about what happened last night. When I came to your room, you were asleep. Thought I'd come back," she said, as though reminding me of her reason for being here.

I didn't need a reminder. I'd been feeding from Ziana for quite some time now. And yes, I knew I needed to feed because my strength was waning, especially after the bullet I'd taken. I should've been able to remove the bullet myself, but I'd waited too long, gotten too weak to do any good. Because of that, I'd caused Penelope pain, which was another notch on my conscience.

Pushing upright, I leaned against the headboard. Perhaps I could try.

As Ziana moved closer, an unsettling feeling came over me. As though she shouldn't be there.

The instant her hand touched my arm, I hissed, the pain from that brief touch excruciating.

"Out!" I ordered, willing the door open with my mind.

The Fae stared in shock, much the same way the female in the alley had.

"Go," I growled, my voice lower. "Now."

"Of course."

Without a backward glance, Ziana ran from the room. I willed the door closed behind her.

Once again, I couldn't seem to move, staring into space as I sensed the female from the alley, her scent surrounding me as though she was right there with me.

"Hey, it's me," came the soft voice in my mind.

It was her. The female from the alley. In my head. I was connected to her, likely because I'd tasted her blood. While I didn't know where she was, I could feel her emotions, hear the softness of her voice. She was calmer than she had been last night, her heart rate normal. If I hadn't been there as it all went down, I would've never suspected she'd been assaulted. Perhaps she was good at hiding it.

"Yes, Mom. It's me, Orianna. No, I'm okay. He didn't hurt me. This guy ... this guy appeared, killed him."

Wait.

The voice definitely belonged to the female from the alley, the one I'd felt a strange connection to. But the male had called her Amber.

She said her name was Orianna.

Orianna McKay.

My *amsouelot.*

The voice sounded in my head again. "He thought I was Amber, Mom. And he was going to hurt me. Said Dad owed him money." A brief pause. "I know. I'll be careful. But I'm staying here. I can't leave until I find her."

The voice trailed off, and I sank into the pillow, even as a sense of loss took up residence in my chest.

Holy fuck.

This was not at all the way I'd expected this would play out. My *amsouelot* seeing me get shot, watching me eliminate a male, as though it was a natural response.

Was she terrified of me now? How could she ever look me in the eye, knowing I'd killed someone?

Suddenly, an overwhelming heat consumed me. My cock raged to life, harder than I'd ever felt it. And in my mind, I felt a connection with the female. I heard the soft rasps of her breath as well as … it sounded like water. The shower, maybe?

Oh, fuck.

Shoving the blankets down, I reached for my cock, fisting it tightly. With my eyes closed, I dropped my head back against the headboard as I roughly jerked my erection, desperate to find a release I doubted was waiting for me.

I'd already learned what the touch of a female did to me. The pain from Ziana's soft fingers had been like holding a live wire.

I focused on the sounds drifting through my mind as I inched closer to release.

Oh, God!

My eyes flew open as the words whispered in my head. Her voice was familiar, yet not.

Soft whimpers reverberated all up in my gray matter. That was when I realized the sound of water had disappeared, replaced by a subtle vibrating hum.

She was pleasuring herself with a vibrator, likely seeking the same release I was. I wondered whether she knew she would never find it. Not the sort of release that would take the edge off, anyway. She needed me the same as I needed her. Only she wouldn't understand any of it. The female had no clue who I was, much less that the only way to satisfy the hunger was to surrender to me.

I let the sweet sounds of her moans and whimpers fill my

head as I stroked myself. It seemed to go on forever, the release just out of reach. When her moans grew louder, more desperate, I reached out to her mentally, not expecting to connect but wishing like hell I could.

Then I felt her, the connection.

Please. I need to come. Oh, please.

I filled my thoughts with images of her beautiful face, allowed my imagination to take it further, fantasizing about my tongue stroking her, laving her, bringing her the pleasure she sought.

Oh, God! Oh, yes!

I could feel her tension as she reached for her release, desperate for it.

My head dropped back with a thud, my body tensing as I imagined plunging inside the warm depths of her body.

A soft, sensual cry sounded in my head as the female came. Her satisfied moans had my hand stilling, my cock pulsing as I came in a rush, the sensation plowing through my body, unlike anything I'd ever experienced at the hands of another.

It took everything in me to break the connection, to come back to myself.

While my body was temporarily sated, the painful longing was still there, seemingly growing stronger with every passing second. That brief, tenuous connection wouldn't be enough to sustain either of us.

Which meant...

Though I had no idea how to find her again, I knew I had to.

OBSIDIAN

I spent the night entangled in Penelope's arms, soothing myself with the warmth of her body after I'd healed my brother. I was still off, having watched my *amsouelot* endure the pain I'd felt as I removed the bullet from Eclipse's shoulder. It wasn't that I didn't want to help him, but I would've avoided it if there'd been any other way.

Unfortunately, since none of my brothers were home, the burden had befallen me. The *fiestreigh* didn't have the powers to heal as the warriors did. Had Kandarie been there, or even Torak, they would've been able to do it the old-fashioned way, but they were off with Cimmerian and Piceous, searching for the *amsouelots*.

Never again did I want to witness Penelope suffering like that. I couldn't bear it.

Now I was looking for a distraction, anything to keep the memories of those events at bay.

"Where are we at?" I asked the group when I joined them in the sunroom.

Nearly everyone sat up straight, eyes lifting from the laptops in front of them.

Magnar was the first to speak. "We've got no reliable intel on Perfidious, Seraphina, or Sirius. Not since the sighting of them in Flagstaff a few days ago."

Son of a bitch.

I glanced from one male to the next. "Where's Reidar?"

"He's in your office. Said he was going to reach out to Kaj. See if he could get an update on the vampires."

At least the male was working.

"Stygian?" I prompted.

Søren was the one to offer a response. "He's getting ready to take off again. Mordecai's grabbing a few things."

"Is he leaving you behind?"

"He said I'm of better use here than out there."

Since Søren was Stygian's *lieterra,* it was rare for the males not to be together out in the field. On the other hand, I understood Stygian's reasoning. Søren was as gifted with technology as Gryffyth, so his expertise was behind a computer. It made sense for Søren to remain back and run things from here. Granted, I wasn't sure Søren was pleased about it. Like Taayin, the male did enjoy his time in the field.

The sound of footsteps came from behind me, moving quickly. I turned to see Ziana heading toward us at a fast clip, her face pinched.

"Problem?"

She nodded, stopping before me. "It's Eclipse. I think something's wrong. I went to check on him. After what happened last night, I knew he needed to feed." Her amethyst eyes lowered. "He yelled at me to leave."

Not sure what to do with that information, I stared at the Fae.

Her eyes lifted. "When I touched him, he recoiled."

My gaze shot to the ceiling as though I could see my brother above me.

"I think he found his *amsouelot,*" Ziana added.

"Thanks for letting me know. I'll go talk to him." I turned to face the others. "For those of you heading out, be safe. And get back here as soon as you can."

Without waiting for a response, I headed toward the stairs. After using my palm print to get through the secured door, I walked through the living space, down the hallway toward Eclipse's room. I paused there for a moment, glanced at the closed doors to the bedrooms of my brothers. The thought of them out there without me didn't sit well, even though I knew there was no other option. Time was quickly running out for all of them. Eventually, the demons would catch up to them.

Good thing was, we didn't have a set time frame. Bad thing: God could smite them all at any given moment. Which meant we had to work fast because not only did we have to find the *amsouelots*, we also had to complete the *lintamair*. And that ... that was by far the most difficult of all.

Stygian appeared. The second my eyes landed on him, he frowned. "What is it?"

I nodded toward Eclipse's door. "He ran Ziana off when she went to feed him. I think he's found his *amsouelot*."

"That's good news, right?"

"You'd think." I peered at the closed door to my room, allowed my senses to expand until I located Penelope. She was sitting in our bed, watching something on her iPad. "We need to come up with a plan. Let's get everyone on the phone, and we'll hash it out."

Stygian nodded. "I'll grab Eclipse."

While my brother remained in the hallway, I returned to the living room to place the calls to my brothers, getting them all on the line.

The four of them were chatting when Stygian and Eclipse joined me a few minutes later. Eclipse looked a little worse for wear, which made me believe Ziana was right. He'd found his *amsouelot*, but it hadn't turned out how he expected.

"We've got six males we can release," I informed them as my brothers took seats on the sofa, the others going quiet on the phone. "And with Eclipse staying back, that's at least one for each of you."

"If I might make a suggestion," Shadow said. "I think it would benefit us all if Gryffyth would stay back. His tracking's unparalleled, and those of us who haven't pinned down our *amsouelots* could really use his expertise."

"I'm leaving Søren here, too," Stygian informed me. "That should help. I'll have him reach out to your *lieterras*, figure out how they can best assist each of you."

"What about you, Stygian? Where're you heading off to?" Aphotic asked.

"Massachusetts," he replied. "Søren thinks he's pinpointed her."

"That's good news," Cimmerian stated. "You're faring better than I am. We've trekked through the entire Midwest and beyond with no luck. Well, unless you count the demon nest we took out in Idaho."

While that wasn't necessarily a bad thing, it wasn't the end goal right now, but I didn't have to tell him that.

"Shadow?" Stygian prompted. "You still in Canada?"

"For now. But we're returning tomorrow night. She's not here."

I sighed, hating to hear more bad news.

"Aphotic? Any chance you can get your female back here?"

The laugh that rumbled through the phone rang with doubt. "It's a wonder she's even talking to me."

A round of genuine laughter sounded.

"You mean, for once in your life, you have to work to get the girl?" Piceous taunted. "Must suck to be you."

"Hey. Give it time. She'll come around." I could hear the smile in Aphotic's voice. "They always do. What about Eclipse?"

Glancing up, I locked on Eclipse, who had his head back, eyes closed. "I found her."

"That's fucking awesome, brother. Congrats," Aphotic noted.

"Yeah. I wouldn't pat me on the back yet." Eclipse lifted his head, opened his eyes. "I killed a male in her presence. I'm pretty sure she'll be running scared."

Well, that fucking sucked.

No one bothered to ask him who he'd killed because we all knew it had been warranted. Eclipse was one of the most level-headed. He wouldn't take a life unless it were inevitable.

For the next few minutes, we outlined who would go where before disconnecting the call.

"Winnie's been asking for a tour of the mansion. I figured I could get Asmia and Penelope to give her one," I informed Eclipse and Stygian. "While they do that, we'll meet with the *fiestreigh*. Get our shit together so we can get you all back here ASAP."

Stygian nodded as Eclipse pushed to his feet.

"I need a drink," he grumbled.

"Then let's meet in the bar," I told him, referring to the recreation space underground.

"I'll let the others know," Stygian said.

When they disappeared, I made my way into my bedroom. The instant my eyes landed on Penelope, a sense of calm came over me. And when she smiled, more warmth spread through my entire being.

"I heard you out there," she said, dropping her legs over the side of the bed. "I didn't want to interrupt."

"You're welcome anytime," I assured her.

"Is everything all right?"

I went on to explain the statuses of my brothers and their ongoing searches.

"I'm sure they'll find them," she said softly.

"The question is, will they find them in time?" I exhaled heavily, then sat in the leather chair beside the bed.

Penelope came over, allowed me to pull her into my lap.

"In time for what?"

"Before..." I wasn't sure I could say the words out loud.

"Before what?"

I cleared my throat. "Before God eliminates them."

Penelope's sharp inhale had me realizing how harsh that sounded.

"Eliminates them? You mean *kills* them?"

"Like you and me, my brothers' souls are tethered to their *amsouelots*. If Lucifer gets his hands on an *amsouelot*, he gains access to her mate's soul. In essence, we become *his* warrior. Considering our powers, God won't allow that to happen. He's ordered Michael to eliminate the *amsouelot* if the *lintamair* hasn't been completed."

"The mating ritual?"

I nodded.

"You mentioned it's a formal thing," she said, her fingers trailing over my scalp, as though she was trying to soothe me.

"Yeah. And it requires a full moon, which, as you probably know, only comes around once a month."

Penelope's hand cupped my cheek, urging me to look at her. I met her beautiful golden eyes.

"Is there anything I can do to help?"

I shrugged.

"As for this *lintamair*," she said softly. "What does it entail?"

I purposely shook off the thought. No way could I even think about it now. Not if I expected to hold on to my sanity.

"Before Asmia heads out with the others," I told her, purposely changing the subject, "I was going to have her give Winnie a tour of the mansion. Figured you could facilitate."

Penelope's eyes shuttered, her disappointment in my deflection clear. "Okay. And while I do that, what will you be doing?"

"Talking to the *fiestreigh*. Getting their assignments nailed down. Perfidious and Seraphina are on the move. We need to be prepared for their arrival in Darkness. And we have to be at the top of our game."

I exhaled heavily. My body was weary, growing more so by the hour. Considering I'd put off feeding for several days, it didn't surprise me. Between my hand-to-hand with Stygian, healing Eclipse, and the *amnigh* keeping Penelope and me entangled, I knew I couldn't put it off much longer.

Her eyes locked on mine, but she didn't say a word, so I slipped into her thoughts, cringed when I heard her silent question.

Looking away, I gripped the back of Penelope's neck and pulled her to me, her cheek pressing against my shoulder.

"I have to feed," I told her softly. "If I don't..."

"I know. That's why you want Acadia to stay back. You prefer her."

"I prefer *you*, Penelope. But ... I can't. Not yet."

"I know." There was a sadness in her words that had pain coiling in the pit of my stomach.

When she pushed against me, getting to her feet, I didn't stop her. This was something we would have to deal with, but it didn't have to be right this minute.

I stood, feeling the weight of everything settling on my shoulders once more.

"I'll have Asmia come in," I told her, then forced myself to leave.

While this was an important subject, it could wait.

It would have to.

PENELOPE

"First off, let me say it's a pleasure to have you here in the mansion," Asmia blurted the instant she stepped into Obsidian's private quarters. "I've been meaning to sit down and chat, but ... well, as you can imagine, it's been rather hectic."

Oh, I knew all too well. Though I didn't have a job to perform, I hadn't had a lot of downtime either. And while I enjoyed spending every waking moment with Obsidian, I wished I could do more to help his brothers.

"Anyway, I'm really glad you're here."

Realizing I hadn't bothered to respond, I forced a smile. "Thanks. I'm not sure how long I'll be here, but I'm glad I'm here, too."

"What do you mean, how long?" she asked, her voice edged with concern, a wrinkle forming on her forehead.

I waved off her question. "Nothing. So." I forced a smile. "You're going to give Winnie a tour, and they've nominated me along for the ride."

I'd known Obsidian's request was more of a way to occupy my time since I'd seen all there was to see of the place. Winnie, on the other hand, hadn't been out and about much these last few days.

I motioned for Asmia to lead the way, suddenly desperate to get out of the bedroom. I couldn't stop thinking about Obsidian feeding from Acadia. The possessiveness that rolled through me bothered me on all levels. I'd never been that type of girl, and I wasn't fond of the feeling.

When we stepped onto the third-floor landing, Asmia

pulled the door closed behind us. The sound of tumblers locking into place followed.

"Quite the security measures around here," I said, keeping my tone light.

"The warriors value their privacy, but now that you're here, it wouldn't surprise me if Obsidian doesn't add additional security measures."

"Inside the mansion? Why would he need to do that?"

"For a male, an *amsouelot* is their sole reason for existing. It's in their nature to ensure their safety and security above all else. Should something happen, something that took their *amsouelot* from them, the male would cease to exist."

"He would die?" I asked as we took the stairs down to the second floor.

"No. Angels are immortal. However, he would have no reason to live at that point. We spend our entire lives waiting for that one true love, the one person we put above anyone and anything else."

"We? You have an *amsouelot*, too?"

"Yes. We all do."

"But this is all so new," I told her. As in *only-two-weeks-since-the-day-we-met* new. "How's it even possible for him to want to put me above everything else?"

"As a human, you're taught not to rush into things, to allow them to grow and blossom. For us ... the blossoming occurs prior to the meeting. Some humans have the benefit of experiencing different variations of love. For us, there's only one." Asmia motioned behind me. "There's Winnie now."

I turned to see my friend strolling toward me, a wide grin on her face.

"Sorry, I was in the shower when Reidar told me you were going to give me a tour."

Asmia smiled. "No worries. We're in no hurry."

"So, tell us about this place," I said, smiling.

"As you've probably noticed, the warriors built the mansion to be a fortress. While it may not look like it, there're many levels of security. They wanted us all to have a safe place to go, where we didn't have to worry about what might be coming to find us."

"Your enemies?" Winnie asked.

I had to wonder how much she'd learned in the short time she'd been here.

"Yes."

"Are demons your only enemies?"

I giggled. No need to wonder. Looked as though Reidar had given her the details.

"Not our only, no," Asmia answered. "Humans, too. One of the rules of our presence here on Earth is that we're to go undetected by humans. Which is why Darkness, Colorado, isn't on a map. And even if humans knew of its existence, they couldn't find it. Not even if they had the coordinates. For all intents and purposes, this place doesn't exist."

"So if I left, I couldn't find my way back," I asked.

"Correct."

"What if that darkness shield wasn't in place?"

"Still couldn't find it. You could walk the path up to the house, but before you got here, you'd be compelled to take a new direction."

Well, that sounded promising. At least as far as keeping the demons out.

Asmia smiled, leading the way down a wide hallway on the second floor. "You might've already seen this, but it's one of the game rooms. Pool table on this side, couches and television on the other. It's a safe bet you'll always find someone in here."

The large space was set up for entertaining and, at the moment, empty. A red-felt pool table and several recreational chairs and recliners scattered about took up one side of the room. Pool sticks were mounted to the wall, the decor matching the old-world style of the rest of the house. Past the pool table was a U-shaped couch, this one in brown leather, facing a wall with six television screens mounted to it. In the center of the sofa was a square coffee table.

The large stone fireplace separating the spaces was identical to the others I'd seen, splitting the enormous area into two sections. The far side had a plush, U-shaped sofa facing the fireplace and the television mounted above it. A huge cushioned ottoman was tucked in the U, a decorative tray sitting atop it. The outer wall held bookshelves with various knickknacks and books on every shelf. The other side of the room was a wrought iron railing that overlooked the main floor below. I could hear someone moving around in the kitchen.

"I have a question," Winnie said. "Not really related to the tour."

Asmia nodded. "I'll do my best to answer."

"Are there any other angels on Earth?"

I smiled. It didn't surprise me that Winnie was so curious. It was one of the many things we had in common.

"Aside from the warriors and those who support them?" Asmia asked.

"Yes."

"To be honest, that's way above my pay grade. I'm here specifically to support the warriors. The information I receive is what they permit me to have."

We fell into step with the Fae as she led the way toward the front of the house.

"All the rooms on this floor are for the *fiestreigh*. At least in the three wings that branch off. This one is a guest room, though until your brother arrived, we'd yet to have a guest."

When Asmia opened the door, I stepped inside, took a look

around. The space was as palatial as the rest of the house. High ceilings, inset bookcases, a sofa. One wall was dedicated to an entertainment center and another with floor-to-ceiling windows. The drapes were pulled back, offering a view of nothingness since the shield was in place. The bed was king-sized, the duvet a plush, silky blue to go along with the masculine design.

We slipped out of the room, down the hall.

Asmia continued to explain, "Each wing has dozens of private quarters as well as additional bathrooms and offices."

"Where's your room?"

She motioned to the left. "Looks much the same as the guest room. Only less blue, more purple."

We reached another hallway, turned left.

"The only recreational room on the third floor is the movie theater, which you've seen. Down here, we've got the library, the males' hangout, and—"

"The males have a hangout? Like a man cave?"

Asmia giggled. "Yes. No females allowed. On the main floor, you've got the kitchen and community spaces. Dining room, ballroom, office, laundry."

"I saw the indoor pool," Winnie said.

I smiled, remembering an encounter I had with Obsidian in that pool.

"Yes," Asmia explained. "Olympic-sized swimming pool, hot tub, sauna. There's also an indoor basketball court and a fully equipped workout room."

"You never have to leave, huh?" Winnie said.

"Not unless we're going to work, no."

The Fae led the way into the library Obsidian had brought me to when we first arrived. It smelled of furniture polish and paper, an oddly interesting mix. The enormous room was clean and dimly lit.

"About the hangout ... why do the men have their own?" Winnie asked. "They sit in there, drink beer, and belch?"

I giggled. I truly was happy to have Winnie there with me. And perhaps, if we had more time, Asmia and I might be able to build a relationship. I liked the Fae. A lot.

"Pretty much."

"So what do angels do for fun?" I asked, getting on board with Winnie's questions. "Aside from basketball, swimming, and working out?"

"The same things humans do. Aside from our aversion to sunlight, we're not much different."

It was my turn to laugh. "Uh, you forget about the mind control, ability to vanish in thin air, telekinesis, pyrokinesis... Shall I go on?"

"Fine." Asmia's eyes glittered with amusement. "There are a few additional things."

Realizing I'd seen almost everything there was to see, I had one question. "Where do the *heurosp* live?"

"They've got a separate residence that can be reached via the tunnels beneath the mansion. It's part of the grounds, but separate to maintain privacy."

"Beneath?" Winnie's gaze bounced between the two of us. "What else is down there?"

"The warriors built the underground space as a safety measure," Asmia explained. "In the event something happened and they needed to find shelter from the sun. They use it for recreation mostly, but it's more or less equipped to house us all, temporarily or long term."

Before we could launch into more questions, Reidar appeared in the doorway. His eyes locked on Winnie.

"Mind if I steal her away for a few minutes?"

I wanted to tell him to go away because I hadn't gotten to

spend much time with her lately. But I saw the way my friend's face lit up and thought better of it.

I smiled when Winnie blushed. "Not at all."

Winnie ducked her head, a move completely out of character for her, and made her way toward Reidar.

Once I was alone with Asmia, I peered around the library. "Asmia, can I ask you a personal question?"

"Of course."

I turned back to the Fae. "Has Obsidian ever fed from you?"

Asmia's amethyst eyes remained locked on my face. "At some point in my existence, they all have, yes."

I nodded.

"Why do you ask?"

I shrugged. "It's just ... I don't like the idea of him feeding from Acadia. Well, from anyone, actually."

Asmia nodded. "That's a natural reaction."

"Is it?" The words shot out of my mouth, along with my disbelief. "The man I'm in love with has to feed on the blood from a fairy, Asmia. I'm not sure there's anything natural about that."

Asmia offered a small smile. "Maybe not. But it's not something Obsidian can avoid. His existence depends on it."

"Can I—" The words died in my throat as the heat hit me, buckling my knees.

"Penelope!" Asmia grabbed my arm, helped me into a chair. "What's wrong?"

I couldn't speak, the painful need robbing me of breath and thought. Since it had only been a few hours since the last time I was with Obsidian, I hoped this one would pass. After all, it was quite the inconvenience.

"Talk to me," Asmia urged.

I focused on breathing as my nipples hardened, my core pulsed with sexual longing. Once again, my skin was too sensitive, the clothing I wore causing physical discomfort. It took everything in me not to strip it away, to ease some of the ache.

"Leave us, Asmia."

I didn't bother looking up, grateful Obsidian had appeared as he'd promised, finding me when I needed him most.

"Of course, Obsidian," Asmia said softly before vanishing in thin air.

Now that I knew what this affliction was, I turned my full attention to Obsidian once we were alone in the library.

His eyes heated as he kneeled on the floor between my legs. "Looks like I get the pleasure of loving you some more."

The promise in his eyes sent a spark of desire to my core, making me moan. "Yes. Please."

21

OBSIDIAN

With the mansion mostly cleared out, those who remained kept busy, most of them tucked away in the upstairs library, hiding out in the dining room, or even borrowing one of the many offices scattered throughout. Taayin, Søren, and Miklós worked with Gryffyth in an effort to provide support in finding the remaining four *amsouelots*, everyone pitching in the best they could.

Though I spent most of my time with Penelope, I couldn't deny something had put a minor rift between us. Okay, *something* made it sound like I didn't know what it was. Except I did. It was the fact that I was still feeding from Acadia, which had not only put Penelope and me on tenuous ground, it had also put a rift between Penelope and Acadia. I wasn't sure how to rectify the situation aside from feeding from Penelope, so I was doing my best to pretend the problem didn't exist.

Not exactly easy to do when the only priority I had was to make my *amsouelot* happy. Which, right now, I was doing by hiding out, giving her time to spend with Winnie. Since Reidar had filled Winnie in on our existence, the two females had something new to bond over. They never seemed to run out of things to talk about, and when they weren't chatting, they were asking questions. Luckily, Asmia had become the go-to for answers, the Fae growing ever closer to the two humans, hanging out with them when she wasn't out on patrol.

The soft knock on the main floor office door had me glancing up.

When it opened, Penelope appeared, looking scrumptious.

"I'm starting to think you've moved in here," she teased when she paused to lean against the doorjamb.

My gaze traveled over her from head to toe, taking in the little sundress she was wearing. I imagined she was chilled, but as always, she was beautiful, her golden hair hanging down her back and over her bare shoulders. She had minimal makeup on, which made her look even younger than her twenty-eight years.

"Am I interrupting?" she asked from the doorway.

"Never."

"Good." Her eyes sparkled when she stepped inside and closed the door behind her.

There was a familiarity in that look that said she had something on her mind, so I waited her out. My *amsouelot* had been doing this lately, surprising me when I was working. At first, I thought it was her attempt to stave off the heat, but the more times she did it, I wondered if it was her way of ensuring she was front and center in my world. I could've told her no one would ever be more important to me, but I wasn't sure she would've believed me. All because I had to feed from someone else.

For the longest time, we remained as we were, staring at one another.

"Is there something you need?" I asked, hoping what she needed was the same as what I did.

"Actually, there is," she said sweetly.

"What might that be?"

"You."

I was hardly breathing, anticipation amping up my already heightened senses. I noticed the exact moment her breaths became more labored, heard the distinct sound of her heart beating more rapidly, smelled the luscious scent of her arousal. My female intoxicated me, and I doubted she even realized she was doing it.

Figuring she needed a moment to decide what her next move was, I stood, moving toward the sofa on the other side of the desk. Before I could pass her, she pulled me up short, her small hand gripping my forearm. Her smile was radiant, her eyes heated as she stepped in close and reached up. She removed my sunglasses, set them on the desk before turning back to me.

Her eyes met mine, and I felt as though she was attempting to peer into my soul. Her smooth hand curled around my neck, pulling me down to her. When her lips pressed to mine, all thoughts of a slow seduction slipped away. Then again, we'd pretty much left that in the past since her arrival here at the mansion, and I couldn't say I was disappointed.

Our lips melded, my tongue slipping into her mouth, seeking the warmth of hers. She was eager, hungry, and as always, I vowed to give her everything she needed and then some. I felt her fingertips caressing my bare abdomen when she slipped under my T-shirt. Only because I wanted to watch her undress me did I release her mouth. The way her eyes shimmered with heat when she revealed my chest, her hands grazing my skin, it was enough to have my heartbeat speeding up, my cock rock hard.

Rather than rush her, I urged her to explore. She closed the distance between us, her lips grazing my chest, teasing, tasting.

She nudged the cotton. "Take this off."

In the work of a moment, I had the T-shirt over my head, tossed to the floor, forgotten.

Her gold eyes glittered when she looked up at me once more. "It's my turn."

"For?"

"To seduce you."

I held her stare. "*Ayreme*, you don't have to work at it. I'm already under your spell."

That seemed to please her, but it wasn't diverting her from her goal.

Not that I had any intention of stopping her. The female made me burn in ways no other ever could.

I inhaled sharply when her fingertips dipped into the waistband of my jeans, her lips grazing my stomach. Lust burned like hot coals deep inside me when she unhooked the button, lowered the zipper.

The sexy female took my hand, led me over to the sofa.

"Don't stop," I whispered, feeling her hesitance. "*Please* don't stop."

It took effort not to reach for her, but I managed. My fingers itched to touch her, but I wanted to feel her hands on me more.

My jeans fell to my ankles seconds before Penelope urged me to sit. My ass met the cushion, my eyes never leaving her.

"Take off the dress," I urged, toeing off my boots so I could free myself from the denim shackles.

While she slipped the straps of her sundress down her shoulders, I kept my attention on her while I removed the rest of my clothes, enraptured by her every movement. There was an innocence in her, and I fucking loved that I was her first in so many ways.

She teased me, keeping her breasts covered.

"Show me."

It was evident she'd never performed a striptease, but it didn't matter. Her natural grace was all that was necessary to have me riveted. Her slender fingers peeled the dress downward, revealing her rosy pink nipples. I licked my lips, desperate to take them in my mouth, to taste her.

"Keep going. I want to see all of you."

Penelope released the thin fabric of her dress, allowing it to slide down over her slim hips, her sexy legs, before pooling on the floor at her feet.

Once she was clad only in a tiny scrap of white lace covering her sex, my *amsouelot* stepped closer. I could sense her nerves, so I helped her out, reaching for her hand and pulling her forward. She straddled my thighs, her hands resuming their caress of my chest, my shoulders. Her lips finally returned to mine, and I let her lead the kiss, waiting until her tongue slipped into my mouth.

Gripping her hips, I pulled her closer, my erection sliding through the heat between her thighs.

Penelope moaned softly, the sweet, sensual sound driving me out of my ever-loving mind.

With absolutely no finesse, I ripped the scrap of lace, removing it quickly.

I growled when she fisted my cock.

Her eyes shot up to my face. "Do you like that?"

Overwhelmed by pleasure, I could only grunt. Her smooth hand caressed me from root to tip, slowly, reverently. In an effort to show her she wouldn't hurt me, I put my hand over hers, gently squeezed, tightening her grip on me. My cock pulsed, the need growing more rapidly.

I groaned, my hips shifting forward of their own volition, desperately needing more.

"Take me inside you," I growled, hungry for the feel of her wrapped around me.

And when she sank down on my cock, my mind was obliterated. I was consumed by her in every way. Her smooth skin against my palms, her sweet lips on mine, those sexy little mewls as I rolled my hips, burying my cock in her slick heat.

By then, I was past the point of seduction.

I worked her on me, pulling her hips forward, sliding them back. Our breaths rasped between us as sensations outranked skill.

Penelope sat up, her eyes meeting mine as I slid deep inside her before retreating by shifting her hips back. Again and again, seconds felt like minutes, minutes like days. I was so fucking lost in her, I knew I wouldn't survive without her.

I thought back to our conversation in the theater when Penelope admitted she wanted to have babies. I'd thought about it endlessly since then. Every moment I spent with her had me eager for the day to come when I could put a baby inside her.

"Obsidian..." She groaned, her head tipping back.

My gaze fell to her neck, my fangs descending at the thought of sinking into her vein. I hungered for her in a way that scared me. Bloodlust wasn't something my kind endured, but right that moment, I got a glimpse of what it could be like.

Thankfully, she distracted me when her hands shifted to her breasts. She caressed her flesh as I pumped into her.

Deeper, faster. Shifting my hand, I pressed my thumb against her clit, working her higher and higher as she moved over me.

"So beautiful," I groaned, feeling my release threatening.

I slowed her down, not wanting the moment to end.

Her eyes opened, returning to mine. We stared for long moments, our bodies intimately joined.

"You undo me, *ayreme*."

Her hands curled over my shoulders, her nails digging into my flesh as, once again, my control snapped. I drove up into her, jerking her forward, filling her. And when she cried out my name, I lost it. With one deep thrust, I held her to me, my cock pulsing inside her.

We both fought to catch our breaths, Penelope relaxing against me. I slid my hand over her back, moving beneath the silk of her hair, holding her close, never wanting to let her go.

It was in those moments when we were as close as two could be that I knew I would spend the rest of eternity with her, despite my darkest fears. There were things I had yet to tell my *amsouelot* about the *lintamair,* things I was having a difficult time coming to terms with, but I knew in the end, I would persevere because there were no other options.

PENELOPE

After the sensual encounter with Obsidian in the main-floor office, I snuck back up to his private quarters and showered, although I wasn't sure why I even bothered. Before the night was over, I knew I'd need another one. At the rate we were going, I'd be in his arms in the very near future.

Thanks to the strange phenomenon he referred to as *amnigh*, we had sex several times, night and day, didn't matter. The intensity and frequency of the heat were getting more powerful, overwhelming at times. But I was doing my best to pretend otherwise, to act like it was no big deal when, in reality, it was a bit overwhelming. Hence, I'd seduced him in the office. It had been an attempt to head it off at the pass, give a little bit of a reprieve before it hit me again.

I'd been doing that for the past couple of days, ensuring Obsidian didn't have to race to my rescue. According to him, there was a reprieve to be had once he fed from me, but since he'd made it clear he didn't want to, I was being stubborn about it.

Granted, I knew he wasn't feeding from Acadia often. About once every three days, and I could always tell when he'd put it off for too long. He thought he was covering it well, but I knew.

And yes, it bothered me that he felt he needed to protect me in that manner, but aside from demanding he feed from me, I didn't know what to do about it.

After my shower, I made my way to the second floor, searching for my brother. Oliver had been avoiding me since our last heated argument when Obsidian had intervened, and I couldn't necessarily blame him. I understood his frustration. He was a prisoner in this house, even if everyone was doing their best to be hospitable. The fact that Obsidian had done something to ensure Oliver couldn't step outside of the mansion had removed his free will.

I stopped in the doorway of the pool room, watched Oliver line up a shot, take it.

When he stood, his gaze traveled in my direction, stopping when he noticed me. He snagged the chalk, rubbed it on the end of his stick.

"Am I violating some rule?" he snapped. "Humans not allowed to play pool?"

"You know you're not," I told him as I moved into the room, made my way over to one of the bar-height stools. "I'm a bit surprised to see you in here, that's all."

"Yeah, well. I got tired of staring at the walls in that room."

"You have to admit, they're nice walls."

The look he gave me probably should've singed my skin.

"Look, Oliver. I'm sorry you were dragged into this mess."

"Are you?" he hissed, spinning to face me. "Do you really fucking care that my entire life has been upended because you've got a new boyfriend who thinks he's king of the goddamn world?"

"That's a bit dramatic, even for you, Oliver."

"Fuck you, Opie," he grumbled, turning his attention back to the pool table. "I still haven't seen proof that Seraphina's what they claim she is."

"Do you really want to?" I countered hotly. "You want her to show you her demon face?"

He glared at me over his shoulder. "No, I want proof that what your boyfriend says is true."

"It's true," I insisted.

He stood tall, moved around the table. "And you know this how? Because he said so?"

"I believe him, Oliver. Everything he says."

"Why?"

"Because he can't lie to me."

Oliver snorted. "You're too naive for your own good."

Perhaps, but I *did* know it to be true because I'd tested the theory in reverse. Just the other day, I'd purposely placed my hairbrush in the closet, then asked Obsidian to get it for me. No matter how hard I tried to tell him I'd left it in the bathroom, I couldn't get the words out. It was impossible to lie to him, even when it was trivial.

Not that it mattered. Oliver wouldn't believe me anyway. He never did.

With a heavy sigh, I got to my feet, then started back to the doorway before remembering why I'd come up here in the first place. I turned to look at Oliver.

"Not that you care, but Gryffyth asked me to ask you if you wanted to go out with them. They're hitting up some club in Telluride. They claim they need a break from the house."

Oliver's eyes were skeptical when he looked my way. "Are you going?"

I shook my head. I had no desire to go to a club.

"Then yes, I'll go."

I considered calling him out on what his problem was with me, but found I had no desire to hash it out with him. I was too damn tired to fight, and his emotions were already wreaking havoc on mine. Being around Oliver had always been difficult.

"I'll let him know. I think he said they're heading out in an hour or so."

Not surprisingly, Oliver said nothing more, so I started toward the stairs, only to come face-to-face with Obsidian.

"Were you eavesdropping?" I teased.

The thin line of his lips reflected his concern as he watched me.

"It's fine," I told him, knowing he could read my mind if he wanted. "Oliver's just being Oliver. Hopefully we'll get this all taken care of soon enough, and he can go home."

That was the first time I hadn't included myself in that statement.

For the past several days, I'd gone so far as to plan what I would do when I got back home, back to my regular scheduled life. It had taken effort to think about being away from Obsidian, but I figured that was going to be inevitable. My home was in Vegas.

But it was then that I realized I was already home. Wherever Obsidian was, regardless of what issues stood between us, I was home as long as I was with him.

When I met Obsidian's gaze, his expression changed. Softened.

"You're reading my thoughts," I whispered.

The next thing I knew, I crashed into the enormous man who smelled like sin in a bottle. When he gripped my shoulders, holding me firmly, I swallowed the sigh, fisting the front of his T-shirt, not caring that I was wrinkling it.

He stared down at me, those silver eyes fierce with the hunger that echoed inside me. It made no sense, this overwhelming desire, even if Obsidian could explain it away with a story about *amnigh*. This was more than a mere physical desire. It was deeper than a chemical release in the brain. No man had ever made me feel like this, and surprisingly, I didn't want to dissect it. I simply wanted Obsidian to love me from now until the end of time.

"You are home," he whispered harshly. "With me. That's home, *ayreme*."

"I know."

"Then stop thinking about leaving me." There was a hint of pain in his tone. "I need you."

I knew that, too, because I needed him the same way.

"I love you, Obsidian." I was panting, gripping his shirt in my fists, trying to get closer, although it was impossible. "So much, it scares me."

"Don't fight it," he whispered.

"I'm not. I can't." I gripped his shirt tighter. "I just want to be with you. Every second, every day. It's all happening so fast, but ... I want this. I don't know why."

"I do," he said softly, his voice a rough grind against my senses.

I knew he was going to kiss me before it happened. I welcomed it, ached for it. When his mouth settled on mine, all thought fled. The only thing I could focus on was the way his tongue slid past my lips, danced against mine.

It started slow. An exquisite melding of mouths, languid, steady.

Obsidian growled low in his throat, and it spurred the need, driving my lust to a flash point.

The ascent into nuclear wasn't gradual, we simply soared. He growled again, gripped my hair, winding it around his big fist. It was such a forceful thing to do, so brutally assertive, commanding, I found my knees weakening. Obsidian didn't hurt, he controlled, commanded, holding my head still as he plundered my mouth. I moaned, gripping his shoulders, the needy ache between my legs intensifying.

As many times as we'd come together over the past couple of weeks, something felt different about this.

"Obsidian, please..." I found his neck with my mouth, desperate to taste more of him, to urge him to keep going. I was blinded by my craving for him, incapable of thinking beyond how good he felt against me, how I wanted to feel him inside me. It was as though I'd known this man my entire life. My body created specifically for his. Two magnets. North and south poles attracting, the magnetic force inevitable. We would be together.

Obsidian jerked my head back, our mouths separating, his lips hovering over mine. I stared up into those molten silver eyes and willed him to see everything I felt, everything I craved, to find a way to satisfy it.

He growled again, almost a plea, but I was at a loss.

We shared the same air as I grew bolder, tugging his shirt up, wanting to feel his warm skin against my palms. I didn't even care that we were standing in the hallway, that my brother was in the very next room. It didn't matter. Nothing did.

While I was trapped in his hungry gaze, I freed the button on Obsidian's jeans, moved on to the zipper. His breaths were soughing in and out of his lungs as though he was trying to hold back. Blessedly, he pulled his shirt off, giving my lips a place to go. I kissed his smooth chest, licked, teased. The dark taste of him spurred me to continue. Just as I was about to reach into his jeans, his hand snapped around my wrist.

"My turn," he commanded softly.

"Your turn," I confirmed, my lungs burning from exertion.

His hands were on my ass, squeezing roughly, jerking me to him.

"I need you, Obsidian. More than I've ever needed *anything*."

Obsidian slid his hands down my thighs, gripped firmly, and lifted me off my feet. My back met the smooth wall seconds before his lips slammed over mine. The deep rumble in his chest was animalistic, dark thunder. My legs wrapped around his hips, trying to get closer.

"I want everything," he commanded roughly, his words laced with gravel, as though they'd been ripped from his throat.

I was vaguely aware of him walking, ascending the stairs to the third floor. I heard the distinct sound of the security panel.

"Everything," I promised, not even knowing what that meant.

The door opened. We stepped inside. That was as far as we made it when my back once again met the wall. I held his head as he bruised my lips with his, felt his hand move between us, was acutely aware of what he was doing, willing him to hurry. I thrust my tongue against his, my lungs burning as air became scarce. Still, I couldn't get close enough.

I heard something rip, realized it was my panties. I didn't even have time to care that he'd left part of them intact, hanging loosely from one thigh. He shifted, impaling me on his thick erection. I cried out, my head dropping back as overwhelming pleasure crashed into me, driving the remaining air from my lungs as my insides coiled into an electrical storm of sensation.

Obsidian pinned me to the wall with his body, driving deep, hips punishing with every delicious thrust, sending blood rushing to my head as I spiraled into the ether. There was no tenderness in the way he held me, no benevolence in the violence that sparked. Only hunger, passion, an urgency so powerful I was helpless to resist.

"More," I cried out.

"Everything," he growled, more beast than man.

I'd never been so out of control, so completely consumed, and that was saying something considering the past couple of weeks. But something was happening between us. It was a pivotal moment, that inevitable point of no return.

His tongue licked at my neck, his fangs lightly scraping the sensitive flesh, snapping the tenuous grip I had on sanity.

"Obsidian..." A sharp gasp escaped when he lightly nipped me with his teeth, the pain euphoric. "Please. Don't stop."

His head lifted, silver eyes meeting mine.

I tilted my head to the side. "Now, Obsidian."

He growled. But rather than sink his fangs into my neck, his mouth was forceful when it covered mine. He drove deep inside me, retreated, drove in again. I cried out as the first wave of orgasm shattered me, left me reeling as he drove me higher once more, never relenting, taking everything and expecting more.

When the next orgasm hit, it was stronger than the first, leveling me. I was panting, my muscles like noodles.

As though he hadn't just banged two orgasms out of me, Obsidian carried me over to the sofa, dropped onto it. I was still impaled on his erection, and the move had me groaning, shards of pain penetrating my core. But this was the sort of agony that turned into a craving, an unnatural desire. Purely erotic, a dark promise of what was to come.

"Ride me," he bellowed, tugging at my dress, pulling it over my head. It disappeared, leaving me mostly naked in his arms.

The sound of fabric tearing signaled the complete removal of my panties, their tattered remains tossed away. Unimportant.

I rocked my hips forward, back, trying to take more of him. He was so big, so thick, filling me, stretching me. I worked myself on him, selfishly taking the pleasure he offered.

With my eyes locked with his, I willed him to see my true need. What I was desperate for.

Dragging my hair to one side, I tilted my head. His eyes instantly dropped to my neck.

"Now, Obsidian," I whispered. "We both need this."

His big hand curled behind my neck, his eyes meeting mine as though seeking reassurance. I leaned toward him, sighed when his lips pressed to my neck. I could feel him pulsing inside me as I rocked on his erection.

"I love you," I whispered, encouraging him to take what I freely offered. "I want this, Obsidian."

He groaned, his hand tightening on my neck.

I stilled when I felt his fangs, a hint of fear running through me.

He pulled back suddenly, clearly sensing my emotions.

This time, I gripped his head, pulling him toward me as I leaned in again. "Now, Obsidian."

I inhaled sharply when his fangs brushed my skin, a second later piercing me.

There was only a prickle of pain, an exquisite euphoria following quickly on its heels. An inexplicable desire bloomed throughout my entire body, and I came as he drank from me, my body melting against him. Ecstasy, unlike anything I'd ever felt, consumed me, dragged me under. He growled low in his throat as he sucked at my neck for what felt like eternity. I could feel his need for more, but his self-control overruled his thirst. His tongue caressed me once, twice.

When Obsidian pulled my mouth back to his, he was gentle, sucking my tongue before kissing me deeply, thoroughly. His hands moved to my hips, guiding me forward, back. I moaned, once more overcome with emotion, unable to get enough. His lips moved, trailing over my jaw, down my chest. He sucked one nipple into his mouth, his teeth nipping, pain dancing erotically over my skin.

His hand fisted in my hair once more, this time pulling my head all the way back, my chest thrusting forward. I flattened my hands behind me, gripping his thighs to maintain my balance as he propelled his hips upward, distracting me when he sucked my nipple between his teeth, then bit down.

I came again, crying out his name as the orgasm surprised me.

"One more," he growled, rolling us both until he was over

me, pushing me into the cushion as his hips swiveled, then jerked.

He hammered into me, his hands finding mine, lifting them over my head. He transferred one so that he held me captive with one hand, his other snaking between our bodies. When he thumbed my clit, I screamed, another orgasm cresting, knocking the air from my lungs.

And when Obsidian threw back his head and roared, his cock pulsing deep inside me, I gave myself over to him.

Mind, body, soul.

Completely and utterly at his mercy.

From now until eternity.

22

ECLIPSE

I considered not going out with the others even though it had originally been my idea. Right up until I heard Obsidian and Penelope going at it in the third-floor living room. At that point, I figured it was more a means of survival than anything else. The last thing I wanted was to endure the sexual energy that billowed through the mansion when those two came together. I was having a hard enough time, thank you very much.

Luckily, I'd gotten out of there before that happened.

"And what exactly made you decide this was a good idea?" Taayin muttered as we stepped into the overcrowded club, the one that clearly had more occupants than real estate.

Part of me wished I'd left the grouchy *lieterra* back at the mansion. The male was in a mood tonight, and since I was, too, it likely wouldn't fare well for either of us.

"Why don't you grab a drink," I insisted, making my way to the bar, desperate to leave them all behind.

When I made the suggestion of a night out, I intended to slip out of the mansion with Søren in tow. Plans changed when Gryffyth got wind of the outing. Next thing I knew, Gryffyth had invited every male and female in the house. At some point, word must've gotten out because Asmia and Ziana had turned up, as did Acadia and Elina, the Fae as eager to get their drink on as we were.

So, here we were, making a night of it.

Truth was, I wasn't here for a drink or a party. I was hoping to get a lead on my *amsouelot*. Not that I figured she'd be here after the tragic incident she'd endured a few days ago. Still, hope sprang eternal.

"What can I get you, handsome?" the blond bartender asked, her steady brown eyes surveying me as I stepped up to the bar.

"Scotch, neat."

She gave an assessing nod. "Coming right up."

When she walked away to do her thing, I surveyed the jam-packed club. Not my usual choice for a watering hole, but since there weren't many options in Telluride, I figured this would have to do. The populace seemed younger, more energetic. Between the strobe lights and the noise disguised as music, my senses were bombarded from all angles. Not even the dark shades helped much.

The bartender returned, and I traded cash for the drink, then headed toward a darkened corner. I noticed Oliver at the bar tossing back two shots in rapid succession. The male had agreed to the outing because he'd been hoping to make a break for it. And I didn't even need to read the human's thoughts to know that. It was in his body language. He was twitchy, anxious. Little did the fool know, but I had tethered us with invisible rope. Should Oliver get more than fifty feet away, the shock the human would receive would not only knock him on his ass but make him rethink his desire to ditch.

Oddly, I was hoping I was paying attention when it happened because I could use a laugh.

It was when I was taking a sip of my drink that I felt the strange pull deep inside me. I scanned the area, looking for the source, not sure what was calling out to me. Could've been a demon or even a vampire. As an angel, I had a heightened sense of awareness, and when it came to the supernatural, I had an uncanny ability to pick them out.

But this wasn't either.

My gaze came to rest on the female from the alley. She looked just as I remembered. Shoulder-length blond hair, cornflower-blue eyes, high cheekbones, and a dimpled chin. A devastating beauty. My *amsouelot*.

"Holy fuck," I mumbled under my breath as I watched her.

She was chatting it up with a male wearing a belt buckle that said he was overcompensating for something. The black hat on his head and the shiny pearl buttons on his shirt made him blend in with two dozen other cowboys in the club. I watched the two of them, an overwhelming possessiveness burning in my gut. I shoved it down, refused to acknowledge it. Probably not a good idea to make a scene in this place.

I figured it was going to be difficult enough to get close to Orianna, considering I'd offed the male in the alley. Last thing I needed to do was piss her off by leveling one of the males. For all I knew, he could be a friend.

For both our sakes, he *better* be a friend.

PERFIDIOUS

Ever heard the saying good things come to those who wait?

I wasn't a big believer in it. Or I hadn't been.

Until tonight.

Somehow I'd let Seraphina talk me into coming to this backwoods redneck brothel disguised as a dance club. Imagine my surprise when I found not one but *four* of those damned angels chatting it up with the locals.

I knew without searching that Penelope wasn't present, nor was the behemoth she was shacking up with. They were too smart to venture out. I was more than certain they were aware I was on their trail. Didn't matter that I'd changed bodies twice since I left Vegas, they would still have a bead on me. They always did.

Good thing I knew how to be one step ahead at all times.

As I stood, imagining exactly how I intended to slay every last one of them, my attention was snagged by a beautiful blond sitting at a table in the back. She was there with a couple of other females, talking, laughing.

Instantly, the thought of demolishing the angels dissolved like ash, drifting off in the wind as a new plan formed.

Okay, so it wasn't necessarily a new plan. It had been my goal all along. Sirius and Seraphina thought I was marching to the tune of Lucifer's orders, but in reality, I was making my own beat. I couldn't give a fuck less about the *amsouelots* at this point. I had much more pressing concerns.

Namely, getting that damn Fae beneath me where she belonged.

Of course, I wasn't an idiot, so I'd been biding my time, waiting for the perfect opportunity to spring my plan into action.

I'd waited. Good things came.

With a smirk, I set my glass down on the bar and made my way through the throng. After making a detour to the DJ on duty, I started toward her. I came up short when one of the males stopped at the table, whispered something in her ear. The instant he shot across the room in the opposite direction, I marched right up to the Fae and smiled down at her.

"Hello, gorgeous."

Asmia peered up at me briefly before her gaze followed the male who'd walked away.

He's not here to save you.

Personally, I couldn't fathom how the male could even stand to be away from her. I had been watching them all night, saw the way they made eyes at one another, felt their chemistry, yet they maintained a safe distance as though they had no choice. They were most certainly indulging in some sort of relationship, but for whatever reason, kept it on the down low.

As for how serious it was, I didn't know. Nor did I care.

Asmia's big blue eyes scanned my face. I watched as she tried to place me, figure out how she knew me. When she realized she didn't, she offered a smile.

"Care to dance?" I suggested, knowing she'd intended to do that but hadn't been able to talk her companion into taking her for a spin on the dance floor.

She fanned her face as though the heat was too much for her. "I should probably wait for ... my friend."

"One dance. I'll have you back in your seat before he returns." I met her gaze, held it, adding a bit of mind control to ensure she didn't reject me. I wasn't entirely sure it would work on a Fae, so imagine my surprise when a bright smile beamed back at me.

"I hope you're a good dancer," she said as she slipped her long, delicate fingers in my hand.

"You have no idea, gorgeous."

She smelled like roses, a sweet scent that went right to my head, made me wonder what she'd look like sprawled naked on a thousand red petals.

The DJ was making his way back to his fancy setup as I tugged Asmia toward me.

"Looks like we've got some seduction taking place right now," the DJ announced. "How about something sinful?"

The crowd cheered as a rousing beat began.

Bodies embarked upon the dance floor as I drew Asmia to me, one hand flattening against her lower back, the other sliding into her hair as I brought her cheek to mine.

"Such a lovely creature," I whispered against her ear, enjoying the way her long, lithe body molded to mine. "So hot and eager."

With my fist in her hair, I pulled her back so I could meet her eyes.

Deep inside her, there was an urge to resist me, but I maintained enough control to override it. Ensuring she understood I was in charge, not her. I held all the cards, made all the rules. It was ultimately my decision as to whether or not she would succumb to my advances.

And she most definitely would.

Eventually.

Asmia whimpered, her hands gliding over me as she gave in to the subtle nudges I gave her mind.

Perhaps I was indulging a bit more than I intended, but I was unable to banish the thought of feeling her skin on mine. Not since the night I'd met her. Every thought I'd had since was plagued with raunchy thoughts of the two of us together. Now as she ground sinfully against me, her body seeking the pleasure of mine, I knew resisting her was no longer an option.

"I don't even know your name..." She moaned softly, her body moving intimately against mine.

"Perfidious," I whispered into her ear. "Say it. Say my name."

"Perfidious," she purred, her legs spreading as I slid my thigh between them.

I was tempted to take her to a dark corner, to lift that sexy little black dress and push deep inside her lush heat, but I resisted.

It was all about the build-up, after all.

"You can feel me, can't you?"

"Yes." Asmia sighed, tipping her head back, exposing her long, sleek neck as the seductive sounds moved through and around us.

I grazed her skin with my lips, caressing her with my tongue.

I'd waited so fucking long to get my hands on her, my mouth. Her taste went right to my head, made every minute I'd spent thinking about her worth it. But it was too difficult to maintain control of her mind when she was driving me to the point of insanity, which was the only reason the connection broke.

She lifted her head, met my eyes, and I could see the concern. Taking back control was easy enough, just a little push on her mind, assuring her I was the male she wanted to be with. As long as she was looking at me, she couldn't refuse me.

"You want me, Asmia. You want what only I can give you."

Her hips rolled as she ground her sex against my thigh, desperate to get closer. I fed her need, cupping her ass, holding her to me as she sought the release the friction promised. I wanted to see her face when she came, to hear my name on her lips. It became my sole focus. One song blended with another, equally as dark, just as alluring.

Asmia remained in my embrace for long minutes. Every time she came close to orgasm, I refused her, maintaining the control I had over her body and mind.

The male she'd been with reappeared near the bar, drawing my attention. He was searching for her, eyes scanning all the bodies. It wouldn't take but a minute for him to locate her, and for now, I intended to keep my presence a secret. This game we were playing was far too intense for me to out myself yet.

Turning my attention back to Asmia, I connected with her mind once more. "When you walk away from me, you won't remember this moment. You'll forget you were in my arms, but you'll crave me. Your body'll burn for mine. When you touch yourself, it'll be my fingers you feel."

She whimpered softly.

"And you'll dream about me, Asmia. When you sleep, you'll feel my mouth on you. It'll make you hot, desperate. No other male will be able to give you pleasure. You'll use their bodies, but it'll be my face you see when you orgasm, my name that'll whisper from your lips."

"Please ... Perfidious..."

I smiled back at her. "Not yet, gorgeous. We've got time yet. I want you to crave me the same way I crave you. And when it's time for me to claim you, you won't be able to resist me."

I crushed my mouth to hers. She kissed me roughly, as though she couldn't get enough.

I jerked my mouth from hers, refusing her the release she sought.

"Until next time, gorgeous."

With a grin on my face, I turned her away, watched that delicious ass as she sauntered off.

Until next time.

PENELOPE

I woke in a familiar room with a very familiar body next to mine. Somehow I knew night had fallen, the shutters would be rising soon enough, but for the moment, I welcomed the darkness.

And while I was used to this, waking in Obsidian's bed, him beside me, it felt different somehow. I felt different.

The heat I'd grown accustomed to had dissipated, but my desire for Obsidian hadn't waned in the least. My body was drawn to his. And here, protected by darkness, I was compelled to move toward him, wanting to get closer.

He was warm, solid. Naked.

Just the way I liked him.

During our interlude in the living room, Obsidian had been mostly clothed. In fact, now that I thought about it, we'd had sex while he was half-dressed numerous times in the past two weeks. As though getting them off took too much effort. Such a shame, too, considering how beautiful his body was. Every second I could, I openly ogled him, no longer ashamed of the desire he inspired within me.

Ogling him wasn't an option now, but I did the next best thing. Trailing my hand over his chest, I memorized the smooth planes of muscle, the hard angles of sinew and bone beneath his velvet-smooth skin with my fingertips. A soft hum sounded from his chest, his arm coming around me, pulling me closer. He pressed his lips to my forehead, breathed out roughly.

It was a move he made frequently, I realized. Obsidian wasn't ashamed to let me know he preferred to have me close to him. I happened to be quite fond of the position myself.

"I didn't mean to wake you," I whispered in the darkness.

"Glad you did."

I lifted my head. "Seriously?"

He chuckled, pulled me until I was draped over him. "I was tempted to do the same, *ayreme*."

He brought my mouth down to his. The smooth warmth of his lips awakened all my senses, my body keenly aware of the position I was in.

I had no idea what he was thinking, but I could feel him staring at me. As had been the case since the first time we made love in his hotel room, there was a lingering tension between us, one that never fully dissipated. The gentle way his hands moved over me stirred that longing, made it seem ... justified somehow. As though we were meant to spend an ungodly amount of time doing exactly this.

Hard to believe that three weeks ago, I hadn't known he existed. Everything since had seemed to go at warp speed. And somewhere in that time, perhaps even the first night at the hotel, I had fallen head over heels in love with him.

It wasn't normal, I knew. Two people did not give in so easily. To lust, sure. But not to love. And while I knew that, deep down, I couldn't seem to fight my emotions. They had settled over me like a security blanket I'd been looking for my entire life. Obsidian made me feel as though I belonged here. Living in his house, sleeping in his bed, feeling his warmth against me through the day when we slept, the nights when we continued to get to know one another.

His warm hands trailed down my back, curved over my ass, slipped between my thighs. Thick fingers teased my clit before sliding inside me, dragging a soft moan from my chest. The man knew exactly how to touch me to make me burn.

I rested against him, completely wanton in my need for him. I positioned myself so I'd have better access. My lips grazed his neck as his fingers teased and enticed until I was rocking my hips, wanting more.

"Ride me," he whispered.

With his assistance, I worked myself onto him, grinding down, grateful for the freedom of the bed. Just as I was working up my rhythm, his body shifted, his torso elongating.

"Lamp on, ten percent," he said softly.

The next thing I knew, the room was bathed in a soft light, the bedside lamp highlighting his exquisite form.

"I want to watch you," he said, his hands tucked beneath his head in a casual yet arrogant move.

Long and lean, every muscle defined, his biceps bulged, his pecs flexed. His golden skin was dotted with scars he'd gotten through the years, or rather centuries. Yet they didn't take away from the masculine beauty he presented.

"Touch yourself," Obsidian instructed, the soft rumble an aphrodisiac.

My hands moved to my breasts as I worked my hips forward and back. I closed my eyes, taking my pleasure from him. His gaze penetrated through me. He was watching every move, his hips shifting from time to time, pushing up into me. There was no frantic rush, just two bodies moving as one, the friction so intense I could feel every nerve in my body waking to find the source.

Although he appeared relaxed, completely unaffected, there was a slight tremble under Obsidian's skin. He was enjoying this as much as I was, but for some reason, he felt the need to pretend otherwise. Or perhaps he was simply enjoying the show.

Leaning forward, I pressed my hands to his chest, held his intense gaze. I could see through the facade. The way his heart beat just a little harder than normal, thumping against my palms as I used the hard planes of his body to leverage myself up, then drop back down.

He groaned softly, silver eyes glittering, glowing.

I did it again and again, noticing the tension in the lines around his mouth and eyes tighten. He was going to snap any second, I could feel it. And though I wasn't sure that was a good thing, I couldn't stop myself from pushing him closer and closer to that edge.

"Be careful, *ayreme*. You don't know what you're asking for."

I didn't. Nor did I care. This man had turned me into someone I didn't recognize, and I liked that woman. I wasn't Little Red Riding Hood slipping through the forest. I was taking the big bad wolf head on, ready for anything he could throw at me.

I worked my hips faster, taking him to the hilt, but it wasn't enough. I needed more and he knew it.

His hands came from under his head, slowly gliding over

my thighs, stilling me with a firm grip. I groaned my frustration when the blessed friction ceased. He answered by flipping me onto my back, coming over me, and driving deep inside.

I screamed, pleasure and pain obliterating my mind. I reached for him, arms circling his neck as I held on. He pounded into me, savage and wild and utterly depraved, a need so deep I could feel it in my soul. It intoxicated me, made me crave more, never wanting that moment to end. My orgasm crested, unintelligible sounds coming out of me as I reached for another, desperate for him to provide.

Obsidian didn't disappoint, relentless in his pursuit. He ordered another orgasm and I gave. Another and I surrendered again. My body was weak when he demanded one more. I shook my head. It was impossible, but he seemed to believe otherwise. His hand tucked under my thigh as he shifted his hips, changing the angle and proving once again that he reigned supreme over my body.

This time, when I cried out, he followed me over, my name a rough grumble on his lips.

"Sleep, *ayreme*," he whispered, rolling off me and pulling me against him.

Truth was, I was exhausted. The past couple of weeks had been taxing on both my body and my mind, yet I found it difficult to close my eyes.

Obsidian stroked my hair and I sighed against him. It felt good to be held, something I'd never had before him.

I turned into him, pressing my lips to his chest. His big hand curled around the back of my head, strong and reassuring, even though it also reminded me of how incredibly giant he was. He towered over me, surrounded me. It should've been intimidating, but it wasn't.

Needless to say, I was in love with him, my heart tethered to his.

In the twenty-eight years I'd had in this life, I had never met a man who held my interest for longer than a minute. A few I'd considered friends with benefits, even gotten close to. I had always figured it was a fault of mine. A lack of passion that I'd been born to endure. And while I was a woman who knew how to satisfy my own needs, I'd never felt an unbridled attraction to a man.

Not the way I did now. For Obsidian.

Overwhelming, powerful. Distracting.

Eternal.

23

OBSIDIAN

Sitting at the kitchen island, I watched Penelope as she talked softly with the Fae, the females drinking wine while everyone else worked around them.

Although it was Sunday, and they'd all had a late night at the club, the day had passed once again, and everyone was back to business as usual. Laptops and iPads were scattered across the granite top, fingers flying over keys as they worked diligently to identify their targets. With four more *amsouelots* yet to be identified, no one was letting up in their pursuit.

At the same time, we were trying to get a bead on Perfidious, find out if he was close. I was grateful the demon hadn't made a move, but the more days that passed without a hint of him, the more my tension grew. The last thing I wanted was to get lax, to think that the security of the mansion would protect us.

Of course, there didn't seem to be anything lax about Eclipse. Ever since their trek to the club, my brother had been on edge. Whether it was because of his *amsouelot* or the fact that Taayin insisted there had been demons present, I wasn't sure. I could've grilled the male, but I was giving Eclipse space, wanting to give him time to deal with his revelation.

Taayin strolled in, staring intently at his cell phone.

"Did you find out who it was?" I asked, hoping for some news on which demons were close. Though I suspected it was Perfidious, I wasn't about to count any of them out.

"I was able to get a picture. I'm pretty sure this is Perfidious," the *lieterra* said.

I took the phone from Taayin, stared at it, then passed it to Eclipse when he appeared at my side.

"I remember him," Eclipse grumbled, then frowned. "I was too preoccupied, or I would've felt his presence."

I set the phone on the countertop, glancing at it one final time before Penelope pulled it toward her. She passed it over to Acadia, who then handed it off to Ziana.

"He looks familiar," the Fae noted, squinting at the screen. "I've seen him somewhere."

Elina took the phone, nodded. "Yeah. He was at the club." Her gaze swung to Asmia as she passed the phone over. "You remember him, don't you?"

Asmia's eyes widened as she stared at the image, horrified.

"What is it?" Taayin asked, clearly sensing her panic.

"That's... He's..." She shoved the phone away from her as though it had burned her.

"Spit it out," I snarled at the female.

She swallowed hard, lifted her gaze to meet mine. "I met him at the club. He asked me to dance."

I noticed she was avoiding looking at Taayin.

"What did he say to you?"

She shook her head. "Nothing. But..." Her amethyst eyes widened as they darted over to Taayin, then back to me. "I'd like to request to speak to you in private."

"Whatever you have to say can be said here," I told her, not willing to allow her to keep secrets from Taayin. Not because I was worried about their personal interactions. If this was Perfidious, the *lieterra* needed to know what was going on as much as I did.

"I think he did something to me," Asmia whispered, terror in her eyes.

Taayin's body went hard, hands clenched into fists. "What did he do, Asmia?"

She shrugged. "I have no idea. I remember not wanting to dance with him, but then I did. Like he willed me to do it. And ... ever since ... when ..." A tear trickled down her cheek. "I think he manipulated my thoughts."

Penelope's hand was on Asmia's arm, a clear sign of her need to comfort the female. "What did he do, Asmia?"

"Whenever Taayin and I ... this morning, when we were intimate..." She shook her head. "I see his face in my mind. Not like a fantasy because I would never. I think he's doing it. Perfidious is making me think about him."

"Turn around," I ordered, moving to stand behind her.

"I want to see," Taayin insisted.

I met the *lieterra's* hardened gaze, surprised by the rage I saw there.

"Show me, Obsidian."

Penelope was staring at us, eyes wide. "What's going on?"

Rather than explain, I pressed my palm to Asmia's forehead. It took a moment to filter through her memories, locating the one from the night at the club. When I did, I projected the image out of her head and through my eyes, watching as Asmia danced with a male, their bodies pressed intimately together.

A harsh snarl sounded from Taayin as I uncovered the hidden manipulation Perfidious had planted there.

When you walk away from me, you won't remember this moment. You'll forget you were in my arms, but you'll crave me. Your body'll burn for mine. When you touch yourself, it'll be my fingers you feel.

And you'll dream about me, Asmia. When you sleep, you'll feel my mouth on you. It'll make you hot, desperate. No other male will be able to give you pleasure. You'll use their bodies, but it'll be my face you see when you orgasm, my name that'll whisper from your lips.

Please ... Perfidious...

Not yet, gorgeous. We've got time yet. I want you to crave me the same way I crave you. And when it's time for me to claim you, you won't be able to resist me.

The image disappeared when I removed my hand from Asmia's forehead. I waited for Taayin to say something. He didn't.

When the male's eyes met mine, I could see the hatred he harbored for Perfidious. The feeling was definitely mutual, though I had to admit, Taayin's hatred was more personal.

"You mentioned you met him at the casino," Reidar noted. "The night that woman was killed in her hotel room."

Asmia nodded, looking at my *ladeare*. "Yes. He looks different now."

Not surprising. To keep below the radar, Perfidious would need to exchange bodies.

"I think he's fixated on her," Reidar said softly.

"Me? Why me?" Asmia asked, clearly as shocked by the revelation as the rest of us.

A bitter growl sounded seconds before Taayin vanished.

"Taayin!" Asmia yelled, then turned to look at me. "What have I done?"

Penelope got to her feet, hugged the female. "You didn't do anything, Asmia. He did this to you."

"He hates me," the Fae mumbled.

No, he didn't. In fact, the male was so far gone, I had a difficult time believing they weren't mated. I'd never seen a male react this way, not one who hadn't connected with his *amsouelot*, anyway.

"Did you remove it?" Asmia asked, turning to me.

"Yes. I took care of it." No way would I allow the demon that sort of power over any member of my family.

But it had me questioning everything. What exactly were Perfidious's intentions? Was he out to eliminate Penelope? Or did he have a new fascination with the Fae? Not that it really mattered. The demon was still dangerous, and regardless of which female he was after, I wasn't about to allow him to harm a single hair on either of their heads.

"I'll go talk to Taayin," I told Asmia.

Before leaving, I pressed a kiss to the top of Penelope's head, then dematerialized, taking form in the main-floor gym.

Weights clattered where Taayin lay on his back, hefting more weight than any mere human could even fathom.

"Talk to me," I said, keeping my voice calm as I weaved through the equipment, making my way over to Taayin.

"Nothing to talk about," my *lieterra* growled.

"On the contrary, I'd say there's a shitload to talk about."

Taayin sat up, his eyes glowing, fangs descended. He looked ready to rip someone's throat out.

Not sure if his rage was directed at Asmia or Perfidious, I felt the need to add my two cents. "This isn't her fault."

His eyes narrowed. "I never said it was."

"She thinks you blame her."

Taayin frowned as he reached for his discarded shirt and wiped his brow. "Why?"

Surely the male wasn't that dense. "I don't know, Taayin. Maybe because you disappeared. Abandoned her."

The realization flittered across the male's face. "What's his motive?"

I leaned back against one of the many machines. "No idea, but I'm certain he was the one to kill the females at the hotel. Sounds like he was stalking the place."

"Never thought his selection was a coincidence," Taayin mused. "But I figured it had to do with Penelope. What does he want with Asmia?"

Good question. Unfortunately, I had no fucking idea. "No telling with Perfidious. But I doubt he's out to hurt her. If he were, he would've done so at the club."

He'd evidently had the opportunity despite the fact she'd been surrounded by angels.

Taayin's gaze dropped to the floor. "Every time I've been with her since ... she's been fantasizing it was him."

If there was a bright side at all, I figured it was good we'd caught it early. As it was, it had only been a full twenty-four hours since they'd ventured to the club. Not that I wanted to know how many times Taayin and Asmia had been intimate during that time.

"Not because she wanted to," I reminded him. "That's not her fault."

"Doesn't make it any easier to handle."

No, I doubted it did.

"She's not my *amsouelot*, but... sometimes it feels like she is. Or at least she should be."

For as long as I could remember, Taayin had been eager to be mated. Then, when Asmia had joined the *fiestreigh*, it was almost as though he had been, the two growing closer with every passing day.

"Have you ever thought maybe it doesn't matter?" I watched Taayin. "So what if the Fates didn't proclaim she's the one your soul's seeking. Doesn't mean you don't love her. Doesn't mean you're not meant to be with her."

Evidently my response was not what Taayin expected because the male stared up at me, eyes wide, mouth hanging open.

"What?" I asked. "If you're walking through this life worried that the female you love isn't the one you're meant to be with, how the fuck do you enjoy the time you have with her?"

"So what am I supposed to do? Pretend she is?"

"For fuck's sake, Taayin. You're supposed to feel. Whatever that may be. Just fucking feel. I wish I could make it easy for you, but I can't. No one can."

As with any who'd been through this, I didn't know how to fix their problems. Even if I could, it wasn't my place to interfere. However, this was a distraction we didn't need. For all we knew, Perfidious could be up to one of his games again, playing us all by diverting our attention.

Before either of us could say anything more, I felt Penelope's pull from across the mansion.

"I have to go."

Not bothering to waste time walking, I vanished my form, reappearing in the kitchen to find Penelope groaning, slumped over the counter.

"Ayreme?"

Penelope's pained gaze lifted, met mine. "Please ... Obsidian."

The others were sitting at the island, wide-eyed as they tried to figure out what to do to help her.

If we'd been alone, I would have eased her right then and there. Since we weren't, I did the only thing I could think of. Lifting her into my arms, I held her close to my chest, then disappeared us both, materializing in our bedroom.

Penelope gasped when we returned to our physical form. It hadn't even dawned on me that the move would be taxing on her body. While teleporting was a nifty trick, it wasn't easy to do, and for someone who'd never experienced it, it could be painful.

"I'm sorry," I whispered, setting her on her feet.

She moaned softly, her eyes closing. I could feel her need. It was intensifying, more so than I expected so soon after I'd first fed from her. I thought for sure we'd have a few weeks' reprieve, a couple of months if we were really lucky. That didn't seem to be the case. In fact, I'd go so far as to say it was more powerful now than before.

"Get them off me," she urged, tugging at her clothing.

"With pleasure, *ayreme*," I whispered, hurrying to remove her clothing even as I allowed my hands to roam over her smooth, warm skin.

She moaned softly, some of the frustration abating.

Before I could shed my own clothing, Penelope was doing the honors, on her feet as she all but ripped my shirt off. I chuckled, pulling it over my head and tossing it aside as she roughly tugged at the button of my fly.

"Careful," I warned. "Don't want to put him out of commission."

"Definitely not." She went up on her toes, pulling my head down so our mouths met.

Her kiss was intense, making my body burn with the need to be inside her.

Penelope groaned, then pulled away.

Expecting her to get on the bed, I nearly fell on top of her when she spun around and bent over the mattress, her sweet little ass beckoning me.

As much fun as that would be, I'd learned from experience our height difference made the position damn near impossible. So rather than bend her over and plunge inside her heat, I picked her up and tossed her onto the bed, following close behind.

I grabbed her hips, jerking them back toward me as I positioned my throbbing cock at her entrance, guiding myself into the heavenly warmth of her.

Penelope's chest dropped to the mattress, hands fisting the blankets as I drove into her from behind. The sexy female made me absolutely crazy. The way she welcomed me inside her, her soft pleas spurring me on. Sometimes I had to remind myself of how fragile she was. Her spirit alluded otherwise, but my significant strength had the ability to hurt her. And when she met me thrust for thrust, it took tremendous restraint to hold myself back, refusing to cause her even minimal pain.

"Obsidian ... make me come!"

I grinned at the demand in her tone, the need.

Even as I proceeded to do exactly that.

PENELOPE

After my interlude with Obsidian, I felt a tad guilty for leaving Asmia in her time of need. Not that I could've done anything to stop it. The desire had surprised me, thrown me off because I'd expected to have a bit of down-time now that Obsidian had fed from me. After all, that was the very reason he'd been holding off.

But now that I was sated—even temporarily—I was on a mission to find Asmia, to help her in any way I could. Perhaps I wasn't the right person to console her, but I couldn't stand the thought of Asmia having to go through this alone. I'd witnessed the scene with my own eyes. Didn't matter that it was a projection of Asmia's memory, it had been so real. And a cheap shot by that damn demon, as far as I was concerned.

I had taken a trek through the mansion before I located the Fae in the library. Apparently, Asmia had shut herself in, probably seeking solitude. I considered that for a moment. What if Asmia didn't want me to interfere? Would I be overstepping? Did it really matter? Everyone needed a friend, right?

With a sigh, I rapped my knuckles on the door after I inched it open and peeked inside.

"Mind if I come in?"

Asmia shrugged.

Taking that as a yes, I ventured into the room, closing the door behind me. The comforting atmosphere hadn't faded, and I understood why someone would come here to be alone. Surrounded by books and words, I couldn't think of a more tranquil place to be.

Attempting to gauge Asmia's mood, I moved around the room, taking stock of the books on the shelves. I smiled when I came to a section of J.R. Ward's novels, another with Sherrilyn Kenyon's. For some reason, I doubted those had been there prior to my arrival at the mansion. Then again, I knew first-hand the appeal those books held, and I certainly wasn't the only fan of those authors.

"Do you read?" I asked Asmia.

"I've read every book in this room," the Fae said softly.

"Even these?" I motioned to the *Black Dagger Brotherhood* series.

Asmia peered over, nodded. "Twice, actually."

I liked that we had that in common.

I managed to pass a few more minutes perusing the spines of the books before I made my way to the sofa. As I took a seat beside Asmia, I realized I didn't have a clue how to broach the subject. Though I wanted to think of Asmia as a friend, I wasn't sure it was my place to intrude on something as personal as her relationship with Taayin. So, rather than launch headlong into advice, I remained silent, figuring Asmia would talk when she was ready.

"How will I ever look at him again?" Asmia finally said, the torment in her tone breaking my heart.

"It's not your fault," I assured her, though I'd already said that, and I doubted it made a bit of difference in the grand scheme of things.

I could practically taste Asmia's despair, and it pained me. While we weren't all that close, I liked her. She was funny and smart and rather entertaining. I'd come to enjoy her stories, whether they were of past events or mere reports or her nights out. Though she looked the part of a fragile, delicate woman, the fairy had some serious steel in her spine. She'd regaled me with stories of her training, and I'd come to realize there weren't many who could go up against Asmia and survive.

Yet right now, she looked like she could be knocked over with a feather.

"Why would Perfidious do that? Why would he mess with me like that?"

There was only one reason I could think of, but telling Asmia that a demon had set his sights on her didn't seem appropriate. I definitely wouldn't want to come to that revelation.

"Do you think he'll ever forgive me?" she prompted, sniffling.

I got up and retrieved a box of tissues from the table, passed it to Asmia when I returned.

"Of course he will. Taayin cares for you."

While I didn't know the details of their relationship, I'd been at the mansion long enough to see there was a connection between Asmia and Taayin. They cared for one another deeply, were, perhaps, even in love.

"I wouldn't blame him if he never spoke to me again."

With a sigh, I pressed my shoulder to Asmia's. "It'll work itself out. Just give it some time."

"Time seems to be all I have these days," the Fae muttered softly.

Not sure what to say to that, I remained silent, leaning gently against Asmia, hoping to comfort.

"How are things with Obsidian?" she asked with a sniffle, clearly wanting to change the subject.

"Good." I smiled. "Very good, actually."

Asmia's gaze dropped to my neck briefly. "I noticed he's feeding from you now."

On instinct, I reached up and touched the marks he'd left just a short time ago, remembering in vivid detail how he'd sunk his fangs into me as his heavy erection had been lodged deep inside me. I'd never felt anything quite so pleasurable. The euphoria I felt when he fed from me had taken me by surprise in the beginning, but now I found I craved it.

"Just wait until you can return the favor," Asmia noted.

I studied her face as thoughts of feeding from Obsidian

danced in my head. Until recently, I hadn't given it much thought, never truly accepting that I might one day be what he was. While it wasn't a subject I was completely comfortable with, there was a certain appeal to the idea.

"Don't worry. It'll be as good for him as it is for you."

"Why is it you don't have to feed?" I asked.

Asmia's gaze swung over to the windows. "I do, but not on blood. Fae feed on emotions. It's one of the reasons we offer ourselves for the pleasure of the males. It sates both needs at one time. Our craving for sex isn't only about the physical aspect. It's more than the release. We draw from the males, use their emotions to sustain us."

"Wish someone would teach me how to do that."

Asmia's curious gaze swung over to me. "Do what?"

"Convert emotions to ... something else." I exhaled heavily. "I'm overwhelmed by the emotions of others. It's been easier since I've been here because I can't sense the emotions of angels or Fae. I tend to do fine as long as I don't interact with Oliver or Winnie much. But out there ... out in the world, it consumes me."

"So you're an empath?"

I nodded. "That's the conclusion I've come to."

"Well, that explains your relationship with your brother," she muttered.

"How so?"

"Oliver's full of anger and rage," Asmia said. "It's even difficult for me to be around him and he would provide plenty of fuel for my existence. In your case, you'd want to keep your distance due to your sensitivities. I think he feels as though you've abandoned him."

I frowned, confused. "Abandoned him?" That was ludicrous. "Oliver's never wanted anything to do with me. Ever since we were kids. Even after our mother left, I needed him, but he shut me out completely."

"But you're twins."

"Yeah. We shared the same womb. That's about it."

"There's something deeper," Asmia said, her eyes serious. "Something inside Oliver that's eating at him. You're not the source of his anger, merely an outlet. I think he knows you'll distance yourself because you have to. He uses that."

"How do I fix it?" I asked, shocked by this revelation. The last thing I would ever want to do was push my brother away, but it made complete sense.

"You can't. Only Oliver can fix it." Asmia placed her hand on my arm. "He will, though. Very soon."

I stared at the Fae, wanting her to elaborate, but she didn't.

"I need to go find Taayin. I need to apologize."

I remained on the sofa when Asmia vanished into thin air. I'd gotten used to that move. They all did it. Randomly, at that. I could be standing in a room, surrounded by angels, and a second later, they were all gone.

It was a rather cool trick, one I wondered if I would be capable of eventually.

24

PERFIDIOUS

I paced the abandoned warehouse, attempting to find a corner far enough away from Seraphina so that I didn't wrap my hands around her neck and squeeze. I'd been fantasizing about it for the past few hours, the idea of sending her back to Hell the only pleasant thought I'd had since I left Asmia at that club. Not that it would do me any good. I doubted I could send her back to Hell and be far enough away.

But that was a nice idea.

"Why are you smiling?" Seraphina asked when she joined me as I made my way into the small, cramped office.

"Just enjoying the fruits of my labor," I told her, holding out my arms to encompass the room.

Her blue eyes slowly scanned the space, taking it all in. "Planning to make this your permanent residence?"

"Permanent's too definitive. But I think I'll maintain it for the time being."

At least until I made my move. Until then, it was imperative that I made Seraphina believe I was working toward the goal.

Turning to face her, I tucked my hands in my pockets. "Any word on whether Obsidian's planning to kill his female so he can bring her back to life on the full moon?"

Seraphina's glossy red lips pulled back to reveal bright white teeth. "It excites me to think of the female's death. Wonder if he'd be opposed to letting me watch?"

"Not really an answer," I told her, though I couldn't care less as to Obsidian's intentions, or the *amsouelot's,* for that matter. However, I wasn't an idiot, and I knew Lucifer was keeping track of their progress.

She pouted nicely. "No word. Though I'm pretty sure they know you were at the club."

The news made me smile. I was hoping they would put two and two together. I wanted them to realize how close I'd been, how easily I could've taken them out. Unfortunately, that would also mean one of those damn warriors had siphoned my mind control right out of Asmia's beautiful head.

Seraphina moved toward me, her blood-red nail scraping a line down my chest. "While I know you're enjoying yourself, you're running out of time, my lord. Should he mate her, you'll no longer have access to her soul."

No, I wouldn't. It would be safely ensconced in Heaven alongside Obsidian's.

Not that I was worried. There were plenty of others I could seek. And once I had Asmia at my side, I could easily locate every single one of them, keep apprised of their progress. And the two of us together would take down Michael's little army, acquiring all of them one by one. I figured the king of Hell would forgive losing Obsidian's soul as long as I delivered the rest.

I peered down, watched as Seraphina slowly released the buttons on my shirt. She didn't stop there, though, going lower, unhooking my slacks, freeing my cock.

"It gets me hot to think about you slaying the female," she rasped, dropping to her knees as she stroked my erection firmly.

What got me hot were thoughts of that blond Fae, the feel of her body against mine, the soft rasp of her voice as she said my name. It thrilled me to know she'd had no idea who I was while at the club, but now… Another smile pulled at my mouth. Now I could only assume Asmia was appalled to know I'd been so close. But in order to have feelings one way or another, she had to think about me.

Closing my eyes, I imagined the lips wrapped around my dick belonged to Asmia. I would kill to get my hands on that female, to get the chance to do dirty things to that lovely body. Make those amethyst eyes glow as she came while I was lodged to the hilt inside her.

I jerked back as sharp fingernails pierced my balls.

Reaching down, I grabbed Seraphina by the hair, yanked her to her feet. "What the fuck was that for?"

"I know you're thinking about her," she hissed, her hand curling around my cock once more. "Thinking about fucking that human."

Human, no. Fae, yes. However, I didn't confirm or deny. No sense pissing off the demon. She was a possessive little bitch, mistaken in her belief that I harbored feelings for her. I couldn't be faulted for enjoying the pleasure she afforded me, but in the end, Seraphina was simply a means to an end, nothing more.

Shoving her toward the desk, I was behind her in an

instant, yanking the scrap of fabric she called a skirt up over her hips. Digging my fingers into her flesh, I rammed myself into her.

Her cry of ecstasy was proof she'd been pushing me on purpose, wanting me to lose control.

The joke was on her because, as I held her in place, fucking her ruthlessly, I closed my eyes, pretended she was Asmia.

Lovely name, lovely ass, lovely everything.

And very, very soon, she would be mine.

For eternity.

OBSIDIAN

As I paced the living room, I listened to my brothers giving their status updates. Nothing much had changed in the past few days—at least not on the *amsouelot* front—and the building frustration was infectious.

At my brothers' insistence, I was imprisoned within the walls of the mansion, protecting my *amsouelot* from the threat we knew was nearby but couldn't quite put our finger on. While I did my best to pretend otherwise, I was growing restless, antsy. I wanted to be out there, helping my brothers. With every passing hour, the tension was rising for each of them.

"Eclipse? How about you?" Stygian's deep voice came through the phone. "Any progress?"

I peered at my brother, noticed the hard lines on his face.

"Aside from keeping an eye on her, I haven't made any progress," Eclipse admitted, the words a dark rumble of disappointment.

"I'm in the same boat, brother," Aphotic said.

"At least you've located yours," Cimmerian grumbled, his frustration prevalent.

"We've got time," I assured them.

"Yeah?" Shadow's angry word snapped through the phone. "It's been a month and a half, for fuck's sake. Not a single one of us has mated. Full moon's tomorrow, Obsidian. Please tell me you've prepared your *amsouelot* for the *lintamair*," he pressed.

"I haven't. But I will."

For all intents and purposes, Penelope was ready. She'd even admitted as much. I knew if I made the request, she'd willingly walk into that mating chamber and lay down her life for me. Truth was, she wasn't the holdup. I was. The thought of...

"Look, I know we thought splitting up was the right thing to do, but I think we need to make some changes," Piceous stated.

"What do you suggest?" Shadow inquired.

"Personally, I think it's best if we return to the mansion. Combine efforts and send out teams in rotation."

It made sense. I couldn't imagine the difficulty of continuing to move from one place to another only to end up disappointed because their intel was insufficient or downright wrong.

"I agree," Cimmerian said.

"Me, too," Shadow chimed in.

"I'll remain where I am," Aphotic said. "But I'll send Rinc back, keep Decebal with me. It's only a matter of time."

"Of which we have no idea how much we have," Eclipse reminded him.

"I hear you, brother," Aphotic said softly.

"I won't be coming in yet. But I can give you Raksa and Viliam," Stygian offered.

I stopped pacing, stared at the phone. "What?"

"I know where she is," he said softly. "At least the vicinity."

Finally some good news.

"Any word on Perfidious? He made a move yet?" Cimmerian asked.

"No," I told him. "But he's close. Gryffyth is fairly certain he's gone to ground nearby, biding his time."

"Seraphina and Sirius?" Stygian asked.

"Nothing on them, but I figure they're with Perfidious," I explained.

"So the brother's safe?" Shadow inquired.

"As long as he's in the mansion, yes." I exhaled heavily. "Pissed but safe."

"If you mate her, you can let him go," Aphotic noted.

I knew that. Didn't make the decision any easier.

Before I could launch into an excuse, I felt Penelope's pull. The heat consuming her called out to my body like a beacon.

As though he sensed the shift, Eclipse looked up at me, nodded.

Without another word, I marched out of the room, down the hall to our bedroom. With every step I took, I felt Penelope, the painful longing that stole her breath, had her thrashing on the bed. For the past month, it had been growing immensely stronger with every passing day. The reprieve we'd expected when I started feeding from her had long since passed. Now it was merely a matter of staying nearby for when it overwhelmed one or both of us.

Throwing the door open, I made a beeline for the bed. “Penelope?”

My female was naked, lying on the bed, face flushed as she moved around, attempting to get comfortable.

“Why didn’t you call me?” I asked, using my mind to strip off my own clothes before joining her.

“You were busy.”

“Never too busy for you, *ayreme*,” I whispered, pressing my lips to hers as she ran her hands over my chest, my shoulders.

“I just want to feel you,” she answered. “To touch you. Plus, I knew you’d come for me.”

“Always, *ayreme*.”

Before I could align our bodies, Penelope halted me by cupping my face.

“Not yet.”

I frowned, confused.

“I want to touch you first.”

“Touch me, *ayreme*. Whatever you need.”

The next thing I knew, I was on my back, my female smiling down at me, her breaths evening out.

“Let me touch you, Obsidian. I need to touch you.”

Her lips were sweet fire on my skin as she trailed down my neck, my shoulders, moving lower. I could only watch, endure. The way her fingers grazed my skin like butterfly wings, barely there, fluttering over me.

These were the moments I cherished, the times when we could explore. They were rare because the *amnigh* wasn’t giving much reprieve. And while I loved being lodged deep inside her, I loved this just as much.

Penelope kissed my chest, inching lower. Her desire morphed with mine, sending flames licking at me. It was nearly unbearable, but the thought of stopping her didn’t occur to me. I could read her intentions. My *amsouelot* was hell-bent on driving me wild with only her mouth.

I widened my legs, allowing her room to settle between them. As she knelt there, the pads of her fingers dragged over me, across my chest, my stomach, moving lower. I sucked in air when she trailed across my hip bones, her heated gaze locked on my cock.

Rather than take me in hand, she teased me with the gentle sweep of her fingers, grazing the sensitive head, down my shaft. Warmth cupped my balls as she palmed my sac. And when her head lowered, it was all I could do to watch. Her pink tongue licking over the head, circling it. Teasing, tormenting.

A deep growl escaped when the blazing heat of her mouth enveloped me.

Penelope was focused on what she was doing, her eyes never meeting mine as I admired the erotic slide of her lips up and down my cock, taking more of me with each pass. It was exquisite torture, a sensual pain unlike anything I'd ever known. Then again, she'd been growing bolder the more time that passed, and I couldn't deny I loved that she wanted to explore me more.

She hummed, the vibrations rattling through me, causing my hips to lift. Her eyes shot up to mine, and there was approval there. Her goal was to pleasure me. And while I was desperate to return the favor, I couldn't seem to move, didn't want this to end.

Her cheeks hollowed as she sucked me deep, dragged her lips over my sensitive flesh before releasing me. She did it again and again, that slight pause before she returned to her ministrations brutal.

Reaching for her head, I guided her back down. This time when she retreated, I urged her to remain as she was, not wanting her to release me from between her lips. Penelope moaned, making my cock pulse.

"*Ayreme* ... sweet love ... suck me."

I dropped my head back with a groan when she did, her mouth moving over me faster, taking me deeper. My female had no idea how hot her mouth was or how wild she made me when she did this. It was a rare treat, one I looked forward to but would never demand.

"Tell me, Obsidian," she whispered, her breath fluttering over my cock. "Tell me what you want."

Tangling my fingers in her hair, I guided her back down. "I want you to suck me."

She shivered, and it was then that I realized she enjoyed the assertiveness, wanted me to guide her.

"Take more of me," I hissed. "As deep as you can."

My stomach muscles clenched as undiluted pleasure slammed into me, the sensitive head of my cock brushing the back of her throat.

"Like that... Fuck." I inhaled sharply. "Just like that, *ayreme*."

Pumping my hips upward, I met every downstroke of her lips, my hand holding her there as she pleasured me in a way no one ever had.

"I want to come in your mouth," I whispered. "Watch you swallow me down."

Another moan, more vibrations. My entire body hardened, my balls drawing up tight to my body. I was so fucking close. Too close.

"You want that, *ayreme*? For me to come down your throat?"

Penelope nodded, never pulling her mouth from my cock.

Using two hands, I palmed her head, held her in place as I pumped my hips upward, gentle thrusts so as not to hurt her.

A dark rumble started in my chest as my release stole over me, robbing me of all my senses. I held her there, my cock pulsing as I came.

A brilliant smile pulled at her mouth as she crawled over me. I brought her mouth down, licked past her lips, showing her how much her actions humbled me. Never in my two thousand years had I ever had anyone bring me such overwhelming pleasure.

"Did you enjoy that?" she whispered, her eyes glittering with pride.

"Always, *ayreme*."

I rolled us slowly, so that my body covered hers.

"Now it's my turn," I warned, grinning back at her.

Taking my time, I tormented her the same way, licking every inch of her as I worked my way down her body. When I settled between her thighs, I slid my hands beneath her ass, lifting her up to meet my mouth. I tortured her the same way, gentle, probing licks, exploring her slick folds, lapping at her juices.

"Obsidian!" Her hands fisted in the blanket, hips rising.

I buried my face between her legs, focused on her clit. My female came apart, writhing and moaning as I overwhelmed her with pleasure.

"Obsidian … Ob—" Penelope cried out, her clit pulsing against my tongue as she came.

In an instant, I was over her, sliding my cock into the slick, hot depth of her body. She welcomed me, her arms wreathing my neck, her sex clenching around me. I took my time, rocking into her, driving us both up once again.

This time, when I launched us over that fragile edge, I fused my mouth to hers, letting her taste all the love I had for her.

• • •

Ten hours later, Penelope was writhing on the bed, as had been the case since my body had answered her earlier call. Since that first exquisite exploration, we'd come together numerous times. We would make love, and no more than forty-five minutes later, she was moaning again, the heat overwhelming us both. I was exhausted, knew she had to be, yet it wasn't letting up.

"Obsidian..." She groaned softly. "What's happening to me?"

"Come here, *ayreme*," I whispered, pulling her over me.

As she straddled my hips, I guided myself inside her.

She moaned, barely moving as she rested her head on my chest. Her hair was damp from sweat and exertion, her voice raspy from exhaustion.

I rocked up into her, slow, steady strokes deep inside her.

"I don't think it's going to stop," she said, her limbs loose and weak.

I was starting to think she was right. As though it was in tune with her needs, my cock remained rock hard, never deflating. Not even as soon as I came.

"I need to sleep," she whimpered, clutching at me.

"I know."

Knowing she was wrung out completely, I remained as I was, pushing inside her, retreating for as long as I could. In an effort to send her over once more, I shifted her beneath me, continued the gentle, rolling motion of my hips until she was clenching around me again.

Penelope offered no words of encouragement, no desperate pleas. Just soft whimpers before her body clamped down on me, triggering my release.

This time, when she went boneless, I forced myself up, found my jeans.

"I'll be right back."

"Okay," she murmured, sleep already taking her.

Not wanting to waste time, I dematerialized, reforming in the medical room. It was a place used more to store supplies for the *heurosp* since angels rarely required medical assistance. I rummaged through the cabinet until I found the sedatives.

"You're going to need something stronger than that," Taayin said, appearing beside me.

"Like what?" I growled.

"Morphine," the *lieterra* said simply.

I spun around, glared at the male. "You want me to pump narcotics into my female?"

"I assume you want her to rest?"

Of course I did. Fuck.

"That'll do the trick," Taayin said. "Give her a reprieve. Hell. Give us *all* a reprieve."

I frowned. "What are you talking about?"

"It's nonstop, Obsidian. The wave of sexual energy seems to have settled over the entire mansion. Constant. Give her the morphine, let her rest for a bit. Give us some time to figure this out."

He passed over a syringe. I stared at it, nodded. "Fine, but let the record show I'm not happy about it."

Then again, I would do anything to ease Penelope's pain. Right now, it seemed as though I didn't have much choice.

Taayin nodded, then disappeared before I did.

25

PENELOPE

Feeling as though my entire body was weighed down, I fought to lift my head, tried to peer around. I could see the shutters were closed, which meant night had turned to day, but I wasn't sure how many had passed.

"Obsidian?"

"I'm here, *ayreme*. Right here."

Turning toward the sound of his voice, I noticed he was sitting in a chair beside the bed, watching over me. He looked exhausted, as though he'd been holding vigil for months, but I desperately hoped that wasn't the case.

"How long have I been out?"

"Roughly ten hours."

Okay, good. Not too long, anyway.

He reached for something. A glass. Water.

My scratchy throat burned with the need for it even as he placed the straw against my lips. Blessed relief came as I sucked the chilled liquid down, draining the glass.

"What's going on? Why am I so tired?"

The words were barely out when the sexual longing slammed into me, brutally painful in its intensity. I moaned, drawing my legs up, trying to ease the ache that resided there, my need for Obsidian overwhelming me. Oddly enough, tears formed, the desire too much for my overtaxed body and mind to handle.

Then I remembered. The incessant need. No matter what we did, it wasn't easing off. The instant I was sated, it would flare up again, more intense until I was consumed by a throbbing, desperate ache.

I was barely aware of Obsidian stripping out of his clothes, joining me on the bed. My limbs were weak, but I seemed to draw strength from him. As his body covered mine, I managed to lift my arms, pulling him down to me.

Obsidian pressed his lips to a tear as it slid down my cheek. "I'm so sorry, *ayreme*."

"It's not your fault."

The look on his face said he didn't agree with me.

"I love you, Penelope," he whispered softly, his eyes beginning to glow.

I could feel his pain as though it were my own. A deep, throbbing ache in my chest. He hated to see me in pain as much as I hated to see him in pain. Right now, it was a vicious, never-ending cycle.

As he settled over me, I stared into his beautiful eyes, watched the silver churn even as they became glassy with what I assumed were unshed tears.

"What's wrong?"

"Tell me you love me, Penelope," he whispered.

"Of course I do."

His hips shifted as he guided himself inside me, pushing in deep.

The friction provided blessed relief, his warm body the blanket of security I needed.

"Tell me," he urged.

"I love you, Obsidian."

His head lowered, his lips brushing my neck as our bodies moved together as one. My body knew exactly what it sought, my hips shifting with his, rocking, the two of us whole for the moment, complete. His love overwhelmed me. I could feel it, the weight of it as it shielded me from all sides, keeping me safe.

But there was something he was holding back.

Not his body. He gave me that willingly, easing the ache as he brought us both the release necessary to sate the heat. For a few minutes, I allowed it to be my sole focus. Kissing his cheek, his neck, I borrowed Obsidian's strength, willing him to feel the love I had for him. I wanted this. Not just now. For eternity.

It became clearer as we moved together, as his emotions seeped into me.

"Penelope..." Obsidian moaned softly. "*Ayreme* ... love me."

"I do," I promised, holding on to him as the pleasure intensified, my core coiling tightly as it sought the release only he could give me. "Obsidian..."

He lifted his head, his silver gaze glowing brightly as he thrust harder, deeper. I was overwhelmed by it, completely surrounded by his love. It was the most incredible feeling, to know he would care for me, that he would pledge his life to me.

"I want this," I whispered. "You. The mating. I want to be yours, Obsidian."

I wanted it more than air. The conviction surprised me,

almost as though it was coming from a part of myself I'd never connected with.

Obsidian's movements became more frantic, driving deep until I was blinded by the pleasure, driven higher than I'd ever gone before. And when my body shattered, I cried out his name.

His head fell back as he roared. I could feel him pulsing deep inside me as he succumbed to his release. Only then did the ache dissolve, my body becoming my own once more. How long that would last was anyone's guess.

"What's happening?" I asked, realizing his eyes weren't returning to normal. They continued to glow brightly, even as he rolled off me, pulling me with him.

I curled up along his side, draping my arm over his torso, holding him close.

He pressed his lips to my forehead. "I love you, *ayreme*."

"Do you not want this, Obsidian? The mating?"

"It's more than what I told you," he whispered. "Not as simple as I made it out to be, Penelope."

The torment in his voice had me lifting my head, meeting his glowing eyes. "What did you leave out?"

He swallowed hard, held my stare. "In order to turn..." He inhaled deeply, exhaled roughly. "Oh, God, Penelope..."

His breaths rasped harshly, as though he was choking back the emotion.

Cupping his face, I urged him with my eyes. "I'm willing to die for you," I assured him. I knew that was in the plan. But it didn't matter.

"It's not that simple." His chest heaved, a strangled sob escaping. "I have to kill you, Penelope."

Jerking back, I scrambled until I was sitting up. "Kill me? As in ... what?" Because there was a big difference between putting me into an eternal sleep and shooting me in the head. Both were tragic and hard to wrap my mind around, but I was willing to succumb to the former. The latter ... not so much.

He propped himself up against the headboard, stared straight ahead.

"It's not only about you dying," he growled. "It's the act, the sacrifice."

"*My* sacrifice?"

He shook his head. "Mine."

Frowning, I waited him out.

"Death isn't meant to be fun," he growled.

"No. Maybe not. But..." Well, I hadn't really considered the logistics of dying. I'd accepted everything he told me, probably a bit too easily. There was no denying it scared me, but I was willing. For him, I was willing.

"I have to make the ultimate sacrifice," he rasped. "To prove my faith in God."

"By killing me?"

"Yes."

I swallowed, tried to wrap my head around it. I'd heard people speak of a vengeful God, but surely He wasn't expecting something morbid, right?

"Okay. So you prove your faith by taking my life," I said, rationalizing it. "Then maybe something that won't hurt. An overdose. I could go to sleep, and when I wake up, I'll be—"

His eyes were cold when they met mine. "I have to drive a dagger through your heart."

My hand instantly went to my chest as though I could protect the fragile organ from such a brutal act.

"Once I do, I'll stand guard over your body. For twenty-four hours, I'm forced to watch over you, to know that I killed you and trust in the Lord to bring you back to me."

"Twenty-four hours? I'll be dead for *twenty-four* hours?"

Obsidian nodded. “When you wake, you’ll feel like you’re trapped in your own body, unable to move, to speak.”

Oh, boy. It just got better and better.

“How long does that last?”

“Only a few minutes.”

Well, thank God for that.

“While I’m dead, will you feel the loss? Like we felt before?” I remembered that moment in the shower at the hotel when I thought he had left.

He nodded. “You’ll be dead, Penelope. My absolute worst fear realized. And I’m forced to endure, to know...”

His breath shuddered, his pain evident. He did not want to do this, although it was the only way we could be together for eternity.

I swallowed hard, then moved over to him, needing to be close, to touch him, to hold him.

“I’m sorry, Obsidian,” I whispered as his arms came around me. “I don’t want you to hurt.”

He jerked me against him, his arms wrapping unbearably tight.

“What happens after that?”

“You’ll feed from me. At that point, when my blood’s running through your veins and yours in mine, we’ll merge. Your memories will become mine and mine yours. Everything I’ve ever done in my life, every heinous act, will flash in your head, Penelope. You’ll know the truth of what I really am.”

I figured that was the easy part. I already knew what and who Obsidian was. His past wouldn’t change how I felt about him. Nothing could change that.

Oddly, not even the thought of him driving a dagger through my heart.

I suddenly realized it wasn’t my pain I was worried about.

It was his.

"Will I experience anything painful after, you know, I die?"

He chuckled, but there was no humor in it. "Blessedly, no."

"And I won't have to cause you any pain?"

He shook his head.

For the longest time, I remained silent, listening to Obsidian's heartbeat against my ear.

"What aren't you telling me?" I asked, sensing he was still holding something back.

"Only that your death has to be precise."

Lifting my head, I peered into his eyes. They still glowed, his emotions still running hot.

"What does that mean?"

"You have to take your last human breath exactly twenty-four hours before the moon is full."

"I suppose you know when that is?"

"In exactly twelve hours."

I swallowed hard, looking at the bedside clock. It was 6:29 p.m.

Obsidian lightly touched my chin, urging me to look at him. "It doesn't have to be now. There's a full moon every month. We could wait."

"But...?"

He released a long, slow breath. "This won't let up. The pain, the longing. It'll only get worse."

I couldn't imagine worse. As it was, I could hardly function. So much that Obsidian had been forced to drug me to give me any peace.

"I'm helpless in this state," Obsidian said softly. "I can't protect you the way you need to be protected. And the fact of the matter is, the demons are close. I need to be able to protect you."

His eyes were so serious, the silver swirling, churning, his pain evident. It wasn't about the effects the *amnigh* was having on us physically. I realized that was what worried him most. Should the demons strike, Obsidian wouldn't be able to protect me. It was his greatest fear, and now it was mine.

I took a deep breath, exhaled slowly as I relaxed against him. I had to die in order to come back. In order to be with him for eternity. I wanted that. Hell, I wanted it more than air. And I wanted to ease his fears and his pain as much as he wanted to do the same.

It was my sacrifice.

Obsidian wasn't the only one being tested. I was, as well.

"Maybe it's not ideal," I whispered, cupping his face as I lifted my head and met his steady silver gaze. "But I'm ready, Obsidian."

Though it didn't even seem rational, it was true.

I couldn't imagine life, or death for that matter, without Obsidian. And I was willing to do whatever it took to be with him forever.

OBSIDIAN

Because neither of us had the strength to make love, I opted to give Penelope another dose of morphine, enough to have her sleeping peacefully.

Once she was under, I called for Asmia to come watch over

her before heading for the sparring gym, pacing back and forth across the room, trying to come to terms with what I had to do.

We now had ten hours before the deadline came upon us. Thanks to the drugs, Penelope wouldn't spend any more time thinking about what was to come or attempting to soothe me. It hadn't exactly surprised me that she had. I'd seen the fear in her eyes. Not for herself but for me. My female worried about what I would go through, the pain it would cause me to take her life. Her love for me was humbling, making it all the more impossible to do what had to be done.

"Hey, what brings you down here?" Taayin asked when he stepped into the room.

I didn't look up, just continued to pace the concrete box, my steps heavy, anger and fear surging through my veins.

"Obsidian?"

"I need you to inform the others the *lintamair* will occur at dawn," I told my *lieterra* as I kept every bit of my attention on the stones in the floor.

There was no snide comment, not even a hint of amusement in Taayin's tone when he said, "Of course, Obsidian. I'll ensure everyone's aware."

I continued to pace even as Taayin slipped out, off to handle the task of preparing the underground chamber where I would spend twenty-four hours mourning the loss of my beloved, and another twenty-four becoming one with her. If only I didn't have to do the former to enjoy the latter. But when had life been simple for any of us? Humans, angels, vampires ... we were all pawns in the game, moved around at God's leisure, forced to endure in our efforts to prove our worth and loyalty.

Until now, I had never questioned my faith, never doubted my ability to do whatever it took to complete the mission. But when it came to Penelope ... nothing mattered more to me than her health and her happiness.

As I thought about driving a dagger through my *amsouelot's* sweet, fragile heart, the anger bloomed hotter, churning, locating the pain and coalescing into a full-blown rage. The emotions made my muscles tense, my fists clenching at my sides again and again as my breaths kept a steady rasp in my constricted lungs. I moved for as long as I could until the pressure became unbearable.

Stopping in the center of the room, I drew in deep, ragged breaths, my face burning hot with temper until I threw back my head and roared.

The Earth rattled beneath me, walls quaking with the power of my rage, chips of stone falling to the floor, dust drifting down from the ceiling.

"Obsidian!"

I bared my fangs when Eclipse appeared.

"You need to relax, brother," the male warned even as he moved deeper into the room. "The last thing you want is to put your *amsouelot* in danger."

The heavy door swung closed, though not by my doing.

I spun around to face my brother, my heart thundering in my chest, a murderous rage throbbing in my veins.

"And what shall you have me do?" I snarled, the words coming out in a deep, thunderous roar, the beast within me taking over. The ache in my chest was too much to bear, driving me to the edge of insanity.

"Whatever's necessary," Eclipse said, his tone firm, controlled. "You want to fight, we'll fight. If it'll help cool your jets."

I snarled again. "You don't want to take me on."

"If it's what you need, then it's exactly what I want." My brother shifted around the room, keeping me in his sights.

Reidar and Magnar appeared, blue eyes locked on me as they tried to determine what was going on.

Eclipse held up his hand to hold the males back. "Taayin's preparing the mating chamber," he explained for their benefit.

The thought of what would take place in that mating chamber ... having to shove a blade into Penelope's chest...

I howled, the pain unbearable.

"It's going to be fine," Magnar said, as though the male had any fucking clue.

My response to the asinine comment was to send a surge of energy at him, driving Eclipse's *ladeare* back into the wall.

Eclipse had known my intention because the instant Magnar's big body slammed into the wall, he rushed me.

The fight ensued, and for the first time since I'd drugged the female I loved more than life, there was a sense of peace. It came with the impact of fists, knees, elbows. Though Eclipse fought back relentlessly, the male was no match for me. Not in this state.

Even when the others joined in, the three of them coming at me with everything they had, they couldn't take me down. Love was a powerful drug, fear more so. The combination of the two made me invincible.

Something moved behind me, and I spun to see Søren there, his blue eyes glowing.

"I don't want to hurt you," I snarled even as I charged Søren, the male rushing me.

We collided. Seconds later, Søren was on his back, laid out on the concrete as I took the others on. Seconds turned to minutes, the four of them coming back for more, each failing as I put every ounce of my rage into every punch, every kick.

It wasn't until the fifth male joined that it became a fair fight. Gryffyth held nothing back as he drilled one punch after another into my torso before I managed to dodge, sending the male into the wall with the force of my fist.

Time seemed to stand still as the five of them ignored the

pain, giving me an outlet for the fury that consumed me. The fear. The pain. There was no way to bury it, so I resorted to violence, desperate for a reprieve but knowing none would come. Taking Penelope's life would likely kill me. Didn't matter that it was necessary.

Then the violence turned to turmoil. My knees crashed into the floor beneath me, a ragged howl escaping as the pain became more than I could bear.

Magnar, Søren, and Reidar dropped to a knee around me while Eclipse shouldered the burden, holding me up, arms embracing as he attempted to comfort me. It wouldn't work, but I appreciated the effort. These males were my family. As the rage turned into agony, I sobbed, leaning into Eclipse, battling the terror that came with the thought of taking my *amsouelot's* life. Even a never-ending afterlife didn't make the thought any easier.

Nothing would make the pain of my task any easier.

The next eight hours were brutal. I paced the mansion, checked on Penelope, slipped out again. I couldn't sit still. Unable to eat, drink, speak. Throughout, I felt the return of my brothers, the presence of the *fiestreigh*, the Fae. They'd all descended on the mansion in a show of solidarity, though keeping out of sight. At one point, I was even aware of the *dhira* being erected, protecting the mansion with the strength of all my brothers.

I was in our bedroom when Penelope roused again.

As I expected, the instant her eyes opened, the heat overwhelmed her. The only relief I found was when I was with her, buried deep inside her, holding her as she loved me like no other ever had, like no other ever would.

I could tell she was keeping her eye on the clock, knew she

was counting down the minutes to her impending death. I was doing my best to ignore it, wishing there was another option, fearing I would fail her, because as the moment grew near, I wasn't sure I could go through with it.

"Shower with me," Penelope said when we were both sated for the time being.

Lifting her into my arms, I carried her into the shower, took my time washing her, feeling her warm skin against my palms, her sweet heartbeat thudding in my ears. I couldn't seem to stop touching her.

She was the one who shut off the water, took my hand, led me out of the shower.

"Penelope..." Cupping her face, I stared into her eyes, searching for the truth.

"I've come to terms with this, Obsidian," she said softly. "I want you to as well."

There wasn't a hint of fear in her mind, only acceptance and love. She was the strongest female I'd ever encountered, and even now, it was humbling to know she was mine.

There was a knock at the door.

"It's Acadia," I warned Penelope.

She retrieved two robes, handed one to me while pulling the other on, then left me alone while she went to answer it.

When she returned, her eyes were intent. "It's time, Obsidian."

I nodded, knowing the others would take over, perform their tasks. Moving of their own volition, my legs carried me into the closet. I dragged on a pair of jeans, didn't bother with anything else. When I emerged, Taayin was there waiting for me.

I paused beside Penelope, cupping her face and kissing her softly. "I love you, *ayreme*."

"I love you, too."

Feeling as though I was walking to my own death, I followed Taayin out of the room, through the mansion, down below. The hard stones beneath my feet a steady reminder I was about to do the unthinkable.

As we descended deeper beneath the mansion, to the lowest level, my heart began to pound harder against my ribs.

It wasn't until we stepped out of the stairway that I felt a modicum of relief.

All of my brothers and the *fiestreigh* were there, standing tall, each dressed head to toe in black, armed to the teeth, prepared to protect me in battle in the event it came to that. Even the Fae had joined in, the females wearing black silk gowns, the color of mourning. More than sixty who vowed their loyalty and protection, standing guard to ensure our safety.

I swallowed past the lump in my throat as Taayin led the way around to where my brothers stood sentry beside the door.

I paused before each of them, accepting their promises to watch over us both. It was all I could do to nod, their words getting buried beneath the onslaught of emotional pain that consumed me.

Taayin opened the heavy door, allowed me to make my way inside.

As the door closed behind me, I took a deep breath.

Alone with my thoughts was probably not the best place for me right now.

The flutter of feathers sounded seconds before Michael appeared.

I didn't have the strength to offer the archangel the respect he deserved. "Why are you here?"

"To bring this," Michael replied, holding out his hand.

My knees weakened when I saw the Jagdkommando

dagger. It was one of the deadliest knives in existence. The triple-edged blade was seven inches long and curved, thick enough to penetrate quickly. Once impaled in the heart, the victim would bleed out in seconds, death imminent.

The victim being the female I adored.

Ignoring the dagger and the uninvited guest, I inhaled deeply, trying to clear my mind.

"It's the hardest thing you'll ever do," Michael said, his voice low, sympathetic.

"And how do you know this?" I snarled, lifting my gaze and pinning Michael with a glare hot enough to melt steel.

"Because I've been where you are, warrior."

I frowned. I'd known the archangel my entire life, not once had I heard that Michael had found his *amsouelot*. Then again, the male wasn't open about his personal life, not even with me.

"You will survive this. As will she."

"Why?" My voice cracked. "Why must I take her life?"

"To prove your faith, warrior. To prove your worth, not only to God but to your mate. I will watch over her at all times," Michael promised. "I will ensure she makes it back to you."

Though the promise should've consoled me, it did nothing to ease the constriction in my chest. Not even when Michael vanished, leaving me alone.

Dropping to my knees once more, I felt the coldness seep through me as the tears fell unbidden.

26

PENELOPE

"Relax," Acadia urged as she brushed out my hair.

I barked a mirthless laugh. "Easy for you to say."

The Fae met my eyes in the mirror. "You're right. I apologize."

I huffed. "Don't apologize."

While I dealt with the anxiety twisting in my gut, Acadia had spent the past half hour preparing me for this ritual. After dressing me in a gauzy white gown that looked as though a virgin sacrifice should wear it, the fairy had dolled up my face with makeup even as I wondered why she bothered, why Acadia was going through all the trouble considering I was about to die, other than it offered me a distraction I desperately needed.

"Leave it down," I said when Acadia reached for a pin. "Obsidian likes my hair down."

She smiled at me in the mirror. "You're right. He does."

The Fae dragged her slender fingers through my hair once more, settling it over my shoulders.

"I know you're stalling," I told her. "It won't do any of us any good for you to do that."

My belly fluttered with nerves, which seemed a bit awkward for a woman who was about to walk to her death. I should've been terrified, cowering in the corner, pleading for my life. Only, there was a sense of peace inside me that both shocked and confused.

"Not stalling, per se. More like passing time. I saw Obsidian's face. I know he's dreading this. Rightfully so."

I heard the pain in Acadia's voice, felt it echoing inside me. I couldn't imagine what he must be feeling. Nothing in this world could ever give me the strength to take his life. Even the thought made my chest ache.

"How does anyone do this?" I mused, staring at her reflection.

"Love is powerful," Acadia said softly. "Makes us do things we'd never imagined we would do. Gives us strength when it feels futile, gives us hope when everything seems hopeless. It's the one thing so many take for granted."

My gaze flipped to the Fae. "You've found love before, haven't you?"

Acadia swallowed. "I have, yes. But it wasn't meant to be."

"Who is it? The male you're in love with?"

Acadia's amethyst eyes lowered. "Kaj."

"The vampire?"

"Yes."

"Is he your *amsouelot*?"

Acadia shook her head. "Fortunately, no."

"Fortunately?" I didn't understand. "Why wouldn't you want him to be?"

"It's not about want," Acadia said softly. "We all must make sacrifices." Acadia's back straightened. "Speaking of sacrifices, we must go now."

Taking a deep breath, I gave my reflection one last glance, then nodded.

Acadia took my hand, helped me to my feet. It was then that I realized my knees were trembling, my muscles weak. Was I really going to do this?

The answer came in the form of my legs moving as I followed Acadia to the door, out into the hallway, through the living room. I'd been this route a hundred times over the past few weeks, but it all seemed different now.

When we reached the second-floor landing, Zeus and Aphrodite were there, sitting patiently as though waiting for me.

Unable to resist, I took a moment to pet their soft heads.

Acadia cleared her throat, clearly paying attention to the time.

Forcing one foot in front of the other, I followed the Fae down the next flight of stairs, surprised to see the dogs were walking alongside me, as though protecting me.

I came up short in the kitchen when I saw Oliver setting a jug of orange juice on the counter.

His shrewd gaze ran over me quickly. "Where're you going?"

"I'll be back soon," I assured him, not wanting to get into the details. Despite our issues, I wasn't sure Oliver would allow me to go if he knew I was about to die.

As I continued my trek, I was grateful I hadn't encountered Winnie. No way could I look at my best friend and not spill the beans. That was the last thing any of us needed.

"Where are you taking me?" I said conversationally as Acadia led the way to the stairs leading beneath the mansion.

"It's known as the mating chamber. They built it for this purpose. Because *amsouelots* are out of commission during the *lintamair*, they wanted a safe place where no one could bother them. It's the best-kept secret in the mansion. No one sees it unless they're going into it."

"What's in there?"

"You'll see soon enough."

I took a deep breath and exhaled slowly as Acadia opened a door. A dark stairwell led deeper underground. Zeus and Aphrodite waltzed in before us, scurrying down the narrow steps.

"How many levels does this place have?"

"This is the lowest. It's the most protected."

Once we'd descended about forty steps, we came upon another door.

"Protected from what?"

Acadia opened the door, and my breath hitched.

"Everything," she said simply. "We will all remain here until the two of you emerge. At no time will either of you be left undefended."

Down on one knee, heads bowed, were all of the angels I'd met since I had arrived, as well as many I hadn't. The line curved in both directions, disappearing around the circular hallway surrounding what I assumed was a room in the center.

Acadia took my hand, holding it as she led the way around.

When we stopped in front of a closed door, my breath locked in my throat. Clearly sensing my unease, Acadia turned to face me, took my other hand.

"When you and Obsidian emerge, you'll be forever united with the male you love, Penelope. And stronger because of the love that binds you."

I swallowed hard, nodded.

"Remember, Obsidian needs your strength as much as you need his. It's the reason you were chosen for him. Only your soul is strong enough to protect his."

My head bounced with jerky movements, mostly agreement, understanding, mixed in with more than a little trepidation.

Stygian stepped to the side, allowed Acadia to open the door. Aphrodite and Zeus sat on either side of the door, staring up at me as though they knew what was about to happen.

As soon as the door opened, there was a flutter of sound from the hallway. I peered down, noticed the angels' wings had appeared, spread wide, overlapping one another. A protective shield guarding what was behind them.

It sent a reassuring chill across my skin to know they were there even though my nerves jangled loudly.

I forced my heart to slow as I turned my attention to my destination. Just inside the room, I saw Obsidian on his knees, head hanging down. His wings were out, hanging limply behind him, shoulders slumped as though defeated.

In that moment, nothing else mattered except going to him, easing his pain however I could.

The door closed firmly behind me, sealing us inside as I rushed over to Obsidian. His head lifted, eyes glowing bright. He reached for me but didn't get to his feet, as though his weight was more than his legs could handle.

"*Ayreme*," he whispered, his voice ragged and torn.

I stepped in close, cradling his head when he pressed his face against my stomach, arms circling my waist. He remained like that for the longest time, until I began to worry that our time was running out.

I scanned the room, looking for a clock. There, on a small table, was a vintage alarm clock. The short hand was just past the six, the long hand just past the four, which meant we were down to mere minutes. From what I'd gathered, the full moon was at 6:29 a.m. tomorrow. As it was, I was to be taking my last human breaths in the very near future.

"Obsidian. It's almost time." My voice trembled, my anxiety level rising. It took everything in me not to run for the door, escape. The only thing that kept me firmly rooted in place was my love for the angel before me. I knew deep in my heart that he would keep me safe, even now. Even as he took my life to give me another.

He cleared his throat, then pushed to his feet. His wings fluttered and moved, a perfect extension of him.

Towering over me, larger than life, was the most amazing man I'd ever had the pleasure of meeting. Oddly, I didn't fear my own death. Even if I never woke, I knew the time I'd had with him—although far too short—had been worth every second. I wouldn't have traded it for a lifetime with anyone else.

Obsidian was breathing hard, short, raspy breaths that seemed to punch out of him. His eyes raked over my face as though he was converting it to memory.

Taking his hand, I lifted it to my lips. "I love you, Obsidian. I'm not scared and don't want you to be, either."

His eyes met mine, the silver swirling, glowing brightly.

"We'll get through this," I promised him. "Together. When I wake, you'll be waiting for me."

I had no idea where my strength came from, but I got the feeling it was directly linked to this man, the one I loved with my whole heart.

A single tear fell down his cheek, making my chest burn.

I reached up, wiped it away. "This is our destiny. Remember that."

I glanced at the clock. Two minutes, which meant he

needed to take that vicious knife in his hand, or this would've all been for naught. I wasn't keen on the idea of going through it all again next month.

Lifting the long, flowing skirt on my gown, I hurried over to the table, retrieved the knife. It was heavier than I expected it to be, but I managed to keep it in my trembling hand. The light bounced off the swirling, deadly blade, and I faltered but only briefly.

"Penelope..." I could hear the plea in Obsidian's tone. He didn't want to do this any more than I did.

Sucking in air, I passed the knife over to him.

He gripped the handle in one big fist, eyes lifting to my face.

"I love you, Obsidian."

Resigned to my fate, I squared my shoulders, steeled myself for the blade to pierce my heart. I managed to keep my eyes open despite the fact I was now trembling uncontrollably.

He stood there, unmoving, a pleading look that broke my heart.

I could hear the seconds ticking away.

"You have to do this," I said more firmly, needing him to pull himself together.

His silver gaze began to glow even more until the room was awash in a brilliant light. The enormous wings at his back spread wide, as though he needed the power they would provide him.

I drew on my internal strength, my love, because I knew I had to show it to him, to allow him to know this was what was necessary for us to be happy, to be safe, to live an eternity together. It was no longer about my fear; it was about my love for him. My need to protect *him*.

"Obsidian," I snapped, eyes darting over to the clock, then back to his.

He held still, eyes boring into mine. Another tear fell, triggering a few of my own. I hated that they fell, but I couldn't stop them.

"Obsidian!" I screamed.

His trembling hand lifted, his voice a rough rasp when he said, "Close your eyes, *ayreme*."

I did.

Aware of his deep inhale, I braced for impact, but nothing prepared me for the blade as it pierced through skin and bone. My breath escaped as searing pain ignited in my chest cavity, blinding. I forced my eyes open, wanting to see his beautiful face once more. Just in case.

I was vaguely aware of Obsidian holding me, tears pouring down his face, ragged sobs escaping as he gently lowered me to the floor. Those enormous wings curled around us, shielding me. I gasped for air, and even that hurt. My lungs no longer worked to send oxygen where it needed to go. This wasn't pain, it was white-hot agony scorching me. I couldn't stop the tears, though I tried as hard as I could. I didn't want Obsidian to hurt any more than he already was.

"I love you," I rasped, my vision going white as I struggled for the air that never filled my lungs.

Then, finally, after what seemed an eternity, the pain eased, a strange warmth overcoming me. It was almost pleasant, erasing the torment my body had endured.

I stared up at Obsidian, smiled.

The last thing I saw before my vision faded completely was his beautiful, tormented face.

The last sound I heard was Obsidian's ferocious sobs and the thunderous growl of him calling my name.

Just when I thought the moment would never end, everything went black.

But only for a second.

In the next instant, I was surrounded by a sea of endless white. Blinding yet soothing as it chased away the cold that had filled my bones.

"There you are, my blessed child."

It took a moment to orient myself, but I realized I was lying on a bed, a feather-soft pillow beneath my head, sheer curtains swaying in the soft, comforting breeze.

"Who's there?" I asked, glancing around, trying to find the source of the words.

The curtains were drawn back slowly, moving of their own accord, and the most beautiful woman I'd ever seen appeared, the light shimmering around her as though she was the source of it. Probably not a woman, I thought. An angel.

"We've been waiting for you, Penelope Jane Calazans."

"We?"

Two more angels appeared, equally beguiling, almost too perfect to be real.

"Are you the Fates?" I asked.

A pleased smile formed on each of their faces, their iridescent silver eyes shining brightly.

"I'm Nevaeh," the one who had greeted me first said. "And these are my sisters. Adorah and Karma."

"You're a very brave female," Adorah said softly.

Suddenly, panic set in. "Wait. If I'm... I can't be in Heaven. I can't. I need to be with Obsidian."

Nevaeh's soft fingers settled reassuringly over my hand. "This *is* Heaven, sweet child. But don't worry, you're only here temporarily. I assure you, Obsidian's waiting for your return. Trust us."

I nodded, somewhat relieved. If you couldn't trust an angel, who could you trust?

"Come, Penelope. Let's have some tea."

When they moved away, almost as one, I followed,

climbing down from the bed, my bare feet securely planted on the white marble floor. Though devoid of all color, the room was serene and beautiful. Exactly what one would imagine being in Heaven would be like.

Nevaeh opened a set of French doors before stepping out into a courtyard. Overhead was a crystal-clear blue sky, fluffy white clouds moving by, far closer than they should've been.

The structure built up around the serene space resembled something out of Greek mythology. Marble columns loomed high above, disappearing into the clouds. In the center was a beautiful fountain, water cascading over the thick-edged bowl it was contained in. I was urged toward a small white bistro table while two more women—or rather, angels—came over, one carrying a teapot, the other a plate with what appeared to be cookies.

For whatever reason, that delighted me. The thought of the angels sharing tea and cookies made me smile.

Nevaeh chuckled, a lyrical sound like the softest of lullabies, so sweet and gentle it made me wonder if I'd actually heard it.

"I can certainly see why Obsidian's so enthralled with you."

"You can?"

The angel nodded, then lifted the delicate teacup to her lips, blew on the liquid before sipping.

"Well, the feeling's quite mutual," I assured her. "I love him."

Nevaeh smiled warmly. "There's no need to convince us. It's in your eyes, Penelope. Your strength is your most powerful feature."

I dropped my gaze to the table. "I've never considered myself strong."

"Oh, but you are," Karma said, the soft intonation of her

voice soothing. "Think about the things you've endured. Your mother leaving, your father's denial. You supported the men in your life without receiving their kindness in return. Yet they've always known you were their rock, their strongest support. And you've persevered, shown Obsidian a love beyond all expectation."

"It all seemed to happen so fast," I admitted.

"In the grand scheme of things, time is irrelevant, Penelope," Adorah said. "Humans have irresponsibly learned to measure the depth of their emotions based on the passing of time. In truth, love knows no bounds. Not time, not distance. It merely is. You knew you loved Obsidian the moment you set your eyes on him, and he you. That's true love. The kind not steeped in measurement of any kind."

"It's true," I admitted, perhaps finally accepting it. "The moment I saw him, I knew he was important to me." I studied each of their faces. "But I thought that was your doing. You selected me for him."

Nevaeh smiled, set her cup down. "That's a misconception, sweet child. We have no say in the matter. We don't select one's mate. Your soul connects with the one meant to make you the strongest. And when it does, we simply seal your fate, guide you toward one another. From there, we guard your souls."

"But I'm human," I countered. "How did my soul seek Obsidian's?"

"Because you're special, as are all mortals who'll mate with a warrior."

"I miss him," I admitted.

"As you should. He misses you, as well."

"Is he all right?" I asked, needing to know.

Adorah lifted her hand. A vision appeared. Obsidian kneeling over my body, his head resting on my chest as though listening for my heartbeat, wings covering me like a blanket. He wasn't moving, but I could sense the pain in him.

Adorah's hand lowered, the image fading.

Tears formed in my eyes. "I don't like the idea of him being alone for so long. He has to endure a full day of this."

The smile that formed on their faces confused me.

Nevaeh reached over, touched my hand. "My sweet child, your day is up."

"What do you mean? I just got here." Panic set in. What if they weren't sending me back? What if I was stuck here for eternity? I didn't want to be without Obsidian. The thought had more tears springing forth.

"Relax, sweet child. Time simply moves much faster here."

Something caught my eye, or rather someone. My attention shifted to the man moving toward us. He had wings spread wide, armor covering his chest, metal faulds hanging down to protect his hips and thighs, a sword tucked into a sheath at his side. His gaze skimmed briefly over me before he looked at the others, nodding ever so slightly.

Nevaeh reached for my hand, then got to her feet. I followed suit, standing before her as she took my other.

"Take care of that dear boy, Penelope. In the coming years, he'll need you more than he ever has."

Before I could ask what that meant, a flash of light blinded me. I felt as though I was free-falling in darkness. There was no sound, no light, but there was also no fear. Suddenly, I came to a halt, still immersed in pitch-black, but I felt at peace, as though I was home.

"Penelope."

Obsidian's ragged voice drew me to him, though I couldn't move, couldn't see. It was as though I was entombed. My eyes wouldn't open, but I could hear him.

There was no pain, no sadness. I could sense the comfort of the room I'd been in with him, his warmth, his love.

I'm here, Obsidian.

Above all else, I needed him to know that.

OBSIDIAN

"*Ayreme* ... come back to me. Please. I need you." Though I spoke the words aloud, I could hardly hear them over the pounding of my own heart.

I could feel Penelope's presence. It had eliminated the brutal, devastating cold that had seemed never-ending.

My bones ached as I attempted to move from the position I'd remained in from the moment she drew her last breath. As my wings retracted, I forced the pain away, gently sliding my arms beneath her. I stood tall, staring down into her beautiful face, awaiting the moment she would open her eyes.

The door to the mating chamber appeared, the one only *amsouelots* were allowed to enter. As I approached, it opened, revealing a room right out of a fairy tale.

Well, technically, it was a room right out of Penelope's sweet, considerate mind. One that encompassed all the dreams she'd ever had for a moment such as this. A gift from Heaven.

The enormous round bed stood in the center of the room, a curved, upholstered headboard on one side, sheer curtains hanging down from silver rods overhead, concealing the plush comforter, which was a sparkling silver with thick white pillows tossed about. There was a solid wall of windows, the thin curtains revealing the sun as it rose beyond. For only this moment in time, I could feel the sun on my face the way Penelope obviously wished for us. The connected bathroom was an exact replica of the one in our room now, and it filled me with pride that my *amsouelot* found pleasure in it.

Settling her on the bed, I moved beside her, brushing her hair back from her face. The blood stain that had marred the gown she wore disappeared, no longer a stark reminder of the pain I had inflicted.

When her eyes drifted open, they immediately settled on my face, glittering gold and washing away a little more of my despair.

"There you are," I whispered, smiling as another tear fell down my cheek. Those tears had been present from the second I'd lifted that blade, driven it into her precious beating heart.

Penelope didn't move, didn't speak, but I knew she had come back to me. I remained close, ensuring she knew I was there with her. Never would I leave her. Not ever again. And I would see to it that there was no more pain, either.

The minutes ticked by as I felt her strength returning, her body coming to life slowly. First, her heartbeat sounded loudly in my ears. Her chest began to rise and fall with her breaths. Her arms twitched, fingers, too. Until finally, she turned her head and smiled at me.

I couldn't have fought the emotion if I'd wanted to. Having spent the past twenty-four hours watching over the female who owned me, heart, body, and soul, it was surprising there were more tears, but I couldn't seem to stop them.

Penelope's warm hand lifted, wiped the wetness from my cheeks before she brought my head down, our lips brushing.

"Obsidian... I love you."

Her voice was the sweetest sound, filling my chest with warmth, chasing away the last of the cold loneliness.

"Oh, how I missed you," I replied.

"I'm here now."

I pressed my lips to hers, a soft brush of my flesh to hers. I found I couldn't stop, loving the way her breaths fanned my lips. She moaned softly when I slid my tongue into her mouth, licking against hers as her strength returned, her body shifting ever so slightly beneath me.

"I can hear your heartbeat," she whispered. "It's so loud in my ears."

Pulling back, I stared down at her. "You need to feed, *ayreme*."

She smiled, her hand moving to her lips. It was then she slid her tongue along the pointed canines inside her mouth. She giggled softly, as though pleased with the idea of having fangs.

Her eyes dropped to my neck briefly, then lifted.

The next thing I knew, I was on my back, chuckling at her brute strength. My beautiful female straddled me, her fingers lacing with mine as she raised my arms over my head, pinning me there. I could only stare, letting the life I saw in her comfort me.

My skin prickled with warmth as I thought of her mouth at my vein. I wanted nothing more than to supply the blood that would give her strength.

"I love you, Obsidian."

I smiled. "I love you, too, *ayreme*."

Her steady gaze raked over my face, her eyes glowing as her fangs descended.

Turning my head to the side, I bared my neck for her. "Feed from me, love."

Hesitantly, she lowered her head, her tongue sliding over my skin, hardening my entire body. There was a slight scrape as she teased. And when her fangs sank into my flesh, I went rock hard, a euphoric feeling coating my mind, leaving me breathless. Had I been inside her, I would've come. Something I intend to do in the very near future.

For the longest time, Penelope fed from my vein, and I could feel her more intensely as my blood began flowing in her veins, uniting with hers. I remained still until she sealed the wounds on my neck, her mouth trailing along my jaw, finding my lips once more.

With her fingers still linked with mine, I rolled us, coming over her and kissing her softly.

"Are you ready?"

Her eyes narrowed, curiosity glittering in her brilliant gold gaze. "Where're we going?"

"Trust me?"

"Always and forever."

Love made my chest expand. Somehow I managed to shift my legs off the bed, pulling her along with me.

Taking her hand, I led her into the bathroom. With the power of my mind, I lit the hundreds of candles placed throughout, extinguishing the light overhead so that the candle glow was all that remained.

After removing my jeans, I turned to face her, taking both of her hands in mine. I stepped backward, leading her into the thigh-deep water, admiring the way the white gown molded to her perfect curves as the sheer fabric left nothing to the imagination. Easing myself down onto the wide ledge, I turned her so that she faced away from me, guiding her onto my lap. It was the same position I'd held her in that night at the hotel in Vegas, back when she'd taken a chance on me for the first time.

"This is the ritual?"

I grinned, kissing her neck as I ran my hands down her body, gripping the gown and inching it up her calves, her thighs. With the drenched fabric in my fists, I raised it upward, drawing it over her head and tossing it aside.

"I'm leading us into it," I assured her. "No need to rush."

Holding her against me with one arm banded around her ribcage, I reached for the rose-scented oil, poured some into my hand. I took my time, massaging every inch of her. Fingers, palms, wrists, working my way up her arms to her shoulders. I'd thought about this for the past twenty-four hours. Touching her, feeling her warm skin against my hands. The sight of her lying there, lifeless and cold, had almost killed me, and I vowed never to take her for granted.

When the oil wore off, I added more, coating her glistening skin, working my hands over her breasts.

"Mmm."

"Like that?"

"Very much."

Penelope rested her head against my chest as I allowed my hands to glide beneath the water. I gently kneaded the muscles in her thighs, spreading them wide, stroking her only briefly with the barest brushes of my fingers against her clit.

"You're a tease," she groaned as I shifted her so that I could access her feet.

"I'll make it up to you, I promise."

With her eyes closed, I admired my mate, the way she relaxed as I worked the tension out of her, ensuring I didn't miss anything along the way.

Once I completed the full-body massage, I carefully dried us both, then carried Penelope back to the bed. Her eyes followed me as I moved around the room, retrieving the stones before joining her.

"Lie back."

Penelope centered herself in the bed, then rested her head on one soft pillow.

After tossing the others to the floor, I reached for her. "Give me your hand."

She held up her right hand, and I positioned her arm, elbow turned, wrist near her head, palm up, before setting the color-changing gem in the center of it, then closing her fingers over it. I did the same with her other hand, another gem tucked in her palm.

"What are they?" Penelope asked.

"Alexandrite," I explained. "The gem representing my birth."

"They're warming," she said, watching as I crawled onto the bed, kneeling between her spread thighs.

As she lay there, positioned so seductively, I couldn't resist the urge to touch her. I teased her sensitive flesh with my fingers, dipping one inside her briefly, making her moan. My tongue itched with the need to lap at her sweetness, so I gave in to the desire. Keeping my eyes on her face, I leaned down, pressed my lips to her hip, then slowly inched lower, caressing her smooth, hairless mound. When I separated her slick folds, Penelope gasped. And when I dipped my tongue through her slit, she whimpered. I feasted on her for long minutes, building her desire but not pushing her to the brink.

"Obsidian ... please. I need to feel you inside me."

Not wanting to deny her, I worked my lips up her body, pausing at her nipples, licking, suckling, before inching higher. Once I was positioned over her, I guided my cock toward the entrance of her body. As I pushed in deep and slow, I groaned, her warmth consuming me, sending chills skating down my spine. She humbled me, the way her body accepted mine so easily, greedy in its need for more.

Penelope moaned softly, her eyes never leaving my face.

Holding myself above her, I worked my hips, pushing in, retreating slowly. I could've remained like that for eternity, sinking into the glorious heat of her, feeling her soft flesh against mine.

"I love you," I whispered, watching as her golden eyes brightened, the color igniting from within, brightening until the room was bathed in brilliant gold.

I let it all in, the emotions building within me as I absorbed her warmth and light, her love.

I retrieved the moonstones I'd set aside, one in each hand. Resting my weight on my forearms, I twined our fingers, feeling the magic of the stones combining. The alexandrite gems and moonstones sealed in our joined palms. I did the same with the second stone, and when both of our hands were clasped together, I felt the power.

Penelope's beautiful eyes widened as the warmth radiated through her and into me, hearts, bodies, and souls joining for eternity.

"Obsidian..." Penelope's head tipped back, hips bucking as her fingers tightened on mine.

Retreating slowly, I pressed my lips to the center of her chest, then rolled my hips forward, thrusting deep. Her knees drew up, clutching my hips as I rocked forward, back, taking us both higher. I drove into her, barely able to breathe for the overwhelming intensity of it all.

"Look at me," I commanded.

Her head tilted, eyes opened.

"Let me in, Penelope. All of me. I want to feel you."

Her warmth infused me from the inside out.

"Love me, Penelope," I whispered, though I doubted she realized it for the plea that it was. There was still an underlying insecurity within me, probably would always be there.

As I moved inside her, I met her gaze, held it.

"My heart and soul belong only to you," I whispered. "From this night until eternity, it is I who will ensure your strength, provide you with light, and accept the same in return should you willingly accept me."

Penelope's eyes turned glassy with unshed tears. "My heart and soul belong only to you, Obsidian. From this night until eternity, I will accept your strength and your light, and give you mine in return."

Fusing my mouth to hers, I kissed her, our bodies joined as one.

In that instant, images began flashing in my mind. All of her memories, every second of her existence, came into my head. She tensed beneath me as I covered her body, continuing to move inside her as we merged, minds, bodies, souls. First, the memories, then our combined strength. Her fingers tightened on mine as she thrust her hips upward. I drove into her, deep and slow, cherishing the feel of her. Her body vibrated beneath mine as she absorbed my energy, my powers.

For one breathless instant, my strength was depleted, draining out of me entirely, leaving me completely vulnerable. For that brief moment in time, I was as human as she had been. Mortal, defenseless.

"Obsidian!" Penelope cried out as I ground my hips against hers, burying myself to the hilt in her tight sheath.

"Drink from me, *ayreme*," I commanded, bringing her wrist toward my mouth as I lowered my head closer to hers.

As though she'd been waiting for that moment, Penelope sank her fangs into my neck at the same time I pierced the vein in her wrist. It was then that we merged completely. The shockwave that hit me was so powerful I nearly lost my grip on her hands. I clasped her fingers firmly as my strength returned with a vengeance, far more powerful than before.

Penelope whimpered, then her body clamped down on me

so violently I hissed, unable to stave off the release that threatened. I bucked my hips, driving into her once, twice. When I came deep inside her, I threw my head back and roared, the thunderous echo extinguishing the candles, leaving us together in darkness, the only light coming from within.

Penelope was panting, her eyes wide as she stared up at me. The slow smile that pulled at her mouth kick-started my heart, my breaths slowly returning to normal.

I licked the wounds on her wrist, closing them. "That was..."

"Incredible? Cataclysmic? Life changing?" she supplied as she sealed the wounds on my neck.

I chuckled at the giddiness in her tone.

Releasing her hands, I gathered the stones, set them aside before rolling, bringing Penelope with me. I was still hard, still lodged deep inside her. When she was straddling my hips, I sat up, holding her tightly as she began to move, grinding her hips, taking all of me inside her.

Her arms curled around my head, fingers sinking into my hair as our bodies moved together once more. Two halves of a whole, intimately joined, completing one another in a way nothing else ever would.

This time, when I came deep inside her, it was with the knowledge that I would spend the rest of eternity with her at my side, and me at hers.

A sense of peace settled over me, perhaps the most compelling emotion of all.

27

PENELOPE

I had to admit, this newfound power left me awestruck, even though I had no clue what to do with it, how to harness it.

Every one of my senses was heightened. I could smell the sweetness of the rose oil in the adjoining bathroom, the heady aroma of sex, along with the potent, musky scent of the male I adored. I could hear the gentle lap of the water, the strong, steady beat of Obsidian's heart. I could see the silver fibers in the comforter beneath us, the dust motes drifting in the air. And I could still taste the richness of Obsidian's blood that had passed over my tongue.

But it was my sense of touch that mesmerized me most. Obsidian's smooth, warm skin against my palms and my cheek. It would take time to acclimate to this heightened awareness, but for now, I relished it, seeing the world as Obsidian did.

A tremor danced down my spine, following the gentle sweep of Obsidian's fingers as he brushed them over my back. I didn't want to move, my body sated and heavy, content to remain where I was, draped over Obsidian's enormous body right here in our own paradise.

Of course, I knew the real world was taking place on the other side of the door. We would emerge eventually, join the others. Only this time, I would be strong enough to ensure my *amsouelot's* safety, protect him the same way he protected me. Loving him, cherishing him...

A tear trickled down my cheek, dropped onto Obsidian's chest.

His head lifted, silver eyes watching me. "What's wrong, *ayreme*?"

I felt it then, the wash of his emotions as they stole over me. Love, admiration, gratitude. He was as content in this moment as I was. I smiled to myself, loving that I had that connection with him. While I'd always retreated from the empathy I felt for others, I didn't feel the need to do so with Obsidian. In fact, I wanted to explore it because it meant I would be able to protect him in all ways, offer him strength, love.

"Nothing," I assured him. "Absolutely nothing."

Truth was, I'd never been happier in my life. For the first time, I felt as though I truly belonged.

When Obsidian moved me to his side, I propped my head on his chest, ran my fingers over the taut muscles of his abdomen. It was then I noticed a glimmer of light coming from the stones where they rested on the bed.

"They're glowing," I whispered.

"They're still working," he said simply.

When Obsidian moved, I went with him. He repositioned so that he was propped up, leaning against the headboard, and I was sitting in front of him, his warm arms embracing me.

Before my eyes, the four stones rose from the silver comforter. They came together as though magnetized, glittering as they spun rapidly, suspended in the air before us.

Obsidian brought his finger to my lips. "Score it."

Confused but intrigued, I pierced his finger with the sharp tip of my fang. When blood pooled at the tip, Obsidian held out his hand, allowed two drops to spill onto the stones as they swirled. I had no idea what was happening, but I couldn't look away. There was a brilliant flash of light an instant before the stones fell to the soft comforter. This time there were two.

"Pick them up," he instructed.

I reached for them, giggling when I realized they were no longer free stones but rather rings, the black metal shimmering in the light from the gems. Obsidian plucked one from the set, then took my left hand, holding it up.

"Angels don't have weddings," he informed me. "However, there are a few human traditions we get behind."

I spread my fingers as he slid it onto my ring finger. In the center was the stunningly beautiful alexandrite gem surrounded by tiny chips of moonstone.

I retrieved the other ring, then did the same with Obsidian's finger, sliding it on and positioning it so we could admire the thick band embedded with tiny chips of both stones.

While I didn't need a material item to remind me of my love for him, I knew I would cherish the ring for eternity. And every time I looked at it, I would remember the sacrifices we'd made for one another and the love that brought us back together.

Reclining against him, I turned my head so I could look up at him. "I met the Fates."

He smiled. "Did you? And?"

"They were kind to me. Provided a distraction from my worry. They allowed me to see you while I was in Heaven."

"I'm glad they took care of you," he whispered.

"There was a man, but he didn't speak to me."

"Michael," Obsidian said.

"He nodded as though giving the Fates his approval. Then Nevaeh took my hands and sent me back here to you."

Wanting to be closer to him, I shifted onto my knees, then turned in the circle of his arms, straddling his thighs.

"I'm so sorry you had to go through that." I pressed my lips to his neck, his collarbone, his shoulder.

I could hear his ragged breaths as I trailed my tongue over him, relishing the salty taste of his skin. His entire body hardened, spurring me to continue my exploration.

"How about a shower?" he proposed, his arms tightening around me, the muscles rippling as he moved.

The sound of the water dropping onto the tile in the bathroom had me lifting my head, smiling. "You'll have to teach me all those nifty tricks of yours."

"I will, *ayreme*. All in due time."

A few minutes later, we were beneath the warm spray, wrapped in one another's arms, a fumble of hands and mouths as we fought to get closer.

And when Obsidian lifted me off my feet, I wrapped my legs around him. My back met the cool tiled wall seconds before he filled me so exquisitely. I held on to him, but it wasn't only our bodies that were joined as one.

Hearts, minds, and souls were connected.

Two halves of a whole.

Now and forever complete.

OBSIDIAN

Although I could've spent an eternity in our very own paradise, I knew we had to return to the real world. Still, as I lay in the bed, Penelope's head resting on my chest, I couldn't find the energy to get up.

"I've been thinking," Penelope said softly, her head shifting, eyes seeking, ensuring I was paying attention.

"About...?"

"What I want to do."

My body stiffened, a hint of unease settling over me.

"Don't worry," she said with a chuckle. "I'm not talking about going back to the casino and serving drinks. However, I do need something to do. I can't sit around all night, twiddling my thumbs."

"What do you enjoy doing?"

"Well, I was thinking maybe I could help with the search for the other *amsouelots*. I'm decent with a computer. Probably not as good as they are, but I'm a fast learner."

"I know my brothers will appreciate all the help they can get."

"Then I was thinking that perhaps I could start documenting things. One thing I noticed was there weren't any books in the library noting your history."

"Document our history?" I wasn't sure I understood.

"I even checked the Bible but found nothing."

No, the Bible didn't have a section devoted to us. Michael had done his best to keep our existence a secret throughout history. According to the archangel, there were certain things even angels didn't need to know.

"Why would you want to do that?"

"Well, I figure it's safe to say there'll be more warriors in the future. Probably wouldn't hurt for them to understand their heritage, where they came from."

I twisted my head so I could look down at her face.

Penelope turned and smiled up at me. "I'm talking about your children. Your brothers' children. The next generation, Obsidian."

My heart did a hop, skip, and a jump in my chest at the thought of her carrying my son or daughter.

"As I told you, I've always been fascinated by mythology." She chuckled softly. "Though I'm not sure that's an accurate term based on the definition. Considering what most consider myths are probably facts."

"And you want to use this for what?"

"Education. Within your family, of course. Not with humans. I don't think they can handle this sort of knowledge."

"They can't," I agreed. "Which is the reason we're restricted from interacting with them if at all possible."

"And that leads me to another question," she said, her fingernail sliding over my stomach. "Will I be able to visit my father?"

I considered it for a moment. "Is that what you want?"

"Eventually, yes. He's still my father. Our relationship might be strained, but I do miss him."

"I'll speak to Michael about it. See what rules he wants in place."

"I can document those, too," she said. "Since it seems most of that information is locked up tightly in your head."

I smiled.

"Do you think Oliver will ever be able to leave?"

Her question didn't surprise me, but I wasn't exactly fond of the subject. "That's the plan."

"Do you think he'll be safe?"

"Eventually, yes. Lucifer can no longer get his hands on your soul," I explained. "It's now safely ensconced in Heaven alongside mine."

"But the demons could still use him for leverage," she noted.

"They could. But it wouldn't get them what they wanted."

"Maybe we could let him go now."

I tucked my finger beneath her chin, tipped her head back so I could meet her eyes. "Is that what you want?"

"I want him to be happy. He thinks we're doing this to punish him."

"Then we'll talk to him. If he wants to leave and you're comfortable with that, we'll let him leave."

Penelope nodded, dropped her head back down, pressing her lips to my stomach. "I think it's time we get out of here. Back to the real world. Are you ready for that?"

I smiled. "More than ready."

Two hours later, I was rethinking that.

After we emerged from the mating chamber, we were overwhelmed by congratulations. Not that I minded them, but even now, after we'd indulged in a feast created at Acadia's insistence, I was being bombarded by questions, most of which I couldn't answer. They were all aware of the secrecy behind the *lintamair*. What happened in that mating chamber was meant only for *amsouelots,* and I warned Penelope of that before we exited. She promised to keep the secret, though I wasn't sure how that was possible with Winnie practically climbing the walls in an attempt to get information.

"All right, love," Reidar said to Winnie. "Why don't we give her a break?"

I smiled at Reidar, a silent thank you. When Winnie reluctantly marched off with him, I scooted closer to Penelope, putting my arm over the back of the sofa and around her shoulders.

"How're you feeling?"

"Strange, actually."

I stared down at her, attempting to read between the lines, to no avail.

"It's odd. I can feel your emotions now when before I could not. So, I assumed that meant I'd feel everyone's. But I can't. Still no reading from the angels or Fae. Not even from Winnie." She peered up at me. "It's strange but nice. I'm hoping it lasts."

I figured it would because we were connected on a deeper level, so it was natural for her to feel me in every way. Even humans had those abilities, though most of them never had reason to feel it. However, I'd heard stories of humans who knew when their significant other had been injured or when their child was in pain. I figured angels felt it more significantly because of our other abilities.

"The real test will be with my brother," Penelope noted. "Since he's apparently locked himself away in his room, I'm guessing it won't be today."

"Speaking of day," I said softly, "it's probably best we get some rest while we can."

Penelope's golden eyes twinkled. "I'm not really tired, but I can think of something that might do the trick."

I laughed as I got to my feet. In one swift move, I lifted her into my arms. "You're insatiable, you know that?"

"It's your fault."

"I don't mind taking credit for it," I admitted as I took her up to our private quarters to see if I could quell that urge.

EPILOGUE

Two weeks later

OBSIDIAN

I walked into the war room, eyes scanning the rows of tables and equipment, the *fiestreigh* occupying all available seats as they worked diligently on their mission.

Prior to its conversion, the room had been nothing more than storage for the overflow of furniture. Because of its size, Penelope had decided it would work perfectly for a dedicated workspace. It had taken her only two days to have it converted into what looked a lot like mission control.

"I was beginning to wonder whether you'd come down for an update," Penelope said, moving toward me with purpose.

"Well, your text sounded important."

Thanks to Penelope's drive and dedication, the *fiestreigh*

was hard at work, focused entirely on completing their priority mission so they could get back to what they'd initially been sent here to do: eliminate demons. As far as drill instructors, my female was quite the force to be reckoned with. Granted, she did it gracefully, so no one seemed to mind that she'd taken charge. Not to mention, we were seeing progress, so she was doing something right.

She'd even enlisted Winnie's help, putting the female to work on what they were calling the "woman cave". Using most of the furniture and decor they'd relocated from Penelope's apartment in Vegas and Winnie's in LA, the females designed a space that was off-limits to the males in the household. According to Penelope, it was only fair that they had a quiet place to spend time together. Thanks to my keen sense of hearing, it hadn't taken long to realize it was more a place for them to giggle and gossip and introduce the Fae to something they called *Supernatural.*

But she was happy, and I damn sure wasn't going to interfere.

I briefly scanned all six enormous television screens mounted to the wall, noting the different information on each one. CNN, the local news, the rest reflecting the last known location of the *amsouelots* we were still searching for. Despite our best efforts, we'd yet to locate four of them, but based on what I could tell, we were getting closer.

"If you'll look here"—Penelope motioned toward one of the screens on the wall—"I'm happy to say we've narrowed down the location for Darina Azelmar."

A.k.a. Stygian's *amsouelot.* Two weeks ago, my brother had thought he was closing in on her, only to find out his female was actually in hiding, slipping through his fingers at every turn.

"She was last seen in Salem," Penelope explained. "That

was three days ago. But she's still there, and we believe she's keeping a low profile for a reason."

"Any ideas as to why?"

Penelope's golden eyes locked with mine. "Truth?"

I chuckled. "Can you tell me otherwise?"

She laughed. "Touché. Truth is, we've got reason to believe Darina's a witch. Yes, a true-blue, queen-of-dark-and-light witch. As are her sisters and her mother."

Interesting. Not surprising, either.

I nodded. "And the other *amsouelots*?"

"We've successfully identified Orianna McKay's apartment." Penelope glanced across the room. "We have Oliver to thank for that."

Turning my attention to the human sitting alone in the far corner, I watched the male. We'd given Oliver the opportunity to leave the mansion and the human had initially been ecstatic. Right up until he overheard Reidar and Søren talking about following a lead. I wasn't quite clear on what happened past that, but the next thing I knew, Oliver Calazans had become an integral part of the undertaking to locate the *amsouelots*. Turned out, his computer skills rivaled Gryffyth's.

"I'm sure Eclipse is thrilled about that," I said, turning back to Penelope.

She peered up at me, worry glittering in her eyes. "You'd think that would be the case."

More accurately, I had hoped. Eclipse seemed to be keeping his distance from the female. I only prayed that didn't backfire on my brother. We were still under the gun, not sure when or if God would call an audible. It was the very reason Penelope insisted we focus all efforts on locating the females while keeping an eye on the demons but not engaging them if at all possible.

"Right now, we've got three teams out," Penelope

explained. "Rinc, Valterri, and Mordecai are in the field. Malak's, Shiloh's, and Magnar's teams are in and resting. Reidar's covering the techs."

I was grateful to know Penelope found a way to keep my *ladeare* busy while not forcing him to go out in the field. Eventually, he'd have no choice, but for now, keeping Reidar close to Winnie was in everyone's best interest.

"And Taayin?" I asked, curious as to how things were going for my *lieterra*.

Penelope sighed. "He's with Aphotic in Texas. Giving Decebal a few days off."

I knew Taayin was spending as much time away from the mansion as he could. Ever since the incident with Perfidious and Asmia, the male had been in a dark place. For whatever reason, he couldn't seem to get past what had happened, though we'd all told him it wasn't Asmia's fault. As for the Fae, she was putting one foot in front of the other, pretending she wasn't bothered by Taayin's absence, but it was clear to everyone that she was.

I turned to face Penelope. "Well, it sounds to me like you've got it all covered."

"They do, actually." She smiled. "I'm simply their cheerleader."

I laughed. She was far more than a cheerleader, even if she didn't realize it.

"I was just thinking about going upstairs to grab lunch," Penelope told me, linking her fingers with mine.

"I was thinking along those same lines," I said, leading her out of the war room. "Although, I had a different type of feeding in mind."

"Did you now? And what? You were too good for my offer last night?"

When we reached the elevator that would take us up to the

third floor, I leaned in and nuzzled her neck. "I recall a feisty female latching onto my neck when we woke up."

Penelope giggled as I pulled her into the elevator. "You can't blame a girl. It's a very tasty neck."

It took effort, but I managed to keep my hands mostly to myself until we were in our private quarters, behind closed doors. Once inside, I bypassed the sofa in favor of the bed, though I honestly didn't intend to do more than feed at the moment.

Well, not much more.

I got situated with my back against the headboard, Penelope sitting between my legs, reclining against me. The moment she was in my arms, I felt immensely better. As though her touch alone could fuel me.

Her head tipped back, resting against my chest as I ringed my arms around her. "Have I told you I love you lately?"

"Maybe once or twice. But I still like hearing it."

"I love you, *ereswa*," I whispered in the dimly lit room.

"I love you, too, husband."

"*Reuthet*," I told her. "That's the word for husband in the ancient language."

"*Reuthet*," Penelope whispered. "I like that."

As she relaxed against me, I couldn't resist touching her, allowing my hands to wander over her chest, her belly, sliding lower, cupping her through the jeans she was wearing.

"I thought you were here to feed," she said on a soft moan. "Not to play."

"I fully intend to feed. I promise. But I see no reason not to multitask."

Penelope dragged her hair to one side, tipped her head so that her neck was available to me. Though I had every intention of feeding from her, I had something else on my mind as well.

"What are you doing?" she asked as I worked the button on her jeans free, lowered the zipper.

Brushing my lips over her ear, I smiled. "Touching you."

I slid my hand into her panties, seeking the warmth between her thighs. When I found it, she moaned again, spreading her legs wide, giving me access to her slick folds. I kissed her neck as I dipped one finger inside her sweet, welcoming warmth.

"Obsidian..." She rolled her hips, attempting to take my finger deeper.

I added another, teasing her, tempting her. "I want you to come on my fingers, *ayreme*."

I fingered her as she rocked against my hand. There was no urgency to the ministrations, just a slow, lingering desire. While Penelope focused on what I was doing to her, I kissed her neck, licked her skin. My fangs elongated, seeking the sustenance only she could provide.

"Feed from me," Penelope said on a soft moan, her hips grinding as she took my fingers deep within her.

I pierced her neck with my fangs, her blood warm as it filled my mouth. The power was instant, her blood fueling my strength, reigniting it. And while I tasted the sweet richness I'd grown accustomed to, there was something different about her blood. Something stronger.

"Obsidian!" she cried out, her body clamping down on my fingers as she inched closer to orgasm.

Not allowing her to wiggle out of my hold, I fingered her while feeding from her.

"Make me come," she groaned, her body locking on my fingers even as I curled them upward, seeking that spot that would make her scream.

When I stroked her G-spot, her muscles tightened. But I

wasn't finished with her. I continued to feed, driving her to orgasm twice more before releasing her from my clutches.

She relaxed against me, panting.

"Do you feel better now?" she teased.

"Much." I pressed my lips to her jaw and smiled to myself.

"Why are you smiling?"

"Did you know?" I whispered against her ear.

Penelope attempted to turn in my arms, looking up at me over her shoulder. "Know what?"

"That you're pregnant."

Her eyes widened.

Nope, she hadn't known.

"Really?" There was so much hope in that single word, my heart swelled.

I smiled, then pressed my lips to hers. "We're having a baby, *ayreme*."

Soon enough, our family was going to expand. Not only from the love I knew my brothers would eventually find, either.

I was going to be a father.

STAY TUNED

I have always known I wanted to write a paranormal/fantasy book. It took me quite some time to get this mapped out and even that continues to morph and change as I go. I hope you enjoyed Obsidian and Penelope's story. There is a lot more to come for them, so you'll be seeing them in the future books, although they won't be the main romance.

If you enjoyed *Protected in Darkness*, please consider leaving a review.

Acknowledgments

While writing is a solitary task, it's not a completely solo project. Because of that, I'd like to thank those who've assisted in one way or another. As a side note, I received no compensation for these acknowledgments, so they are in no particular order.

This past year has been one I don't care to relive again. With the passing of three of our fur babies, I drifted into the darkness known as depression, and it took nearly a full year to find my way back out. I'm blessed to have my family supporting me, though, and I knew, given time, I would eventually emerge. I'm happy to say I finally have and I never could've done it without my amazing husband. Not only does he put up with me every single day, he knows what I need to keep me afloat. Steven, you are and always will be my anchor in the storm.

Of course, I have to say a huge thank you to my daughter, Taylor, who is also my personal assistant/ manager. She's always on top of things, and I wouldn't know what to do without her.

You, the reader: It is because of you that I can continue what I love. Thank you for reading, thank you for writing a review, and thank you for hopping on social media and telling your friends about the book. You're cool like that.

TERMS FROM THE ANCIENT LANGUAGE OF ANGELS

Amnigh: intense desire, or mating heat, experienced between amsouelots.
Amsouelot: the soul destined for another.
Archsire and ***Archdam***: angels who procreate specifically for angel warriors.
Ayreme: Term of endearment meaning my greatest love.
Dhira: the cloak of darkness initiated by warrior angels. Only angels and Fae can see through, disorients those who attempt to locate them.
Ereswa: loosely translates to the human term *wife.*
Gathenya: the sexual energy produced when angels mate.
Heurosp: an immortal human who works for the angels, managing the mansion.
Lintamair: ancient mating ceremony of immortals.
Neilloh: demon sent back to Earth from Hell.
Reuthet: loosely translates to the human term *husband.*
Sezari: term of endearment meaning sweetheart, baby.

TERMS FROM THE ANCIENT LANGUAGE OF VAMPIRES

Adighrielin: The Alpha's advisor, his right hand. The most honorable position within the Zenith, that which is the first line of defense to the Alpha.
Asyra: term of endearment, translates to *my heart.*
Balisra: term of endearment, translates to *my love.*
Cosrobol: blood whore; vampires used solely for feeding.
Dyrlom: honorific title for a male of same status

Kirlesgun: The current alpha's regime
Leaqua: Queen
Mielix zan: the process of identifying/imprinting on one's sexual mate.
Nehadon: vampire mate.
Phaal: king/alpha
Sonavex: the secretion injected into a mate by a male vampire upon claiming.
Tresmar: Honorific title meaning master, someone higher than.
Vestrahn: housekeeper, groundskeeper, those in service to others.

ANGELS OF DARKNESS HIERARCHY:

Lieterra: the right-hand of a warrior angel, tasked with tracking, doling out responsibilities, as well as performing as the warrior's assistant.
Ladeare: highest rank within the fiestreigh, responsible for soldiers under him.
Fiestreigh: the legion of angels assigned to the Angels of Darkness.
Ritarro: a position held by a Fae. It's the equivalent of a handmaiden and a coveted role.

DEMON HIERARCHY:

Trielair: the three demons who oversee the demon factions: Eevuhl, Mizuhree, and Aguhnee.
Mesonneir: the level of demons beneath the trielair. Equivalent to lieutenants.

Impietan: a human turned demon by a mesonneir.

ABOUT THE AUTHOR

New York Times and *USA Today* bestselling author Nicole Edwards lives in the suburbs of Austin, Texas, with her husband, their two fur babies, and the youngest of their three children, who has threatened never to leave home. When Nicole is not writing about sexy alpha males and sassy, independent women, she can often be found with a book in hand or attempting to keep the dogs happy. You can find her hanging out on social media and interacting with her readers - even when she's supposed to be writing.

NicoleEdwards.me

facebook.com/Author.Nicole.Edwards
instagram.com/nicoleedwardsauthor
tiktok.com/@nicoleedwardsauthor
bookbub.com/authors/nicole-edwards
threads.com/@nicoleedwardsauthor

CONNECT WITH NICOLE

I hope you're as eager to get the information as I am to give it. Any of these things is worth signing up for, or feel free to sign up for all. I do my best to keep each one unique and interesting.

NIC NEWS - If you haven't signed up for my newsletter and want notifications regarding preorders, new releases, give-aways, sales, etc., then you'll want to sign up. I promise not to spam your email; you get to pick exactly what you want to receive.

RAMBLINGS OF A WRITER BLOG - My blog is used for writer ramblings, which I am known to do from time to time.

NICOLE NATION - Visit my website to find exclusive content you won't find anywhere else, including Sneak Peeks, A Day in the Life character stories, exclusive giveaways, cards from Nicole, and join Nicole's review team.

NICOLE NATION ON FACEBOOK - Join my Facebook reader group to interact with other readers, ask me questions, play fun weekly games, celebrate during release week, and enter exclusive giveaways!

NAUGHTY & NICE SHOP - Not only does the shop have signed books, but there's fun merchandise, too—plenty of naughty and nice options to go around.

BY NICOLE EDWARDS

AUSTIN ARROWS

Rush

Kaufman

BRANTLEY WALKER: OFF THE BOOKS

All In

Without a Trace

Hide & Seek

Deadly Coincidence

Alibi

Secrets

Confessions

Bounty

Off Course

Chain Reaction

To Have and To Hold

Missing Pieces

Smoke and Mirrors

CLUB DESTINY

Conviction

Temptation

Addicted

Seduction

Infatuation

Captivated

Devotion

Perception

Entrusted

Adored

Distraction

Forevermore

DEAD HEAT RANCH

Boots Optional

Betting on Grace

Overnight Love

Jared (a crossover novel)

DEVIL'S BEND

Chasing Dreams

Vanishing Dreams

HEREOS & HAVOC

Wait for Morning

Beautifully Brutal

Without Regret

Never Say Never

Beautifully Loyal

Without Restraint

Tomorrow's Too Late

MISPLACED HALOS

Protected in Darkness

Salvation in Darkness

Bound in Darkness

OFFICE INTRIGUE

Office Intrigue

Intrigued Out of the Office

Their Rebellious Submissive

Their Famous Dominant

Their Ruthless Sadist

Their Naughty Student

Their Fairy Princess

Owned

PIER 70

Reckless

Fearless

Speechless

Harmless

Clueless

PRIMAL INSTINCTS

Chase (Volume 1-3)

Capture (Volume 4-6)

Claim (Volume 7-9)

THE JAMESONS OF COYOTE RIDGE

Hot Chocolate Wishes

Rough & Dirty

THE WALKERS OF COYOTE RIDGE

Kaleb

Zane

Travis

Holidays with the Walker Brothers

Ethan

Braydon

Sawyer

Brendon

Curtis

Jared

Hard to Hold

Hard to Handle

Beau

Rex

A Coyote Ridge Christmas

Mack

Kaden & Keegan

Trey

Rafe

Violet

STANDALONE NOVELS

Unhinged Trilogy

A Million Tiny Pieces

Inked on Paper

Bad Reputation

Bad Business

Filthy Hot Billionaire

RULE

NAUGHTY HOLIDAY EDITIONS

2015

2016

2021

www.ingramcontent.com/pod-product-compliance
Lightning Source LLC
Chambersburg PA
CBHW030844030726
47495CB00005B/1371

* 9 7 8 1 6 4 4 1 8 1 2 2 5 *